QUINTESSENCE SKY

QUINTESSENCE SKY

David Walton

Volume **2** of the Quintessence Trilogy

Other books by David Walton

TERMINAL MIND

QUINTESSENCE

for Naomi

who wondered

Acknowledgements

To David Hartwell, Stacy Hill, Marco Palmieri, and all the folks at Tor Books, thank you for taking a risk on *Quintessence* and giving this series a great start.

To Eleanor, agent extraordinaire, thank you for your tireless efforts on behalf of all my books.

To Becca, many thanks for your graphical design tips and advice.

And to my early readers, Mike, David, Chad, and Dad, your insights made this book much better than it would have been without you.

PROLOGUE

FATHER Ramos was sitting at his fireplace, reading Copernicus, when the inquisitors knocked on his door.

It was generally his favorite time of the day. His niece, Antonia, worked her embroidery in the rocking chair across from him. The fire cast a warm glow through the room. The crackle of burning wood combined with the soft scrape of porcelain as Carmela, his old servant, straightened the kitchen.

Copernicus claimed that the world was not round, as the Greeks had maintained, but flat, with oceans that ran over the edge into oblivion, or else were held in by a lip, like a giant bowl. He used the movements of the stars to defend his position, and so far, Ramos had not been able to find a fault with his logic. It was a revolutionary work, and he was enjoying it.

At the same time, though, he found it unsettling. Cosmology was not just an intellectual pursuit; it had spiritual implications. For more than a thousand years, the Church had understood the Earth to be round, surrounded by a series of crystalline spheres to which the heavenly bodies were attached, first the moon, then the sun, then the movable stars, then the fixed stars, then the angelic sphere, and finally, the empyrean, the dwelling place of God. The spheres were perfect circles, as God was perfect. If Copernicus was right, what did that say about God?

At the sound of fists pounding on the door, everyone in the room froze. Antonia's chair stopped rocking, and her embroidery needle poised motionless over the cloth. Carmela held her breath, one arm still reaching for a bowl, and darted a frightened glance toward the window.

Unhurriedly, Ramos leaned forward and dropped the Copernican treatise into the fire. He would find another copy. It wasn't worth the risk that one of these brutes would see it and recognize it for what it was.

"Antonia, please retire to your chamber," he said, keeping his voice even.

Antonia was a sweet child, fourteen years old, though she had seen more than her share of tragedy in that short time. She was exceedingly pretty, with thick black curls that flooded over her shoulders and down her back. There was little in this world as guileless or innocent as she, but she knew enough to fear the men who came knocking late at night. The muscles of her neck and arms were rigid with fright.

Carmela, who had served as Antonia's nursemaid since her birth, crossed the room and tried to take her hand, but Antonia pulled away. She stood, heedless of the embroidery that fell to the stone hearth.

"What do they want?" she said.

The pounding on the door grew more insistent, and Ramos sighed. "Doubtless they wish me to perform some service. Don't let it trouble your rest."

"What if you don't come back?"

"I am no heretic, child. I will return by morning."

"You can't be certain of that." She knew it, and so did he.

"Say your prayers for me, then," he said.

Antonia allowed Carmela to lead her away, but at the last

moment, she pulled away and ran back to him. She threw her arms around his neck and kissed his cheek. "Be safe, Tío Ramos," she said.

"I will. Go now."

"Whatever they want, just do what they say. Don't fight them."

"I won't."

She ran back to Carmela.

"Lie still on your bed and pretend to be asleep," Ramos said. "If anyone comes in, don't open your eyes."

True to his vows, Ramos had never married, but God had seen fit to give him this child anyway, the daughter of his brother Diego. Her mother was dead, and Diego had never been the sort of man to care for a child. He had left Spain two years ago on King Philip's orders, to engineer a marriage between the king and Queen Mary of England. He had left Antonia behind, and Ramos had taken her in gladly. Ramos thought it was just as well for Antonia that Diego had not taken her with him. His brother had never been a kind man.

"Open in the name of King Philip!" bellowed a voice from outside.

Ramos stoked the fire to be sure the pages were completely burned, and then walked to the door. He opened it to reveal three men in crimson cloaks. The tallest of them, whose hand was raised to strike the door again, scowled at Ramos.

"You should not use the king's name so lightly," Ramos said. "King Philip is in England marrying a queen, not here sending lackeys to knock down his humble servants' doors."

The tallest one reddened. "We are the king's voice and the king's fist," he said. "Treat us with deference, or we'll have you put to the question, priest or no."

"By all means, your Excellency. Shall I kiss your ring?"

"Or perhaps we'll question that girl who lives in your house. I'm sure she could tell us some tales, if we worked on her long enough."

Ramos bowed his head. These were petty, vindictive men, and no good would come from antagonizing them. "I am your servant," he said. "There is no need for threats." He stepped outside and pushed the door shut behind him.

The inquisitor nodded pompously. "That's better. Come along, then."

"Where are we going?" Ramos said.

"Valencia wants you."

FATHER Alonso de Valencia was waiting for Ramos in the Catedral de Nuestra Señora de la Asunción. The cathedral was a latticework of wooden scaffolding and stone arches built on the foundations of an older church. It would not truly be a cathedral until it was finished, many years hence, and became the bishop's seat, but that did not stop its cellars from being useful in the work of the Church. Valencia was about sixty, his skin dry and taut around his spare frame. His smile was grim.

"It's good to see you, Ramos," Valencia said. "The Lord has need of your service."

"You know what I think about what you do here," Ramos said. "I'm an astronomer, not an inquisitor."

Valencia made a face like he was tasting something bad. "I don't relish the work either. It's often unpleasant, and it wears on the nerves. But it is important work, necessary to cleanse the realm of Protestants and other heretics."

"I won't help you torture someone," Ramos said.

"This time, I think you will."

Valencia descended into the crypt, leaving Ramos little choice but to follow. He would much rather have climbed to the flat, stone roof of the transept, where he could study the stars and breathe the fresh air, but he went down instead, his footsteps echoing in the stone tunnel. The air was cool but thick, and there was a stink of fear and blood.

The prisoner was no more than ten years old. He was strapped into a heavy, wooden chair in the center of the room. His eyes rolled back and forth, and he thrashed against the straps. His chin was wet with spittle, and vomit stained his shirt. Torches were arranged in such a way as to dazzle his eyes and allow an inquisitor to approach unseen from behind. The chair itself had holes in the back where sharpened screws could be slowly turned, iron nails that could be heated from below by hot coals, and attachments for a variety of other instruments of slow agony. A rack stood against the wall as well, along with shelves of hammers, pincers, vices, and blades.

"No," Ramos said. "Let him go. I will have no part of this."

"The boy is demon-possessed," Valencia said. "He went into convulsions when we brought him down the stairs."

"His mind is sick, and he is terrified."

"You should have seen him, thrashing on the ground and frothing at the mouth. The demons have driven him quite mad."

"A clear indication that his parents are Protestants," Ramos said.

"Or worse," Valencia replied, missing the sarcasm, or else choosing to ignore it.

"What do you hope to gain from this? If the boy is possessed, he's not under his own control. If you torture him, he'll admit to anything. How will you know if he's guilty of heresy?"

Valencia laughed. "The boy's guilt is self-evident. Demons can not enter a Christian soul. No, as you say, we need his witness against his parents. We need to know how deep the heresy goes. It does no good to cut off the plant while the roots remain in place to sprout again."

Ramos watched the boy pulling against his restraints, and remembered the tall inquisitor's casual suggestion that they might question Antonia. He felt sick.

"Just because he tells you something under torture, doesn't mean it's true," Ramos said.

"That's why we need you."

"I don't understand."

"It takes a special kind of man to extract confessions," Valencia said. "Someone with patience and fortitude. I am quite gifted at it, but I can recognize when others have talents that I do not possess. They say you are very good at casting the horoscope."

Ramos was not about to be flattered. "I am the king's astronomer, professor of mathematics at the University, and founder of the Holy Astrological Society. Clearly I am competent."

"I wish you to cast for the prisoner."

"I don't see how that will aid you."

"You're too modest. Think of it as helping me know which questions to ask."

Ramos shook his head. He understood what Valencia was asking now, but he still didn't want to be involved. "I don't think . . ."

"It's an experiment," Valencia said. "If it doesn't work, I'll just go back to doing it my way." He looked pointedly at the instruments of pain arrayed around them.

Ramos bowed his head in assent. If he could spare this boy from torture, or even just delay it a while, it was worth the attempt. "I'll need paper," he said. "And plenty of ink."

RAMOS spread a full sheet of printer's paper on a table and weighted its corners with chips of quarried stone from the chapel above. An arc of votive candles illuminated the blank surface. He began to draw.

The boy's name was Luis. He had been born on May the first, under the star Ceginus.

Ramos dipped his quill and inked a large circle, the celestial sphere, which he followed by lines dividing the ecliptic into the twelve houses. With practiced ease, he consulted his astrolabe, converting coordinates in his head, and paged through his almanac for the tables of oblique ascensions.

"Do they keep an unauthorized Bible translation hidden in the house?" Valencia said in a calm monotone. "Or perhaps a Talmud? A secret book of any kind?"

"No book, no book," Luis said.

"If they did have a book, where would they hide it?"

"Luis don't know," the boy said, rocking. "Luis don't read."

"But you've seen it, surely. Is there a secret box? A secret place where they store it?"

"Luis want to go home."

"Where is the book, Luis?"

"Papa read to me sometimes. Not Mama. She don't read neither."

"Where does your papa put the book after he reads to you?"

"No, no, no. Luis is a good boy. Not allowed to touch it."

"Did you ever touch it, Luis?"

"No, no, no."

While Ramos listened, he calculated, and could almost forget the horrific circumstances of this casting. He had figured countless horoscopes in his professional career, and the steps came easily. At the University of Valladolid, he trained medical students in horoscope-casting to diagnose diseases or determine auspicious times to mix their medicines.

His figures gave him trouble today, however, which was unusual. Detailed horoscopes could take hours to calculate, but Ramos was experienced and quick. Something bothered him about this one, though he couldn't quite put his finger on it. The equations just didn't seem to line up the way they usually did.

He persisted, however, and soon certain associations began to emerge. "Ask him about any letters his parents may have received or written," Ramos said.

"With whom do your parents correspond? Are there friends abroad to whom they write?" Valencia said.

"Luis don't touch the letters. Luis don't read."

"Do they read them to you?"

"No, no, no."

"Where are they from?"

Luis looked suddenly frightened. "Luis not tell. Luis keeps a secret."

Some inquisitors were shouters, bellowing threats at the accused to intimidate them into speaking. Valencia's subdued questioning seemed more effective. Ramos suspected that even if the questioning moved on to torture, he would maintain his serene demeanor, posing questions in calm, conversational tones while those he interrogated screamed and wept.

"We already know the answers to these questions," Valencia said soothingly. "It is for your sake that we ask them. If you are honest with us, it will spare you pain."

"From far away," Luis said. "Many days travel." He had a transparently mischievous expression, as if he thought he had answered the question cleverly without giving his secret away.

"From where, exactly?" Valencia said, and Luis's mischievous expression vanished.

Another association materialized under Ramos's pen: "philosopher" and "demon". Philosopher demon? No. The Demon Philosopher. "Ask him about Martin Luther," Ramos said.

At the name, Luis's eyes bugged out and he tried to stand, though he was still strapped down. "Luis not tell," he wailed. "Luis is a good boy."

Valencia nodded appreciatively to Ramos. If Luis's parents were corresponding with Luther's followers, that implied they were much more than simple Protestant sympathizers. It meant a network of Protestants, sedition, underground worship services—exactly how the unrest had started in the Netherlands. They may have just uncovered a serious cancer in the pure flesh of Spain, one that would have to be ruthlessly excised. Ramos was a Jesuit, devoted to the Church and to the Pope. He knew it was important to root out heresy, and yet he didn't feel proud of his contribution here.

Luis became more and more agitated, until his eyes rolled back, and his body went into convulsions, rattling the chair and knocking his head against the iron bands.

"Unstrap him," Valencia said to the guards, who quickly obeyed, allowing the convulsing boy to slip to the floor. They wouldn't get any more information out of him if he battered himself unconscious in the chair.

While they waited for the convulsions to subside, Ramos perused the horoscope again, partly just to take his eyes away from the child's distress. Something still bothered him about the shape of the calculations. He looked back and forth between his paper and his astrolabe, turning the sphere slightly, and then he saw it. He stared, disbelieving. *Surely not.*

Ramos knew the heavens as well as he knew the doctrines of Holy Scripture, as well as he knew his own name. For thousands of years, the fixed stars had turned in their courses, while the five wandering stars—Mercury, Venus, Mars, Jupiter, and Saturn—cut across them in their own complex patterns, more dynamic, but utterly predictable.

If there was anything he knew about the heavenly spheres, it was this: they didn't change. What he was seeing was impossible.

Yet it was true. A star was missing. It wasn't pictured on his astrolabe, though he knew it always had been, knew it had been there only minutes before. He snatched his almanac and flipped through, but the star was missing from the tables as well. Was he losing his mind?

He glanced back up and saw that, although Luis's fit was over, Valencia himself was staring slack-jawed, not speaking. Something was happening. The air felt thick, the pervasive smell of blood sickeningly strong. Luis laughed from the floor, a maniacal sound. Valencia turned to Ramos, his face a mask of terror. He raised an arm, reaching out, and tried to stand, but his legs buckled and he collapsed. On the floor, he began to convulse, his eyes wide and startled, his mouth gulping like a fish out of water.

Ramos leapt to his feet, overturning the table and sending the ink splashing onto the stones. *Witchcraft.* Somehow, the boy had sent his demons into Valencia. The guards were staring at the convulsing inquisitor, stunned. Luis, looking like a frightened rabbit, bolted for the stairs. No one moved to stop him. Ramos began to tremble. This was wrong, all wrong. He took one more look at Valencia's body spasming on the floor and ran.

He raced up the stairs, tripping twice, and stumbled out into the air behind the boy, who disappeared into the night without looking back. Ramos tilted his head and spun, scanning the sky. He saw it at once, in the constellation Gemini. There was a hole in the sky where a star had been before. It was, if anything, blacker than the night sky around it, a chasm where no stars could be seen. Streaks of light from the surrounding stars trailed into the hole in a spiral shape, like water swirling down a drain, as if the hole were sucking the very starlight out of the sky. Ramos had never seen anything so terrifying in all his life.

In the city around him, lights appeared in windows, accompanied by shouts and cries and curses. Antonia. Ramos started running again. He had to get home to Antonia.

Valladolid was the capital city of Spain, but at night, its streets were as black and muddy as a country lane. Lanterns illuminated snatches of a city gone mad. Shouts and weeping echoed on all sides. A man lurched out into the street chased by a woman. He stumbled toward Ramos, eyes wide, then fell down and convulsed on the road. The woman pulled at his arm, trying to drag him back into the house. Ramos hurried on, keeping to the middle of the street.

He ran northeast along the Calle de la Madre de Dios, toward his home. Another shout came from a house across the road, and a first-floor window shattered. A woman climbed through the broken glass, and then she, too, collapsed in the dirt in violent convulsions. Ramos recognized his neighbor, Señora Cabezas, a graceful mother of three who insisted on the old Castilian manners. *Please God, let Antonia be safe.*

When he reached his home, lights already burned inside. It was a two-story structure of brown stone, large enough to teach students and house his library of books, but not much more. He burst through the door and found Carmela in panic and Antonia, her face and shift bloody, lying on the floor, screaming.

"She fell out of bed!" Carmela said. "I heard her cry, but when I came . . . I didn't know what to do!"

"Tío!" Antonia screamed. "Where are you? Carmela! Tío Ramos!" She seemed utterly terrified.

Ramos wrapped his arms around her and lifted her back into bed. "I'm right here," he said. "There's nothing to fear." Though he wasn't at all sure that was true. "Carmela, bring water and a blanket."

Carmela rushed to obey. Ramos stroked Antonia's hair and spoke into her ear, but she didn't seem to be able to hear him, or even feel that he was there. She kept crying out for him, urgently at first, then with a kind of pitiful despair.

"I don't know," she said. "Do you?"

"Do I what?" Ramos said.

"I don't remember," she said. "Home, I think."

"Antonia, can you hear me?"

"Thank you. My name is Antonia." She said it politely, as if she were meeting a guest at their home. "What's yours?"

Ramos clutched her head to his chest, and a painful knot formed in his throat. He thought of Luis and madness and the zeal of the Inquisition. *Please God, may she not be like that. Protect my little girl.*

Carmela returned, and they draped the blanket over Antonia, as if it were her body that was sick and not her mind. Ramos held the glass of water for her to drink. She couldn't seem to tell that it was there. When he tipped it and poured into her mouth, she drank readily enough, but then she started to speak in the middle of a swallow, causing her to choke and spit water up onto the blanket.

"There, dear, just hush and drink it," Carmela said, and started to cry.

Ramos took Carmela's chin and turned her head so she could see the seriousness in his eyes. "We need to keep this secret," he said. "You must tell no one what's happened here."

Carmela nodded, the terror evident in her eyes.

CHAPTER 1

CATHERINE Parris stepped through the invisible barrier that kept the manticores from invading the Horizon colony. They knew better than to trust their safety to a physical wall anymore, as they had in the early days of the colony. The old wall had been made of beetlewood— the only known substance that manticores could not simply pass through like air—but that hadn't stopped the manticores from scaling it and killing them. Like the manticores themselves, the new barrier operated on the quintessence plane, and thus could not be seen by normal light. It couldn't be felt, either, and Catherine walked right through to the other side without noticing anything different.

Two manticores were waiting for her. They were from the red tribe, as close to friends as it was possible for manticores to be. They were her guides and bodyguards on this trip, protection against the dangers of the forest, and particularly against those manticores who were not as friendly. They were visible, as a courtesy to her, but when she nodded to them, acknowledging their presence, they disappeared.

Catherine was hardly defenseless—she could heal instantly from any wound, could outrun any animal in a race across open ground, and at need, she could channel such a large flow of quintessence that she would shine like the sun and incinerate anything within a few meters. In fact, she would have preferred to go on this trip alone, but Matthew had insisted. As her fiancé, he had become inclined to make pronouncements about her safety. He hadn't wanted her to go at all, but they had worked out this bodyguard as a compromise.

She used the quintessence in her body to make herself lighter, which would allow her to sprint for miles without tiring, and took off toward the interior of the island, not caring if the manticores followed or not. They would have no trouble keeping up with her through dense forest, and she had no doubt they were there, invisibly flanking her or scouting ahead. She had a bottle of skink tears which would allow her to see them, if she wished, but the colony's stores of that commodity were getting low, and she needed to conserve her supply.

The manticores were named Paul and Thomas. They were among the first converts to Christianity that Bishop Marcheford had made when he lived in his little house among them during the early months of the colony. When a manticore converted—as more of them had been doing now that the human colony was strongly established— Marcheford gave it a Christian name. It seemed a shame to Catherine, who loved the beauty of manticore names, however difficult they were to pronounce. These two had been called something like Hakrahinik and Lachakchith, the sound of the names accompanied by motions with their tails that were just as much a part of the manticore language as were the spoken syllables. Catherine had learned to approximate those motions with her hands to communicate in their language, but she had to admit, the Christian names were easier.

Paul and Thomas had reported seeing something unusual—a blight, they called it, a region of forest where the plants were dying. It was just one of a host of strange things that had been happening on the island recently. Ferocious lightning storms blocked the sun and deluged the colony with rain nearly every night. More alarmingly, the salt harvest had been declining for weeks. Salt was the fuel by which they generated a flow of quintessence, and without quintessence, they couldn't make food or fresh water or do any of the other miraculous things they needed to survive.

If this blight could shed some light on the salt shortage, it would be worth the trip. Despite Matthew's concerns for her safety, Catherine knew she was the best person for this expedition. She knew the forest, she could speak the manticore language, and she was one of the best experimentalists in the Quintessence Society.

The manticores reappeared, beckoning her in a new direction. As they ran, she asked them about recent politics among their various tribes. It was always hard to stay current with which leaders were growing in power, which tribes had allied with each other, and which had become enemies.

"A new river is rising," Thomas said in his own language. Manticores referred to their tribes using water imagery, which seemed apt to Catherine, considering that a tribe represented a long stream of memories shared from member to member across generations. Tribe loyalties were based less on physical families than on these memory families, and tribes could merge and split and trade members as alliances shifted. It made it difficult for the humans to keep track.

"What is this new river?" she asked.

"Rinchirith hates the humans, and he draws many to his course. The river of Christ grows wider, but as it does, there are even more who wish the humans gone."

It was bad news, but not surprising. As the colony grew stronger, more manticores were drawn to join the converts—whether or not they truly understood the gospel—and ally themselves with a growing power. That very strength, however, drew the hatred of many others, especially those who had died at human hands in the battle for the colony the previous year. Catherine thought she remembered Rinchirith.

"His brother died on the wall last year, didn't he?" she asked.

"Two of his brothers," Thomas said. "His hatred is strong." Paul was quiet, but his tails waved a grim assent.

By the time the sun had passed its zenith, they had left the beetlewood forest far behind and crossed the plains, where herds of grazing fire buffalo cropped the grasses. In the distance, Catherine saw a puff dragon, a reptile the size of an ox that could make itself light enough to float through the air. It drifted on the breeze, trying to get in position over a buffalo, at which point it would plummet, crushing its prey under its suddenly substantial weight.

The sun grew huge as it moved toward the west, and the air grew steadily warmer. Since Horizon was so close to the edge of the world, the sun was cold and distant in the mornings, but vast and blazingly hot in the evenings, nearly filling the western sky. The animals that thrived in the cool took shelter, while reptiles and others that craved the heat began to appear. More sophisticated animals changed color or extruded spines to help radiate heat away from their bodies, allowing them to remain active all day.

The fire buffalos caught flame, burning away the thick hair they had grown during the night to insulate them from the cold. Eventually, Catherine and the manticores sat and rested for a time, tired after hours of traveling. Catherine caught the scent of burnt hair on the wind.

"I don't understand why some manticores hate us so much," Catherine said. "I know we made some mistakes early on, but there's no reason our races can't be friendly now. You two have learned English, learned to read, even accepted the gospel. Why can't they all be like you?"

The two manticores didn't answer, but she sensed something was wrong. The poses of their tails were—what—disbelieving? And from Paul, a sense even of animosity.

"Can you truly not understand?" Paul said. There was a rough edge to his voice.

"Understand what?"

"You humans have changed everything, our security, our way of life. Hundreds have died because of you. Ancient memory fountains destroyed. The structure of tribes and families shifts, some following human ways, some hating them, but all revolving around you. All choices must now consider, what will the humans do? And how many more will come? Everything is different. And you do not *understand* why some would hate you?"

Catherine was taken aback by the venom in his tone.

"But you're a friend," she said. "You worship God now. You can read and write. You probably know more Greek than I do."

Paul stared straight ahead, not looking at her. "Because I see the writing on the wall, as the king did in your book of Daniel. I know that to survive in this new world, I must know the human language, the human beliefs, the human thought. It does not mean that's what I wish for myself. Or for my people."

"Then, you don't truly believe in Christ?"

"My father sent me to convert, for the benefit of my memory family. It is who I am now. It is what must be done."

Catherine didn't know what to say. The humans had brought culture to this island, hadn't they? They had taught the manticores to read, shared with them the Bible and the ancient writings of the Greeks, taught them the gospel as well as mathematics and rhetoric. They had given them the key to civilization. It had never occurred to her that they might not want it.

"Paul exaggerates," Thomas said. "There is much we have learned from you."

Paul lashed his central tail in the equivalent of a scowl. "My name is Hakrahinik," he said.

THEY RAN on, through growing shadows. The conversation unnerved Catherine, as did the news about Rinchirith, and she was glad Matthew had insisted on her manticore bodyguard. It still irked her, though, that he had tried to prevent her from going. They had shouted at each other, and she'd cried despite herself. He said he expected her to continue to pursue scientific exploration and experimentation after their marriage, but did he really mean it? Or would he expect her to stay at home and give those things up? He'd tried to apologize, but she hadn't given him the chance. She'd simply taken her pack and headed off without saying goodbye.

He worried for her safety; she appreciated that. But she didn't want to be protected, not if that meant keeping her tied up at home. What would it be like when he was her legal husband, and had the authority to command her? Could she trust him to keep his promises? She was afraid that, once married, he might decide that treating a wife as an equal was too much to ask. And what if they had children? Would he take time away from his research to help care for them, or would he leave all the work to her? The closer she got to her wedding day, the more she wanted to avoid it.

Catherine had to admit that a big reason she had wanted to come was to prove to herself that she really could accomplish something on her own. On the ship, she'd been unconscious, a helpless victim to the manticore bond, and her father had rescued her. When the Spanish had captured Matthew, her rescue attempt had gone sour, and her father had rescued her again, using quintessence to resurrect her. When the manticores attacked, she had figured out a way to fight them off, but in doing so, she had burned the settlement to the ground.

Worst of all was Maasha Kaatra, the servant of Christopher Sinclair's whose death she couldn't get out of her dreams. It had been her job to manage the void. Her responsibility. It had been her first time doing so, but that didn't excuse her lapse. The wonder of what Sinclair was doing had distracted her, and the void grew out of control. By the time she noticed, it was too late. Maasha Kaatra had seen a vision of his murdered daughters that day, just before he plummeted into the void. Instead of trying to pull him back, Catherine had pushed away from him, thinking only of freeing herself from his grasp. He had fallen, fallen, tumbling endlessly into the empty space behind the fabric of reality. She could still see his dwindling form in the darkness when she closed her eyes.

This trip was her chance, finally, to do something that mattered and get it right.

They reached the far side of the plains and entered the thicker, wetter forest at the foot of the great mountains. Dark clouds swept in on swift winds, and distant thunder thrummed. The mossy foliage of the treetops grew thicker overhead, leaving the forest floor splotchy with patches of deep darkness. Another storm was on its way.

Catherine fished her bell-box out of her pack and pushed the lever in a rapid pattern. Back at the settlement, the bell on the box's twin would chime just as if she were pulling its string. Matthew would be listening, and would be glad to know she was all right.

The code by which they communicated had improved over the years, and Catherine and Matthew used it often enough that they had developed their own shorthand references. She let him know approximately where she was and that she was safe. When she finished, her bell began ringing in swift patterns, Matthew wishing her luck and urging her to be cautious. She wanted to say more, to make some gesture of reconciliation, but the code wasn't subtle enough to transmit expression or feeling adequately. It would have to wait until she returned.

Catherine checked her compass beetles, as she had throughout the trip, to be certain of her heading. The beetles always tried to crawl toward their home—even across oceans—which made them an ideal tool for navigation. She was carrying two: one that lived in the forest near the settlement, and one from another beetle colony they had found elsewhere on the island. Using a rough estimate of the angle between the directions each was facing, she could calculate her position on the island with fair accuracy.

The beetles were black with wing covers traced with tiny curlicues of pale green. As soon as she opened their box, however, she could tell that something was wrong. They were motionless, not scrabbling against the side as they usually would be, trying to move toward their homes. Tentatively, she reached in and touched one. It was stiff and clearly dead. What had happened to them?

She pulled out a knife and cut one of them in half lengthwise, from its mandibles to the top of its abdomen. Its flesh was laced with layers of salt and stone, just as the sailors of the *Western Star* had been when her father had dissected them so long ago. But that had been in London. These beetles were here, on Horizon, where the sky dipped near the earth and flooded it with quintessence power. They weren't supposed to run out of quintessence here.

Catherine suddenly realized how quiet it was. She ought to hear something—the whir of a Hades helmet fly, the chirp of a honeyguide, the scratch of a marmoset's claws in the canopy above— but the forest was silent. The trees on this part of the island were thicker, the trunks steaming with humidity that blanketed the air, unlike the dry, scuttling sounds of the forests further south that rattled when the wind blew. Still . . .

"Thomas?" she called. "Paul?" Her voice seemed small, and there was no response.

Best to be prepared. She licked her finger and dipped it in the salt pouch at her belt. It came out dusted with the small white granules. She licked again, spreading the salt out on her tongue, and felt a warm tingle as it reacted with the quintessence in her bloodstream. She could feel the salt spark and burn inside her, giving her power. A glowing sheen appeared on her skin.

Dark clouds roiled above her. The ground had been steadily sloping downward for some time, and now it became swampy. Reeds grew in clumps around stagnant pools, and she had to step carefully to avoid sinking up to her ankle in mud. She reached a break in the undergrowth where the ground dropped away more suddenly, affording her a wider view, and she saw corpses everywhere, littering the landscape. Dead fish and frogs floated white and rotting in putrid water. A boarcat lay half submerged in a muddy pool, only matted fur and one ear visible, without so much as a ripple in the pools of water around it.

No natural creature killed this many animals and then abandoned the meat to rot. Catherine had spent enough time in the forest to know what death looked like. Nature cleaned up after itself. The death of one animal was food for others: flies, grubs, and scavengers both on land and in the air. But here, even the flies were dead. They littered the ground like seed sown in a crop field. Carrion birds lay crashed on the ground with their wings outstretched and their bodies broken as if they had died mid-flight and plummeted to the earth. There was even a dead opteryx—a scavenging reptile that, despite its large size, floated high on the breeze like a vulture in search of rotting flesh to eat.

It was as if everything that came within this rough circle of earth had died. Plants drooped, wilted and brown, and mossy clumps rotted on the branches of the trees. The smell of putrefaction was thick and turned her stomach. What had happened here?

She called again for her manticore bodyguards, but got no response. Were they dead as well? Invisible, they could be lying at her feet, and she wouldn't know it. She took a step back and fished a tiny bottle from her pack. The bottle held the tears of a seer skink, a blue liquid which the skink excreted from glands around its eyes, and which enabled it to see and catch its prey, the normally-invisible Hades helmet fly.

Catherine covered the mouth of the bottle and upended it briefly, leaving a small drop behind on her finger, which she smeared into her left eye. Pain seared her eye. That always happened, but once it passed, the world would come alive with light and color. Tiny networks of light would cross through the air, connecting trees and rocks, some stretching out of sight or into the sky. It was like clearing a film from your eyes that you never knew had been there.

The threads of light were quintessence, the foundation of the miracles they did every day: turning sand into food, building homes of diamond and gold, communicating across miles. The threads were everywhere, connecting every living thing, reaching even beyond the grave. There was some disagreement among members of the Quintessence Society about just what quintessence was. Was it really the light itself? Was it something behind the light, something intrinsic to the way the atoms of the material world were stitched together? Or was it spiritual, a matter for prayer and meditation rather than experimentation?

Regardless, it was closer and more powerful here on Horizon. Some said it was because here, at the edge of the world, the sun and stars dipped down close to the Earth. Some said the quintessence came from the animals; some that the animals simply benefitted from it. Sinclair had even suggested that the animals used to be ordinary, and only became extraordinary when their island had floated to the edge of the world. Whatever was true, quintessence was everywhere you looked.

Except here. As the pain subsided, Catherine looked around and saw nothing. No light. No quintessence. That explained all the death, at least. She could picture the opteryx, drifting close, then suddenly reverting to its true weight and plunging to earth. Every living thing on Horizon, from the grass to the insects to the giant bovine herds, relied on quintessence for survival. Including her.

Catherine reached inside herself for the familiar flow of quintessence that would allow her to run quickly for safety or leap to the top of one of these trees, but it was gone. She turned and ran, stumbling over roots. She felt clumsy running without the help of quintessence. But no, it was worse than that. Her feet felt heavy and her ankles didn't bend the way they should. She knew what was happening. Without quintessence, the food and water she had consumed over the last year was transforming back into salt and sand.

She tripped again, and fell on her face. Her legs were stiffening fast. She clambered up again, but she could barely move her knees. It was like walking on stilts. Her legs were turning to stone.

An image flashed into her mind, of Mad Admiral Chelsey and the original explorers, their bodies stiff with stone and encrusted salt. Their bodies had changed more slowly than this on their return voyage, but they had only gradually moved away from the source of quintessence, too.

She screamed for help, but with little hope. Thomas and Paul must have already succumbed, dying before they could alert her. They were, after all, native Horizon creatures, even more dependent on quintessence than she was.

She fell into the mud again, and this time she couldn't get up again. She couldn't bend her knees or get any traction against the swampy ground. Her legs burned with pain. A vine creeper next to her was still green and laced with purple flowers. She knew the variety — an innocent-looking bloom with sweet smelling nectar, safe for insects that would spread its pollen, but bearing invisible poisoned barbs to kill any larger animal (or human) inclined to touch it. Catherine had no intention of touching it. The point was, it was still alive. It must be outside the range of the blight. She was close!

She grabbed an exposed root and pulled herself through the

muck, trying to get her legs out of the dead zone. As she pulled, however, she saw the creeper turn brown and its bright flowers wither. Whatever was causing the circle of death, one thing was clear. It was spreading.

She saw it spread past her to other plants, too fast for her to escape. The stiffness crept up her torso, and she cried out from the pain of it. Then, helped by her skink tears, she saw a single quintessence thread burning, leading from her pack back toward the settlement. Her bell-box. She pulled it out. At least she could tell Matthew what was happening. She worked the handle, beginning a message, but before she could say anything, the bright thread snapped, and she was left with a useless wooden box of bones. She cried out in frustration and flung the box aside.

The rain clouds above blocked the sun, leaving her in near-darkness. She made one last, desperate attempt to pull herself forward, but the ground was slick with mud, and there was nothing to hold on to. The circle of death was spreading too fast. It seemed that Matthew's fears for her safety would prove warranted after all.

The dark clouds broke open, and it started to rain.

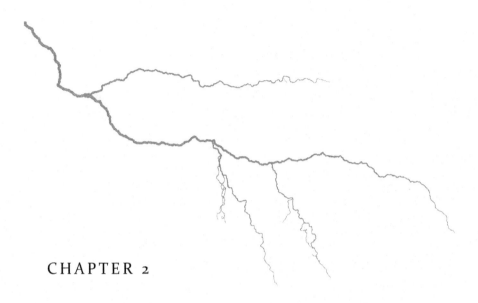

CHAPTER 2

THE RAIN pelted down, drumming against the invisible canopy overhead. Matthew bent and examined the broad, white petals of the flowers arrayed around him like a field of snow. These salt lilies were crucial to the Horizon colony's continued survival, but their yield had been steadily decreasing. He had hoped it was just the recent rainstorms dissolving the salt crystals off of the flowers. He had devised the canopy overhead to keep them dry without blocking the sunlight, but from what he could see, it hadn't helped.

Salt was to quintessence like fuel was to a flame, and every living thing on Horizon needed it, including them. Animals used quintessence in a hundred different ways to hunt prey, hide from predators, attract mates, and protect their young, while plants used it to germinate, gather sunlight, and spread their seeds. Plants like these salt lilies formed salt crystals on their blooms to attract insect pollinators. All of the inventions that kept humans alive on this island required salt, and planting and harvesting these lilies had become their main source of it.

"They're completely dry," Matthew said.

The man in charge of tending the lilies, a tall Scotsman named Ferguson, rolled his eyes. "Of course, they're dry. I told you, didn't I? I watered the soil, just like you said, but the blooms are dry as a desert."

"Then why aren't they producing?" Matthew said.

Ferguson was oddly proportioned, with huge feet, but a tiny head and sunken chin. He glared at Matthew. "Don't look at me. I was a lawyer before we came here. I don't know anything about farming."

Matthew wanted to tell him that it didn't matter what he had been in England, he was a salt farmer now, but that would only antagonize the man. Ferguson thought the work was beneath him—in fact, he had been dropping hints that he would make a better governor than Matthew's father—but he did the job properly. It wasn't his fault there was no salt.

"You'd better tell your father to start paying attention," Ferguson said. "It's just getting worse, and he doesn't seem to care."

Matthew fought back another irritated reply. "First I'll need to test the soil," he said.

The problem was, they didn't know where the salt came from. The animals got it from the plants they ate, and the plants seemed to pull it from the soil, but how did the soil get replenished?

The water in the ocean around Horizon was fresh, despite the fact that it continually flowed over the edge and new water flowed in from the east. That implied that the salt from the ocean was somehow captured by the island and used to feed the local ecology, but how that actually happened, Matthew had no idea. It was hard to solve a problem when you didn't know how it worked in the first place.

"It's the manticores doing it," Ferguson said.

Matthew raised an eyebrow. "How do you figure that?"

He made a snorting noise. "Are you as blind as your father? They don't want us here. They know we need the salt, so they're getting rid of it."

"And how are they doing that?"

Ferguson shrugged eloquently, his shoulders nearly reaching his ears. "You're the smart one," he said.

Matthew ignored him and bent to collect some soil. As he did so, he felt a stabbing pain in his thigh. He frowned and rubbed at the spot. His leg had been hurting him on and off for a week now, and it worried him. Quintessence didn't prevent pain—if he pricked his finger, he would still feel the jab—but it quickly healed all wounds and diseases, even many that would have meant death back in England. What could be causing this pain in his leg to continue, day after day?

He poured the soil into a glass flask filled with fresh, glowing water from the ocean. The outside of the flask was covered with black scales from an opteryx, whose wings and body scales changed color in response to a flow of quintessence. It was part of a mating display, a way the male opteryx had of showing females its strength and prowess. The scales changed from black through a range of colors, sometimes to a pure white, depending on how much quintessence the male had collected in its body. Males with the brightest color attracted the most females.

For the inventors and philosophers of the Quintessence Society, this provided a means to measure and compare a quintessence potential. The salt in the soil would fuel the quintessence in the water, causing it to glow brighter. The quintessence glow would suffuse the scales, which would change color in relation to how much salt had been added.

Matthew stirred the water, and the scales turned a dull red. That meant about 20 Q, which corresponded to less than an ounce of salt. He did the figures in his head. Forty percent less than last week. Not only was the salt concentration still decreasing; it was decreasing at a faster rate.

The numbers didn't lie. Matthew tried to keep the dismay off of his face. Ferguson could be a troublemaker, quick to complain about problems and get people riled up. Matthew wanted to let his father know first, before Ferguson started a panic.

And there would be panic. At this rate, if they couldn't figure out what was happening, all the humans on Horizon would be dead inside a month, with the animal and plant population following soon after. The next expedition to discover the island would find only a colony of statues, petrified like the corpses on Admiral Chelsey's ship.

Catherine had been right to go on her expedition. He worried at the thought of her out in the wilderness, alone, but they had to solve this before it was too late. It went against all his protective instincts for her to be in danger while he stayed safe at home. He had made the mistake of voicing that to her, and they had parted on bad terms. The memory ate at him; he couldn't stand being unreconciled.

Matthew headed back home, bracing himself for a meeting with his father. He walked through the invisible barrier, feeling nothing more than a slight buzz, and on into the settlement. It was more like a city than a village, its buildings tall and beautiful, constructed out of diamond, silver, and various types of wood. Nearly all the homes had running hot and cold water pumped from the river. Most of them were heated without the need for a fireplace, and even cooled by a heat substitution device. It was a tiny city of wonders, with daily comforts London had never dreamed of, but all of those wonders used salt at a tremendous rate. No one would be eager to give up their comforts, but something would have to be done, and soon, if they were going to survive.

The governor's mansion was not cooled by quintessence, nor did it have running water. It could hardly be called a mansion anymore, for that matter, since so many of the newer houses exceeded it in size and grandeur. It was drab and square, a emblem of the Protestant ideal of unadorned piety. Exactly like the governor himself.

Matthew walked in without knocking. This wasn't his home. He hadn't lived with his father since they first arrived on Horizon, when his father had lived in the forest, evangelizing the manticores. But his news was urgent, and he wasn't going to wait to take it through proper channels. He made his way through corridors to the room where he expected to find his father.

It was the largest room in the house, and Matthew found his father there with six manticores, a trusted cadre of Christian converts whom his father was educating. He ran the house like a seminary, housing as many as a dozen, to whom he taught daily classes on Hebrew, Greek, and Biblical theology. In fact, he devoted a lot more attention and passion to this work than he did to the running of the colony, one of the many reasons Matthew considered him ill-suited to the governorship. Matthew had to admit, however, that his father had done a remarkable job of forging a kind of peace with their manticore neighbors after the fighting last year, far more successfully than anyone else could have done.

John Marcheford was dressed exactly as he would have been in London: an austere, black doublet and gray hose, sober attire with a formality completely out of place in a remote island colony. There had been a time, long ago, when Matthew had revered his father as a god. Back home, he had been important and respected, his knowledge vast and his morals above reproach, and Matthew had wanted to grow up to be just like him. In those days, Catherine used to say he was a miniature version of his father, a mannequin who dressed the same and repeated the same phrases.

Now, Matthew had to keep his mouth shut in his father's presence if he didn't want to start a fight. His father's distinguished manner, so suited to London, seemed out-of-place and preposterous here. His clothing was impractical and ridiculous, and worst of all, he denounced quintessence and its use in everyday life as a corrupting and atheistic influence.

"I have to talk with you," Matthew said.

His father lifted a finger and continued his lesson. He was aging, Matthew noticed. The lines of his face had grown deeper, and his hands, which Matthew remembered for their strength and purposefulness, had grown knotted and spidery.

"Please read from verse fourteen," his father said.

A manticore stood awkwardly cradling an English Bible in its pincers. "He causeth grass to grow for the cattle, and herb for the use of man, that he may bring forth bread out of the earth."

Matthew recognized it as Psalm 104, a chapter about God's sovereignty over the natural world.

"*God* causeth the grass to grow," his father boomed in his preaching voice. "It is not the rain or sun which causeth it, however God might please to use them in his service. Therefore, if the grass fail, should we beseech the rain and the sun for help?"

"Nay!" the manticores chorused.

"Should we measure the rain and calculate the angle of the sun to understand why it will not grow?"

"Nay!"

"What then?"

One manticore raised a pincer in a ridiculous parody of a English schoolboy raising his hand. Marcheford called on him.

"We should seek the Lord in prayer," the manticore said.

"Very good," Marcheford replied, his eyes boring into Matthew's. "Only the Lord can make the plants grow."

Matthew sighed. He wondered if they had been studying this passage before he arrived, or if his father had brought it up simply to make his point to Matthew. There was so little they agreed on anymore, and Matthew found it unsettling. Everything he thought and believed came originally from his father. Once, he would have taken every word from his father's mouth as gospel truth.

His father was wrong about quintessence, wrong about the experimental study of the natural world being an atheistic philosophy. But that meant his father *could* be wrong, and if so, what if he was wrong about everything? Matthew still believed his Protestant faith: that salvation was by faith alone; that the bread and wine in the Lord's Supper was a symbol, not the actual flesh and blood of Christ; that God alone was to be worshipped. But he wasn't certain why he believed them. Was it just because his father had always said so? It was only in the last year that it had really occurred to him that his father could be wrong. It was as if the pillar supporting everything Matthew believed had suddenly been swept away, and he wasn't sure if anything he thought he knew would stand anymore.

"We need to talk right now," Matthew said.

His father nodded. "Lessons are adjourned until tomorrow," he said.

He led Matthew to his study, a room which, when Christopher Sinclair was governor, had been strewn with flasks, powders, jars of animal organs, dried insects and bones—all tools in the service of the natural philosophy. Now, the room was filled with rolls of paper, the manuscript of his father's ongoing attempt to translate the Bible for the manticores. The manticores had no written language, but his father had created one, using a combination of Latin letters and pictographs to represent the tail motions that were so important a part of their communication. It had been his father's lifelong wish to bring the gospel to a group of people unreached by the gospel, and no group was more unreached than the manticore tribes. He was living his dream.

"You know we're running out of salt," Matthew said. "I just came from the lily fields. We have a month at most. We need to start compulsory rationing."

His father shrugged. "Why come to me with this? I have nothing to do with your atheist Quintessence Society."

"We're not atheists. And I come to you because you're the governor. You're supposed to be leading."

His father had been offered the governorship with little discussion or objection after Christopher Sinclair died. As a bishop, he had the highest rank and social class of anyone in the colony, so most people accepted his leadership as natural. To Matthew, it seemed ridiculous. His father was the opposite of all Horizon stood for, a man who looked backward instead of forward, who clung to the ideals of London society, who thought young men should respect their elders, women should stay home and be quiet in public, and people should accept their God-given place in life instead of striving to make themselves a new one. What was he doing as their leader?

This was *Horizon*. They could heal any disease, manipulate invisible powers, run for miles without tiring, and practically fly. They were gods. Why should the old rules apply? In this new world, it was Matthew whose knowledge and skill exceeded his father's, not the other way around. His father had been revered by many in London for his religious zeal and his rank in the English church. But Matthew, at only nineteen years old, was the one revered here. Not for his connections or place in society, but for what he could *do*.

"I warned you about this," his father said. "You think you can replace God with no consequences. You think that because you understand how bread is made, you don't need God to provide it. Now God is withdrawing his hand, and what are you left with, after all your wisdom? No bread."

Matthew clenched his fists. "You live in a house forged by quintessence. All the food you eat was created with quintessence." He gestured around the room. "Even the paper you use for your precious Bible translation is available in such quantity because of a quintessence-powered process, invented by people like me."

His father shrugged. "' When ye thought evil against me, God disposed it to good, that he might bring to pass, as it is this day, and save much people alive.'"

Matthew recognized the quote again, this time from Genesis 50. "Evil? You call feeding and protecting this colony evil?" This was why he avoided talking to his father. It made him furious. He felt like pulling all those scrolls down from their shelves and setting a match to them.

"No, son." His father shook his head sadly. "What you have accomplished is truly wonderful, and I praise God for it. The evil is in thinking you no longer need God."

"You're going to lose the governorship, if you're not careful," Matthew said. "Ferguson has been talking to almost everyone, listening to their grievances and blaming the shortages on you. He implies, though he never quite says, that if he were in charge, things wouldn't be so badly managed."

His father didn't blink. "I will not stoop to politics, Matthew. God has given me this role, but I would lay it down gladly if he wishes it."

"I'm not asking you to go door to door and curry favor," Matthew said, though he didn't think it would hurt any if he did exactly that. "I'm asking you to address the problem."

"I am addressing the problem. I preach repentance from the pulpit every Sunday."

"Ferguson calls you a manticore-lover. He preys on people's fears, tells them you're not on their side. He wants to expand the colony's land holdings and drive the manticores out."

"He's a fool."

"He's a fool people are listening to." Matthew searched for a way to reach his father. "'They are as sheep having no shepherd,'" he tried, a reference to Matthew 9:36.

"I am their shepherd," his father said, "and I am feeding their souls. If their bodies should lack in future months, that is no bad thing."

"So you won't call for rationing?"

"I will, if you wish it. But don't be fooled into believing that all you need is more time. What you need is prayer and repentance. You may discover why the salt in the soil is disappearing. You may even discover the mechanism by which it moves from the ocean water to the soil, but the truth will remain that it is God who commands it. 'Thou openest thine hand, and they are filled with good things. But if thou take away their breath, they die and return to their dust.'"

Psalm 104 again. "The rules have changed," Matthew said. "We don't need God to explain why things live anymore, or why they die."

"I know someone else who believed as much."

"Christopher Sinclair, you mean. And you know what? He was right." Matthew pointed his finger at his father's chest. "He was right about this island, and he was right about quintessence. He even brought Catherine back from the dead."

"Nearly at the cost of every life on the island, and ultimately at the cost of his own."

Matthew couldn't stand this conversation anymore. With each of his father's glib responses, hot blood rushed through him, making him want to hit his father or grab his throat and strangle him. His father just stood there, calm and untroubled, which made Matthew even angrier. He threw up his hands. "I can't talk to you," he said. He opened the door. "Sinclair died saving your life, you old fool." He slammed the door behind him.

Matthew stalked through the mansion, furious and, at the same time, deeply ashamed. He wished he could be like Sinclair and set himself completely against God, but he couldn't shake the sense that God really was there, watching him. There or not, however, he would let his father say the prayers. He wasn't going to stand back and wait for God to provide. As far as he was concerned, if there was a way to save this island, it was up to him to find it.

He walked out of the front door of the mansion into darkness. He looked up, expecting that another storm had covered over the sun, but no. Instead of clouds, he saw a rapidly moving stream of blackness, like a river in the sky. An immense whirring sound accompanied it. The river was composed of tiny grains, like pouring sand, and Matthew realized it was made of thousands and thousands of black beetles.

He started to run, ignoring the pain in his thigh. These were compass beetles, the same kind that Catherine's father, and later her mother, had used to navigate across the ocean to find Horizon in the first place. A huge colony of them lived in the beetlewood forest that surrounded the human settlement. The creatures had the unusual trait of knowing the direction to their home regardless of how far away from it they were, which made them immensely useful. Put one in a box and it would point toward home, even across a thousand miles of water.

But now, they were leaving their home behind, migrating en masse toward the interior of the island. What did it mean? Was there not enough food in the forest? Or were the leaves they ate no longer providing enough salt to keep them alive?

Matthew reached the invisible barrier around the settlement and ran through it into the forest. It didn't take him long to see what he had feared. Littering the earth around him were what looked like stones, rounded pieces of rock the size of a silver half crown. He picked one up. It was like a compass beetle, perfectly carved out of stone. It was solid, not a husk like molting cicadas might leave behind back in England. These beetles had petrified, and the others had fled before they met the same fate.

He looked up. High above him, the mossy branches of the trees bent with the weight of similar stone beetles. Hundreds of them.

Matthew had been sixteen—it seemed like an eternity ago—when the mysterious ship had sailed into London harbor filled with human statues and chests of sand. They knew now that the sailors had food made with quintessence in their flesh, and it had transformed back to salt and sand when they traveled too far from Horizon. To see these beetles, petrified like this, here on Horizon, was like reading a death sentence. If it could happen to the beetles, it could happen to them.

CHAPTER 3

RAMOS should have reported Antonia to the Inquisition. It was his duty as a priest and a Christian. The Inquisition was overwhelmed with reports of demon activity, however, since hundreds had been taken with fits in the night. Most of the afflicted were now mad, babbling nonsense and falling down repeatedly with the shaking fits. A rumor spread that the madness was contagious, and fear overcame reason. Several of the mad were dragged from their homes by mobs and stoned or thrown into the river.

Ramos kept Antonia hidden and tried to keep her madness secret. He stayed at home, feeding and caring for her himself. Her babbling was sometimes cheerful, sometimes despairing, and she often cried. Sometimes it even seemed to make a strange sort of sense, but never had any relation to the people or things around her. If he led her by the hand, she would walk along with him, though he had to lead her around obstacles. When she convulsed, he made sure she didn't knock into hard or sharp edges that could hurt her.

Pope Julius III declared the madness a judgment from God,

directed at those who had harbored secret heresies in their hearts. The Inquisition started burning the mad, twenty or thirty at a time. The mass public trials drew thousands, both from the city and the surrounding area, to see the spectacle. Death always drew a crowd, but even more so the death of something the people feared.

As a Jesuit, Ramos had taken a holy oath to obey the Pope in all things. He had always taken comfort in the Church, where truth and falsehood were so clearly defined. As the founder of his order, Ignatius Loyola, had put it, "I will believe that the white that I see is black if the Church so defines it." But how could he believe that Antonia had harbored secret heresies? She was sweet and innocent, more so than many priests he knew. She had never heard the corruptions of holy doctrine taught by the Protestants, or seen the vile practices of the Musselman infidels. And even if she had . . . he loved her. How could he give her up to the fires?

On his own, a mere royal astronomer, Ramos had no political influence to bring to bear. If King Philip had been there, it might have been different. Philip was a devoutly religious man, devoted to the Church, but he was also practical and not given to superstition. He valued Ramos's intellect, especially on matters pertaining to the heavens. Ramos would never presume to think of the king as a friend, but Philip trusted him—a rare thing in a royal court—and he was fiercely protective of those few he could trust. The king, however, was still in England marrying Queen Mary, and was not due to return for months. Spain was in the hands of the Inquisition.

All the while, the hole in the sky grew. Ramos wasn't the only one to notice it. It sucked more of the surrounding stars into its maw, spinning out their light like thread from a spool, leaving them dim specters of their former brightness. Even those with no astronomical knowledge pointed and gawked and cowered in their homes. Many fled to the Church for protection, and the monasteries and convents doubled in size. Everyone could see that the sky was not the same as it had been. They began to refer to the hole in the sky simply by the Latin word for new. *Nova*.

Few people thought to consider any reason for the nova's appearance beyond the judgment of God. Events in the heavens occurred because God decreed them, just as things did on Earth. Ramos, however, wasn't satisfied with that. God might have been punishing the mad, but what if there was another cause? A cause that explained why some had been afflicted but not others? He was determined to find out.

Ramos left Antonia in Carmela's care and began interviewing the families of the afflicted and recording their answers. He made a map of the homes of the mad, hoping to find a geographical pattern. He studied his notes long into the night, barely admitting to himself the secret hope he harbored. If there was a pattern to the madness, then there might be a physical cause. And if there was a physical cause, there just might be a cure.

Word came from Madrid that the madness had struck there, too. When pilgrims arrived from France and the Netherlands, it became clear that the phenomenon was worldwide. Eventually, a pattern did emerge in Ramos's records, a simple strand that linked the thousands of people who had fallen to the madness. They had all been born between May 21 and May 25, the first five days of the constellation Gemini. The constellation in which the nova had appeared.

This provided no cure, of course, since he could not change Antonia's birthday. It did, however, suggest that it wasn't because of heresy that she was afflicted. It also suggested another possible catastrophe for the kingdom of Spain.

King Philip II had been born on May 21. No word had come from England. Was he marrying Queen Mary as planned? Or was he secretly raving in a palace room in London?

If the king was mad, then perhaps it was time for Ramos to take Antonia and flee the country. Spain had not been a unified nation for long. Even the suggestion that Philip might have lost his mind could spark a civil war, nobles vying with each other and with the Church for power, maybe even the division of Spain back into the independent kingdoms of Castile and Aragon, Navarre and Leon. It would mean bloody war and Spanish dead on a massive scale.

Not only that, but King Philip was the Church's greatest champion, the man whose strength held back the growth of Protestant heresy in Saxony and the Low Countries and the ever-fiercer armies of Musselman infidels to the south. If he had fallen to the madness, what would become of Christendom? The Netherlands would be overrun by Protestant rebels; Turkey and then Italy itself would fall to the Musselmen; perhaps even the Vatican would be overrun, its treasures plundered.

Ramos told no one of the pattern he had found, afraid of what the consequences might be. He stopped asking questions and stayed home with Antonia, quietly preparing to leave the country. He wasn't fast enough. Perhaps a neighbor, peering in a window, had seen Antonia in one of her fits, or maybe someone had marked his odd hours and behavior. In the middle of the night—as they always did, for maximum surprise and intimidation—the soldiers of the Inquisition came knocking.

Ramos was instantly alert. He threw off the blanket and went to rouse Antonia, but she was already awake. He helped her up and threw a cloak around her. There was no time to dress, no time to pack. He led her to the back door and opened it quietly, but the soldiers had anticipated him. Two of them pushed through, swords drawn. Antonia fell to the floor, her body convulsing. Ramos tried to go to her, but a soldier yanked his arms behind his back.

"Let me go to her!"

The other soldier slapped him, and he tasted blood. Two other soldiers came through from the front door, dragging Carmela with them. She was shouting at them, but when she saw Antonia on the floor, she started to cry.

"We'll go with you," Ramos said, trying for a reasonable tone. "Let me help her, and we'll go with you peaceably."

The biggest soldier, a scarred man with a broken nose, laughed. "You and your demon child will come with us whether you want to or not." He wrapped his thick fingers through Antonia's hair and yanked her to her feet. She made a high-pitched keening sound, confused and in pain. Carmela tried to intervene, but they knocked her to the floor, where she stayed, whimpering, as they dragged Ramos and Antonia out.

The soldiers threw them into a makeshift dungeon of brick and lime mortar, constructed in the Moorish style. Ramos wasn't even sure where in the city they were. The royal dungeons were in the Castillo de Mota, fifty leagues distant in the old city of Medina del Campo—too far away to bother bringing prisoners who would just be burned in a few days time. Ramos knew that neither his standing as a priest nor his royal connections would save him or Antonia from being convicted in a public mass trial. His home and possessions would already have been seized by the Church to pay for his incarceration and execution. At least they had not been brought to the Catedral and its torture chamber. He held Antonia and stroked her hair. She didn't know what was happening, but she was frightened nonetheless and moaned softly and clung to his arm.

The others in the dungeon were mad as well. They babbled, sang, or simply stared into the distance. They did not seem malnourished, which simply meant they had not been here for very long. The wheels of the Inquisition were turning quickly.

There was a little light coming through cracks in the ceiling and around the door. Ramos traced a circle in the dirt floor and added the lines of the ecliptic. This time, he used his own date and latitude of birth as a basis, because it was his own horoscope he wanted to calculate. He thought he could predict the rest of his short life without such a tool, but there was nothing else to do while he waited to die.

He didn't have his astrolabe or star almanac, but he had done this so many times he didn't need them. The nova lent a new variable to the figures, subtly changing them, twisting them in surprising directions. He moved to a new section of floor and pressed on, surprised at the complexity of the figures surrounding his own life. He almost gave them up as unsolvable, but finally the associations began to emerge.

They were nothing like what he expected. The nova was prominent, with links to madness and danger; no surprises there. But there were figures for treason and heresy, for the love of a woman, for crossing an ocean, and others so unfamiliar he could not understand them.

Ramos scuffed out the figures with his foot, feeling strangely encouraged. Perhaps he and Antonia would escape at the last moment, just as the boy Luis had done. Antonia. He drew another circle in the dust, suddenly afraid again. Just because he would escape didn't mean she would.

Before he could begin, however, the door to the prison burst open with a creak and a bang. The light from the lanterns brought in by the guards seemed unbearably bright, and Ramos covered his eyes. Antonia whimpered, and he wrapped his arms around her. Surely they weren't here to take her away from him already?

When his eyes adjusted, Ramos saw a military officer wearing half armor, an ornate morion helmet with red and white plumes, a red sash, and very white hose. He had a rapier in his belt and a grim expression on his face.

"Father Ramos de Tavera of the University?" he demanded. By voice and bearing, he was an aristocrat, probably highly placed in the army. He seemed quite out of place in the filth and stench of this makeshift dungeon.

Gently, Ramos extricated himself from Antonia and stood to meet the stranger. "I am he."

The officer clapped his heels together and held out a rolled paper tied with ribbon and sealed with red wax. "A letter from His Majesty."

Ramos took it, dazed. "Then his Majesty is not mad?"

"Mad?" The officer looked appalled. "Of course he is not mad. He is married to the Queen of England. He sent me here to gather more ships and soldiers to sail to England and solidify their reign. I regret to inform you, however, that your brother Diego de Tavera died in the king's service."

Ramos's first thought was for Antonia, and he glanced back at her to see how she would react. Now both of her natural parents were dead, though in her mad state, he doubted she even understood the news. "How did he die?"

The officer told a fantastical story, of how Diego had traveled at the king's command to a far-off island in the Western sea, chasing improbable rumors of vast golden fortunes. It was bizarre. Diego was no explorer. He was a priest with political ambitions, a passion for the Church, and too much of a taste for power. He gravitated to thrones and cathedrals, not disease-ridden islands far from civilization. Ramos had never been close to his brother, but the news unsettled him. At least Diego would never see his daughter's madness.

Perhaps the king's letter would shed some light. It must be a letter of condolence, a rare display of generous emotion from a monarch to a member of his court. He tore it open and found that it was nothing of the kind.

> *To Father Ramos de Tavera, Universidad de Valladolid:*
>
> *Your presence is required for a matter of utmost urgency. Depart immediately with the bearer of this letter and proceed by ship with all speed to Whitehall Palace, London. He will provide you with anything you require. Neither illness nor any other responsibility should delay your swift obedience.*
>
> *Sincerely,*
> *Juan Barrosa, Court Secretary*
> *On behalf of His Grace, Philip II, King of all Spain, Portugal, Naples, Sicily, England, and Ireland*

Astonished, he showed the letter to the officer, who showed it to the chief jailor. Ramos lifted Antonia to her feet. "We're leaving now," he told her. "We're going far away."

The jailor blocked his path. "That letter says you," he said, pointing his finger in Ramos's face. "It don't say nothing about her."

"She's my daughter. She's my responsibility, and she's coming with me."

"Look at her," the jailor said in disgust. "Mad like the rest of them, ain't she? Going to burn like the rest of them, too."

Antonia clung tighter to Ramos and tried to hide behind him. Ramos felt his anger rising. He pointed to the letter still in the officer's hand. "That's from the *king*, you fool. It says I leave with anything I require. I require her."

"She's demon-possessed. You can't take her back up to the

streets."

Ramos ignored him, escorting Antonia toward the door, but the jailor grabbed her by the arm and tried to wrench her away. With a ringing sound like a tiny bell, the officer's rapier jumped suddenly from the scabbard at his belt to a point an inch from the jailor's throat.

"Release her."

The jailor dropped his hold. "The Inquisition'll burn you for this."

The officer gave a tight smile. "Let them try."

CHAPTER 4

THE BLIGHT was spreading faster than Catherine could escape it. The stiffness and burning pain had crept up her torso and into her arms. It wouldn't be long now. Her legs were completely immobile, now, and she couldn't feel them anymore. Her frantic attempts to inch herself out of the circle got little traction in the mud, and there was nothing to grab onto.

The rain drenched her clothes and spattered mud into her face. The smell of rotting plants and putrefaction was overwhelming, gagging her. With a desperate heave, she managed to move her body enough to grab onto a slim tree, but now her muscles weren't working. She could hold on to the trunk, but she couldn't pull herself any closer.

"Look what we have here," said a voice.

She nearly cried with joy at the sound. It was a manticore voice, speaking in their language; it must be Thomas or Paul. "Hello!" she called. "I'm here."

The speaker stepped into her field of vision: a large, gray

manticore. The gray's pincered hands were raised and two of his tails slid sinuously over his shoulders. "The star-bird, caught in a net," he said. The sharp sounds his mouth made were punctuated by movements of the pincers and tails, adding specifics to the imprecise ideas that the sounds alone communicated.

Her joy disappeared. This was not a rescue. The gray's manner was challenging, triumphant. Many of the manticores had referred to Catherine as "star-bird" since the manticore attack the previous spring, when she had used a flood of quintessence power to drive them away. It was generally spoken with wary respect, but this gray used the term mockingly.

Still, this was no time to be shy. "I can't move. I need a rope, or something I can hold onto, so you can pull me out."

"My brothers died on your wall," the gray said.

"I'm sorry. I'm going to die right now, if you don't help me. I'm not sure I can even hold on to a rope. Please."

The gray gesticulated and chattered briefly at a lower volume, apparently to other manticores she couldn't see. It was all she could do not to cry out from the pain. All the salt she had eaten, the fresh sea water she had drunk, the bread made from sand: it was all changing back. Her tissues were turning into salt and sand, and it *hurt*.

Something fell near her head. She focused on it. It was a vine, still green and supple, but dying fast. At the other end, a half dozen manticores held on, ready to pull her out. She wrapped loops of it around her stiff fingers and grabbed hold as best she could. As they dragged her away from the circle, the pain receded, and first her arms, then her legs, became loose and movable again. She lay weak and panting at the feet of the big gray, too exhausted to move.

When she could speak, she said, "Thank you."

They hauled her upright, but the pain now surged back into her legs, and she couldn't stand. She tried to use quintessence to make her body lighter, but it was still out of reach, and she slumped back to the ground when they let go.

"Catherine Parris," the gray said.

Catherine frowned. "Who are you?"

It lashed its tails through the air, irritated. "Don't play games."

"Should I know you?"

The gray hissed. "I am Rinchirith, as all know. But perhaps you truly do not remember. A failing we shall soon remedy."

Catherine thought fast, remembering Thomas's warnings about Rinchirith. Was it coincidence, he of all manticores appearing here to rescue her? She didn't think so. "This was all your plan, wasn't it? You arranged for Thomas and Paul to bring me here, so you could capture me."

Rinchirith made the manticore equivalent of a smile. "Are you surprised? They are my memory brothers. Their loyalty to earth and sky runs deeper than their devotion to this *Christ*."

"They're dead, aren't they?"

Rinchirith's pincered hands shut with a snap. "They are as alive as I am. I do not kill my own."

In any other circumstance, Catherine could have leaped over them all, could have run away before they knew she had moved, could have blinded them with a blaze of quintessence energy that set the forest on fire. Now, weakened by the blight, she could barely lift her head. "What do you want from me?"

He laughed, a kind of clicking sound deep in his throat. "I don't want anything from you, star-bird."

"Then why am I here? Revenge for your brothers?"

Rinchirith bent and thrust his face into hers. "They are all my brothers. They all cry out for blood. But that is just the dew on the grass, not the ocean. The dreams of the earth snakes are rising, and you do not understand them."

The "earth snakes" were a common concept among the manticores, whose mythos seemed to associate the underground as the place of gods, rather than the sky. They referred to snakes and worms under the earth in mystical tones. Catherine thought it was hardly surprising, given the power of the shekinah flatworms as sources of quintessence. In this context, however, she had no idea what Rinchirith meant.

"That blight is a danger to all of us," she said. "It's growing. I need to get back to my friends, so we can figure out why."

"We already know why," Rinchirith said.

The other manticores seized her arms with their hard pincer-grips. She struggled, but they were too strong. Rinchirith pulled her wrists together behind her back and began wrapping vine around them.

"And we know how to stop it," he said.

THE STORM that night raged like only a Horizon storm could. Towering black clouds whirled through the sky, thrown against each other by unpredictable winds. They struck with sounds like buildings colliding, sending out billows like exploding masonry and hurling lightning like spears of falling flame. In such a storm, most people had the sense to stay inside, Matthew thought wryly. Instead, he stood precariously on the peaked diamond roof of the church, the tallest structure in the colony, drenched with rain, and holding up an iron rod.

"Matthew!" Stephen Parris, Catherine's father, stood on the ground below, bellowing up at him. Matthew could barely hear him over the pounding of the rain and the crashing of thunder.

Parris leaped, making his body lighter, and flew the several stories up to join Matthew on the roof. His lightened body was more easily tossed by the wind, however, and he had to grab hold of the gold cross on top of the church to keep from being blown clear out of the settlement. He quickly made his body heavy again to anchor himself down.

"You're going to widow Catherine before you even marry her," Parris said. He had to shout over the rain to be heard.

Matthew was busy lashing the iron rod to the cross, and didn't look at him. He didn't want to lose track of what he was doing. "We have to understand why the salt is disappearing," he said.

"How is standing on a roof in a thunderstorm going to answer that question?"

Matthew straightened and leaned toward Parris to be heard more easily. "How long has it been since we noticed the change in salt levels?"

"About five weeks."

"And how long have we been having these thunderstorms?"

Parris grunted. It apparently hadn't occurred to him that the start of the wild, nightly storms corresponded with the beginning of the salt shortage. Matthew didn't know which was the cause and which the effect, or if they were both the result of some deeper cause, but he was trying to find out.

"What are you doing?" Parris asked.

Matthew showed him. He had strapped the iron rod to the cross to hold it upright. The bottom end of the rod rested in a glass flask filled with salt water. The water flask was set inside a slightly larger flask filled with mercury, so that the mercury was trapped in a thin layer between the two flasks. He had covered the outside of the mercury flask with black scales from an opteryx.

The storms had plenty of lightning, and they had seen lightning striking the ground, the trees, even the roof of this church. What if the lightning was destroying or using up all the salt? If a lightning bolt hit the iron rod, whatever quintessence effect it had would be transferred into the water. If it used up the salt, the water would glow, and the opteryx scales would measure the amount. Mercury, however, reduced the strength of quintessence, so the mercury would act as a filter, dampening its power before it reached the opteryx scales. That would allow him to measure quintessence on a level far greater than what a single opteryx could store in its body.

"Two fingers of mercury means a thousandfold decrease," Matthew said. "If it reaches violet, that would be around 7000 Q, which would mean that if lightning strikes in a particular acre of ground once a night, forty percent of the salt in its soil would be consumed."

Matthew was doing what he always did: suggest a hypothesis to explain a phenomenon, then perform experiments to see if the hypothesis was true. It was a strange way of thinking to many, particularly those of the older generation. For centuries, learned men had relied on the ancients for their knowledge: the writings of Aristotle and Hippocrates, Galen and Ptolemy. They didn't see the point of his experiments. After all, who was a nineteen-year-old young man to disagree with the ancients? It was radical thinking, and it was Protestant thinking—rejecting authority in favor of self analysis and understanding. Which was why so many of those who thought this way had fled from England when Queen Mary took the throne.

"Say your experiment works," Parris said. "Lightning hits this rod and registers in the violet."

"That would explain what's happening to the salt," Matthew said.

"Then how would we stop it?"

Matthew shrugged. "I don't know. But at least we would know where the problem was coming from."

It would actually be encouraging, he thought, if the current shortage was due to the lightning. Thunderstorms didn't last forever. That would suggest it was a seasonal thing, a regional event that occurred once every several years and then recovered its balance naturally. If they could ration what they had left until the storms abated, they just might survive.

He opened his mouth to say so when the lightning struck the iron rod.

Fire exploded in his vision. He fell backward, off the roof. He made his body lighter just before he hit the ground. Parris clung to the edge of the roof above him, then clambered up again. Matthew joined him.

"That was close," he said.

"Maybe you should have found a safer way to test this," Parris said.

They looked at the flask. The opteryx scales had barely turned a dark green.

"It's not enough."

Matthew shook his head. "It's a lot of power, generally speaking, to blast through that much mercury. But it's not enough to account for the salt reduction on the island. Not nearly enough."

A strong breeze blew across the rooftop. Matthew grabbed the iron bar to steady his balance, then realized what he was holding, and hastily released it. A light from above caught his attention, and he looked up. At the same moment, he fell to his knees, crying out and clutching his leg. The pain in his thigh had increased a hundredfold.

Parris leaned over him. "Are you all right?"

"Look!" Matthew pointed up to the sky. Some of the black clouds had blown away, opening up a patch of night. A few stars shone through, huge because of how close Horizon was to the celestial sphere. Light trailed away from the stars like ribbons, spiraling into the black chasm where a star used to be.

They had noticed it weeks earlier, just before the thunderstorms came and obscured the sky. Most of the familiar constellations were skewed this far west, and barely recognizable, but the Zodiac constellations, the ones that passed over the center of the world, were the least affected. So when a star had disappeared from Gemini, a gap that seemed to suck the light from the surrounding stars, they took notice. It had been a curiosity, although a spectacular one, one of thousands of unexplained mysteries they had encountered since coming to Horizon. Remembering it now, however, the timing of its appearance with the salt shortage didn't seem like a coincidence. Perhaps it was more important than they had realized.

A bubbling noise drew their attention back to Matthew's experiment at their feet. The water in the flask was aglow and boiling furiously. The opteryx scales on the outside were a bright violet edging toward white. The white color became brighter and clearer, the violet less prominent, until it was such a pure white it was hard to look at. The flask rattled violently, and then the scales burst into flame.

AFTER tying her hands and legs, the manticores wrapped Catherine in a net made of vines, like a hammock rolled around her body. Her limbs were no longer petrified, but she was wrapped so tightly she could barely move.

She could just barely feel a warm glow in the center of her body that meant her quintessence connections were coming back. The manticores had taken her salt pouch, but even without it, she should be able to break out and escape, given a little more time to get her strength back.

"Where are you taking me?" she said.

Rinchirith sat on top of her and leaned into her face, his breath nearly choking her. His eyes burned with hatred. "Only where you deserve," he said.

He shoved a pincered hand into her mouth and forced her jaw open. She screamed and struggled, but the sharp ends of his pincers dug into the soft flesh of her gums. Another manticore approached with a the hollow, cylindrical stalk of a plant. He bit open the top and poured it into her mouth.

She choked as the thick, metallic liquid filled her mouth. Mercury. She tried to spit it out, but Rinchirith clapped her mouth closed, and she swallowed painfully. She couldn't breathe. She writhed back and forth until he released her, and she lay on her face in the dirt, gasping and coughing.

Her quintessence connections were gone. Mercury acted in the opposite way from salt, scouring her clean of quintessence instead of increasing the flow. She was completely in their power, and as long as they kept forcing mercury down her throat, she would stay that way.

Two manticores lifted the ends of her vine hammock and leaped up into the trees, carrying her between them. She was jostled and yanked back and forth as they effortlessly climbed through the branches, sometimes facing the sky, sometimes spinning around to face the ground. After a while, the skink tears wore off as well, and she couldn't even see them.

She was terrified, but after an hour of this kind of travel, she just felt battered and exhausted. She couldn't imagine what they planned to do with her. They could hold her as a hostage to force the humans to some concessions. They could cut her up piece by piece and send the pieces to the colony until they agreed to his terms. Only, Rinchirith didn't seem to her like the bargaining type.

What did he want? Catherine realized that they had never understood the manticores, not even the ones who claimed to be their friends. The humans were the trespassers on this island, a place where a hundred generations of manticores had lived and died without knowledge of humanity. Maybe it was arrogance to think the manticores should welcome them with grateful respect. Maybe humans didn't belong here at all.

And now, what would happen to her? She tried to distract herself from fear by thinking about the blight. She had found it in a swamp, a low-lying area compared to the higher ground around it. It was almost as if the blight had been spreading like a flood, seeping up from the ground and filling up the low areas. Would she have been safe from it if she had climbed a tree? There had been flying animals among the dead, but she didn't know how low they had flown before succumbing.

The whole concept of quintessence transformation was something they still didn't really understand. Quintessence turned salt water into fresh and sand into bread, but in some sense, the salt and sand were still there. In a quintessence field, her body could digest it and pass the nutrients to her tissues and keep her alive. Outside the field, the salt and sand would reappear, suffused throughout her flesh. So which was real? Was her body filled with fresh water and nutrients, or with salt and sand? Was quintessence just an illusion? How could both realities exist at the same time?

The manticores gave her neither food nor water, though every few hours, they stopped and forced more mercury down her throat, an even more terrifying ordeal since they were now invisible to her. Her stomach cramped and her vision blurred, but she tried to keep track of where they were going. No human had ever explored this deeply into the island, and she saw new kinds of foliage everywhere. Mostly, though, she looked for landmarks that might help her get home again.

When they reached the foothills of the mountains, the mossy trees thinned and were replaced by stout shrubs like umbrellas with sprays of root anchoring them to the bare rock. Herds of a mouse-like creature with multiple grasping trunks scattered from the shade as their troop passed through. She saw goats, too, with hooks on their hooves that could pass into solid rock and latch on. In this way, they could run up cliff faces or even upside-down on the roofs of caves and overhangs.

They were moving in a general northeasterly direction, toward the center of the island, with the tallest mountain always somewhat to their left. Several times they had circled far out of their way to avoid a low-lying region of ground, and she wondered if these were more quintessence blights.

Where had the blights come from? Were they related to the dwindling availability of salt? Manticores were quick to blame the humans—and not without reason—but the humans were also the most likely to be able to figure out what these blights were and where they had came from. If the manticores would just tell them what they'd seen and give them access to the sites, Catherine was confident they could discover the reason behind them. Did they always form in the areas of lowest altitude? Could it be caused by a miasma, something heavier than air seeping up from a chasm underground? Given the chance to experiment, they just might find out.

At the rate it was spreading, though, it might cover the island before they got a chance. But no, she didn't have enough information to estimate that. Without knowing the cause, she couldn't tell if the rate of spread should be measured by distance on the ground, like a moving object, or by volume, like a spreading flood, or even if the rate was constant. It might be months before it reached the settlement, it might be only weeks, or it might never get there at all.

The manticores brought her higher, up steep slopes where there were no more trees, sometimes actually climbing up cliff faces. Her precarious litter lurched as invisible hands dragged her higher, and more than once she thought they would lose hold, and she would fall to her death.

By the time they stopped for the night, she was exhausted and crying with hunger. She begged Rinchirith for food, or at least to untie her hands, which were still lashed painfully behind her back. His voice came out of the darkness, speaking in English. "You do not need food. Food comes from the earths, and they will judge you. They can feed you just as easily as they can kill you."

"What do you mean, the earths? You're not making any sense."

"Because your language is a child's language, with no way to say what must be said." He switched to his own language, and rattled off a clatter of sharp syllables too fast for Catherine to understand.

"What are you going to do with me?"

He switched back to English. "Me? I will do nothing. It is not for me to decide your fate."

She closed her eyes. Whatever was to come in the morning, she wanted to have her full senses working for her. She hoped she would be able to sleep despite her hunger and discomfort. Moments later, however, pincered hands closed around her arms and yanked her to her feet again. They untangled her from the netting and forced her to walk forward. Apparently she was not yet allowed to rest.

It was never entirely dark on Horizon. As the stars drew close in the western sky, they grew enormous, casting as much light as the full moon in England. The place where they'd stopped, however, was high on the eastern face of a mountain, and the peak blocked most of the western stars. It was darker outside than she had seen in two years, which, combined with the invisibility of her captors, made her suddenly very afraid. She was led forward, but she couldn't see where she was going.

The manticores jerked her to a halt just as her leading foot felt air instead of ground. She felt forward with her toes, but could feel nothing. In front of her, a deeper darkness seemed to suck the air from around them, breezing her hair gently forward. It wasn't a cliff. It was a hole in the mountain.

"Mighty lords of the earth," Rinchirith said in his own language. He spoke slowly and gravely, so Catherine was able to make out the words. "We have seen your wrath in the deep places. Judge if this creature and her kin are the cause. We sacrifice her to your pleasure, that your anger may abate, and your life power spring up again from the earth."

He shrieked, a long, ululating cry that echoed far below her feet, gradually more distant until the sound faded. Then, without warning, he pushed her over the edge.

CHAPTER 5

IT TOOK a week to travel from Valladolid, landlocked in the center of Spain, to the harbor at Cádiz, and another several weeks to make the trip to England. They sailed on a huge galleon at the head of a small fleet. Ramos was uncomfortable for much of the time, appalled by the language and manner of the sailors, and sickened by the poor food. Nevertheless, he cared for Antonia's needs, feeding her and changing her and continually speaking to her in both Spanish and Latin in the hopes that she might understand. Many on the ship, seeing his priest's cassock, came to him for confession or spiritual advice, and he was glad to listen to them.

He was free from the Inquisition, summoned by the greatest monarch in Christendom to do a great work, but he grew more melancholy as the trip progressed. Of all the Geminis Ramos had found, only King Philip had escaped the madness. If he had been spared, why not Antonia? Was he more righteous than she? Perhaps Philip was vital to the Lord's work, and had thus been granted special mercy.

He brooded on the meaning of the nova, what had caused it to appear, and why it had brought such grief. Most people considered it a harbinger, merely a portent of the madness, rather than its direct cause. Ramos didn't think that way. When two unlikely things occurred at the same time, he assumed one was probably the cause of the other. That or both were the effect of a third cause, as yet unseen. He wasn't content to shrug and blame the whims of an unknowable God. Instead, he spent his days in prayer and meditation, following the spiritual exercises taught him by his mentor years before, and asking God for insight.

Finally, they arrived in England, where a river guide came on board and guided the ship's captain through the ever-changing currents and shoals of the Thames. They tied up at Greenwich, where a vast shipping yard crawled with workers. The air was filled with the sounds of ringing hammers, creaking pulleys, splashing water, and the shouts of men. Ramos held Antonia's hand and stood on the dock, blinking in the sunlight.

"Ramos? Ramos de Tavera!" A thin Spaniard with a trim, triangular beard rushed forward and gripped Ramos by both shoulders. He kissed Ramos on both cheeks and laughed. "My old friend, you look half starved."

Ramos grinned. It was Juan Barrosa, secretary to the king, and an old friend. He returned Barrosa's embrace and introduced Antonia.

"Antonia! I remember you when you were no bigger than my knee. My, what a beauty you've become."

Antonia seemed pleased, but whether she understood the words or not, Ramos couldn't tell. "I've never been to Africa. It must be a fascinating place," she said.

"Ah," Barrosa said sadly. "She is . . ."

"Yes," Ramos said.

"I am so sorry."

Ramos was bursting with questions about his summons by the king, but Barrosa waved them away. First they had to get back on a boat, he said, a wherry this time, and travel the rest of the way down the Thames into London. Once they were aboard, he continued to shrug off Ramos's questions, saying only that the king wanted Ramos to cast Queen Mary's horoscope.

"Truly? It is permitted to forecast for the queen?" In Spain, it was illegal to cast the king's horoscope or predict the day of his death.

Barrosa shrugged. "It is if their Majesties command it."

"Are there no trained astronomers or physics in all of England, that he dragged me a thousand miles from home for so simple a task?"

"Do not press me, friend. There is much more to tell, but without the king's permission, I dare not speak."

Ramos remembered that for Barrosa, coming here with the king was something of a homecoming. Though a Spaniard, he had been born in England to one of the ladies-in-waiting of Queen Katerina, the Spanish first wife of Queen Mary's father, Henry VIII. He wondered how much of the country Barrosa remembered.

The watermen pulled on their oars with the strength of a lifetime plying their trade. The wherry rounded the Isle of Dogs, and London came into view. It was Ramos's first sight of the world's largest city, and he wasn't impressed. Sprawling, dirty, and vast, it had none of the glory of Madrid or Granada. The decaying St. Paul's Cathedral was big, certainly, but with none of the pure white splendor of the cathedral in Toledo. London Bridge sagged out over the river, top-heavy with layers of shops and houses. The massive starlings that held up the bridge were so wide they nearly dammed the river, leaving a visible difference in the water level from one side to the other. The water sluiced through the passage, forcing the wherry to fight its way against the current, lurching sickeningly and throwing up sprays of water. Ramos gripped the side and clutched his stomach, but in a moment they were through. On the far side, they maneuvered through a labyrinth of boats and approached Whitehall Palace, where the queen's swans sailed gracefully near the bank, snapping up morsels tossed to them by the royal swanherd.

The wherry pulled up to the palace dock and was met by servants who took their ropes and tied them fast. Barrosa stood to disembark, and Ramos noticed what he should have seen earlier.

"Your limp," Ramos said. "It's gone!" Barrosa had walked with a bad leg since childhood; now he crossed the uneven dock with ease.

"God has been good," Barrosa said, but an impish smile played across his face.

"What is it? What are you hiding?"

Barrosa's smile vanished. He helped Ramos step out of the boat, but held onto his arm, and his voice was grave. "When you read Her Majesty's horoscope, and the king asks you what you see, do not lie."

Ramos shrugged him off, stung. "Of course not."

But Barrosa didn't let go. "No matter what the horoscope shows you. Tell the truth."

THE QUEEN'S privy chamber was packed with courtiers: an ocean of silk, velvet, taffeta, camlet, pearls, tinseled satin, and cloth of gold. A few of the courtiers were the queen's attendants, loyal friends who had stood beside her in the difficult days when her father, King Henry VIII, had thrown her Spanish mother aside for the Protestant Anne Boleyn. Most, however, were Philip's gentlemen, the vast retinue of Spaniards who had traveled with him from home.

Queen Mary sat at one end of the room in a high-backed chair. She was a small, plain woman with red eyes and deep frown lines at the sides of her mouth. She was noticeably with child. Her dress was purple, embroidered with silver, and bulged forward over her abdomen. This pregnancy was crucial to the future of Philip and Mary's new dynasty, and the whole point of their marriage. A son would inherit the kingdoms of both Spain and England. Mary's eyes locked on Ramos, waiting to hear what he would say. Ramos swallowed, wishing for his quiet home in Valladolid.

Not far from Ramos stood a quiet man in his mid-thirties, tall and slender, with a long, pointed white beard draped over a gown like an artist might wear, with long hanging sleeves, and a black cap. Ramos recognized him as John Dee, the queen's astrologer and mathematician, essentially the same post that Ramos himself held under Philip. Why hadn't Dee been asked to cast this horoscope? Ramos had met him once, years before, in Paris. He had delivered a brilliant lecture about the use of new trigonometric ideas to calculate the distance to the stars. Why such a learned man would want to return to such a backward country as England, Ramos had no idea, but the man was certainly competent. Why was he overlooked in favor of Ramos? Didn't the king trust him?

Ramos was just stalling, and he knew it. He completed his calculations, and Mary's horoscope lay spread before him, as accurate as Dee or anyone in Europe could calculate it. The problem was, it held nothing but bad news. It made him wonder if Dee had somehow slyly avoided the job, for just this reason.

Barrosa's warning came back to him, and he had to admit he was tempted. He could say that all was well, that this pregnancy would end in joy and celebration. Who would know the difference? But Ramos was no flattering courtier, to tell the king and queen only what they wanted to hear. Philip had brought him all the way from Spain to cast this horoscope, so he would tell him and the queen exactly what he saw.

He looked down at his paper, took a deep breath, and spoke confidently. "I see no child. Not now or ever. I see two lines cut short, two pregnancies, but no children. Only sickness and sorrow. There will be no heir."

Queen Mary barely reacted. Her eyes grew distant and looked past him to some distant horizon. She was no stranger to grief, having spent most of her childhood abandoned and disgraced by her father and pushed to renounce her faith. She had endured those years, had held fast to the Church, had regained her rightful throne, had married Philip, all for this purpose: to bear a son who would rule in the name of the Church, as her father had not. Only there would be no son.

Ramos looked to King Philip, standing silently beside her, and tried to gauge his reaction. Philip was not tall, but he dominated the room, resplendent in a black cloak lined with leopard fur and a silvered doublet that reflected the light. His pale blue eyes missed nothing. This was the most powerful man in the world, the champion of Christendom, his armies devoted to driving out the Musselman threat in the south and the cancer of Protestantism eating its way through France, the Netherlands, and the Germanic states. His rage was fearsome, and Ramos had seen him punish messengers for bringing bad news.

But Philip did not look furious, or even surprised. He clapped his hands and waved his fingers in dismissal. The courtiers who jammed the room began to file out, Ramos along with them, but Philip stopped him. "Not you," he said in Spanish. "You stay."

Ramos waited, worried, while the room emptied. He noticed a finely-worked leather pouch around Philip's neck, black as night. Barrosa had worn an identical pouch. It looked out of place on both men: too elegant for Barrosa's dress and too plain for Philip's.

"Do not fear," Philip said to Mary in Latin. Since Philip spoke no English, and Mary only a little Spanish, they communicated mostly in Latin, and when that failed, fell back into French. "I bring you a relic from the chapel of Santiago de Compostela," Philip said. He took the odd leather pouch from around his neck and held it out by its chain. "It contains an ancient worm that once feasted on the flesh of Saint James. From that blessed flesh, it received such life and health that it has not died in over a thousand years." He draped the chain around Mary's neck. "For you. For the health of our son."

The moment he gave it to her, something twitched. Ramos wasn't sure what it was, but something in the corner of his vision had moved. He caught sight of his astrolabe on the table, and thought maybe it had moved in some subtle way, but he couldn't tell. Not again, he thought. Not another nova. Then his eyes drifted to the horoscope, and he saw the mistake.

It wasn't possible. He didn't make mistakes, certainly not one so basic as this. Venus would be ascendant in July, not Mars, as he had written. His eyes darted between paper, astrolabe, and almanac, trying to find an explanation, but there was none. The horoscope was wrong.

Heart hammering, he dipped his pen and drew a new line across the paper, correcting one he had made before. But no, that couldn't be right. He consulted his almanac, and found another discrepancy. Another blunder. But this couldn't be. Either he had been mad when he made these calculations, or he was going mad now. Could he have turned to the wrong page in the almanac?

Angry now, he flipped over the parchment and began again. He redrew the figures, accounting for the distortion caused by England's higher latitude. He worked in a fury, finding mistake after mistake, errors he could not possibly have made. A very different horoscope formed under his pen.

By the time he finished, he knew that some new miracle had happened, not another nova, but something else. Something far beyond the mathematical understanding of a simple astronomer-priest. He gazed back up at the king and queen, shaken. The black pouch rested against the purple and silver of Mary's dress, tiny and ordinary. Ramos believed in miracles, but he had never seen one before now. Somehow, at the moment Philip draped that tiny pouch around Mary's neck, the very lines of force in the universe had shifted. The sovereign will of God, communicated through the immutable revolutions of the heavenly spheres, had changed.

"I see a child," Ramos said, unable to keep his voice from trembling. "Your son will live."

WHEN the king dismissed him, Ramos returned to the apartments that had been given him in order to check on Antonia. He had hired a nurse to sit with her, and the old matron, three times a grandmother, was kind and gentle. Antonia had eaten her supper, and was calm for the moment. A half-buried idea that he would return to find her miraculously healed died, and he cursed himself for foolish hopes.

He left again and prowled the halls until he found Barrosa. He cornered him, snatched the pouch at Barrosa's neck, and held it in his face.

"What is this thing? What is happening?"

"Steady, brother," Barrosa said. "The king gave his permission to tell you everything. In the morning, I'll . . ."

"Morning? Look at me. Look at my hands. They haven't stopped shaking. My horoscope *changed* in front of my eyes. One moment, the lines were in one position, the next moment they had moved. I'm afraid to go out and look at the stars, because I don't know what I'll see. If you can explain what's happening, take pity on me."

Barrosa glanced up and down the passage. "All right. I can't explain all of it, but I can explain some. Tell no one where we go or what you see."

Whitehall Palace was a labyrinth—hundreds of sumptuous rooms that sprawled over acres of land in haphazard arrangement. Secret passages and shortcuts abounded, and Ramos had heard tales of plots and intrigues hatched in this royal warren. After a dozen turns, he was lost, and completely reliant on Barrosa to lead the way.

Barrosa opened a door to a cavernous library still decorated in the Italian Renaissance style. Palace renovations had begun under Mary's father, but had not yet reached this far. Tall gilded mirrors faced ancient portraits over acres of red carpet. On the ceiling, English kings of old in poses of regal glory stretched out their arms to grateful masses, while the twin cherubs Victory and Britannia looked on in approbation.

Barrosa crossed to an elaborately carved wall and leaned his weight on a piece of molding, which rotated down like a door handle. A portion of wall swung inward, mirror and all, revealing a stairwell leading down. Ramos raised an eyebrow. Barrosa beckoned.

Once inside, Barrosa pushed the secret door shut, then led the way down the stairs. A light shone from somewhere below, but Ramos couldn't identify it. It was clear and white, not yellow or flickering like light from a candle or torch. Like starlight.

When they rounded the corner, he could see the source: an elegant glass ewer, made for water or wine, from which a pure light poured as if a star was captured inside. Ramos was so taken with the light that it was several moments before he noticed the other marvels in the room.

It was a large cellar, with driven beams between earthen walls, and it smelled dank. Three stout oak tables were cluttered with books, glass retorts and spiraling alembics, wooden boxes with bells on top, knives and basins, braziers, a dozen odd structures of iron whose purpose Ramos couldn't guess, and more gold than he had ever seen in his life. Gold nuggets, gold bars, gold coins, gold crosses, gold rings, and odder still, gold flowers, leaves, fruits, bones, and one tiny, intricately-fashioned golden mouse, every hair individually carved. Ramos spun, dumbstruck, and noticed diamonds, some as big as his fist, scattered on the table or even the floor, as if someone had dropped them in the dirt but hadn't bothered to pick them up. Did England have such hidden wealth that jewels like this could be discarded and forgotten?

"A year and a half ago," Barrosa said, "a Spanish ship called the *San Salvador* was sent west by King Philip in pursuit of ship full of Protestant heretics and traitors."

Ramos peered into the ewer, and saw that the light was produced by an ordinary worm crawling around the inside surface of the glass. Ordinary, that is, except that its body shone with a pure and beautiful light.

"A month ago, the *San Salvador* returned, with less than half its crew and none of the ship's officers, nor the inquisitor who had been sent with them.

"My brother Diego was the inquisitor, wasn't he?" Ramos said.

"Yes, that's right. I'm sorry. They claimed to have found the heretics at an island called Horizon, at the edge of the world, where the ocean flowed into the abyss. What you see in this room is what they brought home on their ship."

So this was why the king had sent Diego so far away. For gold and miracles. Ramos drifted between the tables, trying to understand what he was seeing. A movement caught his eye, and he squatted to peer in a wooden cage that had been blocked from view before. Inside, a white-furred animal fixed him with startled eyes. It was the size of a rabbit, but there the resemblance stopped. Circling its narrow, naked head was a stiff frill of skin with brilliant red and blue stripes. Its back feet were broad and flat and supported the whole animal, unlike the front feet, which were smaller and sharply clawed. It looked so ridiculous, it was hard to believe it was real, not a stuffed circus sideshow with the sewing thread showing through the seams.

"What is it?"

The creature, startled by the sound of his voice, rose like a balloon to the top of its cage, where it bobbed, defying gravity. Ramos gaped.

"We think it's a defense mechanism," Barrosa said, clearly enjoying the effect this was having on Ramos. "It can't hide from predators, not with that frill, so if it's threatened, it just floats up into the sky, out of reach."

"But how?"

"That's what you're here to find out. How all of this works. It's the real reason the king summoned you from Spain."

Ramos stood, his knees cracking. "And what does the king hope that I will find?" He was already yearning to put his hands on these things, to examine them and test them and tease out their secrets. There was so much to understand.

"That's no mystery. He wants weapons. Power that he can use in the fight against the infidels and heretics. That and a source of gold to finance his armies."

Ramos looked around him, dizzy. It seemed Philip had already found a source of wealth. Though it was true, he would need a lot more than this to conquer France, the German heretics, and the Musselman infidels.

"The pouch Philip gave to Mary. It came from the ship, too?"

It wasn't really a question, but Barrosa confirmed with a nod.

"What was inside it?"

In answer, Barrosa reached to his own throat and pulled the leather pouch out from under his rough habit. He worked the mouth of the pouch open and tipped it so Ramos could see a point of light, glowing from the black interior. He leaned closer. It was a tiny sphere, like a pearl, that glowed with a pure, white light like the one illuminating the room, only much fainter. Barrosa took a dropper from a nearby table, sucked some clear liquid into it, and deposited one drop onto the pearl in the pouch. Instantly, the pearl's light increased.

"What did you put on it?"

"Salt water."

Ramos stared at the pearl, so ordinary a shape, but so beyond anything he'd ever experienced. He felt shaky, not just physically, but in a more central way. He knew how things worked. He had studied the physical world, and anything not explained there was in some way answered by the Bible or the Church. But this . . .

The existence of strange creatures from distant lands was no
surprise; Aristotle had described such beasts, as had Pliny. He had
read of the camelopard, the rhinoceros, the salamander that thrives in
the midst of flames, the catoblepas that kills with its eyes. No, what
disturbed him was what seemed like magic: light without fire,
levitation, the horoscope altering itself before his eyes. Barrosa had
said the island sat at the edge of the abyss. Was this black sorcery
from the pit of Hell? Or was it a miracle from God?

Ramos was reeling, but at the same time, the gears of his
mathematical mind were turning. It was a relatively new idea,
philosophically speaking, to consider secondary causes. God was the
primary cause for everything in creation, but Ramos, as a scholar,
wanted more. Yes, God made the dew form on the ground, but it also
formed because the water in the air condensed when the surface
cooled. Yes, flies were created by God, but they were also created by
rotting meat, as one could tell by leaving meat to rot until the flies
generated from its flesh. Many in the Church thought it was
blasphemy to think this way, but that's why the Church needed
reform, starting with the education of the clergy. It was one of the
principles that had drawn him to the Jesuit order in the first place.

"So, that pearl," Ramos said. "What happened when the king put
it around the queen's neck?"

Barrosa, grinning, hopped up and down on the foot that for so
long had given him his limp. "The pearl cures anyone it touches," he
said. "Just wearing it around my neck makes injuries heal instantly
and keeps me in perfect health."

That could explain why the king, of all Geminis, was unaffected by
the madness. Ramos thought of Antonia. Could this pearl heal
madness after it had already begun? "How many pearls are there?"

"Only four. Originally, Philip kept one for himself and gave the
other three to trusted men, educated philosophers who would study
them and report what they found."

"You are one of those, then. Who are the other two?"

"Perez and Peinado."

"I remember them. The king chose well. They are both wise and clever. Where are they now?"

Barrosa grimaced. "They're dead."

Dead. The word hung in the air. Men who were impervious to injury and illness did not die of natural causes.

"I never said this job was safe," Barrosa said. "Perez was killed by a creature that burst into flame, immolating him before we could pull him free. The pearl didn't save him. Peinado broke open a wooden box to see what was inside, and fell into a hole in the air."

Ramos raised his eyebrows, though he could tell his friend was in earnest.

"You'll believe me soon enough," Barrosa said. "I was there. It was just a hole, black and empty and devouring everything it touched. Look—" he pointed to a corner of the room. "You can see what it did."

There was a circular indentation in the wall and the floor, as if cut to make room for a large sphere. The end of the table was similarly sheared away.

"So the king gave one of their two pearls to the queen, to heal her and her unborn son?"

"That was Peinado's." Barrosa reached into his pocket and pulled out another black pouch, this one seared and twisted by fire. "I am to give Perez's to you."

Ramos accepted the pouch. The moment he did so, he felt the weariness lift from his body. He felt stronger, younger. A small cut on his hand closed up, and the pain he always felt from a bad tooth at the back of his mouth vanished. He uncinched the pouch and peered inside. The bright pearl lay nestled in its black cavity. Ramos closed the pouch again and tucked it under his shirt with the reverence he might have shown a piece of the True Cross.

"Does this magic have a name?" he said.

Barrosa nodded. "It's called quintessence."

◦───

The moment he left the cellar, Ramos went straight to his apartments. He could feel his heart beating against the pouch resting on his chest. He felt conspicuous, as if he had stolen something precious and any moment he would be caught.

He found Antonia as he had left her, sitting by the fire. He sent the nurse to wait outside; he had been charged with secrecy, and couldn't risk her learning of the miraculous things Barrosa had shown him. He and Antonia were alone.

Ramos held his breath and tied the pouch around her neck. He felt the weariness of the years settle back on his own shoulders. Surely this would work. Of all the Geminis he knew, only King Philip had escaped the madness brought by the nova, and only Philip had been wearing a quintessence pearl around his neck. It must be the reason he was preserved.

"Can you hear me, Antonia?"

The apartments were dimly lit. A fire burned low in the hearth, and shadows flickered over her beautiful face.

"Antonia? How do you feel?"

She opened her mouth. His heart surged; he was certain she was about to say his name, to speak sense again.

"I was always afraid of my father," she said. "He was rarely home, but when he was, I hid in my room."

Ramos waved his hand in front of her eyes. No response. "Can you hear me?" he said.

"That's sad. I was lucky enough to be taken in by someone who loved me. My uncle." Antonia started to cry. "I miss him so much."

Ramos held on to her and cried himself, tears of frustration and guilt. If only he had been there that night, instead of participating in an inquisition. It was foolish to think he could have done anything to stop it, but a part of Ramos blamed himself. If he had stayed by her side, then maybe God would not have brought this misery on her.

She spoke as if she were living in a dream. As if there were other people in her head with whom she held conversations. But there was no intelligence in her gaze, no body language that tried to be understood. It was like her mind was walled off in another place, trapped in her imagination.

He took the pouch back again. Her only reaction was a slight drooping of her shoulders and a slackening of her features. She continued to talk to herself, half conversations that no one ever answered. He returned the pouch to his own neck, feeling the corresponding sense of health and well-being, which only heightened his shame. But he couldn't leave the pearl here with her, in the hopes that it would in some way ease her plight. It was not his to bestow. He was tasked with learning its mysteries, and he would not cross the king's will.

CHAPTER 6

"SO it's the nova that's depleting all the salt," Parris said.

"It's worse than that." Matthew sat on a chair with his leg propped up in front of him, his hose rolled down to reveal the skin. There was nothing to see. The skin was unbroken, and looked as healthy as ever. The pain had lessened since they had seen the nova, but it was still intense enough to keep Matthew's attention.

"If we run out of salt, we'll die slow and painful deaths," Parris said. "Along with every other creature on the island. How can it be worse than that?"

"Because the scales only registered the effect of the nova when the clouds parted." Matthew looked at him expectantly.

"Which means?"

"Which means the clouds can block the effect of the nova. Which means all the salt depletion we've measured so far has been *despite* the protection of the clouds. Which means—"

"—once the storms blow over, we're doomed."

"That's what it looks like," Matthew said.

They were in the Quintessence Society's experimentation building. The first building they used for that purpose had been small, only a single room topped with a garret that Matthew had made his home. That building had burned down along with the rest of the settlement in the battle with the manticores. When they rebuilt, they had made it larger, divided into four rooms on the ground floor, with two rooms on the second floor where Matthew had taken up residence.

Though not for much longer. Soon he and Catherine would be married. A new home had already been built for the purpose, glittering with freshly poured diamond walls, not yet dimmed by the everyday assault of smoke and dirt and rain.

Parris examined Matthew's wound. He had been a physic back in England, but there hadn't been much call for medical skill on Horizon. "I want to try substitution," he said.

Matthew frowned. "Why?"

"There's something strange about that wound. I don't understand it."

"Go ahead, then," Matthew said. "I don't mind."

Substitution was a central law of quintessence that they had only begun to understand. It was the principle by which bell-boxes worked, as well as the manticores' ability to share consciousness and memories. The idea was that two pieces of a thing would retain a quintessence bond, regardless of how far apart they were separated. Changes to one would affect the other. It was also the principle behind the heat exchanger that heated and cooled their homes.

When the principle was applied to two human beings, however, it caused an interesting effect. Parris spat into a glass of water and handed it to Matthew, who drank it down. The saliva, until recently part of Parris's body, retained a bond, though not as permanent a one as if Matthew had swallowed a hair or a drop of blood. This bond would only last about ten minutes until it broke down.

As he finished the drink, the pain from his leg faded. Parris, on the other hand, grimaced and clutched at his own thigh. The wound itself hadn't moved, but Parris now felt Matthew's pain, and vice versa.

Parris grunted. "That's bad," he said.

Matthew allowed himself a small smile. Back home, there was no way to tell if you were brave or cowardly in the face of pain, because no one else could ever feel what you were feeling. It was gratifying to have someone else feel the same thing and acknowledge that it was bad. Though it was odd to feel someone else's body, to feel Parris's clothes around him, and to feel a coolness on his head where Parris's hair was thinning. Parris cracked his knuckles, and Matthew felt the sensation in his own hands.

"It feels more like a laceration than a bruise," Parris said. "Never mind the fact that quintessence should be healing it, a wound that feels like that should be visible on the skin."

"Maybe something's hurting me just beneath my skin?" Matthew suggested.

Parris pulled his mouth to one side, looking doubtful. "I'm concerned about something else. You remember back on the ship, when that mutineer sailor stabbed you in the leg?"

Matthew nodded, a chill passing through him. "You don't mean . . ."

"Was it this same leg? The same spot?"

"The exact same. It didn't occur to me, but I think you're right." That wound had been deep and bloody, but a drink of quintessence water had healed it.

"We know the changes quintessence brings aren't permanent in some ways," Parris said. "Quintessence turns sea water fresh, but if we go home, it transforms back into salt in our bodies. We turn sand into grain, but outside a quintessence field, it turns back again."

"So away from the island, my leg would still be wounded?" Matthew said.

"That's what I'm suggesting. The wound never healed in the normal sense; it was just transformed into healthy flesh by quintessence. I think the pain you feel is further indication that the quintessence field around the island is weakening."

"But why?" Matthew felt an itch at his neck and scratched at it, realizing belatedly that it was Parris's neck that itched, not his, so scratching it accomplished nothing. A thought struck him then, and he gasped. "Catherine's been complaining of headaches."

Parris's eyes widened. "She was shot in the head by Tavera," he said, giving voice to what was in both of their minds. "If she goes out of a quintessence field . . ."

"The wound would still be there. She would die."

Parris stood and began pacing. "What would cause something like this to happen? What could affect the sky?"

"We've always suspected that it's the proximity of the stars that gives Horizon its wealth of quintessence," Matthew said. "If something happened that removed quintessence from part of the sky . . ."

Parris raised both hands, frustrated. "What on earth could cause something like that?"

The effects of the substitution were wearing off, and the pain was settling back into Matthew's leg again. He rolled his hose back into place and put his foot on the floor. "I don't know," he said.

"What if we can't stop it?" Parris said.

Matthew shrugged. "We have three choices. We figure out how to stop it, we figure out how to go home, or we die."

Going home was problematic. They still had a ship, the *Western Star*, the one that had brought them to Horizon, but the way home was hazardous, and once they arrived, they would be utterly dependent on the shekinah flatworms they brought with them for survival. Eventually, the salt and sand in their bodies might work its way out as they ate normal food and drank normal water, but would that happen before the worms died?

Besides, they had fled from England because, under Queen Mary's rule, Protestants were being imprisoned or exiled. To return would be to run right back into that danger. He supposed they could return to a different country, one with a Protestant king, but there was no guarantee that English exiles arriving with unexplained magical powers would be well-received.

The door to the outside opened, letting in a draught of heat and the smell of rain. Parris's wife, Joan, appeared in the doorway, water glistening on her clothing. She was a small woman, dressed traditionally in a full gown with squared cap and a shawl around her neck. She was out of breath. Parris jumped to his feet. "What's wrong?"

"Catherine rang in an hour ago," Joan said, her voice sharp. "I've been searching the colony for you. Where have you been?"

"What was the message?" Parris said.

"I don't know your fool code," she snapped. "That's why I was looking for you."

They followed her back to the house, where the bell-box sat silent. Parris tried it, a quick greeting. There was no response. He tried again. Patiently, minute by minute, he pressed the lever, then waited in vain for the bell to ring. Matthew watched, his dread growing. Of course, there were explanations. Perhaps Catherine had lost the bell-box, or broken it, or was sleeping and didn't hear it.

"Let's not jump to conclusions," Parris said.

"Why doesn't anyone listen to me?" Joan said. "You send a young woman, all alone, into a dangerous wilderness, and then you're surprised when something happens to her. Fools, both of you. And you say you love her."

Matthew felt a flash of anger, but he kept it inside. He hadn't wanted Catherine to go either. It was she who had insisted.

Parris glared at his wife. "You go too far. It's not love to keep her locked in a cage."

"Is it love to see her dead?"

Matthew barely heard them. Where was she? What had happened? She was too smart to lose her bell-box. And it was too simple a device to break easily. They had to go out after her, right away, while they still had an idea of which direction to find her.

The door flew open, and Blanca ran into the room. She was young, Spanish, and exceptionally beautiful, with dark eyes and long, dark hair. Matthew thought Catherine was pretty, and all the more so because he loved her, but Blanca made heads turn whenever she entered a room. She wore a long skirt and a man's loose-fitting doublet, and her hair flowed in lustrous waves down her back. In England this would have been scandalous, a look reserved for the bedroom and only seen by a woman's husband, but on Horizon, the rules were different. Catherine wore her hair the same way, and called it the only practical choice.

Blanca's eyes were wide, and she was breathing hard. She looked panicked.

"What is it?" Matthew said.

"There are manticores at the barrier," she said. "They have news about Catherine."

MATTHEW'S father was already at the barrier, to Matthew's annoyance. "Let me do the talking," he said. "This is a delicate conversation."

"I already talked to them. They say they know where Catherine is," Blanca said.

"Even so," his father said. "We don't want to alienate them. They're our allies for the moment, and we want to keep it that way."

It was obvious to Matthew that Blanca didn't much like his father either, and he didn't blame her. The ratio of men to women on Horizon was about ten to one, and half the unmarried men between the ages of seventeen and fifty had at one time or another proposed marriage to Blanca. This far from England, with no parents or social structure, there was no one to tell her what to do, and she had rejected them all. It had been a subject of much resentment and debate in the colony, many believing that she had no right to refuse when there were so few women available. Matthew's father had tried to intervene and commanded her to marry a forty-five year old salt farmer whose wife had died. She had refused to cooperate. His father had been ready to throw her in the stocks, but Matthew had argued him down—shouted at him, really—and it caused enough dissention that eventually his father had let the matter drop.

Three red manticores crouched on the other side of the invisible barrier. Once Matthew put a drop of skink tears in one eye, however, he could see it clearly, like a shimmering fence made of parallel lines of light. The lines stretched between posts of split beetlewood, and had been fashioned using one of the basic principles of quintessence: that two pieces of a living thing, separated by any distance, would retain a connection. Matthew and Catherine had first discovered that principle onboard the *Western Star* by playing with broken ironfish bones. They hadn't been able to see the threads then, only observe the effect one broken piece could have on the other, even across the length of the ship. It had led to the invention of the first bell-box.

The barrier had been constructed by pulling apart split beams of beetlewood and then wrapping the halves around each other, tangling the quintessence threads. When the halves were stretched apart and pounded into the ground, the threads stretched to cover the distance like crisscrossing beams of light. Since the beams were formed from the essence of living beetlewood, manticores couldn't cross it. Humans, on the other hand, could walk through without even noticing it was there. It was much easier to build than a physical wall was, and much more effective. It couldn't be climbed.

The manticores tested it regularly. The reds remained on friendly terms with the colonists, but many of the other tribes, and especially the grays, wanted nothing more than to see them dead. Every few days, a troop of manticores would try to scale it or break through. They hurled tree trunks at it, drove poles into the ground and scaled the poles to jump over the barrier, and tried to dig underneath. Sentries inside the barrier walked around it, guarding it night and day with matchlocks, the bullets dipped in beetlewood wax so they would pierce manticore flesh. Marcheford had strictly banned the sale or trade of matchlocks and ammunition to the manticores, even their allies. It was impossible to prevent the occasional weapon from falling into their hands, but the rule had prevented any significant manticore armament.

So far, the barrier had held. Though Matthew had to admit, they still had only a poor idea of why it worked. By wrapping themselves in a mesh of quintessence threads, they could duplicate most of the manticore's miracles, even walking through solid stone. And yet humans could pass through the barrier, and manticores could not. What was different? Were the manticores actually made of quintessence in some intrinsic, atomistic way? Or perhaps the difference was the quintessence pearl: the tiny pinprick of quintessence that all Horizon creatures had hidden in their bodies, allowing them to use the power naturally.

"You have news of my daughter?" he said. Parris spoke English, which most of the reds understood, though speaking it was difficult for them.

The manticores answered in their own language, accompanying the sounds with sinuous movements of their tails. "She was taken by Rinchirith and his clan to be judged."

Matthew understood the words, mostly, but he still looked to his father for the translation. Since his father had lived among them for so long, he knew the language better than anyone, with the possible exception of Catherine. But his father said simply, "Rinchirith has her."

"Who is that?" Parris said.

"He's a gray, a human-hater. He blames us for everything bad that's ever happened to his tribe."

A lot of it probably true, Matthew thought. Human arrival on Horizon had hardly been good for the manticores. Besides nearly sending the whole island over the Edge, they had disrupted the balance of politics among the tribes, causing all manner of problems.

"We insist on being present for her trial," his father said formally, in the manticores' own tongue, using his hands and fingers to mimic the movement of their tails.

"It is not the gray tribe, nor the council of tribes, that accuses her," the manticore answered. "Rinchirith blames her for the death of his brothers, and many who mourn the dead follow him."

"What will he do to her?"

"He will let the earth judge her for her crimes."

Matthew didn't know what they were talking about, but it didn't sound good. "What does he mean, 'let the earth judge her'?" he said.

"I've heard them speak of it before," his father said. "It's a response to terrible offenses, for crimes that harm the whole tribe. The offender is brought high into the mountains and dropped into a chasm they call Judgment Gorge."

"They're going to throw her down a cave shaft?" The mountains lay farther away than any human had yet explored. Even if she survived the fall, they would have no hope of finding her without manticore help.

"They believe the Earth itself will determine guilt or innocence."

"What, by smashing her body against the rocks?"

Matthew turned to the manticores and did his best to speak in their language. "Will you take me to her?"

"You can't stop them," the manticore said. "Rinchirith's followers are many."

"Take me anyway."

"No, Matthew," his father said. "You can't do her any good. Stay here and wait."

"And do what?"

"Pray for her safety."

"I don't want to pray. I want to save her life."

"If God wishes her life to be saved, it will be saved. If not, then it will not, except if by humble supplication you obtain his mercy."

"Good idea," Matthew said. "You try that route. In the meantime, I'll go rescue her. We'll see which works better." Without waiting for an answer, he stepped through the barrier and addressed the manticores. "I'm ready. Take me to her."

"At least bring a pack," Parris said. "It's a two day journey to the mountains; you'll need food and supplies."

Blanca, however, had anticipated the need. She appeared with two packs from the storehouse, her quintessence powers making it easy for her to carry both. She stepped across the barrier after Matthew. "Don't tell me I'm not coming with you," she said. "Catherine's my friend, too."

Matthew nodded, then faced the manticores. "Let's go."

The manticores, however, did not move. "We will not take humans to the Gorge."

"What do you mean?" Matthew said. "Catherine is there already."

"She is the accused."

"And I'm her fiancé. I want to speak for her."

"We will not take you."

Matthew hurled his pack to the ground. "You don't trust us with your sacred spot? Is that it? You think we'll spit on it or take it for ourselves?" He knew their concerns were probably warranted. After all, several of the manticores' sacred places *had* been destroyed since the humans arrived—though not intentionally—and many villages as well. But he wasn't going to sit by and let everyone tell him there was nothing he could do. "This is nonsense," he said. "You're going to kill Catherine, you savage bastards, now tell me where she is."

"Matthew!" his father said, a shocked rebuke. He started to gesture an apology.

The three manticores hissed and took fighting stances, bodies low to the ground with pincers extended, their many tails fanned up and over their heads. Blanca jumped back behind the safety of the barrier, but Matthew was too angry to heed the warning.

Parris dashed through the barrier and tackled him. He dragged him to the ground just inside the barrier and made his own body heavier to pin him down. Matthew thrashed, but couldn't lift himself free.

"Let me go!"

"You're no good to her if you get yourself killed."

"I'm no good to her if I can't find her, either."

The red manticores disappeared into the trees. When Matthew stopped struggling, Parris stood and helped him up. "We'll find her. But antagonizing the only manticores who don't already want to kill us won't accomplish that. We need a plan."

CHAPTER 7

BACK in the cellar room, Ramos set to work. Barrosa wasn't there to tell him what had been tried before, but he didn't want to know anyway. At least for now, he wanted to discover and see for himself.

He took careful stock of the room, examining each cage, each shelf, each golden artifact. The room was a disorganized clutter, something that would have to change, but for now, he just left things where they were. He didn't know enough to organize sensibly.

He found a lot more gold carvings than he'd spotted the day before: not only the flowers and leaves and mouse, but a host of other ordinary objects carved in gold: a book, a trencher, a pair of spectacles, a shoe. He was starting to suspect that these things had not been carved after all. Only a few people in the world could carve with such incredible perfection, and what would be the purpose? That implied that these objects had once been ordinary, but had been transformed into gold.

Then he found a golden inkpot engraved with the initials J.B. Juan Barrosa. The find gave him a little shiver of excitement. If these objects had been transformed, then it hadn't been done on the island. It had been done right here. It was the alchemist's dream, to turn base material into pure gold. But how was it done?

On a table, he found a shallow tray of water with an eel swimming in it. At the bottom of the tank, on one side, was an ordinary gold ring; on the other side, a feather, each barbule intricately formed in gold. The features were so tiny and precise, he knew it could never have been carved. He wondered if the gold would splinter away if the feather was stroked. He was about to reach into the water when he remembered the fates of Perez and Peinado. Caution would be wise. Instead of reaching with his hand, he went back and found a pair of tongs he had noticed earlier, and reached them into the water to grab the feather.

He was glad he had. As soon as they entered the water, the ends of the tongs changed color and weight. Astonished, he pulled them out. The top half was still iron; the bottom half gold wherever the water had touched. Was it the water that was special? The eel? And why was all this gold just piled up here in the cellar? If the king had a way to turn any object into gold, why didn't he use it to mint himself a fortune? Philip had the armies, the influence, the intelligence, and the will to take over the known world in the name of Christ. All he lacked was the gold.

"I wouldn't bother pocketing any of that, if I were you," said a voice from the stairs. It was Barrosa.

Ramos set the tongs gingerly on the table, noticing small gold specks in the wood where the water from the eel tray had dripped. He was careful not to let it drip on him. "Why is that?"

"Because halfway up the stairs, it turns back into whatever it was before."

"Up the stairs? You mean the cellar itself is what makes them gold?"

Barrosa sat heavily on a wooden bench. "Not at all. It's the worm."

Ramos glanced at the shining worm in its glass ewer. "The worm isn't anywhere near this water."

"It's the source of everything. If you picked up the worm and walked out of this room, then everything fantastic in here would become ordinary. All of the animals would die."

"The *worm* is the source? What about these pearls we each have in our pouches?"

Barrosa sighed. "There's a lot we don't understand. But the pearls store up the quintessence when they're here, and then use it up when they're not. If we don't come down here every day and recharge from the worm, the power runs out."

"The king comes here too?"

"Once a day. And he usually wants a report on what we've found since the last time."

"I'm still missing parts of this story. Where are the men who brought all this back from the island? Surely we could interview them and find out more. Was this the only worm they could find? Where did the pearls come from?"

Barrosa looked uncomfortable. "They're all dead." He wouldn't meet Ramos's eye.

"Dead?"

"Your brother Diego led them out, two years ago. When they returned, half the crew was gone, including your brother, most of the officers, and an English lord named Francis Vaughan. The ship had all this gold and treasure, and the king suspected a mutiny. Everyone did."

"What was their story?"

"They claimed most of the officers had been killed by invisible manticores, your brother had been killed by the Protestant renegades, and Vaughan had been plucked off the ship in the night by a giant sea monster."

Ramos gave a nervous laugh. "You're kidding."

"The surviving men were huddled in four groups around the four pearls they had brought, refusing to be separated. They said they used to have a chest full of the worms, but shortly after they set sail, Vaughan had opened the chest and attracted the sea monster, which leaped out of the sea, snatched him and the chest of worms in its mouth, and dove back down into the deep." Barrosa pantomimed the monster's movements with his hands. "Only one worm was left."

"No one believed them?"

"Why would they? They were filthy and raving and their stories were fantastic. They were in perfect health, but acted terrified of dying. None of the gentry were left to corroborate their tale, and who would believe a bunch of superstitious sailors?"

"But you believe them now."

Barrosa spread his hands. "What they brought back is as fantastic as their stories. And they were right to be afraid of death."

"They died when they were separated from the pearls?"

"Not at first. They were in agony if we took the pearls away, and their limbs quickly became stiff as stone, so we kept them in four cells, each with a pearl, while we interrogated them. Once we learned what they knew—which wasn't much—Philip ordered us to take the pearls for ourselves." Barrosa pointed a finger at Ramos. "Don't look at me like that. I was following a direct command."

"They all died?"

"Some that day; some held out as long as three days. It was like a room full of statues at the end."

Ramos nodded slowly. If it was Philip's command, Barrosa didn't have much choice. A Christian monarch had the responsibility to make hard decisions, decisions for the good of Christendom and the spread of the True Faith, not just for the good of individuals. It was not for men like him or Barrosa to question commands from a holy ruler. And yet, the decision made him uncomfortable. He wondered if he would have done the same in Barrosa's place.

As any rate, it was now Ramos's duty to make the suffering of those men worthwhile, by harnessing quintessence to Philip's holy cause. If quintessence was worthless, they had died in vain. On the other hand, if it increased the might and influence of the Church, then they were martyrs who would be rewarded in glory. It all depended on what he and Barrosa could accomplish.

"Let's get to work."

THE FIRST thing Ramos accomplished was an inventory. His

predecessors had left the cellar room a shambles, with miracles scattered underfoot and no organization. Ramos wanted to know exactly what they had, what was known, and what was unknown.

The large quantity of gold miscellany filled a fish barrel. There were six kinds of animals, the names of which Barrosa had recorded from interviews with the returning soldiers before they died. The worm was called a shekinah flatworm, and seemed to be the actual source of the quintessence magic, or at least critical to its working. The eel Ramos had seen was called a Midas eel, for obvious reasons, and the bizarre frilled creature that floated to the top of its cage they called a puff weasel. The creature that had killed Perez was called a sooty toad, and it was still alive. It had appeared to immolate itself along with Perez, but Barrosa had later found it in a corner, croaking lustily. He had managed to coax it back into its cage with a scattering of dead crickets. There was also a bird—or at least, they assumed it was a bird. It sat on a perch, squawked, fluttered what sounded like wings, and ate seeds from a dish. It was however, entirely invisible.

Finally, there were the compass beetles. These were the only animals of which they had more than one specimen. The soldiers had brought back a dozen from Horizon, but they ate any green leaves and bred readily, so that now they had many more. The glass cage in which they were stored was a strange sight, however, since all of the beetles were pressed to one side, scrabbling to get through the glass. If Ramos turned the cage, the beetles moved, too, so that they always faced to the West. This was how the Spanish ship had found Horizon, Barrosa explained. The glass had been waxed, since the beetles could fly right through just about any other material.

There were plants, too, some with invisible, poisonous spines. All together, despite the wonder of everything he saw, Ramos was a bit disappointed. The collection had not been gathered by scholars. There were no rubbings, no dried flowers and leaves, no drawings, no written observational accounts. The choice of what to bring back had been made based on what would most be most impressive to look at, not by what would yield the most understanding about quintessence and Horizon.

Barrosa and King Philip quickly became impatient with Ramos's approach. The old trio of philosophers had shown the king new wonders every week, sometimes every day. So far, all Ramos had done was organize the room, make drawings, and write long lists. As far as Ramos was concerned, however, it was the only way to proceed. God had created an ordered universe. In the study of the natural world, just as in the study of theology, the whole could be comprehended only by understanding each piece.

Once everything was organized and labeled and written down in Ramos's tiny, neat hand, he began to study it systematically. The shekinah flatworm was the center of everything, the source. As Barrosa had described, the power of the pearls would gradually dissipate the longer they stayed away from the shekinah. Their light and influence would increase with the application of salt water, but that increased the dissipation, too. The farther away the pearl was from the shekinah, the faster it lost its power, and Ramos recorded that quintessence power had an inverse relationship to both time elapsed and distance traveled from the shekinah.

It occurred to him to wonder about the light. Standard light, from the sun or a flame, had no healing or transformative powers. The shekinah flatworm, however, blazed with light, as did the pearls. Was the light different than ordinary light? Did the light itself contain the power, or was it simply an offshoot of it? In the Holy Scriptures, the glory of God was always associated with a bright light—the face of Moses on Sinai, the transfiguration of Christ, the appearance of the risen Lord. Was this a heavenly light?

He began testing it. The first thing he discovered was the light's ability to shine through most objects. A piece of wood held in front of it cast no shadows. Metal was similarly ineffective in blocking the light, as was ordinary gold, although interestingly, the transformed gold did cast a shadow. Which was a significant discovery: it meant the transformed gold wasn't completely transformed. There was an aspect of it, not seen or felt, that was different from real gold. The black pouches effectively blocked the light of the pearls, but Barrosa said the pouches had come from Horizon, and thus were probably fashioned from the hide of some Horizon beast. If he placed a pearl in an ordinary leather pouch, it shone through the material just as brightly as ever.

Finally, he tinkered with the strange boxes that had bells mounted on the top. It appeared as if the lever on each box was meant to ring the bell, but when he pressed it, nothing happened. He sawed carefully through one of the wooden sides to see the interior and found, oddly enough, a set of old bones. At first he thought it might be a fetish from an aboriginal tribe, like a shaman's bone bag. But no, the bones were carefully attached, one to the lever and one to the bell. The one attached to the lever was a jawbone. Based on the shape, and the lack of teeth, Ramos guessed it belonged to a fish of some kind, perhaps a herring or a carp. But, no, that couldn't be. This was the jawbone of a *Horizon* fish, and thus it would be special in some way, just like the eel or the other animals in the room. The other bone, hanging from the bell by a string, was nothing more than a fragment, and whether it had belonged to the same fish or not, he couldn't tell.

He moved the lever up and down, watching how the hinge of bone inside opened and closed as a result. Open, closed. Open, closed. The odd thing was, the lever and the bell were not attached in any way. So what was the point? Perhaps they used to be attached, and the bones had broken apart during the journey. That made some sense, though it still didn't explain why someone would attach a lever to a bell through a collection of fish bones.

Finally, he stopped playing with it and just sat there, contemplating the mystery, but not touching it. It was only then that, with his hands nowhere near the mechanism, as if invisible fingers had grasped the bone fragment and pulled it sharply downward, the bell rang.

CHAPTER 8

CATHERINE fell.

It took much longer than she expected. She screamed and covered her face, expecting at any moment to smash into jagged rocks.

She kept falling. The deafening wind fluttered her hair and clothes, and she pitched dizzily end over end. She wondered how deep this cave shaft could possibly be, since even if she had jumped off the highest point of the mountain, she would surely have hit bottom before now.

Then she noticed she was falling more slowly. The air didn't buffet her as violently, and the blur of rock walls to either side became easier to distinguish. She tried to control her tumble, and found that she could, falling roughly feet first.

Still she slowed. The experience was, if anything, like throwing a ball high in the air. As it flew higher, it would slow down, losing speed gradually at first, and then more swiftly, until just at the peak of its arc, it stopped. She felt like a ball thrown, but upside-down.

When at last, below her, a flat rocky floor appeared, she was no longer falling so much as floating downward, and at the moment her feet touched down, her speed fell to nothing, so that she hardly noticed the impact at all.

For a moment of violent vertigo, her sense of direction reversed, and she expected to plummet head first, back the way she had come. Instead, she swayed slightly, regained her sense of balance and gravity, and realized that, against all expectations, she was still alive.

She couldn't see the top of the shaft. The walls were rough and covered with what looked like a wet lichen, but they rose more or less vertically until they met at a point far above her. The walls stopped just short of the floor, however, creating a low roofed cave that stretched in every direction, high enough that she could walk under it if she stooped. Water dripped from the roof, and jutting spikes cast eerie shadows.

In one direction, a dim yellow light glowed, which must be the only reason she could see anything at all. She ducked low enough to clear the ceiling and began to make her way, bent uncomfortably, toward the light.

The light came from a doorway. An opening anyway, roughly square, without a door. Before she got close enough to make out any details, she heard voices. Human voices.

"Hello?" she said. Her own voice sounded thin and weak in this vast underground space. "Who's there?"

A TREE stood in the center of the settlement, and colonists used it to post notices, offer services, and advertise needs. Walking by, Matthew saw a prominently placed poster with a cartoon drawing of his father, bishop's hat on his head, dropping his pants to copulate with a manticore. It was crude, offensive, and shocking—such attacks on politicians occurred in London, but he had never seen anything like it here.

Matthew tore the poster down and tore it to pieces. There was no question in his mind who had put it there.

"Hey," said a rough, Scottish voice. "What do you think you're doing?"

Matthew turned to find James Ferguson glaring at him. "Removing a vulgar drawing," Matthew said.

Ferguson gave a mischievous smile. "That was mine," he said. "Funny, eh?"

"It's not at all funny. It's crass, and it's slandering a good man."

"Come on, though. Your father, he's a bit of a prude, isn't he? Imagine him with his pants down. Can't do it, can you? I don't think he even takes them down to piss."

Matthew wasn't in the mood for this. He advanced on Ferguson, fists clenched.

"Whoa, slow down." Ferguson raised his hands in surrender. "Your father's a good man. He is. Best man in the colony; nobody doubts that. He's just in a bit too deep with the enemy. Too kind for his own good, that's what he is. And for our good, too."

Matthew shook his head. This was how Ferguson won men's hearts. Not by railing against his father, but by making him look ridiculous and weak. He never challenged him to his face, nor did he put himself forward as a rival leader. He wasn't a fighter; he was a poisoner.

Matthew pointed at the tree. "No more pictures," he said.

"Okay, whatever you say." Ferguson raised his hands again.

"And leave my father alone. He's your governor. Show him some respect."

Ferguson shrugged. "He's not really a governor. Just acting, as it were. He's got no royal writ."

"What difference does that make?"

"Well, if Princess Elizabeth shows up and proclaims him governor, then that's what he is. Until then, he's just filling a vacancy, isn't he? Anyone could do it."

Like most of the colonists, Ferguson thought of the Protestant princess Elizabeth as the rightful queen of England instead of her Catholic sister Mary. "Princess Elizabeth isn't likely to pay us a visit any time soon," Matthew said. "That doesn't mean you don't owe him your obedience."

"Spoken like a diligent son," Ferguson said. "But come now. Haven't you ever thought someone else could do a better job than your old dad?"

Matthew shoved Ferguson out of his way and kept walking. He didn't want to hear any more. Ferguson was too close to being right.

"The manticores aren't our friends!" Ferguson called after him. "Either we conquer them, or they'll destroy us."

Back in his rooms on the second floor of the Quintessence Society building, Matthew fed the torn pieces of poster into a candle flame, watching each one burn down until it nearly singed his fingers. Catherine's bell-box lay silent on the table in front of him. He'd rung it for hours, with no response. He knew it was futile, but every time he decided to give it up, he tried it just one more time, just in case. He needed to do something, but anything else he could do was just as useless. He could try searching for her in the forest, but there was little point in that—the forest was vast, and he had no idea where she was.

It was dark outside, though a single shekinah in a jar provided him with plenty of light. In a distant way, he knew he was hungry, but had little motivation to eat. He was supposed to be so clever. The whole colony looked to him for daily miracles. But when it really counted, he could no more alter his circumstances than a child.

His only hope was that Catherine still had her bell-box but was unable to answer it, or that her captors had it and she might find a way to reclaim it. If so, he wanted to be here when she called. It was his only link to her, and if it had been destroyed or left behind, he had nothing. Not even hope. He stood and paced to the window, looking out into the darkness, waiting for inspiration.

A bell rang.

He whirled and rushed back to the workbench on which Catherine's bell-box sat, but the bell sounded again, once, like a chime, from his left. Where was it coming from? He opened a cupboard and began pawing through it, knocking aside pieces of gold, bones, and fragments of fur. It was full of oddments, items he'd saved for some later use out of broken or discarded inventions. The bell kept ringing, and finally he found it, pushed to the back. It was an orphaned bell-box, one to which the pair had long since been lost. He'd kept it to use for spare parts.

His first thought was that Catherine had somehow found its pair and was using it to contact him, despite how ridiculously unlikely it would be for her to stumble upon a lost bell-box in the middle of the mountains, farther away from the colony than humans had ever ventured. He tapped a quick greeting on it, using their code: three taps, then a pause, then three taps again. Silence. The bell-boxes, including this one, had a damper on them to allow the bells to make only short rings: lift the lever up, the bell would ring, push the lever down, it would stop. This allowed them to deliver messages quickly. After trying the greeting again, the bell rang, but it was a single, continuous ring, with no dampening. Which meant nothing.

Stupid. It was just a phantom, a random fluctuation of the quintessence thread. It happened sometimes—an orphaned box would ring for no reason, sometimes even when they knew its pair had been destroyed. Perhaps it had been lost in the forest, and an animal had gotten a hold of it. Or maybe the loose thread, flapping in an extradimensional breeze, somehow wrapped itself around some other thread that cued the ring. They had no idea, really. It was just a mystery, one of thousands.

Matthew threw the box across the room, where it smashed against the wall. They would never understand quintessence. Not in any real sense. They were fish who, after studying a sunken ship, thought they understood the world above the water.

He heard footsteps on the stairs. A light knock on the door. "Come in."

The door swung open to reveal Blanca's somber face. "What are you doing?" she said.

"Trying to contact her."

Blanca eased the rest of the way into the room. Even on Horizon, where many of the old world's social taboos had disappeared, there would be a scandal if they were discovered alone in his apartments at night, but he didn't ask her to leave. He was despondent, and the company was welcome. She set a sunfruit and a chunk of sandbread in front of him. "Eat."

He bit into the yellow fruit. It was delicious, and he bit again, feeling guilty for enjoying food when Catherine was out there, perhaps already dead. He ate it all anyway, driven by hunger.

"Catherine is strong," Blanca said. "She knows the manticores better than anyone."

Matthew tried for a smile. "You're right. She's probably fine."

"I wouldn't put it past her to come walking in tomorrow without a scratch."

It was just talk, but it made Matthew feel better all the same. Blanca was an inherently empathetic person, feeling the emotions of others sometimes more deeply than she felt her own. Catherine would have told him to stop moping and do something. She had no patience for melancholy. Blanca was so different than Catherine in some ways: gentle where Catherine was brash, quicker to listen than to talk, always understanding. Though in other ways, they were much alike. They were both independent, with a plan for their own lives that didn't take much stock in what others thought they ought to do.

It was that quality that had put Catherine in this situation in the first place, maybe even gotten her killed. Why hadn't she listened to him?

"She'll come waltzing into the settlement with a manticore entourage to tell us they've named her their queen," Matthew said, trying to match Blanca's light tone, but failing.

Blanca smiled back at him, and Matthew could see that she was suffering, too. "Even so, isn't there anything we could do"—she waved her hand vaguely around the room, indicating the various implements and paraphernalia—"with this stuff? To find her?"

Matthew slumped, dropping his chin into his hands. "It's not sorcery," he said. "There are specific things we know how to do. Finding a person across miles of forest and mountains isn't one of them."

"You have her bell-box, right?" she said, pointing. "There's a quintessence thread connecting the boxes, and you can see it using the skink tears. Can't you just . . . follow the thread?"

Matthew shook his head. "You'd think so. It looks like a thread, and it seems to go straight, but it really doesn't. It's not part of our world at all, not really. We tried following a thread before, thinking we wouldn't have to bring the compass beetles with us on expeditions—we'd just follow the bell-box connection home. When the boxes are close together, it works fine. But the farther they get apart, the stranger it gets. The thread points off in a random direction, not toward the other box. Trying to follow it takes you on a path that, while it may not actually be infinite, might as well be. We walked for a full day and never reached a box that we knew to be only two miles away on a straight course."

"There's got to be a way," Blanca said. She put a hand on his arm. "You're the cleverest person I know. You can figure it out."

Matthew shook her off. "It can't be done."

"Well, how does it work?"

"What do you mean?"

"Explain it to me. How does the bell-box work?"

Matthew sighed. "We take a jawbone from an ironfish and separate it from the skull, where the quintessence pearl is. When we . . ."

"I know how you *make* it," Blanca said. She tossed her dark hair. "Tell me how it *works*."

He was quiet for a moment, thinking. "Living things are anchored to their spirits with threads of quintessence. Horizon animals have pearls which link their thread to some part of their body—a jaw, a leg, an eye—that allows them to tap into the quintessence and use it."

"And the bell-box?"

"We simply stretch one of those threads and make it work at a distance. The threads seem to stretch indefinitely—as I said, they're not really part of our universe. It's some kind of energy, like light or heat." He kicked the table. "Or gravity. Or magnetism. Who knows what it is, really. We've debated these things a thousand times. We don't have time for philosophy."

"Could you look through a connection to see what was happening on the other side?"

Matthew thought of the time, more than a year before, when Catherine's spirit had traveled back from beyond the grave on such a thread. He hadn't seen it himself, but her father had described it sliding along the thread like an endless snake swallowing its meal. Did that mean the threads had an inside layer, like a tunnel? Might there be some way to connect to her now in the same way?

He pinched his lower lip. "If you could split open a thread . . ."

You couldn't cut such a thing with a knife or a sword, of course. It was invisible and intangible. He had walked through a hundred of them just by crossing the room. But was there something which might?

He crossed to a workbench, put a drop of skink tears in his eyes, and blinked past the initial burning. He strapped a pair of boarcat paws to his hands. Boarcat claws were unique in that they could actually interact directly with quintessence threads, which was how they wrapped threads around their bodies, enabling the special powers they enjoyed.

"What are you trying?" Blanca said.

"The obvious." He found the quintessence thread emanating from Catherine's bell-box, grasped it firmly with the boarcat claws, and picked at it, trying to find an edge or some strand he could get hold of to unravel it. There was no such thing. It was as pure and unbroken as a beam of light.

He sat back. "*Why* do they have an inside layer?"

"What?"

"Things always have a reason. If quintessence threads are like a tunnel, what's the purpose? What moves through the tunnel?"

"Information?" Blanca said. "When you close the ironfish jaw in the one box, the bones in the other box get the message that they should turn to iron."

"More than that. The power to transform must travel, too, because the other side doesn't need to have a pearl, or even be in a quintessence field. The *energy* for the transformation must travel through the thread."

Matthew snatched up another bell-box pair and placed them one on either side of the long work table that stretched the length of the room. In the center of the table, between the two boxes, he placed a black opteryx scale. He pressed the level on one bell-box, ringing the bell on the other. The scale stayed black.

"Hmm. Maybe it's too small to register?" He poured a little salt water on the scale and tried again. This time, when he pressed the lever, the scale flared a dull reddish color before fading back to black.

"So it's true," Blanca said. "Quintessence flows through the thread."

"Not a lot," Matthew agreed. "But it does."

"Unless it's the flow of quintessence itself that makes the thread? Like a river in a stream bed?"

"No, then the scale would glow all the time. The quintessence only flows for a moment." Matthew paced, considering it. The thought of Catherine in danger and the need to do something about it distracted him, making it hard to hold on to a thought.

"We know a spirit can be sent this way," Matthew mused. Catherine's spirit had come back from the dead along such a thread. It wasn't something they could do again, as it required someone else to die, and risked destroying the world besides, but at least they knew it was possible.

"What if spirits are made of the same energy?"

Matthew sucked in his lips. "So this is spirit stuff we're sending back and forth." A thought struck him. "What if I could send my spirit to her?"

Blanca's face turned grave. "What are you suggesting?"

"Sinclair brought Catherine's spirit back by pulling her thread out of the void and tying it back to her body. What if I opened up a void in the end of this thread, and sent my spirit through it. Would it come out on her end?"

Blanca's eyes were wide. "Or would you just die?"

"I have to try something."

"No. Suicide won't help her, Matthew."

"I won't be reckless. It's a good idea. We'll just try it a little bit at a time."

He pulled a vial of vitriol from a shelf. Vitriol was made from sulphur, which was the most dangerous of the three alchemical substances. Salt and mercury merely altered the flow of quintessence through the world. Sulphur opened up a hole in the world itself, a void of pure emptiness that could be difficult to control.

Rather than risk experimenting with Catherine's bell-box, Matthew crossed the room and picked up the broken bits of the orphaned one he had thrown against the wall.

CATHERINE approached the square of light hesitantly.

"A bheil Gàidhlig agaibh?" a rough man's voice spoke out of the darkness.

Catherine jumped and backed away. She couldn't see anyone, and yet the voice had sounded right in front of her.

"Que parla català?" said a different voice.

"Spreekt u Nederlands?" said a female voice behind her. Catherine whirled, still unable to locate a speaker.

"What about English?" the female voice said again in a lilting accent.

"Where are you?" Catherine said.

"Do not be afraid," the voice said. "My name is Griele. I come from Flanders. I am a weaver. I have two daughters, Anke and Ilesabet. What is your name?"

"Where are you?" Catherine said again. "I can't see you." She took a slow step forward, toward the square of light. As she did, she heard other voices, fainter and more distant.

"No, of course," the voice said. "We can not be seen. You are new here?"

"Yes."

"We are—how you say? Ach, not good English."

"I speak Latin, too," Catherine said.

"Ah yes? That is good. Pietro!"

At this, the voice of a young boy spoke out. "Sì?"

"The Latin, please," Griele said. "Introduce yourself."

"I am Pietro Morosini, son of Girolamo Morosini, Captain of Brescia," the boy announced formally, in Latin. "I am held prisoner against my will. It is proper for you to address me as 'lord'. It is also proper for you to tell us your name."

Catherine's head was spinning. She was surrounded by a crowd of invisible voices. "My name is Catherine Parris," she said. She reached the square opening and stepped through. On the other side, the cavern was even larger than the one she had left. This one had a high ceiling, invisible in the darkness. All around, as far as she could see, there were smears of light—not enough to actually illuminate anything, nor seeming to come from any source. Just thousands of diffuse patches, some gathered together in great bright auras, some set apart on their own. They were all moving.

She heard all kinds of languages, most of which she didn't recognize.

"There are so many of you," she said.

"This is only one room," Griele said. "There are many more."

"Are you . . ." Catherine cringed to ask it, but she was, after all, deep below the ground. "Are you the dead?"

"That is the question, isn't it?" said yet another voice. Catherine had trouble telling how many people were a part of her conversation. There were lights all around her—were they all listening to her? This new voice was a man's, deep and old, with a native speaker's command of English. "You see, we all came here on the same day. On the evening of the August the tenth. If it were one at a time, here and there, maybe. But all at once? No. I am Hayes, by the way. From Sussex. At your service."

"What are you saying?" Pietro demanded irritably in Latin.

Hayes explained in Latin.

"We could have died on the same day," Pietro pointed out.

"True," Hayes said. "But from every country in the world? All at the same time?" He switched back to English. "Pietro insists we're all dead. He won't stop talking about it."

"Perhaps the Lord came for us," Griele said.

Hayes made a coughing noise. "Does this seem like heaven to you?"

"Please," Catherine said. "Why do you all look like lights?"

There was silence. "You can see?" Hayes said.

"Of course. I see little patches of light that seem to represent each of you. There's a great crowd of you in an enormous cavern of rock."

"We're underground?" Griele said.

"Wait," Hayes said. "Do you still have your body?"

"Yes."

"How did you get here? Did you just wake up here like the rest of us?"

"I fell down a hole." The details seemed like too much to explain.

"A hole . . . from where?"

"From Horizon. An island to the west. At the edge of the world."

There was a stir at the far end of the cavern. Lights began to swirl and eddy upward, as if they were motes underwater. She heard distant screams.

"They're coming," Griele said. There was a sudden note of panic in her voice.

"What's coming?" Catherine said.

"We don't know what they are," Hayes said. "But they—"

"Flee!" Griele shouted.

The disruption surged toward them with incredible speed, lights scattering toward the roof. Catherine saw a giant pink body, moist and glistening, that ran and leaped high in the air, a creature twice her size, with splayed feet on the sides of its body and a mouth gaping wet and wide. Its mouth closed around a fleeing light—Catherine couldn't tell if it was one of those she had just been speaking to—and snapped shut. It landed, yawned, and licked its toothless mouth. The light it had caught was gone.

Its pink skin was hairless and translucent, like a salamander's, and it pulsed with the effort of its exertion. It had no ears or eyes. It leaped again, and she caught sight of a fat tail balanced on the ground. It closed its jaws around another light and brought it down.

It had happened so fast, Catherine hadn't even moved. She backed slowly away, hardly daring to breathe, until she had reached the square entrance through which she'd come. She slipped through and pressed herself against the wall on the other side, hoping the entrance was too small to admit the monster, but doubting it. There were no other exits from the cavern except for the sheer, vertical shaft down which she had fallen.

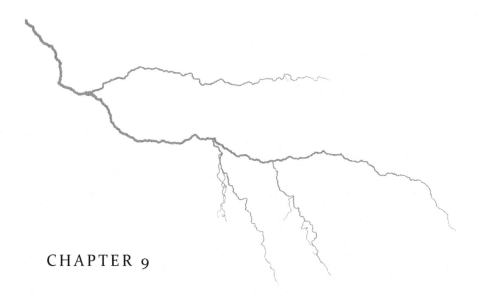

CHAPTER 9

"I'M telling you, it rang," Ramos said.

"It couldn't have." Barrosa picked up the bell-box and looked at the bottom, as if he might find some answers there.

"More than that. It rang in a pattern. Three rings quickly, then a pause, then three rings again. It did that same pattern twice."

Barrosa narrowed his eyes. "That doesn't make any sense."

"I know. You can see, the lever and the bell aren't even connected, and I wasn't touching it. And don't tell me there was an earth tremor; there was no such thing."

"I believe you," Barrosa said. "But that pattern—I didn't even think this one worked at all."

Ramos stared at him. "What do you mean, worked?"

Barrosa touched the jawbone. "When you press the lever, this bone changes material. It becomes very heavy, like metal."

"I've noticed that. But it's not connected to the bell."

"It's connected to the fragment of bone on this box's twin. When you pull this lever, the *other* bell rings."

A chill ran down Ramos's arms. "And . . . when you push the other one, this one rings?" The implications of such a device flooded through his mind. "But how do you know this?"

Barrosa shook his head. He put the bell-box back on the table and crossed to a corner of the room. He brushed some dirt away from the floor to reveal a plank of wood which, when lifted, revealed a small locked chest. He lifted it free and brushed off the dirt.

"You've been keeping secrets from me," Ramos said.

"The king wanted it kept quiet. You didn't need to know."

Barrosa produced a key and soon had the chest open. Inside was another bell-box.

"We thought the others were broken, or that their pairs had been lost at sea," Barrosa said. "The pair to this box, however, is on *La Magdalena*, one of the ships in the Armada, off the coast of Portugal."

Ramos was confused. "So what—"

"Just watch." Barrosa depressed the lever with attentive precision, first once, then twice, then three times, then four. Nothing happened. He waited. Then, without anyone touching it, the bell on top of the box rang. It didn't ring as if it had been jostled; it rang once, then twice, then three times, then four.

"I don't understand. There's a delay?"

"No."

It came to him. "Someone on *La Magdalena* . . ."

"Yes. When I pressed the lever, the bell on *La Magdalena* rang. Someone there just responded to my message by doing the same thing I did. That's our initial greeting. We use the same pattern every time, to show that it's really us.

"Wait a moment." Barrosa used the lever again, this time with a varying number of strokes. He consulted a tiny book along the way. Once again, an answering series of rings returned, and Barrosa wrote down the numbers: 3, 5, 2, 1, 3. 6, 1, 1, 2, 4. When the bell finally fell silent, he paged through the book again, looking for the numbers.

"It's a code," Ramos said. "You're actually talking with the captain of *La Magdalena*, even though he's at sea."

"We could have done a lot better. The code is very limited, mostly a set of key phrases rather than a true language. It's sometimes frustrating, because the captain tries to communicate something more complex, but we can't figure it out, or the king wants to ask a question we have no way of encoding. Today, however, he reports that the wind is fair and their heading true."

"So what does three rings, pause, three rings mean in your code?" he asked.

"That's the thing," Barrosa said. "It doesn't mean anything. Not only that, we never had a pair for that box. We assumed it was lost at sea, along with all the other worms."

But if *La Magdalena* hadn't been the source of the ringing, where had it come from? Ramos's thoughts drifted to the island where, so it was said, a group of renegade Protestants still survived. Someone had made this box, after all. Was it really possible? Could the other half of this box be half a world away?

MATTHEW laid out the pieces of the broken bell-box. The mechanism wasn't the important part. What really made it work was the quintessence connection, and that he couldn't break by throwing it against a wall. He separated the jawbone and positioned it so he could see the glowing quintessence pearl nestled in the delicate whorls of bone. Carefully, he tipped one drop of vitriol out of the vial onto the pearl.

The glow vanished. It didn't just fade; it winked out, leaving a gap of black nothingness in its place, as if the pearl had been cut out of the world. As far as they knew, that's more or less what had happened. Since Aristotle's day, men had argued about whether the material world was continuous or made of tiny atoms whizzing and colliding through empty space. Their study of quintessence—the fifth essence that alchemists had written about for centuries—more or less proved the atomistic theory. They were able to pass material objects through other material objects—impossible if matter was continuous—and see the underlying void first-hand.

The void grew, first to the size of his eye, then to the size of his fist. Left unchecked, it would continue to grow, destroying everything in its path, until it lost stability and the surrounding matter rushed into and collapsed it. Men had died experimenting with voids, before they knew what they were doing. It wasn't something to rush.

Matthew selected two beetlewood planks and used it to control the void's size, pushing it back a little here, a little there. Just as manticores and compass beetles couldn't pass through this particular type of waxy wood, so the void was confined inside it. Matthew had even built special compartments with voids trapped between two layers of wood, allowing him to conduct experiments inside the compartment with no quintessence field, just as things would be back in England.

The quintessence thread, which had been emanating from the pearl, now seemed connected to the void. The thread didn't pass into the void, or stop at its edge; instead, it seemed to thin out and expand, like a cone, to envelop the void, almost as if the void was the thread itself, being stretched open.

It's like we're looking inside the thread," Blanca said, echoing his thoughts. "It's like the interior of the thread is the void—a black tunnel, with no view of the other side."

"The space inside is huge, though," Matthew said. "Just an infinite nothingness, as far as we can tell. A man could fall into the void and just keep on falling, and never return." That very thing had happened to Maasha Kaatra. He knew it didn't invalidate Blanca's suggestion, though. Concepts of space, of interior and exterior, didn't necessarily hold when dealing with quintessence concepts. The interior of a thread might very well *be* an infinite blank space, for all he could say.

"What happens if you throw something into it?" She picked up a broken piece of wood from the bell-box and tossed it accurately, straight into the void. It was like throwing something off a cliff. It dwindled into the distance until it disappeared.

Now that Matthew was staring into the void, the prospect of trying to feed his own spirit thread into it seemed more reckless. If opening a void at one end of a thread really did create a tunnel to the other side, why couldn't they see through it? No, a void was simply non-existence, the absence of reality, as it always had been.

The void was becoming harder to control, growing more quickly and in odd directions, escaping Matthew's ability to push it back with the beetlewood. He clapped the planks together through its center, and it disappeared. The material that had been inside the radius of the void—the jawbone and its pearl, pieces of the broken box—were all gone. Air rushed back into the area with a sharp pop. Even a small circular depression was cut away from the workbench.

Matthew shrugged, despondent. "I should have known."

"What happened to the bones?" Blanca asked.

"Gone." Matthew fluttered his hand in a vague way. "Out of this world." That's why he hadn't tried this on the pair to Catherine's bell-box. He knew it would destroy it.

"Then what happened to the end of the thread that was connected to them?"

Matthew hesitated. What indeed? Aided by the skink tears, he could see hundreds of threads criss-crossing through the room, passing through the walls without difficulty. At first he couldn't see the one they had been working with at all—had the void completely unraveled it? But no, there it was. It had been hard to spot because, as the thread approached the point where the void had been, its brightness smeared, becoming less distinct. The void had done something to it. But it was still there.

He leaned close to examine it. There were thousands of tiny, bright particles, like dust, clinging to the outside of the thread like a halo, diffusing the light. It reminded him of the way shavings from an iron bar would cling to a lodestone. Was it a similar concept? Were these quintessence particles attracted to the thread's quintessence field? And if so, where had they come from?

"Blanca, do you see these?" he said. At his words, the tiny particles danced, like sand on a struck sheet of metal. Some of them skittered down the length of the thread and out of sight. Matthew gasped.

Blanca leaned down to peer at them, her hair brushing his face. "What are they?" The particles jumped again for her. The moment her voice stopped, they stopped moving, freezing in strange and beautiful patterns.

"One. Two. Three. Four," Matthew said, pronouncing each word sharply and waiting a moment between to let the particles settle again. There was no question; they were jumping in response to his voice.

Then the particles jumped again, although neither Matthew nor Blanca had opened their mouths. A man's voice emanated from the thread, as if the sound was produced by the jumping particles instead of the other way around. "Hello?" the voice said. "Hello? Who's there?" The voice was oddly muffled, as if spoken by someone with a jar held over his mouth.

Matthew looked at the open door to make sure, but they were alone. The night was as still as ever, and there had been no noise on the stairs. He leaned close to the thread. "My name is Matthew Marcheford," he said. "Who are you?"

"My name is Ramos de Tavera."

MATTHEW and Blanca stared at each other. Tavera? It had been a Diego de Tavera who had tortured and killed his way through the colony a year and a half before. So who was this Ramos? Whoever he was, he must be one of *them*, an agent of Spain and the Roman Church, who wanted to conquer and control them. Which meant their technology was in enemy hands.

"How did you get a bell-box?" Matthew said.

"From the ship," the voice said. He sounded excited. "Are you part of the Horizon colony?"

"You answer first. Where are you?"

"In Whitehall Palace. In London, England."

Matthew took a breath. At least he was far away, not somewhere on the island. But it confirmed what he thought; if he was in the palace, he worked for the king and the queen.

"Are you related to Diego de Tavera?"

The quality of the voice, already poor, was deteriorating quickly. The man on the other end responded, but Matthew couldn't make out the words.

"What?" Matthew said. "Repeat that."

"Yes," the voice said, though Matthew had to lean his ear close to the thread to make out the words. "He was my brother. He . . ." The rest of the message was lost.

"What else did you get from the ship?" Matthew asked, but the response was too garbled to make out. He tried several more times, but the voice connection was gone, along with the particles that seemed to transmit the sound.

Matthew was torn between elation and shock. He had sent a *spoken* message across a quintessence thread! The implications of that were overwhelming, though of course, as with everything they discovered, it only revealed more that they didn't understand. What were the little particles? How did they transmit sound? Could they transmit anything else? Had he somehow created them with the void? Or had the man on the other end of the thread created them? It chilled him to think that their enemies might somehow have learned more about quintessence than they knew themselves.

"That was amazing," Blanca said, her pretty face flushed. "You were amazing."

"Just luck," Matthew said. "Like most of what we discover." He jumped to his feet. "Let's try it on Catherine's box. If it works the same way, we could talk to her, even just for a moment, and she could tell us where she is." *If she's alive*, he didn't say.

"How did it work?"

"I don't know. I had no idea that could happen. Somehow those particles transmitted my voice through the quintessence thread. I can't begin to guess why."

"And did you smell that musty odor?" Blanca said.

Matthew raised an eyebrow. "You smelled something?"

"Yes, it was damp and earthy, like a cellar. Didn't you smell it?"

Now that he thought of it, he had smelled something like that, but it hadn't really entered his consciousness. "Are you saying you think the *smell* came through the connection?"

She shrugged. "Why not? If sound can come through, why not smell as well?"

Matthew was about to tell her how different the sense of sound was from the sense of smell, but he stopped himself. What did he know? Both traveled invisibly in the air, and for all he knew, both traveled through that invisible realm between the atoms that made up the material world. Perhaps they *could* both be transmitted along a quintessence thread.

He broke open Catherine's bell-box to reveal the bones inside. Blanca bit her lower lip. "I hope she still has her box with her."

Matthew touched a drop of vitriol to the pearl in Catherine's bell-box and used his beetlewood planks to keep the void in check. What had he done before? Nothing really: he had simply closed the void again. He didn't know if it took a particular amount of time to create the effect, or anything special in what he had done. There was nothing for it but to try. He snapped the planks together through the center of the void, closing the gap. As before, the bones were gone, but the thread remained, its end smearing out where the void had been.

A strong smell of swamp pervaded the room. Not just rotting plants, but rotting meat as well. Blanca, who had been leaning forward to peer at the thread, recoiled and covered her face.

"Catherine!" Matthew shouted, leaning close and trying to ignore the stench. "Can you hear me?"

Oh, but it reeked! It was enough to make him feel a bit dizzy. "Catherine! Just talk near the bell-box; we'll be able to hear you."

They waited, holding their breath. Nothing. Utter silence. The particles on the thread didn't move.

Then Matthew tried to step back and found that he couldn't move either. His legs were stiff, weighted to the floor like blocks of stone. He tried to change his weight, to make them lighter, but nothing happened. "Something's wrong," he said, twisting to look at Blanca. "I can't move."

She rushed to him. "No, stay back," he said. "I think it's something with the connection."

"What's wrong?"

"My legs won't work." He tried again to take a step. He found he could lift them, but it was like walking with a statue's legs. He couldn't bend them at the knees.

She knelt down to examine his legs, and jumped back up with a cry. "It's on the floor."

"What is?"

"Something wrong. I could feel it. Let's get out of here."

"Wait. We have to stop it, cut the connection."

"How are you going to do that?"

She was right. They should get away and then figure out what to do from a safe distance.

"My legs are getting stiff, too," she said.

"Quickly then." They stumbled toward the stairs, leaning on one another. They reached them and started down. This far away from the workbench, Matthew discovered he could bend his knees again, and stiffly managed to navigate the steps. At the bottom, he and Blanca stopped, and he bent to massage his legs. They felt like flesh again, and he could change their weight just as before. They seemed to have escaped the reach of the problem.

They paused, exhausted and breathing hard.

"What happened?" Blanca said.

Matthew didn't know. Something had come through the connection, something that made their legs feel like lead. Some kind of gas, or spirit, or miasma, he supposed. Whatever it was, they couldn't see it, only feel its effects. And whatever it was, it came from the place where Catherine was, or had been. A place with the smell of decay and death. Did that mean that Catherine . . . that her body . . .? He couldn't believe that. *Wouldn't* believe it, not without more proof than a bad smell.

When the first explorers of Horizon had tried to return to England, leaving the effects of the quintessence field, their limbs had become gradually stiffer as the nutrients in their bodies turned back to salt and sand. Was that what had happened here? Was whatever had leaked through the connection somehow causing an interruption in the quintessence field?

And what should they do now? He had opened that thread like a tunnel between two places, connecting his upstairs rooms with this place of death. Now that it was open, however, how was he supposed to close it? A void was the most destructive thing they knew about—

it would obliterate any matter—but the quintessence thread wasn't made of matter, and it was the void that had created it in the first place.

Blanca gripped his arm. "Look!"

On the floor near the stairs, a loose, mesh cage held two puff weasels. The furry creatures lay on their backs, limbs splayed out straight and stiff, twitching. Matthew took a step back. He pulled off a chunk from a piece of old bread on a worktable and tossed it toward the cage. The bread hit the floor as a spray of sand.

"It's spreading," Matthew said. "Coming down the stairs. And somehow, it blocks quintessence. The quintessence field doesn't reach wherever that miasma spreads."

"How can we stop it?"

Matthew tried to think. The miasma seemed to move along the ground, like an invisible stream of water pouring out of the connection and spreading out across the floor. If he elevated himself on stilts of some kind, he might be able to make it back up to the connection. Of course, if he fell, he would die. If he could get to his boarcat paws, he might be able to sever the thread, which would probably—possibly—close the hole and stop the miasma's advance.

In the meantime, it was spreading across the floor toward them. They ran outside into the night.

"Go and wake Parris," Matthew said.

"What are you going to do?"

"I don't know."

Blanca ran off toward the Parris home. Matthew raced to the storehouse and was back in a moment with a copper shovel. It was actually only a thin layer of copper around the outside, and wood in the middle, so it wasn't too heavy to use. The blade of the shovel was much larger than a standard shovel. Matthew plunged it into the ground. The copper acted as a conductor of Matthew's own quintessence field. Normally, he could change the weight and properties of the matter in his own body, but the copper allowed him to extend that power to whatever it touched. He dipped the shovel down into the solid earth as easily as through water, and pulled a huge mass of it free as effortlessly as if it were goose feathers. He tipped it up onto the ground, allowing the earth to run off the shovel, where he turned it to diamond, freezing it into a squat, vertical wall.

He shifted to the left and repeated the process, circling his way around the house, creating a ditch with a short wall on the outside. It was the same way they built their houses, only a team of men did the work with copper shaping tools to make the walls straight and true. He would confine the miasma inside a wall.

By the time Blanca returned with Parris, Matthew had it finished. He climbed out of the circle and explained to Parris what he had done and what he had seen. They circled the wall, tossing bits of diamond and gold onto the ground inside of Matthew's makeshift wall. After a few minutes, they saw the gold objects turn back to their original materials. The miasma was outside the house.

Only then did Matthew realize his mistake. "Get back!" he said. Of course, a diamond wall wasn't going to hold the miasma. As soon as it reached the wall, the diamond would crumble back into dirt. An earthen wall might still dam it for a bit, but it might also seep right through.

The land on which the Quintessence Society building stood sloped gently toward them. "Around to the other side," Matthew said. "Get to the high ground."

They raced around, and here the gold pieces on the ground were still gold. The miasma was all flowing downhill away from the building . . . toward the rest of the settlement.

"Sound the alarm," Parris said. Matthew ran to the alarm box. There were a dozen of them scattered around the settlement, placed there to give warning if the manticores ever breached the barrier. It was much like a bell-box, only it was attached to a large bell on top of the church. The increased weight of a single ironfish bone was hardly enough to ring such a bell, but it was enough to release a catch, which in turn released a much larger weight, which fell, pulling the bell rope. The bell tolled, its low tones resonating out over the colony.

At that moment, the Society building itself, also made of diamond, shuddered and creaked like a ship at anchor in a storm. The bottom of the south wall had transformed back into dirt. Under the weight of the diamond on top of it, it was crumbling away, and the whole structure was leaning. Finally, with a deafening crack, the building toppled and crashed into the growing pool of miasma. The south wall, now on the bottom, instantly transformed into dirt and collapsed in a cloud of dust, bringing the rest down after it.

Colonists began pouring into the street, matchlocks in hand, thinking it was a manticore attack. When they saw Matthew and Parris, they ran to join them. "Forget the guns," Matthew said. He quickly explained what was happening. Most of them weren't natural philosophers and had only the barest appreciation of quintessence, but they had lived on Horizon long enough to accept the idea of an invisible smell that could destroy buildings. The smell of death in London carried disease, after all. Why shouldn't it carry destruction, too?

"We need to funnel it down to the river," Matthew said. "Keep it away from the buildings. Get the shovels."

The others scrambled to help, and Matthew raced back around the destruction. It was now possible to see the miasma, if only a little. Throughout the colony, they had erected shekinah flatworms in glass jars on poles to light the settlement at night. Where the shekinah light hit the miasma, however, it seemed to be swallowed up, showing where the miasma was by the absence of light. It was like a barely perceptible shadow, only visible at certain angles, flowing across the ground. And there was a lot more of it than Matthew had realized.

He ran ahead of it and started shoveling, trying to make a wedge of barricades to direct it into a chute. A few men joined him, and he shouted instructions. They dug fast, and threw up great piles of dirt, but the miasma came faster and higher than they expected. It rushed over the walls and flowed around them, sending them running. The two buildings on either side of them, their foundations undermined, crashed toward each other. One man was struck by a falling wedge of diamond wall, pinning him to the ground, where the miasma quickly rolled over him, transforming him into a crumbling statue of salt and sand.

"Back!" Matthew yelled. "Farther back!"

But it was too late. The miasma was spreading, far beyond their ability to control it. They abandoned their attempts and instead ran ahead of it, checking the buildings for anyone left inside and circling back around to higher ground.

Matthew spotted Blanca running into the small building the colonists used to store common goods and tools. It was one of the few original structures that had survived the devastating quintessence fire of two years before, although its diamond walls were melted thin in some places and its original diamond roof had been replaced with a wooden one. Surely there was no one in there to evacuate.

He ran in after her. The building was one large room filled with odds and ends for general use: split boards and cut stone, small mountains of scrap gold and silver, and a smaller pile of copper. And, of course, the stores of mercury, sulphur, and salt. These three were divided into shares and restricted to one share per family, except by special permit from the governor. Blanca was there, gathering up sacks of salt.

"This is all we have," she said. "We need to save it."

Matthew shook his head. "We need to go. We'll get more salt."

"There isn't any more salt. We need this if we're going to survive."

She was right, of course, but so was he. They didn't have time. "Take what you have, and let's go!"

"Not enough."

Frustrated, he joined her, throwing the bags onto a old canvas sail they used to haul large quantities of materials from place to place. If they could get the salt on it, then between them, perhaps they could drag it out and up to safety. The miasma, however, was too quick for them. Before they had half of the sacks transferred, a spot of light near the door suddenly darkened. He couldn't see how much there was, but he knew they didn't have long.

"Quick," he said. "Up!"

Blanca could be as stubborn as Catherine, but she recognized the urgency in his voice. He saw her bend as if to leap, and jumped himself, making his body both light and insubstantial, shooting right through the wooden roof as if it were made of air, and out onto its peaked top. Blanca didn't join him. He dipped his head back in and saw her, her face turned up with a look of terror. Her legs wouldn't move.

Matthew jumped back down, landing on the pile of salt, hoping it was high enough to keep him safe. He held a hand out for Blanca. She grasped it, and he increased his own weight, balancing her as she dragged herself toward him, barely able to move her legs at all. They were heavy and stiff, and she could no longer lighten them like the rest of her body. There was no way he could leap clear while carrying her. Around the edges, near the floor, the pile of salt began to spark and sizzle. The building creaked and tilted as its foundation was undermined.

"Hurry," Matthew said. Blanca shuffled up toward him, and as she did, she pulled her legs clear and regained their use. "Now jump!"

They both leaped this time, clearing the roof and landing on top. It was no problem for either of them to leap to the ground from such a height, but they had no idea how much ground the miasma covered. Near the shekinah lights, it was clearly visible as a shadow along the ground where none should be. In the rest of the settlement, however, it was invisible. They knew it was safe to the north of the collapsed society building, but even with the help of quintessence, they couldn't jump that far.

The building underneath them lurched and tilted, nearly pitching them off the roof. Blanca shrieked and held onto Matthew's arm for balance. They were out of options.

"The nearest diamond," Matthew said. "Let's go."

The buildings nearby, although they had collapsed, still had pieces of diamond wall jutting up from the mounds of dirt. If it was still made of diamond, that meant it was high enough that the miasma hadn't reached it, and if they could leap that far, they could make it.

Holding hands, they jumped, the air rushing by them, and landed on the nearest diamond. Blanca slipped and slid toward the ground, but Matthew held her up. "Again," he said.

They leaped again, farther up the slope, to another island. Finally, after three more similar leaps, like crossing a river on exposed rocks, they made it back to where they had started. Behind them, the storehouse collapsed like the others, only this time, a rush of white flame engulfed the wreckage and melted it down to nothing.

"The salt," Blanca said. "It's gone."

"Everything is gone," Matthew said. He shook his head in disbelief, feeling a heavy stone settling in his chest. Before this, his experiments had always brought good to the colony: more food, more comfort, easier ways to accomplish work. He hadn't meant to risk such destruction. He had only been trying to find Catherine.

They watched the last of the settlement crumble away.

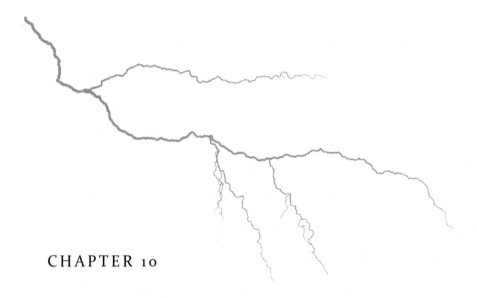

CHAPTER 10

RAMOS kept trying the bell-box, but he got no reply. Either it wasn't working anymore, or else the Horizon colonists, realizing who he was, no longer wished to speak to him. He could hardly believe that it had really happened. He had spoken to someone on the other side of the world! He had only just gotten used to the idea that they could make a bell ring a thousand miles away; that was astonishing enough. Now his voice, his own voice, had somehow been made to travel across that immense distance.

His mind spun, trying to invent plausible theories for how it worked. There was nothing connecting his bell-box to anything else. Nothing that could been seen or touched, anyway. Just to prove it to himself, he lifted the box and waved his hand under it, over it, and all around it. He felt nothing. Yet somehow sound had traveled from Horizon to his little box.

What was sound, anyway? It was invisible. Humans made sound by blowing out air, but sound could also be heard underwater, and could be made by striking with a hammer or plucking a string.

Generally, it only traveled a short distance; even a very loud noise rarely traveled more than a mile. The sound diminished as it traveled; close to the source it might be very loud, but as it traveled, it was changed somehow by passing through the air—dirtied, as it were, and made less. It reminded him of Aristotle's theory of how a prism turned regular light into a rainbow. He said that the light passing through the prism was dirtied depending on how much of the glass it passed through, so that light passing through the thick part of the prism was colored differently than light passing through the thin part.

What if sound worked the same? Perhaps quintessence was just the carrier, the aether, and either light or sound could travel through it like water in a riverbed. If quintessence was a purer carrier than air, then light passing through it would be less dirtied, and thus purer, more white, as indeed the light from the shekinah flatworm and the pearls seemed to be. In the same way, quintessence-carried sound would not be dirtied as it was in air, and thus could travel a much further distance.

As a theory, it left a lot to be desired, but perhaps more details would help flesh it out. Anyway, there was no sense philosophizing when he could simply test the idea. If quintessence light could pass through a prism without changing color like regular light, then that would support the theory. If it did change color, he would keep thinking.

Barrosa had long since gone to bed, and Ramos was alone in the secret cellar. He took his time, gathering what he needed and setting up the experiment. On one table, he directed lamplight through a prism; on another, quintessence light from his pearl. At first he was disappointed. The resulting rainbows looked the same. Red turning to yellow, passing through green, and fading to violet.

He sighed. If quintessence light had passed through the prism without changing, or at least had changed differently, that might have given him a clue, a piece of knowledge that he could pick at and pull into real understanding. He nearly went to bed right then. The revelation came quite by accident. On the red side of the quintessence rainbow, an ordinary candle stood in its holder. The quintessence light was not shining directly on it. No part of the rainbow touched it. The candle, however, melted.

Ramos examined it in confusion. The wax pooled beneath it in a lumpy mass and was still hot and soft to the touch. What had happened? The candle had not been lit. The room was not hot, and none of the other candles in the room were melted. He slid the prism across the table and shone the rainbow on another candle. Nothing happened. He shifted it to the right slightly, then a little more, until the rainbow shone on the wall a few handbreadths away from the candle. When it reached this point, the second candle rapidly melted. Heart pounding, Ramos lowered his hand in front of the candle, then swiftly pulled it back in pain. His skin was red and tender, as if he had burned it in a fire.

A chill rippled down Ramos's skin. *Invisible light.* There was some kind of *light* shining to the left of the rainbow, as if it continued past yellow, orange, and red into more colors, colors that could not be seen. And not just any light, but a kind of light hot enough to burn skin and melt wax. He tested regular light the same way, but as he suspected, it had no such effect. Only the quintessence light could melt candles and burn his hand.

Aristotle had it wrong. It wasn't the prism that produced the colors, any more than it was the prism that produced this new kind of light. The prism, after all, hadn't changed. The invisible colors were a characteristic of the light, and if that was the case, then the visible colors were as well. That meant the prism didn't add colors to the light. The colors were already there.

He aimed at another candle, and this time, he dropped the pearl into a jar of saltwater to increase the intensity of the quintessence light. The pearl blazed into brightness. At first, nothing seemed to happen. Then, with a deep *whoosh*, the swath of air from the prism to the back wall erupted in flame. The candle, the holder, the table— everything in its path—vaporized in a violent explosion of heat and light. An invisible pulse blasted into Ramos, throwing him backwards and knocking his head against the table behind him.

He lay stunned for a few moments. He touched the back of his head, and his hand came back bloody, but the wound was already healing, thanks to the quintessence pearl. He stood and surveyed the damage. The room was a wreck. In a line from the prism to the wall, there was nothing but soot, the black particles still swirling gently through the candlelit air. A hole had been punched in the earthen wall, leaving dirt still crumbling to the floor.

Ramos sat up, letting his head clear, and a slow smile spread across his face. The king wanted a weapon. Ramos had found one.

THE GIANT salamander snuffled and poked its nose through the square entranceway. It was as tall as Catherine, but so thick in the body that the opening wasn't wide enough to admit more than its blunt head. Its pink face was wormlike, devoid of features beyond a pointed nose and that gaping mouth. Catherine was close enough to see a few wet hairs hanging limply from its chin, like a beard. Its wet skin glistened. It was much larger than an ordinary salamander, of course, but its dimensions were different, too. It was shorter and plumper, like a leech with legs.

It planted its feet and squeezed, shoving its body into the too-small hole with a squelching noise. It was coming through after all. Fold after fold of flesh rippled into the room until the whole salamander emerged, its bulk blocking the soft light of the spirits beyond.

Catherine flattened herself against the wall, trying not to be noticed, though the monster was close enough to touch. She hoped it couldn't smell her, or that it preferred eating glowing spirits to eating human flesh. She felt a throbbing in her chest that seemed connected to the pulse in the creature's skin. It was like holding a shekinah flatworm in her bare hands and feeling the pulse of its power, only much greater.

It ignored her, if it even sensed that she was there. It pulled its glistening body toward the vertical shaft. As quickly as it had leaped to catch the tiny sparks in its mouth, it leaped upwards into the shaft, blocking the light. It fit so neatly that she suspected it was the salamander that had made the hole in the first place. She heard it squirming its way up toward the surface. It had a long way to go.

She didn't stick around to watch it. She ran back into the large cavern, where the motes of light still swirled in agitation.

"It's gone," she told those nearest. "It went up the shaft."

At first, none of the closest spoke English or Latin, but eventually one responded in kind and spread the word. Gradually, the eddies of light settled.

"What is that creature?" she asked.

Hayes had found her again. "We don't know," he said. "We can't see anything physical. We didn't even know there was anything physical left in the world, until you arrived."

"It looked like a huge, pink salamander."

"It's a monster, that's all we know. We can feel when it's coming closer, though not always soon enough to escape before it devours us."

Catherine explored the cavern, discovering openings into several more caves. Eventually she would need to find a way out, though she didn't want to think too hard about how unlikely that was. For the time being, her most urgent need was to find some food and water. She stepped through into another cave after using a mound of chipped stone to mark the entrance. She didn't want to get lost and be unable to find her way back to where she had started.

The cavern beyond was darker, but a small galaxy of the spirit lights followed her into it. Although they couldn't see, they apparently had some sense of their environment, such that they could flee the salamander or follow her. It was a good thing, because without their light, she wouldn't have been able to see anything. If another salamander came, of course, they might flee again, leaving her behind in darkness.

The cavern walls were wet and echoed with the sound of water dripping. Spikes jutted down from the ceiling, occasionally met by others reaching up from the floor. It was like walking through an alien forest with stone trees and the occasional crystal flower blooming red or white from a cavity. She found a small stream cutting its way through the rock from one end of the cavern to the other. The way this new cavern dipped and turned and opened into other spaces, she was afraid she would have trouble finding her way back, even given her precaution. She wished she still had her pack.

She drank from the stream, which tasted cool and—to her surprise—salty. None of the water around Horizon was salty. Even the ocean for miles around it was fresh, the salt consumed by all the fish and marine life that used quintessence to catch prey, attract a mate, or camouflage themselves. Anywhere else in the world, this water would have been undrinkable, useless to her, but here on Horizon, both the salt and the water were essential to life. She drank eagerly, and, though still hungry, felt much better.

There were other creatures down here besides the salamanders. She saw pale fish in the water, giant eyeless spiders with too many legs skittering out of the light, and colonies of naked bats hanging from the roof. She needed to catch one of those fish, and she needed a fire to cook it, but she didn't see how she was going to manage either one.

She followed the stream up to its source, a rush of water down a smooth wall marbled with mineral deposits. It flowed out of an opening high above her, but that was no barrier, not with a fresh supply of salt coursing through her body. She leaped, adjusting her body weight to control her ascent, and scrambled up through the opening, soaking her feet.

A smaller cave now tunneled back into the rock, following the water, gradually higher. She continued, reasoning that it was better to go up than down, and that the water must come from somewhere outside, though given how far she had fallen, she held out little hope of climbing to the surface this way.

She climbed further, not sure what she was looking for, but knowing that sitting down in despair wouldn't get her very far either. The lights began slipping away behind her, no longer following, but she could see another light in the distance, beyond a bend in the tunnel. She rounded the bend, and found it was farther away and brighter than she had at first thought. Was it possible it was sunlight? Could she be coming out through the side of the mountain?

When she rounded the next bend, the light was so bright it hurt her eyes, and it definitely was not sunlight. It reflected off the white surface of the cave wall, and she gasped when she realized what she was seeing. She licked her finger, touched it to the wall, and put it back in her mouth. Salt. She closed her eyes and savored the taste.

There was enough salt here to provide for the colony for months. Years, depending on how deep it went. She pressed closer to the light, sliding sideways and shielding her eyes. Finally, she could see where it was coming from. Hundreds of shekinah flatworms lined the walls, their bodies pressed to the salty surface like leeches to a wound. The light from their bodies flared and blazed in time to their motion. She pressed farther in, barely able to see, closing her eyes to slits and blocking most of the light with her hands. The shekinahs surrounded her. She had to step carefully to avoid crushing them.

As she progressed, the shekinahs grew larger. The ones at the entrance to the cave were finger-sized, just like the ones they caught and used for light back in the colony. Farther in, they were the size of her fist, fat and soft. Beyond that, they were as big as her head, then bigger still. The larger ones seemed stretched, pinker and more translucent, and producing less light. She reached a cavern where the walls and ceiling opened up, still glistening white with salt. The light was less bright here, and she could open her eyes. Doing so, she realized her mistake. The largest shekinahs had legs. They were giants three times as large as she was, pink, earless, and eyeless, with flat tails and gaping toothless mouths.

This was the salamanders' lair.

CHAPTER 11

RAMOS stood in a field of yellow wildflowers that stretched to a distant forest line. Thousands of bright blooms swayed in a gentle breeze. The temperature was mild, and thick clouds glided through a blue sky.

King Philip sat on a three-legged stool that his page had carried for him on the four mile walk from town. Philip himself had ridden a horse, as had his guards and his inner circle of advisors. It was a small retinue for the king, who usually rode with at least a hundred. The king's advisors were all generals, battle-hardened men who had commanded armies in France or Italy or Turkey. The government was run by bureaucrats, but the men Philip trusted were those who fought for him.

Ramos tinkered with his device, adjusting the height of the wooden stand, checking its balance, nervous for everything to be just as it should be. He briefly explained the apparatus. The pearl and prism were shut inside a box mirrored on the inside, but a black wooden barrier could be slid into place, dividing the pearl and prism into separate compartments. A hole in the front, set at the proper angle, would let out the invisible light.

One of the king's advisors, a thickset man named Carillo in a cream white doublet, yawned.

"The strength can be adjusted," Ramos said. "This is low power, with no salt used at all." He held one of the flowers in front of the device and lifted the barrier. The petals blackened around the edges, then curled and shriveled until nothing was left but black powder drifting away in the breeze.

Carillo snorted. "Better a flint, my lord, if I wanted to light a cookfire."

Ramos replaced the barrier, ignoring the comment. He explained how he had split the light into colors with a prism, how the candle had melted, how he had deduced the existence of invisible light outside the span of colors they could see. The men shuffled their feet and looked impatient. He was losing them. He had never been good at presentation; the things that seemed crucial to him weren't necessarily of interest to his audience.

He decided to skip the explanation and jump ahead. He had set up a simple wooden crosspiece in the field. He walked over to it and placed a hat on the top point and wrapped an old cloth around it to serve as a cloak.

"This is an enemy soldier," he said, "and this is high power." He opened a hatch at the back of the device and pulled the top off a jar of salt water.

"I hope the enemy is lame," Carillo said, "or you'd be dead by now."

Ramos tipped the jar into the compartment where the pearl sat. He had only used a few drops before, but, irritated at Carillo, he poured it all in, filling the compartment with the white liquid and leaving a slick of wet salt behind in the jar.

Ramos motioned at the men. "Stand back, please."

Some of the men edged back slightly, but Carillo held his ground.

With a flourish, Ramos pulled the barrier free. For a moment, nothing happened, and he feared he had ruined the experiment by drowning the device. Then the stick figure's cloak exploded in a rush of flame, as did a wide swath of flowers around it. In moments, the figure was incinerated, the clothes vaporized, and black ash drifted through the air.

Ramos replaced the barrier, and the remaining flames died away, leaving nothing but blackened, smoldering wood. He was gratified to see a layer of soot coating Carillo's cream doublet.

The military men broke into excited conversation. "The box would be clumsy to transport," Carillo said, dusting off a shoulder and trying to look unimpressed, but the others ignored him, discussing how this might give them an advantage in their wars.

"How many can you make?" asked a man with a thin mustache. "Could you surround a castle with them and keep them continuously supplied with salt water? A wall of fire would be a formidable barrier."

Ramos shook his head. "No, my lord. I . . . to be honest, I can make only this one. Four at the most. I . . ." He trailed off, reddening as he realized how limited this device was. It required a quintessence pearl, of which only four existed in England. He thought he had something marvelous; he had planned to amaze them. Instead, he had wasted their time.

"Look on the bright side," Carillo said. "Just before your enemy cleaves your head in two, you can throw salt water in his eyes."

The men laughed. Ramos's face burned. Surprisingly, it was the king who rescued him. He raised a hand, silencing the laughter. "It is *Ignis Dei*. The Fire of God. You have done well, Ramos de Tavera. Better even than your brother before you. Rest assured, you will be rewarded." He stood, slapping his thighs. "In the meantime, continue your work. You are the power of the armies of God."

Ramos felt a warm, grateful glow. His monarch, this great champion of the Church, was pleased with him. His sense of euphoria remained while the king and his retinue gathered up their things and rode away. Once they were gone, however, the enthusiasm faded. The king was kind, but his demonstration had been a failure. The weapon made an impressive show, but what good was it? They couldn't mass produce it. It was dependent on the pearls, and they only had four of those. Worse, the pearls were dependent on the shekinah flatworm, so they couldn't send one to the wars in Turkey or France. Without the shekinah, they would quickly fade to uselessness.

Barrosa clapped him on the back. "Congratulations! I hope you remember your friends when you're sitting at the king's table."

Ramos shook his head. "It's a novelty, that's all. It won't make any real difference in the wars, and the king knows it."

"It could. You just need to work on the design. Make it more portable, easier to carry and aim."

"That won't help without more pearls."

Barrosa gave a mischievous smile. "What if we had more pearls?"

"What are you talking about? There were only four."

"I'm talking about getting more. An expedition to Horizon."

Ramos kicked the ground. "That would take over a year, even if we sent a ship today."

A slow grin spread across Barrosa's face.

"What is it?"

"You can't tell anyone."

"I swear."

"Swear on the Bible."

"I swear on the Bible and the Blessed Virgin. Now tell me what you're grinning about!"

"Philip sent an expedition of conquistadors to Horizon months ago. Five ships of the line, stacked with cannon and crammed with soldiers. They have orders to kill the heretics and return with all the pearls and shekinah flatworms they can find."

Ramos gaped. "Then, the ship with the bell-box? *La Magdalena*?"

"Yes. We were talking with Alvaro de Torres, captain of *La Magdalena* and Capitán-General of the expeditionary fleet."

"You told me they were off the coast of Portugal!"

Barrosa shrugged.

"How close are they to the island?"

"If the weather holds? They'll arrive within the week."

Ramos felt his pulse rate rise. In less than a week, someone would be in the presence of the source of these wonders, and would be able to *tell* them about it, in limited fashion, from half a world away. But the conquistadors were mercenary soldiers. This Alvaro de Torres would have been given a contract from King Philip to conquer the island, looting and plundering whatever he found, and taking a cut for himself.

Killing the heretics meant murdering those who discovered all these wonders, mastered the use of the shekinah flatworms and pearls, invented the bell-boxes, and who knew what more? If they were killed, their knowledge would die with them. Suddenly, Ramos felt more sympathy with the distant colonists than he did with those of his own country and religion. They understood the value of what they had found. Ramos had sworn to be loyal to his king and country and to the Church, but he knew something else, knew it as surely as he loved Antonia. He didn't want those colonists to die.

CATHERINE found a salt-encrusted crevice in the rock and hid herself there to watch. From this vantage, she could see back along the cave passage through which she had come. She marveled at this discovery: shekinah flatworms and these gigantic salamanders were the same creatures! She had no idea that shekinahs were not the adult form of the animal; they had never seen them grow appreciably in all the time they had kept them in captivity. There must be something about this cave that caused them to mature, perhaps the abundance of salt.

But no, as she watched the shekinahs, she could tell that they were not eating the salt at all, as she had first assumed, but excreting it. In fact, all the salt covering the walls must have been left by generations of shekinahs passing through and growing to adulthood. The thought made her head spin—could this be the source of the island's salt? If there were enough caves like this tunneled throughout these mountains, with colonies of maturing shekinahs, perhaps rainfall washed the salt out to the surrounding land, in streams like the one she had just drunk from, and deposited it in the soil over time.

Catherine decided to keep moving. If she stopped, if she allowed her mind to drift from the immediate problems and mysteries at hand to the fact that she was trapped alone untold leagues below the earth, with no concept of how to get out, then she might lose her mind. One step at a time. She needed food.

She climbed back down to the salty stream, ready to bolt back to her crevice at any sign of an approaching salamander, and made it there without incident. She was greeted again by the swirling lights of the spirits. No wonder they hadn't followed her into the upper cave—the salamanders fed on them. Which was a mystery in itself: the salamanders excreted salt, but fed on the disembodied souls of people? Had there always been spirits here? Was that their main diet, or did they get sustenance some other way? Were they, in fact, eating the spirits at all?

She remembered the leviathan they had encountered on their trip to Horizon the year before, how it had attacked the ship to get a salt-enhanced quintessence pearl, only leaving them alone when her father had thrown the pearl into the sea. The leviathan had caught it in its massive jaws and then plunged beneath the surface, never to be seen again. Were these salamanders like the leviathan? Was it the quintessence power that these spirits represented that they were attracted to, rather than the souls of the people themselves?

She knelt at the water's edge and trailed a hand into the stream, trying to touch one of the eyeless fish. This proved harder than expected, however, as the fish slid smoothly away every time her fingers broke the surface. Perhaps they, too would be attracted by a bit of quintessence. Flush with salt, she made her skin glow white, and sure enough, the skittish fish swam close and tried to nibble her fingers. Once she touched one, it was simple to make it lighter than air and snatch it as it rose out of the water.

Cooking it was no more difficult. A flash of quintessence fire, and it was baked black and steaming. Not the most gourmet dish ever prepared, but it would keep her fed. She was just figuring out how to tear off a piece without a knife, when she noticed that the tiny spirit lights were gone. She turned around to find them, and saw three giant salamanders crouched behind her, their fleshy mouths agape.

Catherine reacted quickly. She leaped high to the cavern roof, altering her weight radically, and grabbing hold of a crag. One of the salamanders leaped after her, its mouth clamping shut just below her foot, before it fell back down again. The salamanders ignored the fish. It was her they wanted. As she'd suspected, they seemed to be attracted to quintessence. Once she evidenced some to catch her own meal, they saw her as another source of food.

She edged along around the spikes, but they followed her. One of the salamanders reached the wall and climbed it effortlessly, cutting off her escape to the larger cavern. There was nothing for it. She dashed for the salamanders' lair, hoping she could get through.

Too late. The salamanders were awake. They loped toward her, grunting and leaping. More of them climbed up the walls, swarming around her. She dropped to the floor again and raced back the way she had come. The two exits to this cavern that she knew about were blocked, but the stream must exit the cavern somewhere. She leaped from rock to rock, just ahead of the pursuing salamanders.

The cavern narrowed, but continued to twist its way downward, following the stream. It closed to a point nearly too small for her, but she splashed through the water, and on the other side, it widened again. She didn't look back. She had already seen how the salamanders could squeeze their bulk through holes that seemed too small for them, so she had no doubt they were still behind her.

The rock angled down sharply and the surface became more jagged, with tortured twists and folds of rock that hid from view what lay beyond. She heard the thunder of a nearby waterfall, though she couldn't yet see it. She had no idea where she was going, or what passages might leave her trapped in a dead end, but she had no choice but to run blindly. The salamanders, close on her trail, were gaining. They seemed just about to catch her when she burst out into open air and the clear night sky.

At least, it looked like the night sky above her. She was in an immense open space with stars high above, and yet, it seemed wrong. The breeze that played on her face wasn't fresh enough, and the smell hadn't changed. Then she saw that the stars were moving. She was still underground, but in a larger cavern by far than any she had yet seen. What she had mistaken for stars were actually thousands of the glowing spirits.

The salty stream ran down into a pool. Other streams joined it, cascading in waterfalls from other rifts in the rock. Salamanders emerged from all of these rifts, filling up the space from every direction. The salamanders who had been chasing her loped past her, ignoring her, and converged with the others toward a circular platform raised out of the rock in the center of the space. The walls of the platform were straight and true, as if fashioned by human hands. It was surrounded with crystals of all colors and shapes: jagged pink blooms, turquoise starbursts, smooth sheets of translucent sapphire. On the platform itself, his arms raised as if to welcome the growing horde of salamanders, stood a man.

Catherine recognized him. But it was impossible.

She ran toward him, heedless now of the gathering salamanders. They seemed less interested in her now, anyway, transfixed, just as she was, by the man at their center. She reached it and climbed up, circling him so as to see his face.

When she had known him, he had been strong and powerful, his bunched muscles sliding seamlessly over one another like those of a tiger crouched to spring. He had killed a mutineer with a scimitar blow that had nearly cut the man in half. Now, he carried himself like an old man, hunched and fearful of a fall. His face, once impassive, was lined with pain, his lips dry and cracked, his eyebrows scabbed white. Before, his skin had been so black it was difficult to see the creases, and she had marveled to stand next to him and compare her fair skin with his. Now, like a black-bottomed boat crusted with barnacles, his skin was layered with chalky, white lesions.

"Maasha Kaatra?" she whispered.

His eyes swiveled to take her in, and if anything, grew even sadder.

"Catherine Parris," he said. "You should not be here."

"What is this place?"

He shook his head, but his face was etched with all the despair in the world.

CHAPTER 12

CAPITÁN-GENERAL Alvaro de Torres leaned against the stern rail and let his bosun take command of the ship. Against all odds, they had made it, and with all five ships of the fleet intact. Torres was no stranger to difficult sea voyages. He had sailed around the Horn of Africa as far as the Pacific, and he had fought in the Mediterranean against France in the Italian Wars. But nothing had tested his sailing expertise like setting out across the Western ocean with no land in sight and nothing but a scrambling beetle in a box for navigation.

The trip had been made three times before, once by Admiral Chelsey, once by Christopher Sinclair, and once under the command of Diego de Tavera. The first and third had returned, though no survivors had lived to tell of it. The second had never returned, and the *Western Star* was reportedly still here on Horizon Island, its sailors and passengers the kings of a rich colony. A colony he was here to destroy.

The fleet sailed into the quiet bay, apparently unobserved. A carrack, presumably the *Western Star* itself, floated at anchor, unmanned. Torres scanned the shore with his spyglass, and saw a roughly-built pier and a well-worn track leading into the forest.

When King Philip first gave him this charter, Torres had scoffed at tales of miraculous water and creatures walking through walls. The king's court secretary, Barrosa, had shown him enough to convince him, however, and he had seen enough on this journey already to think the stories probably fell short of the reality. If he succeeded in his mission, Spain would be the greatest nation in the world, its military undefeatable. Even the bell-box, that apparently simple device by which he communicated back to Barrosa and the king, would be enough to give Spain a crushing advantage in warfare if they could construct enough of them. He envisioned multiple forces on land and sea, their movements coordinated precisely across hundreds of miles. No one would touch them.

But there was more, far more, that could give riches and military might to the country that controlled this island. Which was why Torres planned to take all possible precautions in approaching the settlement. By all accounts, he should have five times as many men as the colonists, professional soldiers trained and armed against exiled shopkeepers and theologians. But he didn't know what they could do. He would assume the worst, and plan accordingly.

Back in his cabin, Torres genuflected before the crucifix mounted on his wall and made the sign of the cross. This was God's mission, like the crusades of centuries past, and God had granted him, Alvaro de Torres, a central role. He would vanquish the heathen and apostate alike and return victorious with the power to convert the world to Christ.

In his heart, though, he had to admit he was nervous. There were unknown powers at work on this island, powers that, until now, had been used only in the service of the devil. What horrors might he encounter here? Would not the devil resist the conquering of this stronghold of evil with all his wiles and might?

Torres was no saint, and he knew it. There had been that girl in Mindanao, whose lithe brown body still invaded his dreams. He kept a whip of leather straps under his pillow with which he lashed himself those evenings when his imagination strayed to the memory of her flesh. The penance was a welcome relief to his conscience, but it never seemed to fully cleanse him, and the next night he would find his thoughts pulled once more toward desire for what he knew to be sin. He was weak. Why had God chosen such a man as he for this holy work?

He bowed his head to the crucifix. "God give me the strength," he said.

When he returned above decks, a rising column of smoke over the trees caught his eye. He trained his spyglass on it and could make out the tops of buildings. The buildings were *tall*, and they glinted in an odd way, like they were made of some strange material. It looked more like the buildings you might find in a city than in a frontier settlement. He had been led to believe there were no more than five dozen people living here. As he watched, however, flames leaped up around the buildings and smoke billowed up to the sky. The tallest of the buildings toppled and collapsed out of view, with a crash that echoed clear out to the water.

He whispered a quick prayer of thanks and repented his lack of faith. God was judging the heretics already. Perhaps this mission would be easier than he had thought.

THE COLONISTS watched their settlement burn. Matthew's father organized an operation to gather and count everyone. Everyone in the colony was ultimately found and accounted for, except for one man who had died in the flood of miasma.

They made for the *Western Star*, which was still at anchor in the bay. Surrounded by water, they would be somewhat protected from manticore attack, and it would give them shelter from the daily rainstorms until they could start to rebuild. The water in the bay was fresh, and they could make food onboard from sand. They could live there for a long time, if need be.

He heard James Ferguson loudly blaming manticores for the destruction, claiming that they had developed a new weapon. Eventually, Matthew would have to tell the truth about what he had done, but at the moment, it seemed prudent not to make an announcement: Ferguson might even claim that, as a manticore-lover, he had done it on purpose at the manticores' request.

They never made it to the beach. At the tree line, they were intercepted by a company of Spanish conquistadors in pointed metal helmets, their matchlocks aimed and ready. There were probably two hundred of them. When had they arrived? There was no time to consider. An officer with a raised sword bellowed, "Down on the ground, all of you!" Another hundred soldiers emerged from the trees behind the colonists, cutting off their escape, pointing their weapons and shouting.

Five Spanish ships of the line stood at anchor in the harbor, pennants fluttering, rows of guns protruding from their flanks. Matthew still had salt on his fingers from their attempt to rescue it from the fire, and now he licked it off. He made his body heavy and his skin like iron. He could barely move, but he didn't need to move. The other colonists threw themselves to the ground as instructed, but Matthew just stood there. He started to glow.

"On the ground!" screamed the officer. "I warn you, we will fire!"

Matthew ignored him. He drew quintessence, as much as he could. It wasn't a lot, not like the jar full of salt water that Catherine had drunk before driving back the manticore armies. He just hoped it would be enough.

At the officer's order, a row of matchlocks opened fire. Iron balls pinged off of Matthew's skin, doing no harm. He closed his eyes and released the quintessence he was holding, and a dazzling white light blazed out from him in every direction, not enough to burn anything, but enough to blind anyone looking at him, at least temporarily.

"Run!" he shouted. "This way!"

He led them toward the north, into the trees. Their best chance was to try to make it to the salt farms, the only human habitation outside the settlement, and now the only human habitation left on the island. At the center of the farmed area was a cluster of buildings, surrounded by a miniature version of the settlement barrier. There would be some supplies there, at least, and some protection from the manticores.

Where had the Spanish come from? The memory of his conversation with Ramos de Tavera flashed through Matthew's mind. Had it been a trick? Perhaps Tavera had been on one of those ships, only a few hours' sail away, and had lied about being in England. The bell-boxes required a quintessence field, after all. That meant he either had a shekinah flatworm, or he was in the vicinity of the island. How much did they know?

They should have prepared for this, Matthew realized. They knew someday the Spanish would be back. They had put all their faith in the protections around the settlement: the barrier, the alarm bells, their stores of weapons and salt and mercury and vitriol. Now all of that was lost, and they were helpless, with no backup plan, no shelter they could run to. They should have built another settlement, or stored supplies in a cave somewhere. Of course, they hadn't planned for someone's botched experiment to destroy the entire colony.

When they reached the farm buildings, Matthew examined the supplies. No weapons. Some salt. Enough food for a day or two.

He sat down in the dirt and covered his face. Quintessence had always been his ally, a willing servant that brought good to people whenever he touched it. His inventions had provided food, shelter, safety, and comfort to everyone in the colony. Now he had destroyed everything he had ever made, and everything else besides.

Blanca sat with him and put her arm around his shoulders, but he shook her off. He didn't want comfort. He wanted to make it right.

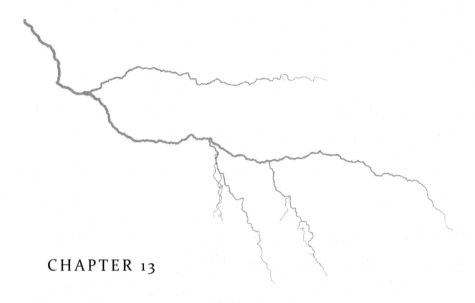

CHAPTER 13

RAMOS slept late, having spent most of the night experimenting in the cellar. He broke his fast with Antonia, a spread of cheese and fruit and thin bread, and gave her nurse instructions for the day. It was mid-morning by the time he descended to the cellar, expecting to find Barrosa already at work. Barrosa, however, was missing, as was the *Ignis Dei*. Ramos searched to be certain, but there weren't that many places it could have been hidden. It was clearly gone.

Only the king or Barrosa could have taken it. If a thief had discovered the room, he would have taken the gold, not the *Ignis Dei*, which was useless at any rate without one of the pearls they kept in their pouches. Ramos felt a chill. Barrosa would only take it on the king's orders, and if the king took it, it was because he planned to use it. But for what? Was it valuable as a weapon after all? If he had just wanted another demonstration, then why didn't he ask?

Ramos charged back up the stairs and made his way to the king's privy chambers, a lavish wing of the palace that also housed the king's menservants and most favored courtiers. The queen had her own chambers in another wing. He found the vice-chamberlain, the member of Philip's court responsible for organizing his schedules, travel arrangements, and paying the expenses of his retinue.

"Where is his Majesty today?" he asked.

The vice-chamberlain peered through tiny French half-glasses as if examining a bug. "What is your business with the king?"

"I am his court astrologer and advisor on natural philosophy. I have a special commission from His Majesty, and I need to know where he is."

The vice-chamberlain pressed his lips together. He shifted papers on his desk from one pile to another. "Are you a member of the king's privy council?"

"No. I just told you, I'm . . ."

"Are you on the king's medical staff or a member of the nobility above the rank of earl?"

"Are you even listening to me?"

"This is my job, sir. Only certain people are permitted to know the king's location."

Ramos pounded the corner of the desk. The Spanish government was full of people like this. King Philip ruled his kingdom through a vast bureaucracy that generated enough paper to fill the English Channel, all of it managed by minor functionaries who guarded their fiefdoms with weasel-like ferocity. Each of them considered themselves indispensable to the running of the empire, and none would share information if they had an excuse to withhold it.

He tried another tack. "What about the court secretary? Juan Barrosa? Are his whereabouts so tightly protected?"

The vice-chamberlain shifted papers again—Ramos could have sworn he moved the same stack back to its original location—and cleared his throat. "What is your business with His Majesty's secretary?"

Ramos leaned forward. "Listen," he said. "In about a minute, I'm going to push all your papers off of this desk and scatter them on the floor. That is, unless you can give me a straight answer to this very simple question. Do you know where Barrosa is?"

The vice-chamberlain swallowed. He opened and closed his

mouth a few times, then said, "He went to Smithfield. For the execution of the Protestant conspirator."

"Thank you," Ramos said with a short bow. "You've been most helpful."

He strode quickly away, heading for the stables where he could saddle a horse.

"The king will hear of this!" the vice-chamberlain shouted at his back.

SMITHFIELD was a large, grassy clearing, lovely compared to the mud and filth of most of London. It had been used for jousting tournaments for centuries, and once every year it transformed into a fairground, with rows of tents, mummers, jugglers, sword-swallowers, minstrels, and hordes of laughing children. It was also an execution ground. A generation ago, those saints of the faith who had refused to acknowledge Henry VIII as the head of the church had been burned alive here for their resolve.

Mary had been continuing this tradition as of late, only she was executing Protestant heretics instead of the faithful of the True Church. John Rogers had been the first, executed back in February, for preaching heresy day after day in St. Paul's Cross. Despite many warnings, he had made reference to "pestilent Popery, idolatry, and superstition" before a large crowd, and had earned himself quick passage to the fires of hell for his blasphemy.

The criminal to be executed today was even worse, a Bible translator named Charles Shiveley, who not only preached insidious doctrines, but called on Englishmen to cast Queen Mary aside in favor of her Protestant sister, Elizabeth. Heresy and treason both.

When Ramos arrived at the field, hundreds were already gathered, lining the path down which Shiveley would take his final walk. The sky was bright and clear, with a strong wind blowing out of the east. Soldiers held back the crowd, and Woodroofe, the sheriff, trotted up and down the grounds on horseback, scanning the crowd worriedly.

Shiveley's wife was there along with her ten children, the older ones holding or helping the younger, waiting for Shiveley to appear. Mrs. Shiveley held the littlest girl herself, a tiny thing no more than three, and murmured in her ear.

In the execution yard, a stout pole with a crossbar had been driven into the ground. The pole was a freshly-stripped green, but the ground around it was blasted black from prior execution fires. Two carts of logs and kindling were trundled into the yard, and men began to stack wood in heaps around the pole. The brisk wind ruffled Ramos's hair.

On the other side of the crowd, sitting high on a curtained dais, were the king and queen. Philip reclined in a high-backed, lacquered chair, a small smile on his face, watching the crowd. Mary had eyes only for her rounded belly, which she patted and stroked incessantly. A coterie of maidservants followed her everywhere now, making sure she was comfortable, offering food and drink, helping her to walk as delicately as possible so as not to harm the all-important child. She was withdrawing from public life more and more as her son grew. Officially, Mary was the monarch of England, and Philip only her husband, but she adored Philip and yielded power to him as she readied herself for her anticipated role as mother of the prince. Before long, she would go into her confinement in preparation for the birth and leave the ruling of the kingdom entirely to him.

This execution was, of course, happening at Philip and Mary's command, but Ramos was surprised they had actually come to witness it. Maybe Shiveley was more important or influential than he'd realized. And where was Barrosa? Ramos couldn't reach the dais through the tightly packed crowd. He would have to wait until the execution was over.

Woodroofe spurred his horse down the path and met a group of soldiers advancing the other way. The crowd waited, restless but not loud. Some children, oblivious to the morning's grave occasion, darted across the path, chasing each other and laughing. Ramos scanned faces, looking for any he recognized. So many people. He guessed that few of them actually knew Shiveley, or cared about him. They had come to see the spectacle.

A moment later, Woodroofe stepped aside, revealing Shiveley, barefoot and chained, and the crowd roared to life. Many did call words of consolation and strength to him, but many more elbowed their neighbors and pointed and laughed. Shiveley held himself straight despite obvious physical weakness, and began his walk to the stake, singing the Psalm Miserere.

They stopped him when he reached his wife. She stood clutching her family and weeping, but he gazed at her with a determined calm. Woodroofe said, "Even now, sir, if you will but recant . . ." He had a showman's eye for drama, positioning Shiveley just out of reach of his weeping family. His wife tried to reach him, but the soldiers held her back. Shiveley turned aside and continued his march. His wife screamed his name. At the pole, he took his place, allowing them to shackle his hands behind him without a word of complaint.

Ramos had seen it before, but he still found it hard to understand. What drove such a man? How could he hold to heresy with such a stubborn and evil will? The man knew what was coming, and that was just a taste of what would follow for all eternity. Why would he not recant?

Across the yard, Ramos spotted the triangular beard and slight frame of Juan Barrosa, bustling back and forth behind a screen, conferring with servants. A creeping feeling of dread gripped him. Something was amiss. He renewed his efforts to circle around and reach the dais.

When Shiveley was secure, Woodruffe raised his voice above the crowd and the wind. "Charles Shiveley, you are convicted of denying the Christian character of the Church of Rome and the real presence of the sacrament, and of plotting to overthrow her Majesty, Queen Mary, in favor of her sister, the Princess Elizabeth. For this, your body is to burn to serve as a warning, to those who watch, that the greater fires of Hell await."

"It waits for you, Woodruffe!" a man's voice shouted. A soldier pushed into the crowd, but the man who had spoken was already gone.

"Hold! A pardon from the queen!" A soldier ran up to Woodruffe and held out a parchment to him. Woodruffe read it and then raised it above his head, fighting to keep hold of it in the gusting wind, until the crowd quieted.

"I hold here a pardon for Charles Shiveley, signed and sealed by Her Majesty, the Queen," Woodruffe said.

Ramos was surprised, thinking at first that the man had truly been pardoned, but then he recognized the ruse. This was no free offer. The deception annoyed him. There was no need to battle heresy with lies.

Woodruffe held the flapping paper out to Shiveley. "Only revoke your abominable defamation of the Holy Sacrament and swear eternal fealty to Mary, your queen, and you shall live."

Shiveley stared at the paper, and for a moment, Ramos thought he would relent. Then he lifted his eyes to the sheriff's, and spoke in a bold voice that reverberated through the yard. "My fealty belongs first to God, whose glory I shall soon see. Second, to Elizabeth, the trueborn Queen of England!"

The crowd roared, and it was impossible to tell whether more of them shouted against his words or in favor of them.

"So be it," Woodruffe said. He opened his fingers, and the paper fluttered out of his hand, dancing erratically out over the crowd. He gestured, and a man stepped forward with a torch to light the fire.

Before he could do so, King Philip stood and raised a hand, his raised position on the dais making him clearly visible to everyone. The torch bearer stopped short. Everyone fell silent. Woodruffe looked as astonished as everyone else.

"Douse the fire," Philip ordered. "Remove the wood from around the stake."

By the time they did so, Ramos knew what was coming. The screen underneath the dais, where he had seen Barrosa, had a small hole cut in it, and Barrosa was now nowhere to be seen. Ramos pushed his way into the crowd, trying to make it to the royal platform before it was too late.

"These are troubled times," Philip said in his rich and commanding voice. He was not a tall man, but his presence arrested every eye. Woodruffe looked surly; this was his show, and he hadn't been expecting an interruption.

"The poison of heresy has leaked into many corners of the world," the king continued. "In this land especially, many doubt the True Church and fall into wickedness and treason. Yet God has not changed. Bear witness, all you who gather here! So that there may be no doubt that we rule by divine order, and that Charles Shiveley stands under condemnation not just by man, but by God, we will not light the fire today. Instead, we look to God to bring his own judgment. If this man has sinned, let God himself light the fire!"

Woodruffe looked stunned. His head swiveled comically between the king and the piles of logs, uncertain how the show should proceed or if he had a part in it any longer. The crowd stared at the stake, hushed and expectant.

Ramos started running, shoving people out his way, knowing he couldn't get there in time. This was wrong, a far worse deception than the fake pardon. Philip was fabricating a miracle on the scale of Elijah's fire from heaven before the priests of Baal, but it was nothing more than a charlatan's trick. Worse, he was using Ramos's discovery to do it. Ramos wanted no part of this hoax.

In the center of the clearing, Shiveley suddenly cried out. He looked around, trying to find what had hurt him, and then screamed, twisting his body as if to escape some invisible fire. His face bore the terror not only of the pain but of its apparently miraculous cause. He screamed and writhed, while the crowd looked on in silent awe. There was no fire, and yet he burned.

"Stop this! Turn it off!" Ramos said, still trying to push through, but his shouts only broke the silence, prompting the crowd to erupt into noise again. Those who loved Shiveley wailed and begged God for mercy, while others railed against heresy and spat at him.

Shiveley lived for a horribly long time. When Ramos finally reached the platform, it was too late to save him. He found Barrosa behind the screen, aiming the *Ignis Dei* through the hole and peering through to view his handiwork.

"For the love of mercy, add more salt!" Ramos said.

Barrosa looked up. "The king's orders were . . ."

"He will burn in Hell soon enough. Give him more fire and end this charade."

Barrosa still didn't move, so Ramos grabbed the jar himself and poured salt into the pearl compartment. Shiveley's clothing flared up in a rush of bright flame. The smell of meat filled the square, familiar from a hundred inquisitions.

As Shiveley's screams fell silent, so did the shouting of the crowd. They watched mutely as the impossible flames devoured the flesh. There was no need for Philip to say any more. They knew a miracle had taken place.

Ramos slammed the barrier down, blocking the prism from the quintessence light and thus turning off the fire. "This is vile deceit," he said. "Do you think you are God? Can you stand in His place and bring fire from heaven?"

Barrosa didn't flinch. "Apparently I can."

"It's a lie. This is Aaron, forming a golden calf and giving it to the people to worship. You have called God what is merely a work of man."

"Is it?" Barrosa flushed and his voice rose. "Is this your work, Ramos de Tavera? Did you create quintessence? Did you bottle it up in this pearl? This is fire from heaven, if ever there was."

"Lies. You stretch the truth until it breaks. This is a natural force, found by men, brought home by men, and directed by men. By me. And you use it for falsehood."

"It's God's work, Ramos. Why do we burn heretics? To terrify the rest into contemplating the just and miraculous and very real, eternal fire of God. Isn't that what I'm doing? Just a little better than most."

"Look where you are. Out in the open? No. You hide here like a thief, hidden from view, and you tell me your motives are just? If this is God's work, then stand in the light, for all to see!"

Barrosa bit back a retort and spun away. When he turned back again, his face was set in hard lines. "Do you think I had any choice? This was neither my invention nor my idea. Maybe you should have thought of the consequences before you showed this to the king."

"I gave the king a weapon to fight the Protestants, not a tool to gull the simple into believing they'd seen a miracle," Ramos said. He would have gone on, but Barrosa was looking past him with a grim smile.

"I *am* using it to fight the Protestants," said a commanding voice behind him. Ramos whirled. It was the king.

"Your Grace," Ramos said, dropping to one knee.

"You object to this charade," Philip said.

"I do, your Grace. It puts false ideas in the people's minds."

"And will you leave this place and tell the English I am a liar and a fraud?"

Ramos gasped. He bowed his head lower, almost touching the dirt. He was acutely aware of the power of the man before him, and the command he held over life and death. It would be nothing for Philip to make him the next victim tied to that stake. "No, my lord. I beg pardon."

"Will you destroy this weapon or refuse to make more like it?"

"No. It is not my place to question. And yet, I dare to ask, as your spiritual advisor, whether it is wise—"

"Good. We are agreed." Philip crouched beside him and placed his ringed hand on the back of Ramos's neck. Ramos could see his embroidered shoes and smell his perfume. "For those who are faithful, we accept certain irregularities. The presence in a household, for example, of one possessed by a demon, can be overlooked. This is not the case for those who fall from favor."

Ramos struggled for breath, thinking of Antonia sitting innocent and unprotected in his apartment. Though who could protect her from a monarch's will? "Your Grace," he finally managed to say. "I am your humble servant."

The king stood and walked away, leaving Ramos shaking. He lifted his head and caught Barrosa's eye, who gave him a look of pity. "We have no choice, you and I," he said.

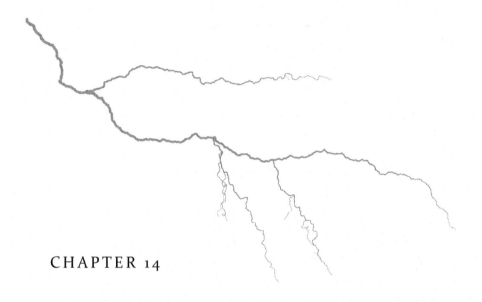

CHAPTER 14

THE VOID grew larger, and Catherine beat at it frantically with the beetlewood planks. "I can't control it!"

"Yes, you can," Sinclair said. "I'm almost done."

Vibrations thrummed back and forth along the void's edges, forcing her to take a step back. She tried to slap the planks together and close the void entirely, but it was too late for that. She could no longer reach the center.

Sinclair saw. "Run!" he said.

She stumbled backward, dropping the wood. Sinclair abandoned his work and ran. Maasha Kaatra, however, stood transfixed by the glowing vibrations, not seeming to hear. "Father?" he said.

Catherine tugged at his arm. "Get back!"

His unfocused gaze snapped to her. "Murderer," he said in a terrible voice. "My daughters. You killed them." He gripped her wrist painfully.

She tried to pull away, but he was too strong. "Maasha Kaatra!" she shouted. "It's me, Catherine!" The void was enveloping them. She *could see nothing in its darkness. "Let me go!"*

She screamed and pulled again, this time yanking her wrist out of Maasha Kaatra's grasp. The vibrating strand reaching into the void blazed like the evening sun and then broke.

The whole room lurched, and she fell. She looked up from the floor in time to see Maasha Kaatra toppling backwards like a crumbling tower. Where he should have struck the floor, the void was there, and he kept falling, tumbling farther and farther, like a rock into a bottomless well. The void collapsed with a pop, and he was gone.

THE SCENE had repeated itself over and over in Catherine's mind for the last year and a half. She had hardly known Maasha Kaatra, though he had traveled with her the whole journey from England. He had been a dark shadow at Sinclair's side, a silent threat, rarely speaking. She didn't know his history beyond the fact that he had been freed from Portuguese slavers by Christopher Sinclair. He had lived a whole life before that, as a prince in Nubia, with two daughters of his own. They were dead now, she thought, though she knew nothing about the circumstances. All she knew for sure was that she had been responsible for his death. And yet here he was, standing on a stone platform deep underground, looking about a hundred years old.

"How can you be alive?" Catherine said. "What happened to you?"

"Look," Maasha Kaatra said.

She followed his pointing finger to the large pool into which the underground streams were all pouring. It seemed to be extraordinarily deep. At first, she couldn't tell what she was supposed to be seeing about it. Then she saw that at one end, where overhanging rock left the pool in deep shadow, a familiar shimmer hovered over the water. It wasn't a shadow at all. It was a void.

Even after all these months of working with them and learning to control them, Catherine found voids disturbing. Aristotle had taught that matter was continuous, but it wasn't. It was made of tiny particles they called atoms, and behind those particles was the void.

Nothing. The absence of reality. Opening windows into that void was terrifying, because it demonstrated how tenuous reality actually was. What appeared to be solid was only the interactions of tiny particles at a distance. Change the interactions slightly, and you could slip right through. Lose control, and you might lose reality altogether. Sometimes, Catherine wished Aristotle had been right.

"So, more than a year ago, when you fell out of the world . . ." She struggled to understand what he was implying. "You fell back in through that void right there? Have you been here ever since?"

"I do not know how long I fell." Maasha Kaatra's expression grew distant. "Days? Years? But at the end was water, deep water, and drowning, until finally, I emerged on this shore. I wandered through endless caves, exploring, losing my way, but always finding myself back here."

"What is this place?"

"Hell, or Purgatory, or whatever name men might choose. The place where all paths lead. I thought I might find my girls here, but I have called long and searched deep, and have not found them. Perhaps they went to another place, a happier one, where there is laughter and good food in the perpetual bright sun."

"You've survived all this time, just wandering in the caves?" Catherine said. Is there no way out?"

He arched a scabbed eyebrow. "Out?"

"Out. Back up to the surface."

He was silent.

"This isn't Hell, not really. We're underground, deep in the mountains. It's very far down, but perhaps there's some way out."

Maasha Kaatra looked up, and she followed his gaze. Directly above them, high in the ceiling where the spirit lights gathered, was another cave shaft. It led upward, straight as a line. It was very high, but since it was also very wide, she could see the opening far, far above, and through it, the stars. Not more spirit lights, but the real stars—she recognized the constellation Aquarius.

"Never the sun," Maasha Kaatra said. "Only stars and darkness."

"Well, yes, of course," Catherine said. "Unless the sun was directly overhead, the light couldn't penetrate this deep. It probably does shine all the way down the shaft, but only twice a year, and for a few minutes at most."

Maasha Kaatra gazed at her, uncomprehending, or perhaps just not listening. She looked back down to see that the crowd of salamanders was much closer. "Maasha Kaatra?"

A deafening sound, both deep and shrill at the same time, echoed through the cavern. Catherine covered her ears. "What's happening?" she shouted.

The salamanders turned to face one direction, and Maasha Kaatra did the same. Something began to force itself through one of the largest of the tunnels carved by the streams of water. A gigantic black creature, slick with moisture. Its flesh rippled and seemed to burst out of the hole as it shoved itself through in rhythmic pushes, bellowing its terrible cry. Finally, it emerged.

It was a salamander, but a hundred times larger. It had the same fat, glistening body, the same face, the same open-mouthed gape, but its front legs had grown stubby and formed into fins; its back legs had fused into a massive tail; and most disturbing of all, its snout had lengthened, and in that open jaw were dozens of teeth as tall as a man. It was not pink anymore, but jet black. She had seen a creature like this before.

"Leviathan," Maasha Kaatra said in tones of worship, his voice dark and rich. "He is the god of this land."

"It's not a god. It's just a really big fish," Catherine said. A member of this species had attacked and nearly capsized their ship on the way to Horizon.

"It's the devil himself. You should not be here, Catherine Parris."

She glared. "I don't want to be here either, when it comes down to it. You don't know a way out, do you?"

"Hide yourself." He closed his eyes and raised his hands. His skin began to glow white. "Our epic struggle begins."

Catherine looked around, trying to understand. Epic struggle? Had Maasha Kaatra gone mad from a year of living alone underground? When the leviathan attacked their ship, it had been attracted to a glowing quintessence pearl that her father had in his pocket. Once he realized what the leviathan wanted, he threw it into the water, and the leviathan ate it and left them alone. Which made sense—salamanders were ravenous for sources of quintessence, so if leviathans were just another stage in the life of the same creature, it stood to reason that they would be attracted to the same food.

The leviathan surged forward with surprising strength, opened its jaws and slammed them shut into the crowd of salamanders. Three of the soft, pink bodies were crushed in its maw. Those nearby squealed piteously, but made no move to get away.

Catherine recoiled and took a step back. "Why don't they run?"

Maasha Kaatra was paying no attention. His body was blazing with light now, and she could hardly look at him. Then it occurred to her what that meant. He was making himself the most brilliant source of quintessence in the room.

The leviathan looked toward them, the light reflected in its black eyes. It was clearly a sea creature, unsuited for life on land, but its whole body was a spring of hard muscle. It slapped its tail and propelled its huge bulk, awkwardly but effectively, directly at them, its giant mouth open wide.

Catherine screamed and threw herself off the platform, heedless of the salamanders. The leviathan landed like a falling tree, smashing the rock and crushing salamanders underneath it. Maasha Kaatra disappeared into its mouth.

Catherine struggled to stand, crying despite herself. She had been so glad to see Maasha Kaatra, alive after all this time. Together, they might have found a way to the surface. Why would he commit suicide in this bizarre way just moments after meeting her? He seemed to have planned it for some time, perhaps even constructing that platform somehow for the purpose. He must truly have gone mad.

She scrambled out of the crowd of salamanders, who seemed equally intent on self-destruction, and cowered along the wall of the cave, gasping for breath. What would cause a living creature to sit still while it was devoured? Every animal in her experience—or plant, for that matter—did everything in its power to survive. It made no sense for the salamanders to sit there, unmoving, while their older brother ate them whole.

An idea struck her.   What if, when eaten, the individual salamanders *did* survive? Just as two manticores could share a bond of connected consciousness through quintessence threads, perhaps two salamanders could share a more direct bond, the smaller one contributing both its flesh and its consciousness to the larger. The whole salamander group would live on, part of one large body, which would then slip into the deep pool, and from there, find its way to the sea. Perhaps this was how it had grown so large in the first place—by eating its own kind. If she only had some skink tears, she could have seen whether it was true. If it retained the quintessence anchors of those it devoured, she would be able to see them, and that would prove that the leviathan was in fact not a single creature, but many, sharing the same body.

A breeze fluttered her hair. Swirls of dust eddied at her feet. The wind picked up, blowing steadily along the rock wall. She looked up and saw that the spirit lights were caught in it, too, propelled around the cavern in counter-clockwise circles. Dark clouds began to form. A deep rumble echoed through the cavern.   A rain storm, underground? Catherine huddled into a niche and held her knees as lightning flashed from cloud to cloud over her head.

A glow appeared in the cave shaft above, its rays shining through the swirling dust straight down onto the leviathan on the circular platform. Its illuminated sides heaved with its labored breathing. The crowd of salamanders was similarly still. The swirling wind intensified, rippling Catherine's clothes and sending her hair streaming out to one side. Curiosity got the better of her. She stepped out of her niche and staggered through the wind, back toward the center of the cavern. From this vantage, she could see straight up the shaft to the stars. At the center was the nova. The hole in the sky.

But how could that be? It was Aquarius she had seen through the gap, not Gemini. Half a day would have to have passed for the nova to become visible. Either time itself had passed with impossible speed, or else a second nova had formed.

Now that she thought of it, she could see that this one was different. It was smaller than the other, more like when the other had first appeared. How long had this second nova been there? She hadn't seen it when she first looked up through the shaft. Had it formed just at this moment?

Oddly, the leviathan itself seemed the only thing illuminated by the stars. The crushed platform around it, the other salamanders, and the rock floor all remained dark. It was almost as if the leviathan was sucking the light down out of the stars, instead of just being shined on. It grew brighter, and she could hardly look at it.

A brilliant shock of lightning tore out of the clouds and struck the monster, sending up liquid sparks like molten metal. The wind gusted, nearly knocking Catherine down. She pushed through it back to her niche and held on to the rock, peering out at the unfolding scene.

Lightning struck again and again, like a blacksmith's hammer falling in a forge. The leviathan drew the light down from the sky, making the nova pulse and the stars dim, and all at once, Catherine realized what was going on.

She checked off the things she knew or guessed. One: When shekinah flatworms were full-grown, the largest of them ate the others and grew into salamanders. She hadn't actually seen this happening, but it stood to reason based on what she had seen. Two: When salamanders were full-grown, the largest of them ate the others and grew into a leviathan. That meant that a leviathan represented the combined spirits of thousands of shekinahs, and all their quintessence power. The growth of all of those creatures culminated in a single, magnificent predator that ruled the seas.

It fit with the rest of the island's ecology. Humans tended to think of spirits as inherently individual, one spirit for one body, but that's not how things worked on Horizon. Manticores split and connected their spirits. Boarcats intentionally sacrificed their spirits, then brought them back from the void. As Christopher Sinclair had taught her, everything that animals and even plants did was for a purpose. The purpose of this was clear: presumably the deep pool actually provided a route to the sea, and once the salamanders were all eaten, the leviathan would slip into the depths and spend the rest of its life prowling the oceans, too large and powerful to be harmed by anything.

But the most important realization was that Maasha Kaatra had not committed suicide. He had allowed himself to be eaten, just like the others. He was joining the leviathan.

What about the lightning storm? And the nova? She didn't know. Was this a normal part of the birth of a leviathan? It didn't seem so— the novas were a recent phenomenon, and she suspected the fierce storms that had plagued the island since the first nova appeared might have had their origin in this storm as well. That implied that the nova and the storm were not naturally connected to the formation of a leviathan, but were connected instead to Maasha Kaatra's interference with it.

The lightning strikes increased to such a rapid rate that the leviathan appeared to be connected to the clouds by shifting, jagged lines of light. The noise was deafening, and the sharp smell of burning air filled Catherine's nostrils. The creature's skeleton glowed red through its flesh, like a log in a cookfire burned down to char. Finally, its body exploded, fountaining ash into the wind. The storm boiled and swirled, then rushed upward into the shaft with a roar, spiraling up and out of the cavern. For a brief moment, there was utter darkness, then the shaft cleared and the light from above shone down again.

Spirit lights traced gentle circles around the ceiling, only now there seemed to be more of them. In fact, hundreds of new spirit lights were drifting down from the shaft, filling the room. The new ones darted and zagged, full of energy, like fireflies. Many sought the caves from which the streams spilled and made their way up. Other flitted about the ceiling and into nooks and niches. Finally, when all the lights and smoke and ash and cloud had cleared, she saw Maasha Kaatra.

The leviathan was gone. The salamanders were gone. He stood alone on the platform, strong and proud and erect. The posture and gait of an old man had left him; he was young and powerful now. His muscles bulged, and he moved lithely, like a stag. The chalky lesions and scabs had disappeared. Instead, his skin glowed with a pure white energy. The platform, crushed and broken by the weight of the leviathan, was whole again, its sides straight and true.

"Catherine Parris!" Maasha Kaatra roared. His voice echoed through the cavern. She stood, afraid. "Come," he said.

She approached slowly, unsure what to expect. Closer, she could see that the light moved like fire under his skin.

"Now I have power, for a while," he said. He pointed to one of the rocky spikes extending down from the roof. Lightning fired from his pointed finger and struck the spike; it shattered and fell to the floor in explosions of falling rock and powder.

Catherine gaped. "And this power will fade?"

He nodded solemnly. "But it is the only way to survive."

She looked up through the empty cave shaft, and saw the newest nova, larger now, a great gap in the sky where the quintessence had been torn away. "The novas," she said. "*You* made them."

How long had he been doing this? The first nova had appeared six weeks ago, but Maasha Kaatra had been here more than a year. Had he been killing leviathans all this time, but only recently learned how to draw the power from the sky? Or perhaps he had first been eaten by salamanders, before learning how to entice and then defeat the leviathan itself? Catherine shuddered to think how close she had come to being similarly devoured. How had he discovered this as a means of survival? Surely he hadn't allowed himself to be eaten on purpose the first time. Perhaps it had been an accident, simply an exercise of his will to survive as an individual spirit among the thousands inside.

With this power, could he help her reach the surface again? The idea gave her pause. As much as she wanted to return to the colony and her family, she wasn't sure if she should talk Maasha Kaatra into taking her there. Once he reached the surface, with the power of lightning and more at his command, what would he do? Whose side would he be on?

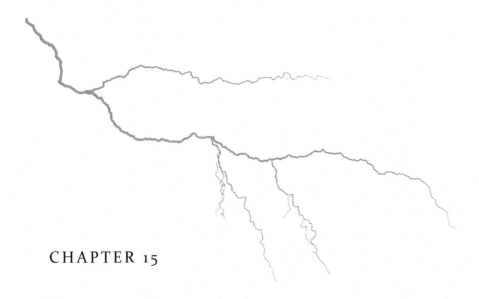

CHAPTER 15

NEWS of the miraculous burning of Charles Shiveley spread through London like fire through a wooden shantytown. The effect was more dramatic than Ramos would have imagined. It divided Englishmen into two camps: those who fanatically worshipped Philip and Mary as God's representatives on Earth, and those who called them devils and plotted to overthrow them and put Elizabeth on the throne. Some of the lords of questionable loyalty had already disappeared from London, and there was some possibility that, like the rebellion by Thomas Wyatt of a year before, they were gathering a force to march on the city.

The unrest only increased when the second nova appeared in the sky. Hundreds more joined the ranks of the mad. The country was in chaos. Ramos quickly determined that all of the newly mad had been born in a five day span under the constellation Aquarius. He told King Philip, but if the intelligence interested him, he didn't show it. Philip continued to use the madness for his own purposes, making proclamations about God's judgment on the faithless and the need for heretics to submit to the Roman Church.

The missives sent from Rome were more or less the same, denouncing the madness as the judgment of God. Those who remained should repent and return to God lest the same judgment fall upon them. It shook Ramos more than he wanted to admit. How could it be true that everyone born at a certain time of year had earned God's judgment? Of course, all had sinned, and so all were deserving of God's wrath. Perhaps it was a sign to the rest of them not to be complacent. Perhaps God would continue to bring random judgments until the Church was reunited and the apostates returned to the fold. He clung to that explanation, but it didn't sit comfortably in his mind.

It didn't sit comfortably with the rest of the population, either. Demonstrations for Elizabeth sprang up throughout the country, despite Philip and Mary's attempts to suppress them. Finally, Philip commanded that Princess Elizabeth be brought back to London from her house arrest in the royal residence at Woodstock. After a rebellion the previous year, Elizabeth had been imprisoned in the Tower. Philip had originally argued for her release, suggesting that her power was better neutralized by taking her away from public view and finding her a Catholic husband. In the fervor after Shiveley's execution, however, the chance that she would be rescued from Woodstock and assault London at the head of a Protestant army was just too great.

At first, Elizabeth said she was too sick to come, until Philip insisted she be brought even if she die on the way. When she finally did leave, she turned a four-day journey into six with frequent stops and requests for rest. Common people thronged her way, giving her flowers and sweets and prompting Mary's jealousy.

Ramos woke on Palm Sunday to the news that Elizabeth had finally arrived. Ramos had been born on *el Domingo de Ramos*—Palm Sunday—making it his birthday of sorts, though of course the date of the holiday was different every year. He went out with the crowds, wanting to get a glimpse of this young woman who inspired such hatred and such love.

It became clear that the holiday had been at least partly the reason behind Elizabeth's delay. The symbolism of her entering the city on Palm Sunday was lost on no one: she was the savior of her people, coming to be killed by evil men. It was a religious analogy in which she played the part of Christ, and Philip and Mary the parts of the wicked Roman and Jewish leaders, and the people ate it up. Her carriage windows were open wide, and she waved at the massive crowd that gathered.

It was the first time Ramos had seen the young princess. She was pretty after a fashion, with a strong chin and striking red hair, but her cheeks were drawn and her skin was unnaturally pale. Either she had genuinely been sick, as she claimed, or she had powdered her face to give that impression.

In fact, prisoner or no, Ramos realized Elizabeth had thoroughly orchestrated this whole affair to turn public opinion in her favor. Her arrival was supposed to be a secret; Philip had wanted her safely stowed in the Tower before anyone knew she was there, but somehow the word had spread. Her claims of illness, her plain dress, her appearance now as a weak and suffering maiden with no one to protect her: all were calculated to stir the hearts of young patriots to rush to her aid. Ramos could see why she was so dangerous.

The crowd lined the road all the way to the Tower. When they reached it, Elizabeth drew back in fear at the sight of the fortress prison she had only so recently left, and Ramos thought the terror on her face was genuine. She certainly had good reason to think she might not leave the Tower grounds alive, as her cousin, the Lady Jane, had not. Or was she that shrewd, to play to the crowd even now?

As they took her inside, the crowd pressed forward, crying out comfort to her, until the yeoman warders standing guard fired their matchlocks in the air. Mounted soldiers rode through, forcing the people to disperse.

Despite the king's desire for secrecy, everyone in the city now knew that the Princess Elizabeth had arrived. If anything, it only heightened revolutionary feeling. Every day, more rumors came to London of this or that lord calling his people to arms, of the Queen's tax collectors attacked by mobs, of rotting vegetables hurled at Catholic priests in the street. Every day, Ramos feared he would look beyond the wall to see an army of peasants marching on the city.

It was hard to respect a people that could be so fickle. Less than two years before, it had been Mary who was washed into London on a tide of popular approval, to throw down a pretender to the throne without a shot fired. Had she lost their love, simply because she had married a Spaniard? Or had this country been so thoroughly corrupted by Protestantism that they now hated anyone of the True Faith? Somehow the miracle of the burning of Charles Shiveley had galvanized them. The story was on everyone's lips, and even at court, three times as many people claimed to have witnessed the event than could actually have been there.

Ramos had to admit that King Philip's plan had misfired. He had intended to use the miracle to claim divine sanction for his rule and thus earn submission and awe from the people. In Spain, it would have worked. But most Englishmen had been raised in the age of Henry VIII. They had learned from their youth that Popes could be defied, that sacred laws could be rewritten, and that if you wanted something badly enough, you could simply take it, and ask for forgiveness later. It was a totally godless country, degenerate in ways Ramos had never dreamed of before coming here. King Henry's blasphemy ran deep, and now his sins were being visited on the next generation. At this rate, the Church would be ousted from England once again, and another generation of sinners would be lost to the devil.

To combat this threat, Philip and Mary needed power. The king dreamed of establishing the True Church permanently, not just in England, but across the world. To do that, he needed military might and vast quantities of gold, enough to quell heresy not just in the cities, but in a thousand towns and hamlets. And he was looking to Ramos de Tavera to give him that power. Ramos had failed the first time, but he would not do so again.

He returned to the cellar and determined not to leave it until he had succeeded in producing a weapon worthy of the king's vision. For the Church to prevail, it had to fight against wickedness in any way it could. This was why God had brought him to England: so that the armies of the True Church could overrun the Protestants and

Musselmen and put an end to war and heresy forever. So they would all finally see whose side God was truly on. The fact that Ramos himself had been tempted to doubt the Church as of late was all the more reason to focus his energies.

When he was a boy, Ramos had admired the brightly clad soldiers who battled the infidels and drove them from the land, but he had never had the strength or courage to be a soldier. He was an intellectual. But now, God had called him to fight in a different way, a way that could ultimately make a greater difference to the spread of the Church through heathen lands. He would use this divine gift to create an army of God, devout and invincible.

From now on, he would not doubt. No more following his own ideas of right and wrong; no more secret investigations to satisfy his own curiosity. From this day forward, he would live a life of service and obedience as he had always known he should: first to God, then to the pope, then to the king. Fortunately, all three were in agreement. It made his path clear.

Perhaps if he was faithful for long enough, then someday God would see fit to give Antonia back to him again.

MATTHEW saw the second nova appear just before the storm blackened the sky, an event that a few days ago would have seemed crucially important. The salt would now be leached out of the soil at double the rate. For all he knew, there might be no salt left anywhere on the island in a few days time. But it hardly seemed to matter. With the loss of the settlement, their needs were more immediate. They needed shelter, food, water. They couldn't stay at the farms. There wasn't enough room for all of them, nor enough supplies. They would have to leave in the morning and find somewhere else to go. Only there wasn't anywhere else to go.

The dark clouds opened and rain pelted the landscape. In a flash of lightning, Matthew saw a few gray shapes outside the barrier. Manticores. It was dark, and besides, he had no skink tears, so he had no way of telling how many of them were out there. They must have seen the burning of the settlement and come to investigate. Now they knew the colonists were vulnerable and were only waiting for them to venture out.

The colonists crowded into the largest room, arguing about what to do. There were no good solutions, and tempers flared. Some favored running for the bay and surrendering to the Spanish. With no settlement left, they argued, they couldn't survive on the island anyway, and the only way off was on those Spanish ships, in chains. Perhaps the Spanish would give lenient treatment in return for knowledge about quintessence or the island.

Others considered that option nothing less than treason. They favored running for the woods, or the mountains, or the cliffs. If they moved quickly, perhaps they could be gone before the manticores gathered in large numbers. They could go into hiding, live outdoors. The island was huge; they could travel for days until they found another spot to build again. By the time the manticores or Spanish found them, they would be strong again, and ready.

"Remember, you are Englishmen!" Ferguson said. He was a coward, but he could talk big when he wanted to. "Englishmen do not surrender. Our nation suffers under the rule of her enemies, but it will not be so forever. Sometimes I wish we had stayed at home. Surely by now good men are rising up to fight the oppression of Rome and Spain and raise the Princess Elizabeth to her rightful throne! We are far from that war, but the war has come to us. We must do our part. We must not give in!"

He was cheered by some, but others shouted him down, protesting that they had no weapons and no food. Matthew brooded in the back, not participating in the argument. What right did he have to offer an opinion? In former days, he would have done so readily, and many would have listened to him. They might still. But what made him think his ideas had any merit? He might just get them all killed.

Finally, he tired of listening to them and slipped outside to be by himself. The thunderheads had rushed down from the north like a blanket thrown over their heads, completely obscuring the sky. He wondered how it was for Catherine. If she could see the same clouds.

If she was even alive.

A gentle hand touched his cheek. He looked down to see Blanca, her face a picture of compassion. She melted against him, fitting perfectly in his arms, and he held on to her like a life raft. He should not be touching her, he knew, should not even be alone with her, but he was losing everything, including any sense of who he was or what mattered. He could no longer think of himself as the capable young miracle worker who commanded the respect of everyone who knew him. He was a fraud. Just a child who had fooled everyone into thinking they could trust him. Only now his secret was out.

He needed Catherine, but Catherine wasn't here. Blanca tilted her head back and looked up at him with wide, dark eyes filled with concern. "You did the best you could."

He grunted angrily. It was just what he wanted to believe, but he knew it wasn't true. "I experimented with something when I had no idea what it would do, without any help or advice. It's exactly how Sinclair killed his servant and nearly destroyed the island. And it's only by the slimmest of luck that I didn't kill you."

She pressed closer to him. "Hush. I'm all right. Besides, I was there, too. I'm just as much to blame."

He shook his head dismissively. "I was the one who—"

She laid a finger against his mouth. "We had no way of knowing what was on the other side of that connection. We'd never seen or heard of anything like that miasma. Catherine hadn't either, or she wouldn't have gone into it."

"You think—"

Her finger against his lips again. "Hush."

He shouldn't be here, alone in the dark with this young and beautiful woman while his fiancée was missing. She was telling him everything he desperately wanted to believe: that this crisis wasn't his fault, that he was worthy of admiration, that the future was bright with promise. Holding her, he could almost feel that everything was all right. But none of it was true, and he knew it.

He pulled away. "Catherine is still alive," he said.

There were tears in her eyes. "I want that to be true as much as you," she said. "She was my only friend."

He felt exhausted, too overcome with sadness to speak anymore. He shook his head. "I can't," he said. He left her and circled to the other side of the building, where he dropped down and sat in the dirt, ashamed and overwhelmed. What if Catherine really was dead? What if they never even knew for sure?

A memory surfaced, down at the shore of the bay with Catherine, unchaparoned. In England, it would have been impossible to spend time with her like that, at least not without a great scandal, but on Horizon it was easier. The two of them were so often exploring in the forest that their absence caused little notice.

It had been before the storms started, and the bay was still, the weather cool. They sat together on some of the soft moss that was more common than leaves in Horizon forests, and watched the sand tortoises lumbering along in the surf. When they used their tongues to kiss—something he was sure his father had never done and would denounce as lewd behavior—they traded enough quintessence-infused saliva that the principle of substitution came into play. For a few minutes, he could feel what she felt, and vice versa. If he brushed his own arm, he felt nothing, but she could feel it clearly. If she licked her lips, she felt nothing, but he could feel the sensation on his own mouth. It didn't last long, but it was deliciously intimate, and the thought made him flush with guilty pleasure. He missed her so much.

A hand clasped his shoulder, too large and strong to be Blanca's. It was his father. Bishop Marcheford didn't say anything, just sat down in the dirt next to him and squeezed his shoulders in a tight, one-handed embrace. At first, Matthew felt a flare of anger—he didn't want to deal with his father right now—but then it left him in a rush and he found that he was crying. He had felt so superior to his father, so certain that he knew what was best.

"I'm afraid she's dead," Matthew said. "I was just trying to find her. I was supposed to rescue her, and instead, I destroyed everything."

The anger came back again, as fast as it had gone. Why was he saying this? His father would just tell him that he shouldn't have messed with quintessence in the first place, that if Matthew had just listened to him, it never would have happened. He would spout platitudes about Catherine being in a better place and about submitting to the perfect will of God.

"We have to kill them," his father said.

Matthew gaped at him. "What?"

"The Spanish. At the very least, we have to force them off the island. If quintessence gets into the hands of King Philip, then the Papists will sweep across the world and the fledgling Protestant churches scattered throughout Europe will perish. Another thousand years may go by before someone else has the courage and conviction to stand against them again."

Matthew hardly knew how to answer. "Father? There are maybe sixty of us left alive. The Spanish will have hundreds of armed soldiers and heavy weaponry. With the colony intact, with a large store of salt at our disposal, we might be able to do it. But now? We have no homes, no salt, no store of weapons. We couldn't take twenty paces away from this spot without being killed by a manticore sentry. How do you expect us to drive off the Spanish? We should be begging them for mercy."

"Mercy? You saw the kind of mercy the Spanish showed the last time they were here."

"And what do you want me to do about it? Don't look to me for a miracle."

"I've seen what you can do. If Catherine were here, you wouldn't be sitting in the dirt licking your wounds. You'd be mobilizing for war."

"She's not here. She's either turned into a statue in a pool of miasma, or she's lying dead at the bottom of a cave shaft." Matthew let all his bitterness show, all his frustration and helplessness. "And there's nothing I can do about it."

His father released his shoulders and turned to meet his eyes. His voice was hard. "You don't know that. You're giving in to the devil's lies. You're believing that there's no hope, that you're a failure, and it's just not true. Wake up! Your enemies are *out there*, not in here."

"You don't know what I did. This whole disaster, it was—"

"I don't care what you did. It was the gray manticores who took

Catherine. It wasn't me, and it certainly wasn't you. And it's the Spanish who are going to kill anyone the grays leave behind, and then use all your inventions to enslave the world. Take all your anger and pour it where it belongs—not into feeling sorry for yourself and reliving your mistakes, but in destroying the evil that's all around us."

An idea wormed its way into Matthew's mind, taking shape despite his fury. There was a way. There was still salt in the soil—a lot less than there should be, but it was still there, all around them, underneath the hooked feet of their manticore enemies.

"Tell everyone to be ready to go," Matthew said. "We head for the mountains."

EVER since the snow lilies' salt production had waned, salt farmers had been forced to find better methods to meet the needs of the colony. Their latest technique had been invented by Catherine's father using fire buffalo bones. A buffalo jaw and a connected piece of its skull were separated to make a long quintessence thread. These threads were stretched out radially from the cluster of buildings, through the soil, to form a large circle around them some two hundred paces away in every direction.

When fire buffalo grazed, they drew salt up out of the ground through the roots of the grass. The grass itself had salt content, like the rest of Horizon life, but they needed more to fuel their daily pyrotechnic displays. Inside one of the buildings, a circle of buffalo jaws could be manipulated to perform the same function, drawing the salt up out of the ground along the line of the quintessence thread that normally connected the jaw to a portion of its skull. The only difference was that the colonists had stretched that line to be two hundred paces long.

The salt farmers would manipulate the jaws in the morning, which, once the dew dried, would leave a crystalline layer of salt across the ground like a gigantic white wagon wheel. They spent the rest of the day collecting it, then unearthed the skull bone fragments and buried them slightly farther along the circle, so as to draw salt from different lines of earth the next day.

Of course, salt-drawing was not the only thing a fire buffalo could do. For safety, certain portions of the jaw had been removed, but Matthew knew how to get at those spots anyway. He prepared each one, having no way to test it, but fairly confident he had it right. If he was wrong, then even more colonists would die, but he couldn't let himself slip down that mental path again. He thought about Catherine, dying alone in a black pit, and his anger grew hot again.

"Tell them all to go," he told his father. "Run due north and don't look back." Then he pressed all the jaw mechanisms at once.

Lines of fire erupted from the ground in every direction as the salt was consumed. This was quintessence fire, white and bright. It gave off little heat, but it was deadly, and caught on any quintessence-formed material with uncanny speed. If any manticores had been patrolling, they were likely already dead, or at least trapped between two walls of silent flames, unable to cross to see where the colonists were escaping.

Matthew pushed out of the building just as it, too, erupted in flame, and raced north after the others.

CHAPTER 16

FOR the second time, the king and his officers gathered at Ramos's request in a field outside London. Carillo was there again, his cream doublet laundered, as were a dozen others of the king's trusted men.

"On your left are six trained soldiers," Ramos said. "Veterans of many wars. As you can see, they are armored and hold weapons with which they have killed before. I do not know these men, and they were not told ahead of time what to expect. We are going to stage a melee. These six men . . . "—he paused for effect, then drew an ordinary carpenter's hammer from his belt and brandished it— "against me."

He expected laughter and was not disappointed. He was not an imposing figure. He was neither strong nor tall, and to be honest, he had developed a bit of a paunch from eating the king's food. But that was the point. They were meant to understand beyond doubt that what they were seeing wasn't the result of skill or physical strength.

The men ranged about him in the traditional tournament style, laughing and readying a variety of weapons: sword, mace, and axe. Ramos removed his priest's robe, leaving only a long undertunic.

"This is a farce," Carillo objected. "He's paid these men to take a fall for him."

"Ten gold sovereigns to any man who spills the priest's blood," the king said calmly. It was much more than Ramos could possibly have offered them.

Ramos's adversaries grinned broadly. Ramos swallowed. This had better work. "Begin," he said.

Generally, this kind of fight was staged for entertainment, to show off the prowess of a champion who could defeat two or three men at once. No one man could defeat six, however strong and skilled. As his adversaries approached, sneering and clearly enjoying the idea of being paid a fortune to beat a priest bloody, Ramos started to have second thoughts. If this went sour, he doubted these men would let him go with just a scratch.

The first approached, a square-jawed brute at least two span tall, and drove a spiked fist into Ramos's gut. Ramos flinched, but as intended, the blow went right through him as if he were made of smoke. The soldier, off balance, fell on the ground, and Ramos struck him on the side of the head with the hammer. It was an awkward blow, but hard enough to make him howl in rage and pain.

In an instant, the others were on him. Ramos swung the hammer with abandon, heedless of the other men's weapons. Swords and axes passed through him without harm, but his hammer blows fell with crushing force. His biggest danger was that the hammer might be yanked from his grasp, so he held onto it with all his might.

The fight ended quickly. Wiser men might have regrouped or even run from such an invulnerable adversary, but these soldiers had been trained from childhood that cowardice was worse than death, and unyielding, savage onslaught was the only way to survive. They battered futilely away until Ramos had five of the six lying unconscious on the ground.

The sixth must have been cleverer than the rest. He was the smallest, carried a short sword, and probably survived by his wits on the battlefield more than brute strength. As Ramos delivered a final blow on the fifth attacker, the sixth darted forward and grasped the pouch at Ramos's neck. With a mighty yank, he snapped the leather cord and threw the pouch far away.

Ramos knew he was done for. He tried to run, but he tripped over one of the prone bodies and sprawled to the ground. His attacker was there in an instant, fury twisting his face. He stepped hard on Ramos's wrist, and lifted his sword high to strike off his arm. Terrified, Ramos tried to roll away, but he was held fast.

It was the king who saved him. One moment, the brute's sword was swinging down toward him; the next a jeweled and shining blade was buried in his neck. The soldier toppled and fell in a gurgling rush of blood, revealing Philip standing behind him.

"I can't have my brightest inventor losing an arm," he said. He held out a bloody hand to Ramos. Ramos clasped it, and Philip hauled him to his feet. "Besides, I have no desire to waste ten gold sovereigns."

The watching generals applauded. A page retrieved Ramos's pouch and returned it to him, and Ramos demonstrated once again how his body could be completely insubstantial while appearing just as solid as ever. Even Carillo approached and slapped him on the back, and exclaimed as his hand passed through Ramos's shoulder. After that, they all had to reach a hand through him, staring in wonder as they felt no resistance. Some were disturbed by the experience, crossing themselves and murmuring wards against witchcraft, but no one dared denounce it in light of the king's clear approval.

Afterwards, the king dismissed his advisors, all except Barrosa, and made Ramos explain how it worked.

"I figured it out from the bird, Majesty," Ramos said, bowing low.

"That invisible one that makes such a racket?"

"Yes, Your Grace. We can't see it or touch it, but somehow it's there. We might think it a spirit, and yet it eats the seeds we give it. I wondered where the seeds went when the bird ate them."

King Philip laughed. "The room is probably littered with bird droppings that we can't see or touch."

"Just so. And I found them."

"How?" Barrosa said.

"I embedded tiny iron filings in the seeds that I fed to the bird. Then, after a time, I searched for them with a lodestone."

"If you could neither see nor feel them, how did you know you had found them?" the king said.

"The lodestone weighed more."

The king's eyebrows shot up. "The filings are no longer material . . . and yet they weigh more? It makes no sense."

"They are still a part of the material world—the bird can eat and digest the seeds, after all. It's just that something has been done to them. Two things, in fact. They have been changed so that light will pass through them unhindered, and they have been changed so that other matter will pass through them unhindered."

The king nodded. "And today, you duplicated the second feat. Can you also duplicate the first?"

"Alas, no. Not yet, Your Majesty."

"But how did you do it?" Barrosa demanded.

"I obtained a quantity of the bird's saliva," Ramos answered, enjoying the consternation on the faces of both king and friend. "Yes, I know the objections. How did I extract saliva from an invisible bird? How could I possibly get enough to cover my body with it? It was the obvious step, though, you see. Something in the seeds' passage through the bird caused the change. Since we did not see the seeds, after they were eaten, sliding in mid-air down the bird's throat, I concluded that it must be its saliva."

King Philip grinned and squeezed Ramos's shoulder. "It's enough for me. You are a genius, and you will be rewarded."

Barrosa's face showed clearly that the explanation was not enough for him, but he could hardly say so until the king had left.

"It still requires a shekinah," Ramos said, shrugging. "So it is only of limited use."

"That may soon change," the king said. "Continue this great work. You are the sword of God, bringing light to the world."

Barrosa was beside himself with impatience while the king and his retinue prepared to leave. When they were finally gone, he rounded on Ramos, who couldn't contain a smirk. "Tell me the rest!" Barrosa said. "My curiosity is not so easily satisfied."

"You mean the part where I got the bird to kiss me?" Ramos said, grinning.

Barrosa punched him on the arm, but of course, his fist passed right through. He grunted in frustration. "Come now, it's amazing. How did you do it?"

"It's like a conjuror's trick. If I tell you, you'll realize how simple it is, and you'll lose all your wonder for the trick itself."

"Just tell me!"

"Collecting the saliva required no miracle. I floated the seeds in a measure of water. The bird plucked them up, naturally leaving a tiny amount of saliva behind in the water."

"And you isolated it?"

"No. The water itself took on the quality of the saliva. When I dipped a rod into it, the rod became insubstantial. It can, apparently, be greatly diluted and still have the same effect. Only a tiny amount is sufficient."

"But then, why didn't you turn invisible?"

"I don't know. Maybe that's accomplished through a different means. Maybe the saliva needs to be less dilute to achieve invisibility."

"Can you change back? Now that the saliva is on you, can you become substantial again?"

Ramos laughed. "It would be a big problem for me if I couldn't. No, I tested that on the rod before using it on myself. It takes a lot of scrubbing, but it can be taken off. Besides, it wears off by itself in a few hours. Evaporates, or just loses its potency."

Barrosa gripped his head and shook it as if trying to dislodge something inside. "But it doesn't make any sense. If only your skin has touched the saliva, why didn't one of those swords pass through your skin only to pierce your heart?"

Ramos lifted his hands and shrugged. "Perhaps it's not allowing things to pass through my skin, exactly. Perhaps it simply deflects the sword into another space when it touches one side of my skin, and then back into our space on the other side."

"Another space? What are you talking about?"

"A space behind the material world. The void behind the atoms."

Barrosa grew quiet. "That's atomism," he said. "It's not orthodox church doctrine."

Ramos brushed the idea aside with an awkward motion. "Just an example," he said. "There are many explanations. Which one is the right one, well . . ."

"Next thing you know, you'll be reading Copernicus," Barrosa said.

There was a tense silence, then Barrosa laughed and Ramos joined in with him. "I can't believe you put on this show," Barrosa said. "If you had missed a spot with that stuff, you could be bleeding out on the grass."

Ramos relaxed. "Something else interesting I found with the rods. If you dip two of them in the saliva water, then strike them together . . ."

"They touch each other," Barrosa guessed.

"They do."

"Even though either one of them would pass through any other material thing."

Ramos nodded. "As if both were material after all."

"Or . . ." Barrosa couldn't finish the thought.

Ramos did it for him. "Or as if both, encountering the saliva on the other rod, were deflected into a space outside the elements of the material world around them, and there struck each other, just as materially as ever."

They looked at each other. The Church had opposed ideas like this for centuries. Atomism was at its root an atheistic philosophy. It suggested that the world was a machine, a mere byproduct of atoms crashing together in random ways, and that everything that we called a tree, a chair, a star, or a man, was bound by the same rules and governed by the same random interactions. If the universe was nothing more than a machine, then what room did that leave for God?

It was a chilling, dizzying thought, and Ramos felt his heart racing. If heretical musings like this were heard by the wrong people, he could go up against the Inquisition. Much worse, however, was the question of what he, Ramos, believed in his heart. Did he really think the world worked in such haphazard fashion? Didn't that go against the whole idea that God had made the Creation exactly as it should be, with all the mountains and oceans and stars perfectly in place? But then, he had already seen the stars change. Perhaps the mountains and oceans could change, too, given enough time.

Ramos pondered these things, disturbed, as they made their way back to Whitehall. No sooner had he returned, than a liveried runner found him to say that the king wanted to see him, alone, in his privy chambers.

KING PHILIP was never alone. He had menservants to dress and shave and coif him, cupbearers and waiters to bring him food and drink, a chief groom of the toilet to see to his necessaries; he had bodyguards and door sentries, scribes and translators and harbingers, a chief historian to record his life story (which twice already he had burned in pique), and jugglers and minstrels and clowns. His most favored friends and advisors rarely left his side. Today, however, he was in his most privy chambers, alone, without even the most lowly servant to attend him.

Ramos trembled with anticipation. Such an honor was unheard of, and would be buzzed about the court for days, since all those who had been sent out of the room would be jealous to know what had transpired, and fearful for what it might mean for them. If he were an ambitious man, he could easily turn such a meeting to his political advantage, by hinting this, suggesting that, or intimating that favors done for him might mean a favorable word in the king's ear. Ramos had no such intentions, but he still quaked to think of what difficult or dangerous task the king might ask of him.

The king sat in a straight-backed chair. To his left, on a small service stool, sat a porcelain dish and a tiny pair of silver scissors. Ramos understood that he was meant to assume a duty generally performed by the groom of the king's toilet, that of clipping the king's fingernails. For any other man, this would be a lowly task, but for the King of Spain, Portugal, and England, it was an honor, a private intimacy that involved touching the king's own person. It was a mark of the king's favor and trust.

Ramos knelt by the tool and took up the silver scissors, terrified that he might mangle the job or cut the king's hand by mistake.

"You have shown your faithfulness and devotion," the king said.

"Thank you, Your Grace." Ramos took the king's fifth finger in his own trembling hand and delicately snipped off the edge of the nail. Better to leave too much, he thought, than to cut too short.

"I have another service to ask of you," the king said.

"Only speak it, and I will fulfill it to the best of my humble abilities."

"Have you ever met the Princess Elizabeth?"

"Never. I only saw her once, on el Domingo de Ramos."

"Ah yes. Her secret arrival in the city." The edges of Philip's mouth turned up slightly. "To which everyone in the kingdom turned out."

"Just so, Your Grace."

"Elizabeth is a conundrum. She appears innocent and guileless to the people, yet she is shrewd as a snake. She knows more than she should, and she manipulates those around her—even her jailors—like a master puppeteer. If there is anyone in this kingdom who threatens our sovereignty, it is she, and yet I cannot kill her, lest the people revolt. The best would be to marry her off to a Spanish nobleman, thus nullifying her claim to the throne, and yet this, too, would strain our command of the English people, who hate foreign rule. She is a spark from which the fires of rebellion can spring, and yet I cannot be rid of her."

Ramos finished trimming the nails on one hand, but the king did not offer his other. Ramos noticed a file partly obscured by the bowl, and picked it up, tentatively running it along the nails to smooth out the rough edges. "What would you have me do, Your Grace?" Ramos said.

The king frowned down at him. "Put some strength in it, man."

"What? Oh. Yes, Your Grace," Ramos said and applied the nail file more vigorously.

"I want you to hear the Lady Elizabeth's confession," the king said.

Ramos waited to hear more, but the king was silent. "She is a Protestant," Ramos said. "Will she not refuse to confess?"

"Your task will be to convince her."

"Does England have no priests? Surely she would sooner confess to one of her own countrymen, if to anyone at all."

"England has priests enough, but they are all English. The hearts of this country are rash and too easily captured by a pretty young woman. I wish Elizabeth to be attended only by my own countrymen. Besides, you worked with the torturers in Spain, I believe?"

Ramos swallowed. "Briefly, Your Grace. But the sacrament of Holy Confession . . ."

The king waved his free arm. "Still your fears. I do not want her body touched. That would only fuel the fire were it to become known, as I have no doubt it would. Somehow, it always does. You should speak with her only. Manipulate her. Learn her fears and insecurities. Gain her trust, and find out how much she knows. You are an intellectual, the sort she admires. Argue with her. Insinuate doubts about her Protestant faith into her mind. Try to discover with whom she communicates, and how.

"There are few people I can trust to this duty. With anyone else, I would fear betrayal, that they would themselves become the means for Elizabeth to communicate with her allies. I know you are loyal to the True Church and to me."

The king met his eye. He wasn't just talking about Ramos's faith. He was talking about Antonia. He knew that Ramos's dedication to the Church was strong, but more than that, he knew that Ramos could silenced by any threat to Antonia. He was an exotic pet, but a safe one. A tiger with his claws clipped.

Head bowed, Ramos accepted the king's other hand and trimmed and filed the nails, troubled by his thoughts, but knowing he would obey.

CHAPTER 17

IT was the largest gathering of manticores in the memory of Rinchirith's family, and his family went back hundreds of years. There was unrest in the deep places, and the tribes were afraid. Rinchirith was not afraid: he knew that marvelous things were happening, which was why, at long last, the tribes were looking to him to lead them.

They gathered at Judgment Gorge, the largest of the great rifts in the mountains, where the deep places sometimes glowed red, and steam rose from vents in the rocks. Cracks like this had been opening more frequently as of late, emitting foul odors and sometimes gouts of hot water. One of the fountains of forgetting had actually boiled.

All of these things increased fear among the families, and more memory bonds had been traded than Rinchirith could remember. The tribes were becoming one unified nation, and he—he, Rinchirith!—was at its head, finally earning the loyalty and respect of them all. Even the reds, those weak advocates of the humans, had sent a delegation. Soon, the manticores would rid themselves of the human plague and become the powerful people they were meant to be.

Perhaps they would even travel across the sea to the human land. It must be a small place, compared to the vastness of Horizon. The manticores would build their own ships and, in time, conquer the humans, as well as any other new lands and creatures they might discover. It was their birthright. And it would all be because of him, because of Rinchirith!

"The earth snakes are rising!" Rinchirith yelled. The Gorge made low groaning and cracking noises from deep inside, loudly enough that it was hard to hear voices. Others relayed Rinchirith's words through the crowd, so that every time he spoke, an echo of shouts carried what he said through the gathering.

"They have accepted the star-bird as our sacrifice," he said. "Now they urge us to finish the work. We must eradicate the human plague from our land!"

There was a surge of noise from the manticores at that, some disagreeing, but most roaring their approval. As they should. They owed nothing to the humans, who had brought only death and destruction. Those who had joined the cult of Christ, worshipping a human god, were the worst of all. Who ever heard of a god that lived in the sky? It was ridiculous. The converts were not ridiculous, however. They were traitors to their own race, and deserved a traitor's death.

He would not suggest that to this crowd, however. One victory at a time. First, destroy the humans and solidify his own primacy. Then he would have the power to kill whoever deserved it.

Rinchirith lifted high a hollowed plant stalk. Behind him, the Gorge rumbled. "Witness the dance of the lords of the earth!" he screamed, and drank the contents of the stalk.

A thick, sticky liquid filled his mouth. It was a diluted quantity of a poisonous sap, lethal in larger quantities. Rinchirith had drunk it so many times that he could handle a dose that would kill a younger manticore. When it didn't kill, it gave the drinker strong and powerful visions which, if he were wise, he could interpret and communicate to the rest of his tribe. Rinchirith drank it now in order to see the earth snakes and know, for certain, what they wanted him to do. He also did it because it was expected; without this rite, the manticores would never follow him. If he was to be their leader, he had to be in communion with the spirits of the deep.

He choked the liquid down and coughed violently. It wasn't long before he felt its fire ripping through his bones, his tails, his skull. His head felt like it was lifting off, stretching up and away and out of his body. His limbs jerked, and he fell on his face. He stumbled up again, and his body convulsed, stiff limbs moving of their own accord. The world swirled and twisted through his vision, changing shape, stretching and smearing like sap. Somehow, he kept his balance, and began the spasmodic, involuntary dance of the earth.

Faster and faster he danced, raising his arms and tails and shrieking as he spun. He felt vomit soaking his fur, but it was nothing to him, unimportant compared to the rush of motion. "The lords of the earth speak!" he shouted. Then the visions began.

CATHERINE put her arms around Maasha Kaatra's neck and climbed onto his back. It was like climbing a rock face; his muscles were granite, and he barely shifted to support her weight. His black skin glowed, and he was hot to the touch.

"Hold tightly," he said.

"What if I can't?"

"I will not leave you," Maasha Kaatra said, prompting another twinge of guilt on Catherine's part. It was her fault that any of this had happened to him.

"I'm sorry," she said. "It must have been awful for you down here, all alone."

"But I am not alone," he said.

He raised his arms. She clung to him. His skin glowed, but the light was warm, not harsh. From above them, the swirling river of spirits suddenly dipped and flowed directly toward them. It rushed around them like a flock of birds, each one darting and veering but moving together as a group. More streams of the spirits poured in through every crack and tunnel, lighting up the cavern like the evening sun.

The spirit lights began to alight on Maasha Kaatra's skin, and on Catherine as well, like moths touching down, soft and delicate. She could hear them all speaking like the noise of a faraway crowd, a murmur without words or meaning. Before long, they were covered in lights.

"Now," Maasha Kaatra said, lifting his arms still higher, "we rise."

At his words, they lifted into the air. The walls of the cave shaft glowed bright with their ascent.

THE growling of the earth behind Rinchirith grew louder. The gathered manticore assembly started to snap their pincered hands together in steady rhythm, and the sound was like rocks breaking. Rinchirith danced and screamed, screamed and danced. Others wailed and danced, too, and the beat of their snapping pincers gradually sped up and intensified.

The Gorge was like a great beast's mouth, rising to swallow him. As he watched, it grew eyes and claws and clambered out of the earth. It was a vision, real and yet not real, and Rinchirith faced it without fear. He danced for its delight, and it snapped at him, but he was not devoured.

A red glow came from the mouth of the Gorge beast, like a furnace of flame. The grass under Rinchirith's feet split and formed a chorus of a million tiny voices, shrieking and biting at his ankles. He screamed and fell again, and the grass-mouths tore at his flesh as he writhed. These were the visions. If he endured them and did not quail, he would eventually gain mastery over the spirit and force it to answer a question.

The combined tribes were with him, the relentless snapping of their pincers audible even through his anguish. The rhythm gave him strength, and he rose, crushing the grass-mouths under his feet. The snapping raced ever faster, speeding him toward the moment when he would take control.

He saw, in his mind's eye, the human nations far away. He saw their spirits, millions of them, covering an endless land far larger than Horizon, more land than he had ever imagined could exist. He saw the humans landing on Horizon in great numbers, ship after ship after ship, inexorable. There were so *many* of them. He had hoped to destroy them, but no one could destroy this multitude.

The earth shook. At first, Rinchirith took it for part of the vision, but the pincer rhythm faltered, and many of the manticores in the assembly fell down. The ground bucked again, harder this time, and Rinchrith went sprawling, suddenly afraid. What sort of spirit had he summoned?

He sat up and found that the human spirits were here, already surrounding him. Tiny, diffuse patches of brightness whirled everywhere, spinning and fluttering and landing on him. He leaped to his feet, trying to brush them off, but he couldn't. This was unlike any vision he had ever had before, but he couldn't show fear, not now.

The ground shook hard enough to rattle his teeth in his skull, and the Gorge started to tear, the edge shifting back like a huge flower opening. Rinchirith tumbled down the slope, and suddenly a geyser of the spirit lights erupted out of the hole. They filled the sky and the air around him. The crowd of manticores panicked, running in every direction. And in the densest cluster of lights . . . it couldn't be.

A human man stood on the edge of the Gorge, a man Rinchirith recognized and had thought long dead. And on his back, the star-bird, Catherine Parris. Only now did Rinchirith succumb to the fear. It bubbled up in him like boiling water, and he knew that this time, he would not be taking control.

The lords of the earth had spoken, but they had not spoken for Rinchirith.

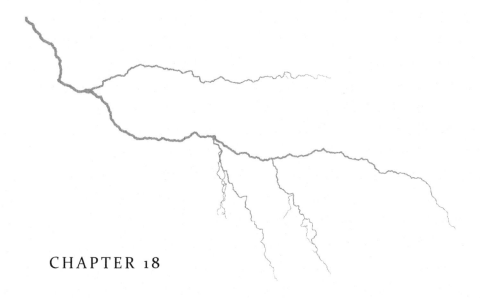

CHAPTER 18

PRINCESS ELIZABETH huddled wretchedly in a corner of her cell, her face drawn and pale. This time, she had not been allowed to bring her ladies-in-waiting into captivity with her, so she was alone. The cell, if it could be called that, was comfortable, with a large fireplace, windows looking out on the keep, a large bed, two chairs, a table, and a writing desk.

"Why does she look like this?" Ramos asked her jailor. "I thought the king ordered that she be given food from his own table."

"Indeed he has," replied the jailor, an old veteran soldier. "But she will not eat it. She will take only water and bread, and the meats and dainties lie spoiled on her tray."

Ramos asked to be left alone with her, and the jailor retreated, locking and barring the door behind him.

"Your Grace?" Ramos said.

A pair of brown eyes peered out at him from the corner. Ramos felt awkward. This was, after all, a princess, a woman of royal blood. He didn't know how to address her in this circumstance. 'My child' seemed too intimate.

"I'm sorry to intrude, Your Grace," he said.

"It is no intrusion, Señor Ramos de Tavera," Elizabeth said. Her voice was soft, but clear.

"You know my name?"

"And your trade, Master Astrologer."

"Then we are on even ground," Ramos said. "For your name and title is all I know of you."

She chuckled softly. "But this is marvelous. Are you the equal, then, of a princess?"

Ramos blushed. "You know I am not, Your Grace. I meant only—"

"I see. You meant only that your knowledge is equal to mine."

"Not at all. I meant only that I know little of you."

"And you presumed that I share the same ignorance."

Ramos shut his mouth, exasperated. Finally, he said, "My apologies, Your Grace."

"I accept your apologies, and forgive you gladly. Why have you come?"

Ramos took a deep breath. "To hear your confession. To allow you to unburden yourself before God."

"Do they plan to strike off my head, then?" Her voice wavered at this, and Ramos thought she truly was afraid to die. As well she might be, since she had chosen a path of heresy and rebellion. Elizabeth must know where it could lead; her own mother had lost her head not far from where they were sitting.

"I don't know their plans for you," Ramos said. "I'm a priest, not a politician. But should not your heart be prepared for that possibility? It is a dreadful thing to enter the presence of God with the black of sin still on your soul."

Elizabeth's mouth curved in an almost imperceptible smile. "And who will hear *your* confession, Master Astrologer? Are you not the murderer of Charles Shiveley?"

Ramos gasped. "Surely not, my Lady. Shiveley was executed by the will of the king and queen."

"Did you not create the foul device that deceived my people and blasphemed God? There is no need to reply. I see by your face that my information is correct."

Now it was Ramos who was afraid. How did she know these things? "My sins are not at question here," he said. "I am come to hear yours."

"Hear mine then: I conspired to wrest the kingdom from the control of evil rulers who will drain her treasury and enslave her people in fear." Elizabeth emerged from the corner, the light catching her fiery hair as her voice grew louder and more confident. "I plotted to free my people from the abuse of wealth and power, from religious prejudice and hypocrisy. I schemed to make England independent and strong instead of vassals of the Pope and the King of Spain. Do you absolve me of these sins, my father?"

"These are sins indeed. King Philip and Queen Mary are granted their authority by God. To defy them is to defy God."

Her brown eyes were pitying. "Good Father," she said. "Do you not fear what Philip will do with your latest discovery? Will he not use it again to crush the people through deception and terror, the way he did with your first?"

His *latest* discovery? How did she know these things? Was she truly a witch? Could she read his mind? "The king is the arm of God to dispense justice and chastisement," he said. "It is right for him to punish where necessary, and wrong for us to judge him false."

"And Antonia?" Elizabeth almost whispered it. "How long before the chastisement of the king's justice falls on her?"

"No more," Ramos said. The woman knew everything about him. "We are talking of you, not me."

"But what if she is not demon-possessed, as the Roman Church would have you believe? What if there is a natural explanation for her condition?"

"The Holy Father has already spoken on this subject. The mad are under the judgment of God for harboring secret heresies in their hearts." The words tasted like mud in his mouth, and he knew, even as he said them, that he did not believe them, and Elizabeth knew it.

A profound look of disappointment came over Elizabeth's face. Ramos squirmed under her gaze, which seemed to see right through him to the uncertainty inside. He had come to instill doubts in her mind, but it was happening the other way around. The walls he had so carefully constructed around his misgivings were crumbling, and he was finding them grown even larger than before.

"There is a man I trust," she said, "a mathematician and philosopher like yourself, who believes that the spirits of the mad were caught up in the novas, that they still live, and with enough knowledge about the stars and the deeper mysteries, we might return them to themselves again."

Despite himself, Ramos was interested. It was the very hope he had harbored through all his investigation of quintessence, despite what the Pope said. He knew he should not agree to this meeting. It would be a betrayal of his allegiance to the king. It would be admitting the possibility that the Pope could be wrong, just because his heart desired it to be so. And yet, even as he argued with himself, he knew that he would meet the man, whatever the risk.

"I will not tell you his name," Elizabeth said. "If he deems it safe, he will find you."

THE NEXT morning, an elegantly folded and sealed note was slipped under Ramos's chamber door. The message was brief, written in red ink in a precise hand.

Meet me in the old library. D.

There was no time specified. Ramos could only assume he meant at once. He also had no idea where the "old library" was, and didn't dare ask anyone, since he didn't know what he would find when he got there. Not even counting the mysterious agent of Princess Elizabeth he was supposed to meet, an old library might contain books of a politically questionable nature, or hold a significance of which he was unaware.

The queen had a library, mostly religious, with a handful of rare illuminated manuscripts, but it wasn't available for common use, and could hardly be the location the letter had meant. Ramos wandered through the acres of Whitehall Palace's many rooms, hesitant to ask anyone for help, but afraid of wandering through the wrong door. Whole wings of the palace were given over to be used by various of the great families, guarded by their own soldiers, and staffed with their own liveried servants. He didn't want to find himself in an awkward situation.

What kind of a man was this he was meeting, who would send him on such a chase? An educated man, Elizabeth had made clear, and one who had the freedom of the palace. A brave man, who would swear fealty to Mary and yet consort with Elizabeth. Ramos wondered if he was being foolish, stumbling blindly into a situation that could get him executed. But his devotion to King Philip was faltering, and even—could he say it?—to the Church. He had thought the king the very definition of what was moral and just, and the Church the definition of what was true, but his doubts about both had grown too strong to be ignored. He had questions he needed answered—about the novas, about human souls, about the way the universe worked—and the answers that Church doctrine constrained him to did not satisfy.

Perhaps the doctrine was all true, and it was his understanding that was faulty. But he couldn't live with the uncertainty. He had to know.

Finally, with the aid of an elderly serving man, he found the room. It was more like a dusty closet with walls lined with cubby holes stacked with old scrolls. There was barely room for two people to sit down, and in any event, there were no chairs. The mysterious agent stood inside, holding a manuscript close to a candle flame, the point of his long, white beard resting on the yellowed parchment. Just as he had been when Ramos first cast the queen's horoscope, the man was wearing a long artist's gown with sleeves that hung down over his wrists, and a black cap on his head. It was John Dee, the queen's astrologer.

"Come in and close the door," Dee said.

Ramos did so. It left them standing close together in the musty dimness. It was a meeting place unlikely to be discovered by anyone, and no wonder. Dee held a trusted position in Mary's court, privy to many of her secrets. If he was passing information to Elizabeth, he was risking torture and death. But then, why was he talking to Ramos? Ramos was a Spaniard, after all, and a Jesuit, loyal to the king. Wasn't Dee afraid he would reveal his duplicity?

"The question to consider," Dee said, not looking up from the manuscript, "is why does the position of the stars at the moment of a person's birth affect his future? The stars are distant, and the moment fleeting."

Ramos's head spun at the sudden launch into metaphysics. "You're asking if horoscopes work?"

"Certainly they do," Dee said, setting down the paper. "It's the basis of astrology. Someone born in March under Saturn has different loves, different strivings, and a different future than someone born in July under Mars. But why? What is the connection between a person and a star?"

"First things first," Ramos said. He held up the folded note. "Did you send me this letter?"

Dee pursed his lips, annoyed. "Of course I did."

"But you are loyal to the queen."

"I'm loyal to the truth. A mutual friend told me you were as well. Is that not so?"

"Yes. But I wish to know what kind of conspiracy I'm getting involved with."

"No conspiracy. No plot. I seek only to learn the truth of matters kept hidden by the strictures of politics."

"Or of religion."

Dee cocked his head. "Is there a difference?"

"Why didn't Mary ask you to cast her horoscope instead of me?"

"She did. She didn't like the result."

"And Philip doesn't trust you."

Dee sighed. "I have a cousin, Blanche Parry, who is a maid to the Princess Elizabeth."

"Leading Philip to doubt your total devotion to Mary."

"Quite."

"So despite the fact that the king's fears were well-founded, and you are passing information to the princess, you want me to believe that this conversation has nothing to do with Elizabeth's desire to take the throne from her sister?"

"It may have everything to do with it, but we must set aside such questions and consider only what is true. Enough of politics. My question?"

Ramos wasn't accustomed to being treated as a pupil, but he hid his irritation. "The connection between a person and a star? Perhaps there is none at all. Perhaps each heavenly body emits rays of force which influence a spirit at the moment it comes into the world, more or less, depending on its place in the sky. The nature of that spirit is permanently set by that initial influence."

Dee carefully rolled the manuscript he had been reading into a tight cylinder. "But can the spirit not change? Is its essence fixed?" He held the manuscript near the candle. "Can I not change this parchment into ash, and thus change its essence?"

"The essence of a soul must be immutable."

Dee nodded. "I used to think so. But my thoughts were overturned by recent events."

"You mean the novas."

"Of course."

Ramos considered before answering. "The appearance of a nova in that constellation affected the people born under that constellation. So you are right; there must still be a continuing connection between the people and the stars."

"Yes. This is the crux of the matter. The nature of a soul may, in fact, change, but no matter how much it changes, the connection of force still remains."

Ramos felt something click in his brain, like a padlock opening. The bell-boxes connected to each other invisibly across great distances as well. Just as the spirits of the mad must somehow have been connected to their constellations. Were the two types of connections the same? The stars were in the heavens; the boxes on Earth. Could they really be driven by the same rules? And yet, quintessence had come from Horizon, where the heavens and the earth almost met.

Ramos felt dizzy, like the whole earth was spinning with him at the center. Though perhaps it was just the foundations of his life that were spinning. He should walk away right now. He had met this man, and heard his thoughts; he shouldn't get any more entangled. It would mean his life, and Antonia's life as well. But if they could get to the heart of the matter . . . then Antonia's life might be saved.

The next step, however, was to share with Dee what he himself knew, and that was a line over which he could not return once he crossed it. It was one thing to meet with another astrologer in a library and talk about the stars. It was quite another to share state secrets with a man he knew to be a spy. In the end, he didn't hesitate very long. He wanted answers, and he wasn't finding them himself. Not fast enough, anyway. Already, from only ten minutes conversation with Dee, he had learned more than he knew before. He needed a collaborator.

"Come," Ramos said. "I have some things to show you."

RAMOS paused at the cellar door. On the way, he had prepared Dee with the history of the *San Salvador* and its voyage from Horizon, the wonders the sailors had returned with, and some of what he had so far discovered. Dee merely raised an eyebrow at the story of the *Ignis Dei* and its role in the burning of Charles Shiveley, and Ramos remembered that Elizabeth had already seemed to know. Had she learned it from Dee? Or had she been the one to tell him?

This was the point of no return. So far, he had only exchanged some philosophical banter with a member of the court. To lead him into the secret cellar, however, was advancing into willful disregard of the king's command. He descended first, to be sure neither Barrosa nor the king was already there, and when he found it deserted, returned for Dee.

Ramos showed him the animals, the gold, the shekinah and pearls. He explained how he had come upon the idea for the *Ignis Dei*, and demonstrated the power of the invisible bird's saliva. Dee became more and more animated, ruminating on the nature of matter and the likelihood of other planes of existence. When they reached the bell-boxes, Dee agreed with him instantly that the quintessence connection that joined the boxes must be of the same kind as that which joined people with the stars of their birth.

They were interrupted by the sound of a door opening and footsteps descending the stairs. Both men froze. They were trapped; there was no other way out of the cellar, and no place to hide. Ramos had not yet mastered the bird's trick of invisibility. It could only be one of two men on those stairs, and either one meant disaster.

It was Barrosa. He reached the bottom before he noticed them, and he froze as well, joining the tableau of shocked discovery. Then he laughed.

Dee laughed as well, and the two men embraced. Ramos watched them, still unable to move, his mouth slightly agape.

"I told you we could trust him," Barrosa said.

Ramos sank into a seat, feeling weak. "I don't understand."

"I told Dee you loved truth more than politics. I told him you were smart, that we needed your mind, and that you would understand the importance of considering the question of the novas without political interference. But I never dreamed . . .!"

Ramos was starting to feel like he'd been tricked. "Dreamed what?"

"I've been sneaking around, meeting with Dee for a month, but I never dreamed of actually bringing him down here. I barely even told him about these things; I just dropped hints, because I knew if any breath of them leaked out, the king would know I was the source. The risk was just too great. And here you are, the first time you meet, giving him the full tour!"

"I have to know the truth," Ramos said. "Antonia . . ."

Barrosa clapped him on the shoulder. "I know, old friend."

Comprehension dawned. "You!" Ramos said. "You're the one talking to Elizabeth. That's how she knew so much about me."

Barrosa nodded with a chuckle.

"But . . . why? You're a Spaniard. Why spy for an English woman?"

"This has nothing to do with politics. It's no conspiracy to put

Elizabeth on the throne. But she's not like other monarchs. She cares about what's true, not just what serves her interests. She's not content with shallow, thoughtless explanations that protect the status quo. And she knows people." He indicated Dee. "She brought us together, and she'll find more. If the madness is just a curse from God, there's nothing we can do about it. But if it's a natural phenomenon, based on quintessence, then just maybe it's something we can understand and do something about."

Ramos thought of Antonia, and he knew this was the right course. But how could the right course be contrary to the ways of God? Unless God wasn't on the Church's side after all. Ramos felt seasick, as if the solid deck he thought he was standing on was now pitching up and down in the wind, liable to capsize without warning. Who was he anymore? The masts of his life were split and tumbling on either side, and yet he felt oddly sure that he was heading in the right direction.

"Count me in," he said.

RAMOS continued to visit Elizabeth, ostensibly to hear her confession. He grew more and more in awe of her, a young woman barely more than a child, yet wiser than her years, and with the strength of a lion. He continued to try to convince her to recant and swear allegiance to the Roman Church, but she refused.

When the days grew hot, Philip and Mary moved court to Richmond Palace for the summer. Removing anything from the cellar was a terrible risk, but Ramos decided it was worth the gamble. John Dee's mother was still alive and living in Mortlake High Street, not far from Richmond, so Ramos and Barrosa and Dee decided to set up headquarters there. Ramos moved Antonia to Mortlake and began to spend most of his time there, when he was not expected at the palace. Ramos and Barrosa smuggled in as many things as they dared so they could expand their experiments beyond what the cellar would allow.

The first thing Ramos tried was the bell-box again, this time with Barrosa and Dee with him. He was desperate to talk to the Horizon colonists, to find out what they knew, and to warn them of the ships heading their way.

They tried the lever again and again, but with no response. The bell never rang. Either the colonists were dead, or had fled, or were afraid he was their enemy and so refused to answer. They might even suspect that the connection had been a ruse to gain their confidence or discover their position. He knew it wouldn't be easy to gain their trust, but it would be impossible if he could never speak to them.

Ramos told Barrosa and Dee about the brief conversation he'd had with what he assumed were Horizon colonists. They were as astonished as he, especially since the bell-box connection to *La Magdalena* didn't work that way at all. Pressing the lever rang the bell on the other side, which was miraculous enough, but it couldn't transmit a person's voice. The boxes looked the same, and seemed to be of the same design. What was different?

"They're the same on this end," Dee pointed out. "That doesn't mean they're the same on the other end."

Ramos snapped his fingers. "Of course. The colonists must have improved the design. But how?"

It took them three days to figure it out. Once he knew it was possible, Ramos was relentless in trying to discover the secret, and of course, he didn't have many options to try. It did occur to him the colonists could be using some tool only available on the island, a special plant or something taken from a Horizon animal, but that didn't stop him. He tried everything he could think of, until at last, despite Barrosa's warning of the dangers and the likelihood that the box itself would be destroyed, he carefully tipped a drop of vitriol into the glowing heart of the ironfish skull.

The void sprang into being, small at first, but glowing.

"Hello?" Ramos said. "Hello? Is anyone there?"

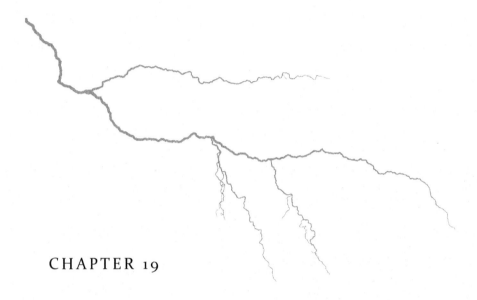

CHAPTER 19

MATTHEW and Parris ran at the head of the line wending its way through the forest toward the distant mountains. They needed to reach the foothills, at the edge of which lived the red manticores, the tribe most accepting, if not exactly welcoming, of the human presence on the island. Whether they realized it or not, the Spanish were their mutual enemy. He needed to convince them of that fact, and enlist their help. If he could convince them to help find Catherine, or at least learn for certain if she was dead, so much the better.

The line was spreading out. With enough salt, they could run without growing tired, but they had long since used up whatever reserves their bodies held. At least there were no injured, since even without a supply of salt, their bodies healed almost immediately. Matthew's father lagged somewhere at the back of the line. Ferguson, on the other hand, walked at the front, sometimes even pressing ahead of Matthew, as if he were leading the way.

Finally, as it grew dark again, Matthew called a halt to the column.

They would have to spend the night under the stars. They posted sentries to watch for the many enemies that could do them harm: the manticores, the Spanish, or even nocturnal predators. Matthew volunteered for the first watch.

When the light of the blazing sun finally disappeared, leaving the forest lit by rays of ethereal starlight slanting in from the west, Blanca found him. Most of the colonists were asleep, or settling down for the night. Tomorrow's journey would be even more difficult: uphill into the foothills of the mountains.

"Blanca," he said. "About the other night. I don't think we—"

"Never mind about that. I brought you something." She held out a broken piece of wood. "He's talking again."

"What? Who?"

"The man from England."

Matthew's mind felt blurred with exhaustion, and it took him a moment to figure out what she was talking about. "Tavera, you mean? The one from the orphaned bell-box?"

She nodded. He couldn't read her expression in the starlight shadows.

"But it was all destroyed," he said. "The jawbone, the box, it was all swallowed up in the void. The end of the thread was still there, but it wasn't attached to anything, and now it's all burned away."

"Remember how I threw a piece of wood into the void?" she said. "I kept the other piece in my pocket. I still have it, and just now, while I was running . . . I heard him talking."

Matthew took the piece from her and turned it over in his hands. Another mystery. A piece of this wood had been thrown into the void. Like any living or formerly-living thing, the two pieces would have been joined by a thread, one side in the void, the other side in the world. But when the void had snapped shut, what had happened to the thread?

He lifted the wood close to his mouth. "Can anyone hear me?"

The response was immediate. "This is Ramos de Tavera."

Matthew's skink tears had long since worn off, but he had no trouble believing that the thread from the piece of wood in his hand stretched all the way back to the spot where the void had closed, where the second floor of the Quintessence Society building used to be. He'd seen often enough the peculiar ways that quintessence threads could stretch and follow an object wherever it traveled, yet without getting tangled with the thousands of other threads stretching through space. The incredible thing was that this thread, apparently trapped and held by the edges of the closing void, seemed to operate as an extension of the thread connecting the old bell-box to England. Like tying together two strings to make one, he was now somehow talking through a piece of wood, connected with a hole in reality, connected to one half of a bell-box on the other side of the world.

"What do you want?" Matthew asked.

Ramos spoke in a deep, accented voice. "Am I speaking with the Horizon colony?"

"You could say that." What did the man want? His gunships had already taken over the harbor. Was he demanding their surrender?

"This is a warning," Ramos said. "There are five ships, galleons of war filled with soldiers and guns, coming to attack you. Their orders are to kill you and plunder your gold and shekinah worms and quintessence pearls. Do you understand?"

"Is this a joke? Don't think this is over. You might think you understand this island, but you have some surprises waiting for you."

"No. What? I make no joke. King Philip sent the ships months ago. He—"

"Do you really not know?"

"Know what?"

"The ships are here. They're in our harbor. We were forced to flee into the mountains." Matthew didn't mention that this was mostly because he had burned down the settlement.

A pause. "Then I am too late."

"I'd say so. Now you answer some questions for me. Are you telling me the San Salvador made it back to England? Are Francis Vaughan and the others alive?"

"No one is alive from that ship. Many died on the way; the rest died shortly after. Only one shekinah flatworm and five pearls remain of what the ship carried when she set sail. A few animals as well, and a few artifacts like this amazing box with its bell and bones. We have been investigating these things. They are quite wonderful."

Despite himself, Matthew felt a flush of pride at the compliment, but he remained suspicious. "Who is 'we'? Are you an agent of the king? You must be, if you're in the palace."

A pause, longer this time. "I am not in the palace now. There are three of us here: myself, Juan Barrosa, and John Dee. We . . . are operating outside of the king's authority. He would not have wanted us to warn you about the ships."

"How do I know you're telling the truth? You could have waited until the ships arrived, and then pretended to warn me to gain my trust. If you could make contact, why did you wait until now to do it?"

"We do not know as much as you. It took many tries to make the void and speak with you."

Matthew's jaw dropped. "You figured that out? To make a void on your end?"

"Now the box is destroyed, though. Once this void is gone, I fear we will be unable to speak again."

"No! You can." Despite his suspicions, Matthew was starting to like this man. A big limitation to their study was that they could only do their experiments on Horizon. Matthew had created a box that blocked quintessence fields, to mimic conditions back home, but it wasn't perfect. If they could communicate with men in England and suggest experiments to try, think about how much they could learn!

"Take something organic," Matthew said. "A stick, a bone, anything. Break it in half, and throw one piece in the void before it closes. Better yet, do it with a few different things, in case you lose one or it doesn't work. Because you're right—once that void closes, we'll never be able to open a new connection between us."

There was a flurry of sound from the other side as Tavera and his friends presumably did as he suggested.

"Have them burn something," Blanca said.

Matthew raised an eyebrow. "Do what?"

"Burn something. Or light a pipe, or something that will make a strong smell. To see if we can smell it."

Matthew grinned and squeezed her arm. "Perfect," he said. He explained to the men on the other end what he wanted them to do, and soon the smell of burning tobacco filled their nostrils.

"It works," he said. "The smell from the pipe actually transmits across the quintessence thread, just like the sound of our voices does."

"More than that," Blanca said. "Look."

She held her hand behind the piece of wood. By the contrast of her pale skin, Matthew could see faint wisps of gray smoke drifting into the air.

THE FOLLOWING day, Barrosa was required at the palace to wait on the king, but since neither Philip nor Mary had sent for astrologers, Ramos and Dee were free to experiment, only now with a lot more knowledge. After seeing the pipe smoke appear, Matthew Marcheford had spoken to them of quintessence threads, and of the invisible world behind the world, where the threads stretched and intertwined. Ramos knew this was the same space he and Barrosa had talked about in the field where he had fought the king's soldiers, a space behind and separate from the material world.

Ramos and Dee spent the day in heady discovery. With the shekinah worm nearby to provide the quintessence field, they recreated a series of thread connections like the one through which they had talked to Matthew. First they broke a stick in half—just an ordinary elm branch they found outside—and put the pieces in different rooms. Then they used a drop of vitriol on each piece to open a void, and found they could talk to each other through the connection, even at a whisper.

They broke a second stick in half and tossed one half into one of the voids, and did the same with a third stick at the other void. Ramos had discovered that with his fingers covered with wax—the same wax that prevented the compass beetles from escaping—he could keep a void from growing too large and close it when he wished. When he clapped the voids closed, the connections remained. As long as they stayed within the quintessence field of the shekinah flatworm—which barely covered the house—they could speak from stick to stick and be heard, even after the voids had been closed.

In the evening, Ramos sat outside with Antonia. They sat quietly together, Antonia sometimes babbling under her breath, but blessedly not falling into one of her fits. There was a small patch of garden between the street and the river, and across the street, the Church of St. Mary the Virgin stood, a solid building of multicolored stone with ivy climbing the walls.

Ramos's faith had once been as strong as that building, built to last, proof against storm or flood. Now it wavered, undermined by contradictory truths. It wasn't just that he didn't know what was true. He didn't even know the ultimate source of truth. Was it the pope? The king? Holy Scripture? What he could see and hear with his senses? The conclusions of his logical mind? Where these things were in agreement, there was no question about truth, but where they disagreed, he didn't know whom or what to believe.

He put his hand over Antonia's. The pope called her a demon-worshipper. Dee said her mind was caught up in the stars. And what did Ramos himself believe? He could no longer say that he believed the pope implicitly. It was just that the implications of that lack of belief undermined everything he had given his life to: the priestly ministry, the spread of the Church, the worship of God.

He didn't think he was an atheist. If the world truly was composed of tiny atoms and invisible quintessence threads, then surely those things were created by God as well. If the world was governed by the movement of tiny particles; if it was a machine with gears that meshed and turned by predetermined rules, then God had created the cogs and gears.

But no, he wasn't satisfied with that, either. That approach pushed God farther and farther out of relevance with life. It treated God simply as a means to explain what was unexplained. The more they learned and understood, the smaller God's sphere of involvement would be. Soon he would be thinking of God as merely the architect of the world, an initiator only, remote and distant from the lives of men. That could not be. Though he couldn't have it both ways, could he? Either the workings of the world were governed by natural laws, or they were governed directly by God.

His musings were interrupted by the sound of hoofbeats. Mortlake was a quiet place, characterized by birdsong and the running of the river. This sounded like a company of riders. They rounded the bend and came into view on the road; four soldiers bearing the queen's colors. Ramos's first thought was that they had come for Antonia. He stood to hurry her inside, but the riders were there before he could lift her to her feet. They jumped to the ground and tossed the reins to the one of their company. The other three approached.

"Where is the astrologer John Dee?"

"What do you need of him?"

"He is under arrest, by order of their royal majesties, King Philip and Queen Mary, on charges of calculating and conspiring with the enemies of the crown."

RAMOS found Barrosa at Richmond Palace and dragged him into an empty side room.

"How much does the king know?"

"Are you mad? Know about what?"

"About Dee. About us. About sneaking his treasures out of the palace from under his nose in collusion with the Princess Elizabeth."

Barrosa was open-mouthed. "Nothing, that I know of."

"Well, they didn't arrest him for the length of his beard!"

"Arrest who? Ramos, what are you talking about?"

It was Ramos's turn to look surprised. "Dee was just arrested. Four soldiers just rode up to the house and dragged him away in chains. You're the king's secretary; you must have seen the papers."

"I saw nothing. He was arrested?"

"At sundown. I've been up all night clearing out our things and moving Antonia to other quarters before they commandeer the house."

"The arrest wasn't at the king's command. He spent the day with his council hearing reports from the wars and dictating letters to his commanders."

Ramos rubbed his chin. "Maybe one of the lords took it upon himself."

"No. Not with someone of Dee's stature. The queen . . ."

Their eyes met. "The queen," Ramos said.

Barrosa nodded. "She must have discovered something, some inkling of what we're doing."

"But how? She hardly takes any interest in politics any more. All she thinks about is her pregnancy. She wouldn't be setting spies on us."

"She's playing some different game. Dee read her horoscope before you did, you know. He said her baby would die."

"Which was true, before the king brought quintessence into the mix."

"Even so, she may hold it against him. Or fear he will perform some sorcery to kill her baby and make his prediction true. He's widely thought of as a magician, you know. What was the actual charge?"

"'Calculating and conspiring with the enemies of the Crown.'"

Barrosa started pacing. "'Calculating'? What kind of charge is that? You and Dee calculate all the time. It's your job."

"It's one thing to calculate inside the lines. It's quite another thing to pursue knowledge wherever it leads you. Then what happens when what you find disagrees with what those in charge tell you to believe? I think 'calculating' is exactly the right charge." Ramos fingered the black box at his throat. "I also think the queen knows about Dee's involvement with Elizabeth."

"That seems likely," Barrosa said.

"What do you think she'll do?"

Barrosa shook his head. He cracked the door and looked out—no one there—and then beckoned Ramos over to the window. "Mary hates Elizabeth," he whispered. "Loves her and hates her at the same time. I was here, in England, when Elizabeth was born." Barrosa had been the son of one of the ladies-in-waiting to Queen Katerina, and had grown up in England.

"That must have been a frightening time," Ramos said. Mary's father, Henry VIII, had thrown the Holy Church out of England, and Mary's mother out of the palace, so he could marry Elizabeth's mother, Anne Boleyn.

"The worst," Barrosa said. "Mary was seventeen years old. There she was, stripped of her titles, forced to acknowledge—after twenty-four years—that her parents had never been truly married. Her father forced her to leave her mother and live in Hatfield House with beautiful little Princess Elizabeth, and to act as her servant. She had to watch her father and his lover—and the whole court, really—fuss and praise and lavish every possible rich gift on Elizabeth while she stood by."

"And through all that, she remained faithful to the Church," Ramos said.

"That's just it. If not for this baby son, Elizabeth would be next in line for the throne, and she's a Protestant. At some level, Mary loves Elizabeth as a sister, but at the same time, she's fiercely jealous of her, and she fears England slipping back into the heresy that took her father away from her. Just by being alive, Elizabeth is a threat to Mary's son. If Mary sees this as treachery, then both Dee and Elizabeth are in grave danger."

Ramos unlatched the window and swung it open. He was finding it hard to breathe. They were on the third floor looking down, so no one from outside would overhear them. "She's going to execute Dee, isn't she?"

"It's quite possible. This may even be the final straw that tips her over into executing Elizabeth. Most of her council advises her to do it. She's refused so far, out of loyalty to family and a respect for what she considers royal blood, but if it looks like Elizabeth is complicit in a plot to kill her baby . . ."

"And what about us? The soldiers came looking for Dee, and found me sitting on the front step. If they didn't know of a connection between us before, they do now."

"We work for the king, though. We're not under the queen's authority."

"If the king finds out we were telling his secrets—"

"Why should he find out? The queen doesn't care about quintessence or know anything about it. Besides, we're useful to the king. We make discoveries that will be useful to his war effort."

"That's true," Ramos said. He thought of the king's veiled threat against Antonia. "He wants us submissive, but still working."

"So what do we do?" Barrosa said.

"We stay in Richmond and act like good king's men. Stand with his courtiers, attend functions, write his letters, tell him what the stars portend. Give him no reason to be displeased with us."

"And Dee?"

"We watch for our chance," Ramos said. "Speak on his behalf, if we can. Find out how much the king knows, and how much he suspects."

THE PRINCESS Elizabeth was called to a hearing before the queen, the king, the Lord Chancellor, and the Archbishop of Canterbury, and sentenced to death by beheading if she would not recant and confess her crimes. After they brought her back to her cell in the Tower, Ramos visited her. She sat on the floor in a corner, away from the window, looking small and helpless.

"I know I am mortal," she said. She sat very still, and her voice was quiet. "I cannot live forever. I should be ready for death, whensoever God pleases to send it."

"Will you not recant?" Ramos said. "Mary would give you your life, if you would convert. Is it not better to work within the Church to reform it, rather than set yourself against it?"

Elizabeth shook her head, and her voice took on a little more of the steel he was used to. "I will never be constrained by violence to do anything I would not do of my own free will. If the threat of harm could make me bend, what kind of queen would I be?"

Ramos took a step closer and kneeled next to her. The stones were hard and cold. He wanted to put a hand on her shoulder, but he knew she would never allow it. She was a royal personage, her body sacred. "This is stubbornness," he said. "Even a queen must compromise. The greatest commander must sound the retreat when the battle is lost."

She raised her eyes to look at him around a lock of red hair, a hint of a smile playing about her lips. "Do you care for me, then, Ramos de Tavera?"

He was taken aback. "Of course I do, your Grace."

"Then listen: There is more at stake than my life or my pride. Do you not understand this? I care not about the divisions and quarrels of Christendom. There is only one Christ Jesus, one faith. All else is a dispute over trifles."

"Then why take this stand? Swear your allegiance to Rome, and live another day."

She held his gaze. "Because it is truth that hangs in the balance. Not the truth of a single doctrine or fact of history, but Truth itself, the very meaning of the word. There are those who believe only what makes them feel good or important or worthwhile. They cling to it, lest they see themselves for the petty and immoral people they are. Truth does not hide or cover up. It stares at the ugliness without shrinking back. It asks not, what would I *like* to be true, but what actually is?"

Her gaze drifted to the window. "To love Truth is to risk everything. There are many who seek to suppress it at all costs, because it would reveal them. To others, and especially to themselves. But I have to believe that Truth is worth the risk, and that, even if I die, it will win in the end."

She spoke with a quiet ferocity, and Ramos didn't answer at first. He knew she wasn't talking about him, not directly, but she had drawn a line in the sand, and he wasn't certain which side of it he stood on. Did he have the courage to seek out truth at any cost? Or did he prefer to tell himself those lies which made his place in the world easy and secure?

"What would you do if you took the throne?" he said. "If Mary died today, and you were freed from this tower and crowned queen?"

She gave a deep sigh, as if all her strength was gone. "I have thought all my life that God had called me to rule. I have prepared for it, considered the glory and the cost, and been in constant danger of my life from those who wish me ill. I have learned how to play this game of thrones."

She sat up straighter, tossing her hair over her shoulder and looking out into the distance. "If I were queen, I would chart England her own course, free from Rome and all the nations who wish to turn her sails. She would be my consort, and I her bride. We would allow no lies in our presence, no deceit, no flattery. We would surround ourselves with men who loved truth above greatness, and honesty above power. Who loved God more than Protestantism, and England more than their own political gain."

She leaned back against the wall. "But now, Mary will have a son, and if God wills it, I will die. Perhaps I was never destined for the throne, after all."

"Do not lose heart, your Grace," Ramos said. "If anyone was destined to rule, it is you."

It was out of his mouth before he realized what it meant. He had already been sneaking around behind his king's back, doing secret experiments, and questioning the actions of the Inquisition. But this was something more. Treason. He owed allegiance to Spain, not England, and to the Roman Church, not the English one. But Elizabeth spoke of a Truth that transcended religious and political lines, and he was loyal to that truth above all.

He realized he had crossed the line. He had seen the differences between Philip and Elizabeth, and he knew whom he would rather serve. What was the Church, if it tortured the innocent? What was Spain, if it was ruled by a selfish despot? He wanted Rome and Spain brought to the truth, but it was the truth he was loyal to above all.

Ramos remembered the horoscope he had cast for himself on the floor of the Spanish prison. There had been figures for treason and heresy, for the love of a woman, for the crossing of an ocean. Those predictions, so bizarre at the time, seemed much more likely now.

He had told Barrosa that they should lie low and not call attention to themselves, but now he had no intention of taking that advice himself. He had crossed the line, and there was no going back. He knew what he had to do. It didn't matter that Elizabeth was English and a Protestant. He wasn't going to let her die.

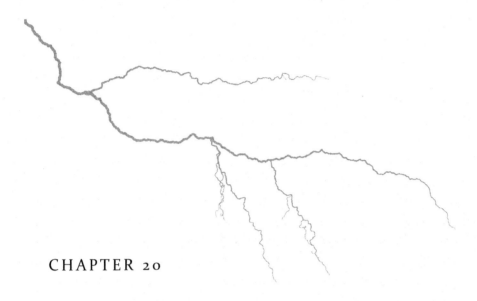

CHAPTER 20

BY THE NEXT nightfall, the colonists reached the caves. It had been another long day, mostly traveling uphill, and everyone was exhausted. Even so, there was work to be done, gathering wood for fires, making sleeping arrangements, digging a pit in the woods for a latrine. Quintessence could make these jobs faster and easier, but many of them were spent from their journey, and almost all of the salt had been lost to the miasma.

Ferguson was the only one who didn't seem tired. He walked from group to group, listening to complaints about the size of their sleeping area or how much of the remaining food ration they were receiving. Matthew knew his father should stand up and make an encouraging speech of some kind, but he also knew he wouldn't do it. His father was a preacher, able to rouse passions when he put his mind to it, but he wasn't connected to how the people around him felt.

These caves were the same ones Catherine and her father and others from the Quintessence Society had hidden in to escape Diego de Tavera after the first Spanish ship had come. Tavera had found them then, and he had no doubt the new Spanish arrivals would find them again, in time. For tonight, however, they should be safe enough.

The caves were complex and jagged, full of twisting fissures that concealed deeper passages. Some of the openings were large enough to march an army through; some too small for a child. No one knew how far back they led. The sound of running water suggested the existence of an underground river, but if one existed, it was out of reach. There weren't many comfortable spots to sleep on the rocky floor, but the night was dry, and there was plenty of room outside under the stars.

He was just about to fall asleep when the voice of Ramos de Tavera came again through the piece of wood. He told Matthew that Princess Elizabeth was sentenced to die. Matthew, in turn, told Ramos about their situation, but he seemed distracted.

"Elizabeth needs help," Ramos said.

It was big news, and would be upsetting to many in the colony, but Matthew was exhausted, and England seemed so far away. "I hope she gets it," he said, yawning. "I'm sure my father will pray for her."

"I mean, she needs help from us. You and me."

"How could I possibly help her?"

"I have an idea," Ramos said. He went on to explain it: a mad, impossible idea that—if they were desperate enough to try it—just might work. Though if it didn't, it might just kill her instead.

MATTHEW slept without dreams and woke later than he intended. His father was already assembling a delegation to visit the red manticores, whose tribal grounds were nearby. He chose Matthew and Parris to accompany him, but not Ferguson.

"That's a mistake," Matthew said. "We should bring him along."

His father raised an eyebrow. "The whole point of this visit is to solidify our friendship and ask the manticores for help. I have no desire to bring someone who is known to hate them, and will only insult them, if not actually start a fight."

"He'll cause trouble here if we don't. Better to have him along, where we can keep an eye on him."

"I'm not taking that fool," his father said. "I can't control what he does, eye on him or no. Our enemies are numerous, and this meeting is crucial. If we have no allies, we won't survive."

The three of them set off at a brisk run. They hoped to find some of his father's Christian converts among the red manticores. They hadn't seen them since the fire and could only assume they had returned to their own people.

Manticore lookouts saw the humans long before they saw the manticores. Matthew couldn't see or hear them, but he knew they would be there, silently tracking them through the trees. Finally, before they came in sight of the primary manticore village, their escort materialized. Nearly a dozen manticores surrounded them, two with English matchlocks.

"We come in peace to treat with your chief," Marcheford said.

Matthew recognized one of the gun-bearers as Tanalabrinu, the son of the red manticores' chief. He was not utterly hostile to the humans, but neither was he exactly a friend.

Tanalabrinu snapped his teeth, a gesture of annoyance. "Why should we treat with you? Your kind brings only death."

"Because of the love we bear you," Marcheford said.

"Was it love that killed Hakrahinik and Lachakchith?" Tanalabrinu said.

Matthew's breath caught in his throat. Hakrahinik and Lachakchith were Paul and Thomas, the two manticores who had accompanied Catherine into the wilderness as her bodyguards. If they were dead, that didn't hold out much hope for Catherine.

"We know nothing of their passing," Marcheford said. "There was another with them, a human girl. We heard she was taken by the grays. Have you news of her?"

"She was judged and found wanting." Tanalabrinu's manner was dismissive.

Matthew couldn't help himself. "They threw her into that chasm?

They killed her?"

"She was judged," Tanalabrinu said.

A stone settled into Matthew's stomach. Even after all this time, he had hoped for good news. Hatred suddenly flared in him, hatred for all the manticores, both those who had killed her and those who could treat her death with such indifference. He wanted to fly at Tanalabrinu and scratch out his eyes, but a shred of reason remained, enough to hold him back. If he did that, he would be killed, perhaps even all of them would be killed.

Some of what he was thinking must have shown on his face, because Tanalabrinu raised his rifle and sighted it on him. "Why have you come here? Give me the truth."

"We would speak with the chief," Marcheford said.

"You are speaking with him. Tanakiki is dead."

That was not good news. Tanalabrinu's father, Tanakiki, had a complex history with the humans, but he had generally supported them. He had been the brother of Chichirico, the only manticore ever to see England and return again to Horizon, the manticore who had brought Catherine into the memory family of his tribe. Tanakiki had never converted to Christianity, but he understood humans as well as any manticore could. He would have almost certainly have helped them in this difficulty.

If his son was in charge now, however, things would be different. The assumption that they would be met with friendship no longer applied. They would have to work for his trust.

"Our settlement is destroyed," Marcheford said. "Our people are scattered. An enemy people has landed with ships and weapons and men. They seek to kill us, raid this island's treasures, and return home with as much as they can take."

Tanalabrinu seemed amused. They continued to talk, but Matthew found it hard to concentrate on their words, despite how important they were to the colonists' future. Catherine was dead. It was impossible to believe. He tried to imagine her body broken in the dark at the bottom of a cave shaft, and the image just swam in his mind. What if it was just a trick by Rinchirith? Just because he said he had killed her didn't mean he had actually done it. Perhaps they were just holding her hostage. Though imagining that was almost worse.

He felt like he needed to see her with his own eyes before he could really believe she was gone. The problem with that was, if the manticores were telling the truth, he would never be able to see her. Her body would be unreachable. There would just be long months of waiting, hoping, watching out the window, hearing her voice on the wind, until hope finally withered and died.

Parris was talking now. "We have knowledge," he said. "You have seen the things we can make. We would share this knowledge with you."

Hadn't he heard? Didn't he know that his daughter was dead? Matthew had a painful lump like an acorn lodged in his throat; he could barely breathe, much less talk.

"I offer myself, as a memory bond between our two peoples," Parris said. He approached Tanalabrinu and pulled his tunic up over his head. He turned, crouched, and presented his back to the manticore chief.

Only then did Matthew see the emptiness in Parris's eyes. For a human to memory bond with a manticore was a dangerous thing, risking madness and loss of self. Parris had done it once before, briefly, to save his daughter's life. Only Catherine herself had endured a prolonged bond with a manticore.

Tanalabrinu grew thoughtful. "Your people are not connected, as we are. This bond would be with you alone."

"Yet from me, you would learn much that would benefit your people," Parris said.

"The rest of us would stand by this bond," Marcheford said, though Matthew doubted this part of the deal had been planned ahead of time. "We are all red manticores now."

Tanalabrinu cocked his head for a moment, then clicked his pincers. "Agreed," he said. With sudden violence, he leaped on Parris's exposed back, wrapping his tails around his torso, and plunged his memory tail, the one tipped with a sharp spike, into Parris's spine. Parris grunted and arched his back, though the tail was not piercing his skin, but merely passing through it into the flesh beneath.

The tail would implant a tiny amount of material from Tanalabrinu into Parris. This material, separated from its source, would connect the two with a quintessence thread. It would then act like a bell-box, only much more sophisticated, sharing not just coded phrases but thoughts, senses, and memories in a flood of consciousness powerful enough to overwhelm a human mind.

Manticore tribes were formed as memory families, in which all the members were connected in this way. This ensured that knowledge was passed down through generations, even when individual members died. Offering a member, usually a child, as a memory bond to another manticore tribe was the strongest means of forging an alliance.

Parris was sacrificing the very privacy of his own mind for the sake of the colony, but Matthew felt unreasonably angry at him. He was escaping his grief, drowning it in the manticore consciousness. Parris was the only person who could understand what Matthew felt, but now his grief would be a distant thing, subservient to his role as spokesman between their peoples. He was leaving Matthew alone.

By the time they left, the manticores had agreed to a treaty. They would help the humans rebuild their settlement near the caves; manticores and humans would fight together against common enemies, whether the grays or the Spanish; and the humans would admit red manticore youths into their English school.

Parris was quiet as they walked back, and stumbled along as if in a dream. Matthew knew he was seeing not just the woods around them, but a host of images from the manticore village as well, experiencing thoughts and memories that were not his own. He wouldn't have volunteered if Catherine were still alive. Though, Matthew had to admit: if Catherine had been here, she would have volunteered herself.

They found the caves quiet. Too quiet. As the returning diplomatic party wound their way through small groups of colonists, the groups fell silent, casting uneasy glances their way. Something was wrong.

James Ferguson stood waiting for them by the largest fire pit, a smug expression on his face. Four thuggish men flanked him, some of his most ardent supporters.

"How are your friends?" Ferguson said. His tone was light, but there was menace underneath it, and something else as well. Triumph.

"They remain our friends, for the time being," Marcheford said.

"And what was the cost of this friendship, I wonder?"

"Only what is just. That we should fight alongside each other against our common foes. That their children should be educated in our schools, while they teach us what forest craft we do not yet know."

Ferguson spat. "You expect our children to learn alongside those beasts?"

Matthew glanced at Parris. There was no turning off the link; Tanalabrinu and the other manticores were hearing all of this.

"I do expect that," Marcheford said calmly. "They have offered us friendship despite many reasons to do otherwise. I expect you to accept them as part of us and keep your tongue civil."

A slow smile spread across Ferguson's face. His eyes glanced behind them, and Matthew turned to see that many of the other men of the colony had gathered around them. "We took a vote while you were gone," Ferguson said. "We've got ourselves a new governor now."

"Who?" Marcheford said, incredulous. "You?"

Ferguson gave a mocking bow. "You had your chance. You're finished now. Our way of life was falling apart, and all you could think about was your precious pet manticores, getting them to pray and parrot Bible verses like a bloody circus act. Now look at where we are. Our homes are burned to the ground, the Spanish want to gut us all, and you're still prancing around making friends with their lot. They're our enemies, if you hadn't noticed."

There were murmurs of agreement from the others. Matthew saw that not all the colonists were part of this mutiny; some held back, and others were absent or inside other caves. The majority, however, seemed to have swung Ferguson's way.

"They're not all our enemies," Marcheford said. "Many of them are principled. Honorable. Trustworthy." He turned his glare on those gathered around, and his implication was clear.

"The only manticore I'll trust is a dead one," Ferguson said, to a chorus of ayes from the men nearest him.

"And what will you do? Kill them all?"

Now Ferguson was positively grinning. "If it comes to that."

"With what? Your fists?" Marcheford said.

Ferguson didn't answer, and it was quickly clear why. His skin was glowing, dimly at first, but then brighter, until the light streaming from him illuminated the cave. This was what Catherine had done to defeat the manticores in the battle for the colony the previous year. It was a powerful display of quintessence, and it required an enormous expenditure of salt. More than Ferguson should have had at his disposal.

Ferguson gestured at the fire pit, and the glow rushed out of him and exploded into flame, tripling the size of the previous blaze into a white furnace that quickly vaporized the remaining wood. As the quintessence fire died away and their eyes adjusted, they could see that all of the men in Ferguson's closest circle were now glowing, too, making up for the fire's light.

"You've been hoarding salt," Marcheford said. "Lying to us all."

Ferguson laughed. "If I had been hoarding it, that would be more than you've managed to do. No, I wasn't stockpiling my own supply. I was just making better use of my time. While you were off befriending savages, I was working on providing for our own people."

Matthew was losing his patience. "What are you talking about?" he said.

Ferguson gestured at one of his cronies, a belligerent Welshman named Craddock. "Show them," he said.

Craddock led them deeper into the cave, through a complex of twisting passages, past remarkable rock formations looming down from the ceiling or flowing like petrified waterfalls over the stone. Finally, they reached a crack they had to turn sideways to squeeze through, one by one. On the other side, embedded in the rock face and glittering with reflected light, was an immense vein of crystallized salt.

Ferguson was grinning. "This is what happens when someone competent is in charge," he said.

It was a ludicrous claim, especially since Marcheford had left instructions for the caves to be thoroughly explored in his absence. But it didn't matter. This explained why all the colonists had so willingly gone along with Ferguson's coup, or at least not challenged him. He controlled the salt. He and his friends were full to bursting with quintessence power. No one could get to the salt without challenging him, and no one could challenge him without getting to the salt.

Marcheford's face was grave. "I promised alliance to the red manticores. They will fight with us and protect us and give us aid, if we keep our promise."

"But we don't need their help. Don't you see, old man? This is more salt than we gathered in a year mining lilies."

Parris spoke for the first time. "Why do you think the manticores haven't already mined this salt? It's right on their doorstep, after all." Matthew gave him a sidelong glance. Did he know something about this vein through his bond with Tanalabrinu? If so, he didn't reveal it.

"I don't know," Ferguson said. "Maybe they never found it. Maybe they're too stupid to know it's valuable. Maybe it's some sacred place in their demon-spawned religion and they don't dare touch it. I don't care what they think. It's mine now."

Matthew noticed that Craddock was now posted in front of the only exit. They were trapped deep in a cave with two men bursting with quintessence power. There might be three of them, but they would have no chance against Ferguson and Craddock, or even against one of them.

"It should be made available to anyone who needs it," Marcheford said. "We should start a rotating duty to mine the salt and bring it out, so everyone can reach it."

"Here's the thing," Ferguson said. "You're not in charge anymore. So you have two choices. You and your four friends can walk out of this cave and never come back."

"Or?" Marcheford said.

Ferguson smiled. "Or you can never walk out of here again."

CATHERINE and Maasha Kaatra emerged into the blazing brightness of the evening sun, surrounded by manticores. The spirit lights flew off in every direction, and many of the manticores, obviously terrified by their sudden appearance, scattered as well. The remaining manticores, despite their terror, gathered close around Catherine and Maasha Kaatra, reaching out to touch them with tentative pincers or tails. Catherine climbed down from Maasha Kaatra's back and walked among them, smiling, reassuring, allowing them to see who she was. They looked up at her with awe, as if she were a god.

She looked back at Maasha Kaatra, who was still standing in the same place, unmoving. His face was lined, and he stooped slightly. White lesions had reappeared on his neck, next to one eye, on the back of his hand. Whatever power he had drawn from the nova, he had used much of it bringing her here.

The manticores drew them gently away from the Gorge and down into a sheltered overhang. They washed the dust off their arms and faces. Maasha Kaatra submitted to this without expression. The manticores were of many different colors and sizes, some of which were new to Catherine. One had pure white fur, some were mottled or streaked with brown or gray, some had blunted pincers while others came to a sharp point. She had never seen such a variety in one place. It must be a gathering of some kind, of manticores from all over the island. But for what purpose?

"I need to get home to the human settlement," Catherine said.

No response but some tail-waving that meant nothing to her. She tried her request again in their language. This time the white one responded with rapid sounds and gestures, which again she could make no sense of. They were speaking to her, but she didn't understand. Was this a different dialect, some variation of the manticore tongue? If so, they probably couldn't follow her stumbling vocabulary any better. She gave up and submitted to their gentle care without any more attempts to communicate.

She fell asleep, only realizing it when she woke in the dark and found the manticores gone. Maasha Kaatra sat next to her, awake, but almost like a statue in his stillness.

"Thank you for bringing me back to the surface," she said.

He nodded gravely. "I was glad to help you."

"I don't see why. It was my fault you fell into the void in the first place."

"Your fault? No. I was drawn to the void ever since I'd seen it. I wanted it. And it wanted me."

Catherine shifted position so she could see his eyes better, but they told her nothing. "You mean you fell into the void on purpose?"

He shrugged, barely a twitch of his shoulder muscles. "Not on purpose, not like that. But it called to me. It calls to us all, eventually. It is where we end."

"You wanted to see your daughters again, didn't you?" she said. Maasha Kaatra was so physically powerful, so reserved, so alien to her that Catherine sometimes forgot he was a normal mortal person, with more pain in his life than most people had to endure. He had been sold into slavery, and survived, had watched his daughters raped and killed by Portuguese slavers, and survived, had fallen into the void between the atoms of the world and had still, somehow, survived. He was so good at surviving that it hadn't occurred to her that perhaps he didn't want to anymore.

"I want them every day, more than life," Maasha Kaatra said. "It is like breathing with lungs full of glass. Every living moment is pain. If I knew where they were, and how to get there, I would go through seven hells to be with them again."

Catherine remembered how her father had been when her brother Peter had died, like a man drowning, but with no will to save himself. Mother had kept the family going in those days, while her father had buried himself in an obsession to heal what he had failed to heal in Peter. Her father probably thought she was dead now. Was he as devastated by her loss as he had been by Peter's? And what about Matthew? If she died, would he be undone, or would he move on and find someone else?

"I'm sorry," she said. "You were hoping to find them in the void, weren't you?"

"It wasn't until you came that I even realized I was still in the world," Maasha Kaatra said. "I thought I was in the afterworld. I thought to find my girls among the lights."

"Who do you suppose they all are?" Catherine said. "They seem to be spirits, but where did they come from? Are they of the living or the dead?"

"If they are dead, they are only the newly dead. They come from all places in the world, but they have memories of recent times," Maasha Kaatra said.

"I know what they are," a voice said.

Catherine jumped and looked around. The voice was soft, young, and female. She saw no one.

"Or should I say, what *we* are," the voice said.

Only then did Catherine notice the tiny light hovering nearby. When they emerged from the Gorge, the spirits had scattered in every direction, but this one had apparently stayed, or else she had found them again.

"I've been talking with the new ones," she said. "They remember being in their homes only yesterday. They remember when the first nova appeared, and some people went mad. They started babbling nonsense, and many of them were killed, at least in Spain. I think *we* are those mad ones. Our spirits left our bodies behind and came here. Now that these new ones have come, I think it must have happened again."

Maasha Kaatra covered his face with his hands and let out a cry. "I have done this," he said. "I have killed these people, separated daughters from fathers."

" Our loved ones may even be hearing what we are really saying, only it doesn't make any sense to them, so they call it babbling," the spirit voice said. "Especially at the beginning, when anything we said would have been panicked, full of screams and crying."

"Who are you?" Catherine asked.

The light bobbed. "My name is Antonia."

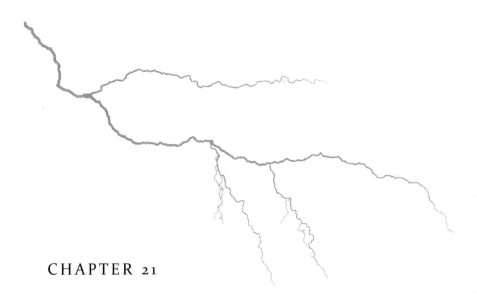

CHAPTER 21

AS her confessor, Ramos was permitted to see Elizabeth in the Tower before her execution. She had shaved her head and wore a simple dress of brilliant white. Kat Ashley, her former governess and now chief gentlewoman, had been imprisoned in Fleet Street, but Blanche Parry, Dee's cousin, was here with her. Blanche was in her forties, dressed stiffly in a black gown with a high neck, the white ruffles almost covering her chin. She stood behind the princess, stroking her scalp and crying.

"It doesn't have to happen like this," Ramos said. "We could make a break for it right now. We'd have a good chance."

"A good chance," Elizabeth echoed, with a quirk of one eyebrow.

"Well, a better chance than we'll have once you put your head down on that swordsman's block."

Elizabeth stood and put a hand on his shoulder. "This is the right path. The people need to see me facing my death bravely, not sneaking off like an escaped convict. Now, are you ready with everything we need?"

Ramos nodded. He pulled a bottle from inside his robes and handed it to her. "It has to cover every inch of your body. Every inch." Then he flushed, realizing what he had just said to a princess.

Elizabeth handed the bottle to Blanche, apparently unconcerned. "I understand. And afterward?"

Ramos spread his arms helplessly. "It is as ready as it could be. But the risks are high, Your Grace."

She brushed his words away. "The risks are always high. My mother died out on that block, you know." Of course, he knew. All the world knew of the death of Anne Boleyn.

Elizabeth stood and approached her cell's small window, which looked down onto the Tower Green. The headsman's block was in clear view, as was the headsman himself, sharpening and polishing his axe. This was by design, of course, to give Elizabeth a chance to think on her sins.

"She had the king my father dancing like a marionette on a string, helpless to resist her," Elizabeth continued. "Until the day it all turned upside-down, and the very feminine allure that had given her so much power seemed to the king like it must have been black magic, a power of the devil used to enthrall him." Elizabeth turned back from the window to face Ramos. "In short, she made the king feel foolish, and that you must never do."

"Never?" Ramos said, thinking of what they were about to do.

That elicited a tiny laugh. "Well, only when you can't help it," she said.

The sounds of voices rose through her window. Ramos glanced out to see that a boat had arrived with the queen's Chancellor, Stephen Gardiner, as well as Cardinal Pole, the Archbishop of Canterbury, and a host of their attendants.

Ramos bowed. "I should leave you to finish your preparations," he said. "I will stand at the door. If any come, I will say you are within, praying for your eternal soul. When you are ready, knock, and I will let them pass."

Elizabeth held out her hand for Ramos to kiss. He knelt and touched his lips briefly to her fingers. He found that he was shaking. "You have been a loyal subject and friend," she said. "Go in peace,

and whatever happens, be strong. A clear and innocent conscience
need fear nothing."

He bowed again and left her.

THERE had been no reason to hurry. Hours passed while crowds
gathered outside. Finally, four Tower guards, resplendent in their red
livery, came for Elizabeth, and Ramos rapped lightly to let her know it
was time. As she stepped out of her room, one of the guards tried to
take her arm, but she gave him such a glare that he pulled his hand
back as if burned.

Blanche Parry was gone. She had not been a prisoner herself, and
had been free to leave. Ramos hoped Elizabeth had told her to get as
far away from London as she could. After today, she would not fare
well if she were caught by Mary's agents.

At the bottom of the stairs, they emerged into bright sunlight.
Two ranks of Tower guards, halberds held high, kept back the crowd
and made a straight path toward the headsman's block. Elizabeth
stumbled as she saw it, but she quickly regained her balance and
made her way forward with poised and regal bearing. She looked
every inch a queen, despite her simple dress and shaved head.

A huge crowd had come to see the spectacle, but most of them
were outside the Tower's outer walls, unable to view the event itself.
The crowd permitted inside were mostly aristocracy and loyal
supporters of the king and queen, though even that was enough to fill
the inner ward from Constable Tower all the way around to
Wakefield Tower and right up to the edge of the green itself.
Elizabeth would have preferred to be executed on Tower Hill, where
everyone could have seen her, but of course Philip had designed it
this way.   He wanted her death to be public, and thus
incontrovertible, but not so public that her final words or actions
could influence the people.

It wouldn't matter, Ramos thought.   If everything went as
planned, today's events would spread through the masses like a city
fire, whether they saw it with their own eyes or not.

The block was on a raised platform, covered with straw to soak up the worst of the blood. Elizabeth mounted the platform without a pause, and Ramos, as the representative of the church, followed behind her. Wind whipped his robes. The Tower's ravens croaked from their perches on the battlements, anticipating that another head would soon be mounted on the wall for them to peck at.

The executioner knelt before Elizabeth. "I beg your pardon, my lady."

It was customary for a headman to ask those convicted to pardon him for his act. Since the swiftness of death was in his hands—a botched execution might take four or five strokes to finally sever the head—prisoners were often quick to do so, and even to pay him for his services. Elizabeth, however, looked down at him with steel in her eyes. "God forgive you," she said in a ringing voice, "but I never can."

Startled, he rose to his feet and lifted his axe. Elizabeth ignored him and faced the crowd. King Philip and Queen Mary sat on a raised platform of their own outside the Chapel of St. Peter ad Vincula, surrounded by all their attendants. There were also Nicholas Heath, the Archbishop of York; Lord Russell and William Paget, Keepers of the Privy Seal; as well as the Chief Justices and Secretaries and Lord Treasurers, the Chief Barons, and the Masters of the Rolls. Beyond them, and in a circle to every side, were all the lords and nobles and their families, with many of their servants, every one of them here to watch Elizabeth die.

"My people," Elizabeth said. "Loyal subjects and traitors both." This was treason, but it could hardly matter at this point. "I stand here accused because I will not recant my Protestant faith. Much blood has been lost over this issue, but that we cannot change. The past cannot be cured. Only the future lies within our power, and for that, I beg you, consider carefully whom you will follow. The powerful are not always the good, and those who appear the most sanctified are sometimes the worst of men.

"As for me, I ask only that God will judge me justly for my deeds. If my crimes are as great as my sister, Mary, deems them to be, let my blood flow across these grounds for all to see and wonder at. If, however, I have not sinned, may my life today be spared, as witness to all of you that my cause is just."

King Philip smirked. Even now, he didn't see what was coming. The deception bothered Ramos, but only a little. It was, after all, exactly the sort of trickery Philip himself had employed at the burning of Charles Shiveley, using quintessence to give the impression of divine intervention. The justice of it pleased him.

Elizabeth drew back her hood and knelt in front of the block. She stretched her beautiful, vulnerable neck across the dark wood. Without her hair, she seemed tiny, like a child, and it was all Ramos could do to play his part.

"Elizabeth, I call on you to renounce your heresy and cling to Christ for mercy," he said in a loud voice. "Acknowledge the Holy Father as God's authority on Earth and your sister Mary as the rightful queen, and even now, you shall be pardoned your crimes."

He looked down at her and saw that she was shaking. She placed her arms behind her back and said, "Never."

Ramos nodded at the headsman and took a step back. The man flexed his fingers and grasped the pole of the axe with a sure grip. Muscles rippled as he took his stance and lifted the axe over his head. When Elizabeth's mother had been executed on this spot, King Henry VIII had sent to France for an expert swordsman to insure that her death was quick and clean. For Elizabeth, however, no such expense had been made.

With a grunt, the headsman swung the axe down, throwing his weight into the blow. The blade flew through her delicate neck and embedded itself in the wood beneath. The head did not fall. There was no blood. The executioner himself was the first to notice that something was wrong. It had been too easy; there had been no resistance as bone and flesh were severed. The rest of the crowd didn't realize what had happened until Elizabeth lifted her head.

Gasps spread throughout the crowd, turning into shouts as Elizabeth stood up, unharmed. The headsman crossed himself and backed away. A few people screamed. Elizabeth raised her hands and spun slowly, letting them see her unmarked neck and her white dress free of blood, for all the world like an angel come to Earth.

Philip was on his feet, shouting. Soldiers ran toward them,

weapons drawn. Ramos took Elizabeth's hand. "Time to go," he said. They jumped down from the platform and ran back the way they had come. Soldiers presented their halberds and tried to prevent their escape, but Ramos and Elizabeth ran right through them, to shouts of fear and consternation.

King Philip had been demanding a supply of this liquid, but Ramos had put him off, saying that he had used all of his supply on his demonstration, and it would take weeks to gather more from the bird. In fact, it worked even greatly diluted, and Ramos could easily have supplied some to the king and still had enough left for himself and Elizabeth. However, he had wanted to make sure that there would be no chance of them meeting a squadron of soldiers whose swords could pierce their otherwise insubstantial bodies.

Ramos hadn't bothered to bring a weapon. He didn't want to kill anyone; he just wanted to escape, and there was no one who could stop them. They raced through the stones of the inner wall to the outer ward. On the other side of the outer wall was the moat, and their quintessence magic wouldn't allow them to fly over that. Instead, they ran around the outer ward to Byward Tower, and through that to the bridge. The portcullis crashed down, but they passed through it without pausing and across the drawbridge, ignoring the hail of arrows raining down on them from above.

On the other side, a Protestant friend of Barrosa's was waiting for them with two horses. They each vaulted into a saddle—treated with wax so they wouldn't fall through—while the man who had brought the horses melted back into the crowd gathered outside the Tower. By this time, Elizabeth had been recognized. A huge roar went up, mostly cheers, and she waved to them from atop her horse. She trotted in a quick circle, demonstrating that she was unharmed, and then rode into the crowd.

The people parted for her, like the waters of the Red Sea. Men threw cloaks down in the mud for her horse to trample. Women called out blessings and shouted her name. Some cursed her as well, calling her heretic or traitor or whore, but most seemed inclined to love her. Even without her hair, she was beautiful, but not like a peasant girl was beautiful. Elizabeth was regal, supernatural, untouchable. She looked like nothing so mundane as an execution could have any hold on her. As if she would be young forever. When the queen's soldiers came racing after them, the gap in the crowd closed, blocking their path.

We made it, Ramos thought. *We really escaped.* Then an arrow flew over the crowd and embedded itself into his horse's flank. The animal screamed and reared. Ramos tumbled off and hit the ground hard. The panicked horse, its hooves flailing, came down on top of him.

FOR a time, everything was blood and chaos. The pursuing soldiers attacked the crowd with swords and arrows, and the people rioted, surging in every direction, sometimes around Ramos and sometimes—since the invisible bird's saliva was still working—right through him. He struggled to his feet. His horse was screaming and twisting on the ground in a pool of bright red blood.

Suddenly, Elizabeth was there, wheeling her horse around him to make a space in the mob. He clambered up behind her, and she galloped away at high speed, leaving him no choice but to put his arms around her to stay on.

By this time, their pursuers had found horses of their own. Ramos knew this escape could be disastrous to Mary's hold on power. Soon there would be dozens, if not hundreds, of men following them. The small advantage that the invisible bird's saliva had given them would soon wear off. If they could not lose their pursuers, they would eventually be found and captured. Barrosa and Ramos would certainly be killed, probably after torture. After a betrayal of this magnitude, Philip would want to make them suffer. Elizabeth might be kept alive until a second execution could be prepared, but it would be swift, and without help, she would not escape a second time.

The most critical part of their escape would be making it to London Bridge before they were cut off. Their destination was a home on Tooley Street in Southwark where a small band of Protestants loyal to Elizabeth were waiting to bring them to

Gravesend, where a ship could take them across the channel to the Netherlands. The Netherlands was Protestant now, and would harbor Elizabeth while she gathered support to reclaim her throne. Ramos had already secretly relocated Antonia to Tooley Street, a risky move that might have doomed the whole plan if Philip had discovered it.

London Bridge, however, was the only bridge across the Thames. If the queen's soldiers blocked it, they would have no easy way across. As a backup plan, they would ride through the city to the horse ferry at Westminster, where Barrosa knew a man willing to take them across to Lambeth. This route took them right by Whitehall Palace, however, and required riding several miles through muddy, winding streets crammed with horsecarts and foot traffic without being caught.

London Bridge was their best chance. Their horse thundered through the streets, throwing up mud, heedless of pedestrians. The soldiers behind them shouted for them to stop. Elizabeth rode hard, avoiding obstacles with prodigious skill, but every time Ramos stole a look back, the soldiers seemed to be closer. The raw sewage smell of the Thames was strong; they must be close. Suddenly, they rounded a corner, and there was the bridge, so crowded with shops and buildings that one feared it might tip over from the weight.

He could tell there was something wrong as soon as they reached it. Normally it was choked with traffic, not just those trying to reach the other side, but those visiting the shops along its length. But the bridge was empty.

"Where are all the people?" Ramos said.

Elizabeth glanced over her shoulder at him. "They all came to watch me die."

"There's something wrong."

"It's too late now," Elizabeth said. The pursuing soldiers had almost reached them. There was no time to change their plans. She spurred the horse forward with a cry, and it thundered across the stones onto the bridge.

The buildings flanked the road, several stories high on each side, giving the impression that they were riding on a city street instead of a bridge. Most of the time, they couldn't even see the water. Some buildings even connected over the road, forcing them to ride through dark tunnels.

They flew past shop after shop, past the rows of latrines that emptied out into the river below, past the Chapel of St. Thomas, a church dedicated to Thomas Beckett that was larger than some churches built on land. When they passed around the chapel and through the narrowest arch of the bridge, Elizabeth wheeled the horse around and turned to face their pursuers. As the first two charged through the arch after them, they exploded into flame. The horses collapsed, blocking the tunnel, already dead. Their riders were blackened ash. The next horse collided into this devastation and went down, catapulting his rider off of his back before he, too, burst into white flames.

The tunnel was black with smoke and barricaded with blackened corpses. Frightened whinnies and shouts could be heard from the other side. Juan Barrosa emerged from the passage where he'd been hiding with the *Ignis Dei* for the better part of the day. "Right on schedule," he said. "Lucky I had it primed."

Elizabeth still stared at the destruction. "I had no idea," she said. "You told me what it could do, but I didn't realize . . ."

"We can't wait," Ramos said. "Let's go."

Barrosa lifted the *Ignis Dei* onto his own horse and jumped into the saddle. They galloped the rest of the way to the end of the bridge toward Southwark. The top of the south gate bristled with pikes on which human heads were impaled, gruesome and covered in tar. These were all that was left of criminals who had been convicted by the crown of high treason. Ramos couldn't tear his eyes away.

If this went poorly, it would be his own head grinning down from there before the end of the day.

As they hurtled through the gate, it suddenly became clear why the bridge was deserted. At least a hundred soldiers stood solemnly in ranks, guarding the gate. They were facing south, away from the gate, though some of them turned as Ramos, Elizabeth, and Barrosa bore down on them. Philip and Mary must have feared a rebellion, that someone would mount an assault on the city to rescue Elizabeth, so they had posted soldiers here to guard the bridge.

The soldiers hadn't been expecting anyone from the bridge, so they were slow to act. Elizabeth spurred her horse on, charging right past them, and Barrosa followed just behind.

"That's the princess!" an officer shouted. "After them!" Soldiers ran to their horses to give pursuit.

Elizabeth, Barrosa, and Ramos turned a corner, out of view for the moment, but knowing it wasn't for long. This was not good. They needed more time, time to board a coach and leave the city without the king knowing which way they had gone. The coach would bring them to Gravesend, where they could board the ship for the Netherlands.

Ramos had never been on this side of the Thames before. He barely saw it now, jostled on the back of the sweating horse as Elizabeth urged it ever faster. It was an ugly part of the city, a place for bear-baiting, gambling, and whoring. Taverns and brothels whisked by along with cheap tenement housing and the occasional playhouse. Finally, they reached an inn on Tooley Street, where the coach was waiting for them with fresh horses.

They handed their mounts to the men who had risked their lives to make this escape possible. "Bless you," Elizabeth said. "Get out of sight now; there are soldiers coming."

"Quickly," Ramos said, and ducked inside. He breathed a prayer of thanks at the sight of Antonia, already seated, mumbling rapid nonsense to herself. He gave her an embrace that she neither responded to nor seemed to notice, but that was all right. She was safe. All the way from the Tower, he had worried that their plan might have been found out, that Antonia would be in a dungeon, or worse, already dead, a victim of the king's wrath.

Elizabeth climbed in across from him, and with a cry from the driver, the horses broke into a run, and the carriage lurched forward with the clatter of wooden wheels on paving stones. The friends who had helped them scattered.

As they drove east out of Southwark and into farming country, Ramos kept checking behind them for signs of pursuit. Cows meandered near the road, and sheep dotted the grassy hills farther south. Could they really have made it away safely? His heart began to slow down, and he dared to hope.

"They say that a star disappeared from the sky, and some people went mad," Antonia said.

Ramos whirled to face her. "What did you say?"

She didn't meet his eye or acknowledge his presence. "They started babbling nonsense, and many of them were killed, at least in Spain. I think *we* are the mad ones they're talking about," she said.

A rush of heat flooded through Ramos's chest. Antonia spoke from time to time, and occasionally her speech made a kind of sense, though never in context. But this was the first time he had heard her actually refer to her own condition, or to the nova.

"Our spirits left our bodies behind and came here. Our loved ones may even be hearing what we are really saying, only it doesn't make any sense to them, so they call it babbling," Antonia said.

This time, Ramos couldn't help it. He started to cry. He snatched up her hands and squeezed them. "I'm here, Antonia!" he shouted. Elizabeth and Barrosa watched in astonishment, looking back and forth between them.

"She is aware," Elizabeth said. "She is alive and thinking and interacting somewhere, just not here."

Ramos passed a hand in front of Antonia's eyes, but she didn't blink. "Could she be in another body? Living somewhere else in the world, but unable to return?"

"Perhaps she is in heaven," Elizabeth said. "Perhaps her soul has passed on to the blessed realm, but something has prevented her body from being severed completely from it."

Ramos remembered Antonia's terrified screaming from the night the nova had first appeared. "I don't think so," he said.

"Do you hear that?" Barrosa said, suddenly tense.

"What?"

"Hoofbeats."

Ramos concentrated. Yes, he could make out another set of hoofbeats, faster than their own. He leaned out of the carriage and looked behind. A plume of dust billowed in the distance.

"We're being followed!" he shouted to the driver. "Hurry!"

The driver cracked the reins, and the carriage picked up speed.

Without a carriage to pull, however, their pursuers were faster. It was hopeless, Ramos knew. They could never outrun them, now that they had been spotted.

"We need to stop the coach," Ramos said. "Your Grace, you must take a horse and ride. On your own, you might elude them."

"No. I will not abandon you," she said.

"Please. It is to save you that we risked everything. If you, at least, were spared . . ."

She held his gaze, her eyes green and clear. "What kind of ruler would I be if I left my friends to die while I saved myself?"

Matchlocks fired behind them, and Ramos heard one ball thud into the wood of the carriage. There were empty fields around them in every direction, with nowhere to run and nowhere to hide.

"Thank you for your loyal service," Elizabeth said.

Ramos grimaced. "Don't give up hope quite yet. I have one last desperate trick to pull." He pulled a chicken bone out of his pocket and began to talk to it. "Matthew," he said. "Are you there?"

***

MATTHEW followed his father out of the cave, with Parris wandering distractedly behind him. Ferguson and Craddock flanked them, making sure they didn't speak with any of the other colonists on their way out. Matthew suspected the others were being given salt only to the degree that they were loyal to Ferguson. Those closest to him were the most powerful; those suspected of disagreeing with his leadership were given short rations, if any at all. It was the feudal system back again: a single lord who controlled the natural resource (in this case, salt instead of land), and thus controlled all the people as well. In retrospect, Matthew realized they'd been foolish to overlook this kind of power grab as a possibility.

Out of the caves, they headed north, higher up into the mountains. Matthew didn't know where his father was leading them, if anywhere. They were three humans in a vast wilderness, driven out by their own people, their home destroyed, and with enemies on every side. They had nowhere to go. They made camp in the shadow of a large rock jutting out of the mountainside, though with no supplies and without quintessence, their shelter was damp and exposed, and all they had to eat was a meager collection of roots and greens that Parris scavenged for them. It demonstrated how dependent they were on quintessence for everything.

Matthew sank to the ground and put his head in his hands. "What are we going to do?" he said.

"God will provide, as he has always done. We will pray and wait on his goodness," his father said.

It was something Matthew himself might have said two years earlier, before coming to Horizon, but a lot had changed since then. He was no longer afraid of his father, nor afraid of disagreeing with him. "Always provided? What does that mean? Catherine is dead. She's not coming back, and I don't know what I'll do without . . . I don't know how to live without . . ." Tears flooded into his eyes, but he gritted his teeth and didn't let himself cry. This was no time to grieve.

"Thanks to me, the colony is totally destroyed," he continued. "Ferguson thinks we need new leadership, and maybe he's right. With your passive piety and my wild experimentation, we haven't done very well by them, have we?"

"We did the best we could, by God's grace. And will continue to," his father said.

Matthew hurled a stone into the trees, where it cracked against a rock and then bounced soundlessly through the foliage. "Continue how? Ferguson threatened to kill us if we come back, which he would be very able to do, since he controls all the salt. The Spanish would kill us for sure, or worse, torture us and make us tell them how to find and kill everyone else. We can't get home, and our best allies are a tribe of manticores who are less than hospitable and only agreed to help us when they thought we could provide help in return."

"For someone who worships reason and logic, you're not thinking very clearly," his father said mildly.

Matthew raised an eyebrow. "No? I think I laid out our situation pretty plainly."

"That's because you're so focused on yourself. You think it's your fault that Catherine may be dead." Matthew tried to object, but his father held up a hand. "I say *may* be dead, because we only have the word of one who did not see it happen. But that's not my point. My point is that you feel like you should have stopped her from going or should have protected her better. And you think it's your fault that the settlement was destroyed."

"It was my experiment!"

His father gave him the sort of glare that had sent him scurrying when he was young. "Close your mouth and listen to what I'm saying. It's not all about you. You're so wrapped up in your inventions that you think the only way a problem can be solved is if you do it yourself."

"So I should sit around and do nothing?"

"You just finished telling me how powerless we are. So instead of despairing and blaming yourself for what you can't do, acknowledge that life . . . that reality . . . is a lot bigger than you are. That there's more to life than you can measure or control."

Matthew stood up, annoyed. "I don't understand this. Didn't you teach me to take responsibility for my actions?"

"Yes. But not to take responsibility for everything that happens. God is telling this story, not you. No matter how much power or knowledge you have, you can't write the ending."

"So you want me to give up."

His father sighed. "I think you know what I'm telling you. You just don't want to listen."

"I am listening. I know what you think; I always have. I just don't agree."

Matthew wasn't sure his father would ever understand. What he saw as the best hope for the future of mankind, his father saw as an obsession with the unnatural and a rejection of the Almighty. His father blamed him for the decreasing attendance at Sunday worship services and the colonists' increasing self-reliance where they should be sensing their need for God. Most people believed in God out of a fear of the supernatural. Storms, lightning, and disease were all ways that God showed his displeasure with the sins of men. But what if those things could be understood and controlled? What was left for

God?

Parris stood up. "Something is happening," he said.

They both looked at him. Matthew had almost forgotten he was there. "What do you mean?"

"Among the manticores," Parris said. "Something big. Loyalties are changing. The tribal structure is being overturned. And something else . . ."

The ground heaved under Matthew's feet, throwing him sideways. He landed painfully, twisting his wrist under his body. The rock they were sheltering under split with a deafening crack. The mountain seemed alive, like a giant waking up. It reminded him of a year ago, when the island had been sliding over the edge of the world.

"What's happening?" Matthew shouted.

"The lords of the earth are rising!" Parris shouted back.

"What does that mean?"

The massive rock above them shifted and leaned toward them. "Run!" Marcheford said. They ran out from under it just as it crashed down, exploding into shards. The whole mountain shook under them. Boulders sheared off from cliffs higher up the mountain, starting avalanches of uprooted trees and rubble.

It started to rain. Sheets of water pelted down on them from above, and lightning split the sky. They ran, the ground uncertain beneath their feet, looking for shelter.

"Matthew!" said a voice. "Are you there?"

It wasn't his father or Parris talking, and there wasn't anyone else around. Besides, the force of the rain was so loud he wouldn't have been able to hear anyone who wasn't right next to him. It took him a moment to realize it was coming from his pocket.

He snatched out the stick that Blanca had given him. "Ramos?"

"Let's do it," Ramos's voice said from the stick. "Just like we talked about."

"Not right now," Matthew said, tripping over a root, and then regaining his balance. "We're a bit busy at the moment."

"It's now or never," Ramos said.

"We're running away from an earthquake. If we survive the next five minutes, I'll give it a try."

"If we don't do it this instant, it'll be too late, and I'll be dead," Ramos said.

"I can't. I don't even have any vitriol," Matthew said.

"You said you'd be ready for us." Ramos's voice was angry, despairing.

"There!" Parris shouted. There was a depression in the mountainside, not a cave, exactly, but a indentation with a narrow rock ledge. They huddled underneath it, out of the rain, but it was barely enough to fit them.

"We can't stay long," Matthew's father said. "This whole mountain could come down on top of us."

"Wait," Matthew said to Ramos. "I shouldn't need the vitriol. The quintessence thread tied to the stick is holding the void open. It never really closed. That's why we can hear you whenever you speak through it."

"It doesn't matter," Ramos said. "I've got a void here, and I have nothing to lose. We'll risk it."

"Who are you talking to?" Parris said.

"Make some room." Matthew set the stick on the ground in the middle of their little shelter. "We think solid matter can travel along a quintessence thread, just like sound can. We saw it happen with smoke, which is just burned particles of matter. We planned to test the theory with larger things, even living things, but we haven't had a chance."

The mountainside shuddered. They could feel it vibrating through their feet.

"We should go on!" Matthew's father shouted.

"We have to wait, just a little longer."

"Why?"

"This stick is tethered to a quintessence thread that reaches all the way back to London. We've been talking to two men there—Spanish by birth, but they're on our side—only they were afraid they might need to escape London in a hurry."

Parris got it right away. "You mean these men are going to try to *travel* from London to Horizon through a void?" The idea obviously excited him, but there was horror in his voice as well. "How do you know it won't kill them? The void is pure nothing, just the space between the atoms. What if the atoms of their bodies just fly apart? What if they go into the void and never come out?"

Matthew spread his hands. "I don't know," he said. "We were going to test it first, and answer those questions, but we've been running for our lives."

Around the edges of the stick, a void began to form, its deep blackness seeming to suck the light out of their little shelter. Parris gasped. "I've never seen it just form like that, all by itself."

"It never completely closed," Matthew said. "They must be coming through right now." He looked at his father. "There's one more thing you should know."

"What's that?"

"There's someone else with them. Someone who desperately needs to get away from King Philip and Queen Mary."

His father gave him a wary look. "You don't mean . . ."

Matthew nodded. "The princess Elizabeth is coming with them."

THE VOID yawned black and terrifying, taking up half of the carriage. It had already annihilated a section of upholstery and some of the floor.

"What is that?" Elizabeth said, terror plain on her face.

"An escape route. I hope," Ramos said.

The soldiers were gaining on them, shouting at the driver to stop. They had only seconds, but Ramos hesitated. Now that he was facing it, it seemed like a terrible idea. The void was rapacious, growing larger and devouring everything it touched. It was like throwing oneself into a dragon's mouth.

Just as he was about to jump, the soldiers shot the driver. Tumbling from his seat atop the carriage, he dragged the reins with him, and the horses veered, pulling the carriage up on two wheels around a sharp turn. They were all thrown to one side of the carriage. They grabbed for handholds, all except for Antonia, who fell silently out onto the road, disappearing from view behind them.

"No!" Ramos shouted, reaching out for her, too late.

The carriage, off-balance, teetered for a moment, and then crashed to the ground on its side, dragged along until the horses, terrified and tangled in their harnesses, tripped over each other and sprawled, neighing in terror.

Ramos scrambled out. Antonia lay on the road, unmoving. Beyond her, a dozen mounted soldiers thundered toward them, on a path to trample her. Ramos didn't hesitate. He ran straight toward the horses, calling Antonia's name.

He reached her first, and lifted her to her feet. She seemed bruised, but unharmed. He dragged her back toward the carriage, and she complied as always, but without urgency, completely unaware of the pounding hooves getting closer every moment.

The void was destroying the carriage. It grew, swallowing the wood and enveloping the wheels. Elizabeth stood nearby, looking helpless in the simple white dress she still wore. Barrosa ran up to Ramos, dragging the *Ignis Dei* along behind him. "Run," he said. "I'll buy some time."

Ramos didn't argue. He propelled Antonia as quickly as he could, back toward what was left of the carriage. Barrosa poured salt into the device, but Ramos could see he was too late. The soldiers surrounded him, pointing their weapons and shouting at him to step away.

It was now or never. Ramos faced the void. "I'll go first," he said to Elizabeth, swallowing. "If I survive, you can follow." But he still could not move.

"There's no time for chivalry," Elizabeth said, and hurled herself into the void. It was as if she had jumped into a well. He saw her falling, the shape of her dwindling into the distance far below.

Mortified at her bravery and his own cowardice, Ramos steeled himself. Whatever she was facing, he wasn't going let her do it alone. A shot fired. He felt no impact, no pain, but when he looked at Antonia, blood was running freely down her neck, bright and red, soaking her dress. He grabbed for her as she sank to her knees. Her blood ran onto the ground, staining the dusty road.

There was only one choice. He lifted her in his arms, stumbling with the weight, and hurled her into the void.

Before leaping after her, he took one glance back at Barrosa, and saw something he should have noticed from the beginning. Barrosa had removed the wooden barrier between the salt-soaked pearl and the prism and had used it to *block* the opening through which the invisible light was supposed to pour. He raised his hands in apparent surrender, but the device was glowing, increasing in intensity.

"No!" Ramos shouted. But it was too late. The *Ignis Dei* exploded. The flame roared like a living thing, devouring Barrosa, the soldiers, and their horses together, leaping high into the air. Ramos felt the heat rush over him like a burning wind. A few soldiers at the periphery screamed and ran, their clothing aflame, but the *Ignis Dei* and Juan Barrosa were simply gone.

Ramos bellowed his grief. The edges of the void shimmered, about to collapse. He hurled himself into its open mouth.

He fell for what seemed like miles, deeper than any hole, farther than a jump off any building or cliff. He fell, and then, before he could steel himself for it, a light flashed up from below and swallowed him. He crashed into rocky ground, hard enough to hurt, but not enough to injure.

The ground heaved under his feet. He was dizzy, disoriented. Rain was falling so thickly it was hard to see, and his clothes were soaked through in a moment. The void he had just fallen through collapsed and popped shut with the finality of a slamming prison door.

Strangers pulled at him. "Come on!" they said. "Run!"

He stood and staggered after them. One of the men was bleeding. No, it was Antonia who was bleeding, and the man was carrying her. Elizabeth was there, too, apparently unharmed. Rocks the size of Ramos's head tumbled down the mountainside, one narrowly missing him as it hurtled past.

Suddenly, they were surrounded by the most bizarre creatures he had ever seen: crouched monsters with orange fur, pincers for hands, and hooks where their feet should be. They just appeared out of the air, all around them in a moment. The creatures grabbed onto their clothes with their pincers and lifted them high. Ramos thrashed and screamed for Antonia, but he couldn't get away. The men he didn't know—presumably Matthew and two other colonists—weren't fighting their captors, so Ramos allowed himself to be carried. Where were they going?

It didn't take long to find out. The creatures brought them into a cave, the opening just a horizontal crevice where one jutting rock face overlapped another. Ramos didn't think he would even have noticed the opening, but the creatures and humans squeezed through. Inside, the rumbling of the mountain seemed distant, and they were blessedly out of the sheeting rain.

Inside was a cavern, larger than he expected, with more of the strange creatures, and two women. The creatures set them on the ground. One of the women leaned over Antonia, tilting her head forward and pouring water into her mouth. Ramos crawled to her. There was a lot of blood, her dress stained red with it, but he could see no wound. The bullet must have struck her in the neck, but there was nothing. To his shock, Antonia sat up and looked around, apparently unharmed.

"She'll be fine," the woman said. "It's the quintessence water; it's healed her already."

Ramos wiped water out of his face and eyes. "Barrosa," he said. He could hardly speak. The image of his friend burning himself to death overwhelmed his mind.

Elizabeth caught his arm. "What happened to Barrosa? Is he coming?"

Ramos shook his head. "Dead," he managed to say.

"Ramos?" Elizabeth said. "Where are we?"

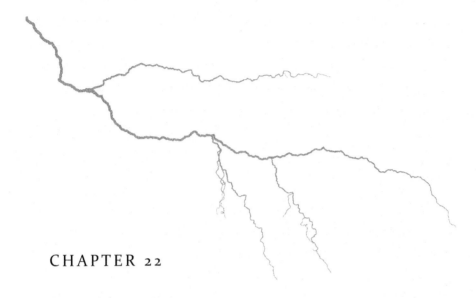

CHAPTER 22

ALVARO de Torres was astonished that the manticore creature could speak. And not only speak, but insist on discussing the terms of an alliance, as if they were equals. He hadn't heard of such a thing happening since Baalam's donkey spoke on the road to Moab. He would catch one of these manticores and bring it home with him, if he could. A talking animal would cause quite the stir at court.

Though it was fitting that the language the creature spoke was English. Torres had always considered the English people little more than animals themselves, so the language probably came more naturally to it than Spanish or Latin. In his one visit to London, Torres had been astonished by the lack of civilization. The English had no sense of art or sculpture, and what little they displayed had been imported from Spain or Italy. Their entertainments were brutal and uncouth. Bathing seemed to have been a lost art form, if they had ever discovered it. And their women hadn't the least sense of proper manners or gentility. In short, they were barely progressed beyond the Celtic savages they had displaced. If they had found common ground with animals, Torres was not surprised.

He had instructed his men to bring this creature, this *Rinchirith*, onto the deck of *La Magdalena*. From here, they could see the conquistadors on the beach, drilling. He didn't yet know what strength the manticore might have, but it seemed practical to intimidate him as much as possible, to get the meeting started on the right footing. If Rinchirith could lead him to where the remaining colonists were hiding out, or assist him in finding and gathering the valuable goods he had been sent to procure, then it would be worth playing the game of collaboration and alliance.

Torres had been to the settlement. He had seen the melted remains of what must have once been grand buildings. He had also seen the defense that even a single colonist had been able to mount to evade capture. If all of the colonists could run like the wind and cast blinding light from their bodies, they would be formidable opponents. Already apostate, they had apparently made a pact with the devil to gain unearthly powers, with the consequence that the powers had come back to destroy them. That was always the way with sin. It seemed so good at the time, but later, it destroyed your life. Buried memories clawed for the surface of his mind, but Torres shoved them back down again.

It didn't matter. What mattered was this moment, this meeting. An officer who spoke English stood by to translate their conversation.

The manticore's gray fur rippled in the breeze. It snapped its pincers open and shut. "Greetings," it said. Its tails moved in a complex way that made Torres feel faintly nauseated. "I am called Rinchirith." The translator stumbled a bit over the pronunciation of the name.

"What can I do for you?" Torres said.

" I believe you can help me, and in return, I can help you. I wish to unite my people into one tribe," Rinchirith said.

"I see," Torres replied. "With yourself as chief, no doubt."

"I have many who follow me. But many more do not. If I am seen to have the friendship of the human people, more will join me."

"No doubt."

"I have seen a vision of the future. I have seen your people coming here in great numbers, relentless. I used to think we should destroy you, but you are like the cacari that lives in our forests. If we cut off your arm, another grows in its place. Instead of fighting, I wish to join my power with yours."

"And what do you suppose that you can do to help me?" Torres said.

"I will fight with you against your enemies, both human and manticore."

It was laughable, really. This creature probably had a dozen warriors fighting with sticks and clubs, and he wanted to ally himself with the most powerful empire in the world. Torres glanced out at his six hundred armed conquistadors marching on the beach. "Yes?" he said. "And how many fighting men can you contribute to this cause?"

"There are thirty thousand manticores who have pledged their lives to mine," Rinchirith said. The translator spoke the words with no emotion, but Torres got a sense of barely suppressed rage from the manticore's tone and body language.

"Thirty thousand!" Torres laughed. "Quite a number. Can he corroborate that?"

There was some back and forth between the translator and the manticore as the meaning of the word 'corroborate' was discussed. Rinchirith bared his teeth.

"He says he can show you," the translator said.

Rinchirith gave a piercing shriek, and all around him, more manticores appeared, literally springing into reality out of thin air. They covered the deck, surrounding Torres and his men, and clambered all through the rigging. On shore, they appeared as well, a host of them all around his men and continuing back into the trees as far as he could see. There were, indeed, thousands of them. Many were the same gray color as Rinchirith, but others were white, orange, brown, and black. The manticores began to snap their pincers together in eerie unison.

Torres tried to back away, but there was nowhere to go that was not covered with manticores. All these thousands had been there, invisible, all the time. His heart thundered in his chest. He was not ready to die. The manticores leaped up and down into the boat's hold by passing straight through the deck, as insubstantial as air. Yet it was clear that those pincers could cut and those teeth bite if they wanted to attack.

"Do we have an agreement?" Rinchirith asked.

"Of course," Torres said. He took a deep breath, got control. "We would be glad to help you fight your enemies in return for your assistance fighting ours. We grant you exclusive trading rights and agree to support you over any rival leadership, in return for which you will furnish us with those goods we wish to take home to our masters."

Rinchirith bared his teeth again, and Torres wondered if it was a grimace or a smile. "Agreed," he said. "As a sign of good faith, we will show you where the human vermin are hiding."

Torres smiled uncertainly. This was good progress, wasn't it? He had barely landed, and already he was on good terms with a powerful local chieftain who would help him find and kill the English. He got the impression, though, that Rinchirith would just as readily apply the term 'vermin' to Torres himself.

<hr />

MATTHEW had never been so happy to see a crowd of red manticores materialize out the air around him. He wondered if Parris had called them through his bond with Tanalabrinu. The manticores lifted them and carried them through the storm until they arrived at a hidden cave entrance and slipped through. Inside, they found Blanca and Joan Parris waiting for them. Parris ran to his wife and embraced her.

Three people had come through the void from England, one man and two young women, and only now was Matthew able to get a good look at them. He had never seen the Princess Elizabeth before, and at first glance, he wasn't sure which of the girls was her. Both were young, bedraggled, and dirty. One was shaved bald, and the other was covered in blood.

Blanca went immediately to the injured one and gave her a drink of quintessence water from a flask at her belt, healing her wounds and washing the worst of the blood from her face and neck. The injured one was younger, Matthew could see now, which meant the one standing, whose head was shaved, was the princess. She looked like a girl, disoriented and clearly frightened by her surroundings.

Joan Parris was the first to kneel. "Your Grace," she said. Elizabeth extended a delicate hand in what seemed like an automatic gesture, and Joan kissed it.

Matthew and the others rushed to imitate her. Whatever, she might look like, this was *Elizabeth*, the Protestant princess and the hope of England.

Her hair had been shaved off for her execution, of course, and the simple white dress she wore was dirty with the dust of the road, but Matthew was surprised he had not realized at once who she was. She held herself erect and moved with the grace and bearing of a queen. The man with her, presumably Ramos de Tavera, seemed just as dazed. He gripped the hand of the first girl, who must be his niece, Antonia.

"Where are we?" Elizabeth asked. She looked as if she were trying not to cry.

"This is Horizon Island," Parris said.

"Horizon?" She looked at Ramos. "How is that possible?"

Blanca reached out and took her hand. "You're safe now, Your Grace," she said. Matthew hoped it was actually true.

"Why are we in a cave? Is your settlement nearby?" Elizabeth said.

Matthew explained to her, with comments inserted by his father and Blanca, of the destruction of their settlement, the arrival of the Spanish ships, the uneasy relationship with the manticores, and the coup by James Ferguson. She asked many questions—how many the Spanish were and how far away, what Ferguson was like, what resources they had. She had been transported thousands of miles from her home and dropped in an unfamiliar land among strangers, and yet her questions were precise, aimed at defining her situation and making plans. She was a survivor, Matthew realized, raised in a political environment where her life was always at risk. She had grown up in luxury, but she knew how to cope with peril. Despite the fact that they were nearly the same age, Matthew felt as if she were an adult with the wisdom of experience and years, while he was only a child.

"When Ferguson threw you out, we went to the manticore village looking for you," Blanca said. "Tanalabrinu knew what had happened, of course, and he had already mobilized this group to find you and bring you back to stay in their village. When the earthquake began and it started to storm, they brought us here instead."

"I'm sorry," Matthew said to Elizabeth. "We have no food to offer you, and no true shelter. If we had salt, we could create some food, produce a fire, and protect ourselves, but we don't even have that. I'm afraid you have escaped one desperate circumstance only to arrive at another."

"That's where you're wrong," Ramos said. He stood and began to untie his tunic.

"You don't believe me?" Matthew said.

"I meant, you're not as short on salt as you might think." Ramos pulled off his tunic to reveal a crude set of leather straps slung over his shoulder. Hanging from these were sacks, fat and heavy with their contents. Ramos reached into one of these and pulled out a handful of translucent crystals. "I came prepared," he said.

There was a combined cry of astonishment from the colonists at the sight of all that salt. Matthew laughed and clapped Ramos on the back. "I can't tell you what this means to us," he said. "Ferguson kept it all for himself, to solidify his power. With this, maybe we can take control again."

"It will be of no benefit to attack your fellow colonists," Elizabeth said. "There are precious few Englishmen on this island, and none to spare."

Matthew looked at the floor, embarrassed. "What then?"

Elizabeth's expression was serene. "We must convince them to join with us."

WHEN the rain had stopped and the ground settled, they

emerged from the cave. Ramos was struck by the alienness of the land around them. Dark clouds covered much of the sky, but not enough to hide the sun, which was too large by far. It dominated the sky, boiling everything in its heat and giving the air a tropical feel. He knew from speaking with Matthew, but could scarcely believe, that it would grow larger still as it sank toward evening, driving men and beasts to seek shelter from its rays. Then, once mercifully set, it would rise the next morning as tiny as a pinprick in the distant east, leaving a chill in the air.

They stood on a rocky promontory on the edge of a mountain, its base surrounded by forest, but the trees were not the elm and oak and ash he recognized. They were taller than seemed appropriate, their tops wreathed with a mossy fluff instead of leaves. Those leaves he did see were the wrong shape: round, or else stretched into long strips that fluttered in the breeze. He even saw a tree with only one enormous leaf lofted high in the air that caught the wind like a kite and collected sunlight far above its bare trunk.

The rocks were more familiar, but even they seemed different, a darker color than he expected, with here and there a jagged stone that shone a glossy black. The air smelled fresher than London, of course; that was to be expected, but there were new smells, too, scents he couldn't identify. He followed the others downhill, toward the forest, and when they entered the trees, he was struck by how differently it sounded than an English forest. When the wind blew, it didn't whisper through the trees so much as crackle, as the lower, dead layers of mossy foliage rattled against each other.

According to plan, Elizabeth, Joan, and Blanca split off in a different direction. Ramos stayed with the other men, leading Antonia by the hand. Before long, they could see a clearing in the trees ahead. Ramos heard people talking and smelled the smoke of fires. They emerged to see about a hundred people, many of them working to erect several buildings out of stone blocks and wooden beams. It was a moment before Ramos recognized what he was seeing.

The colonists were cutting up several large, recently-felled trees for their wood. Instead of using saws, however, they were using their hands. One would drive his hand into the trunk as easily as if it were air, tracing out the desired shape, and then remove the wood, cut with an edge as smooth as if it had been carefully sanded. The stone was quarried using the same method. Ramos had experience with matter passing through other matter, of course, but it had not realized it could be used to separate the atoms making up a material, and to see people doing it in so casual and efficient a manner took his breath away. The other men in his party seemed unimpressed, and Ramos marveled at how easily miracles could become commonplace when you saw them every day.

The work stopped as the colonists noticed them. Bishop Marcheford strode confidently into their midst, and Ramos followed in his wake with the others. "Where is Ferguson?" Marcheford bellowed. His face was thunderous, and Ramos had to admit he could put on an intimidating show. He spoke like a preacher, with the force of Scripture and the threat of brimstone rumbling under the words.

A tall man with such a weak chin that his face seemed to slide straight into his neck without interruption ducked into view from behind a stack of cut stone. "I thought I told you never to come back," he said. He tried to match Marcheford's tone, but he didn't have the voice for it, and he just came off sounding petulant.

"James Ferguson, you are hereby deposed as governor of Horizon," Marcheford pronounced. "By order of the rightful queen of England and this colony."

"Queen?" Ferguson said. He sneered as he advanced on Marcheford. "You have no salt, no friends, and nothing to offer these people. Even if you were here to apologize, I would run you off. As it is, you and your son and . . ." Ferguson trailed off as he saw Ramos. His eyes traveled up and down his body, and Ramos was conscious of his dark hair and Mediterranean features, not to mention the clerical garb he was still wearing. He was clearly Spanish, and a priest besides. "You didn't," Ferguson said.

Now other people were taking notice, and their eyes darted to the edges of the clearing.

"He sold us out!" Ferguson yelled. "He told the Spanish where we are."

Everyone came to their feet now, abandoning their building materials and scanning the trees for signs of attack. This was not going well.

"Listen, you young idiot," Marcheford said, his tone of confident command slipping. "I'm a bishop of the Anglican church. Do you think I would go running to a pack of papists?"

Ramos felt a surge of irritation, but he let it pass. He was, after all, throwing his lot in with exiles and heretics. He couldn't expect them to speak well of the Roman Church.

"Who's he, then? And why are you ordering us about in the name of Queen Mary?" Ferguson said.

"Not Mary," Marcheford said, exasperated. He made an attempt to bring the stentorian tone back to his voice. "I mean Her Majesty, trueborn daughter of King Henry the Eighth, Queen Elizabeth!"

At this pronouncement, a light blazed from the other side of the clearing. Every head turned in time to see Elizabeth striding out of the forest, aglow with quintessence light. It was a trick anyone in the colony could do, with quintessence water in their veins and enough salt to fuel it, but Elizabeth pulled it off with a ceremonial majesty that left no doubt as to her identity. The light streamed over her bare scalp, giving the impression of flowing, red-blond hair. Behind her, Blanca and Joan Parris walked, as if holding her train.

Elizabeth glided into the center of the stunned gathering, as poised as if she were arriving at a ball. Ramos knew she must still be terrified, not just of these people, but of the strangeness of the quintessence light streaming out of her body. But she gave no sign of it. She had slipped on majesty like a mask at a costume ball, and she radiated strength and purpose. "I am Elizabeth," she said. "I command your allegiance."

Ferguson opened and closed his mouth, unequal to the moment. Ramos watched him, knowing that the spell could be broken with a word. But Ferguson seemed entranced. He walked forward like a man in a dream, his eyes only on Elizabeth. She beamed at him, her beautiful face radiant despite the dirt still smudged there. He kneeled, rapt, and kissed her outstretched hand.

The other colonists rushed forward, kneeling in the dirt in front of her and reaching out to touch her hand or dress. Ramos remembered that these were Protestant refugees who had been forced to flee their homeland for their beliefs. To them, Elizabeth was a heroine, a saint, the savior they dreamed would take the throne someday and turn their nation back to Protestantism. And suddenly, here she was, the Protestant princess, impossibly materialized on this island. Most of them knew her face, but even those who had never seen her before recognized royalty in every graceful gesture and angle of her body.

"I will be as good to you as ever a queen was to her people," Elizabeth said. "Follow me, and I will lead you with all my will and power. And be persuaded that, at need for your safety, I will not hesitate to spend my blood."

Ramos already knew she was a remarkable woman, but he was amazed once again. She had done the impossible, simply by walking in and speaking it into being. Never mind that scant hours ago, she had stood on a scaffold, about to lose her head, and then had been thrown into this bizarre land with no preparation, a step ahead of death. She was now the undisputed queen of this colony. Whatever quarrels these people had harbored, they were forgotten, at least for this moment, swept aside in their united devotion to her. Ramos realized that he, too, was in love with her—not the everyday attraction a man might have for a woman, but the veneration of a mortal man for a goddess.

"I require shelter and refreshment, and then I will hold council," Elizabeth said. "We have much to discuss."

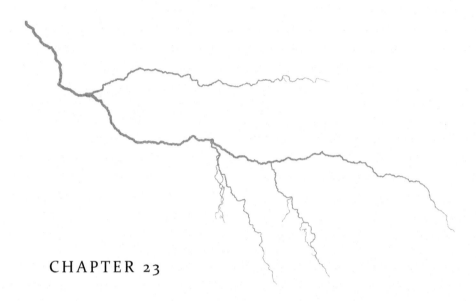

CHAPTER 23

FROM Antonia's description of her experiences, Catherine began to piece together an understanding of what had happened.

"So you were all born at the end of May?" Catherine said.

"The first group of us," Antonia said. "Everyone I asked, anyway. The second group that came was born in early February."

Catherine and Maasha Kaatra were sitting in the sheltered overhang where the manticores had left them, while Antonia flitted above them.

"Their souls must have been linked to the part of the sky that corresponds to your birth," Catherine said. "Maybe even with a normal quintessence thread, like we use all the time. When Maasha Kaatra drew the energy out of the sky, it drew the threads with it. Literally yanking your souls out of your bodies and bringing them here."

Antonia circled closer in lazy spirals. "I don't understand. The stars rotate around the Earth. If our souls were tied to the stars, wouldn't they be pulled out of our bodies every day as the heavens moved in their courses?"

Catherine was amazed. This girl, alone among all these roaming spirits, had been able to evaluate her situation and deduce what was happening to her. She had gathered enough information from talking with the others to realize that they all had similar birthdays, and that those birthdays corresponded to the appearance of the novas. What fourteen-year-old girl had the education to know so much about astronomy? And now she was asking difficult questions about the structure of the universe. She reminded Catherine of herself at that age, but Catherine had benefitted from her father's example. Who had taught Antonia to think of the natural world in so logical a way?

"Quintessence connections stretch as far as they need to. They're not like physical threads; they can stretch across the world," Catherine said.

"Then why were our souls pulled away at all?"

Another good question. Catherine remembered the experiment in Sinclair's house when he had successfully brought a bird back from the dead. The bird's spirit had leaped up out of the void along a quintessence thread and into the bird's body. If it were possible for a spirit to be transmitted along a quintessence thread . . .

"Maybe the connection is still there, between your body and the stars. Perhaps what Maasha Kaatra did just pulled your soul along that connection to Horizon."

Antonia's light bobbed more vigorously. "So there might be a way to send us back?"

Catherine nodded slowly. "We'll do everything we can to make that happen."

It was a compelling thought, that all the souls on Earth were connected to the quintessence generated by the stars. It implied that life itself was a product of quintessence. Which was no surprise, given what had happened when Sinclair had brought Catherine back from the dead, causing such an imbalance that the entire island had started to be dragged over the Edge.

Or maybe it wasn't an imbalance at all. They had assumed it was the weight of her soul that had pulled the island, speculating that in quintessence terms, a single human soul weighed more than the entire landmass of the island. But what if it wasn't the weight of her soul, but its connection to the sky that caused the problem. When her soul was drawn out of the void without the benefit of a flexible quintessence thread connecting Earth to sky, perhaps it was the sky itself that was dragging the island over the Edge, as it continued along its normal rotation.

She had no way of testing the hypothesis experimentally, at least not yet, but it was an intriguing idea.

"Catherine Parris," said a strained voice. She knew it instantly as a manticore voice, from the unnatural way it pronounced the English syllables, but it wasn't until she looked up that she recognized him.

She jumped to her feet. "Tanalabrinu!" She pulled the manticore into an embrace. The gesture was odd to manticores, but they understood its intended meaning. Tanalabrinu had not always approved of her, particularly when she had bonded with his uncle, Chichirico. He understood how much she had valued Chichirico, however, and so he had always treated her respectfully. She wouldn't normally have hugged him, but she was so glad to see a face that she recognized, one who could speak the same language and would have word from home, that she couldn't help herself.

His news, however, was not good. He told her of the burning of the human settlement, the arrival of the Spanish, the attempt by Rinchirith to unite the tribes into a single nation, and more recently, his alliance with the Spanish. Catherine reeled with each new revelation, hardly able to accept them. She had been gone mere days, hadn't she? But no, according to Tanalabrinu, several weeks had passed since her trek into the forest. It didn't seem possible. Had she lost time? Or was it just that hard to judge the passage of days when deep underground?

"What of my parents?" she said. "What of Matthew?"

"Your father and Matthew are alive. I have bonded your father and promised them alliance. Through that bond, I know that your mother is also alive, as is your friend Blanca."

"But where are they living? What are they doing?"

"I will show you. First you must know that all the tribes that did not follow Rinchirith have allied themselves to me, and through me, to you. I fear there will be war. What shall I say to them?"

"Thank them for me, for their friendship. But please let me go now, and join Matthew and my parents."

"You do not understand. The tribes expect you to lead them. To defend us against Rinchirith and the Spanish both."

"What? They expect *me* to lead them?"

"The lords of the earth have spoken. You have been judged, and found worthy for the single, great task that is set before you. What greater task than to restore peace among our people?"

"But I know nothing of war. I'm no strategist; I'm a eighteen-year-old girl. I can't inspire confidence or urge bravery. Any decision I made would be a disaster."

Maasha Kaatra spoke up for the first time from his position on the ground with chin resting on knees. "I don't think he wants you to make any decisions."

Catherine looked between them. "I see. You want me to be your talisman. The star-bird, fallen to the depths and risen again, pointing the way towards victory and a happy future."

"They will see you alive," Tanalabrinu said. "They will know that the earth snakes did not devour you."

"And if I'm killed in battle? Am I just a martyr to further the cause?"

Tanalabrinu lashed one of tails like a whip, a gesture of irritation. "This is your cause, too. Rinchirith wishes to massacre all the humans on the island."

Dry laughter from Maasha Kaatra. "I wonder if he mentioned that to the Spanish."

"I'm not a good luck charm," Catherine said. "I want to see Matthew and my parents again."

The ground shook again, and a loud crack sounded from the direction of the Gorge. Catherine leaned around the edge of the rock to see what was happening. She jumped back, startled, as a thousand spirit lights blazed past her head in whining buzz. One of them circled back and hovered near Antonia. "Flee!" it screamed.

It dashed off after delivering its warning, but it was too late. An enormous salamander, ten feet long and heavier than any three people, leaped over the rock behind which Catherine and Maasha Kaatra were sheltering and snapped its wet jaws around the fleeing light. It crashed down onto the mountain with bone-shaking force, fissuring the rock.

Its head swiveled, and it saw Antonia. Its muscles bunched to leap again, even as Antonia flew upward.

"No!" Catherine shouted. With quintessence speed and strength, she snatched up a log and smashed it into the salamander's head just as it jumped. The blow was enough to save Antonia, but not enough to stop the beast's momentum. It launched itself into the air, mouth closing just short of Antonia's fleeing light, but its giant tail sent Catherine sprawling. It landed half on top of her, smothering her with its slimy, glutinous body. She fought to breathe, unable to shift its bulk, until it moved again, trampling downhill after the other lights. Catherine lay on her back, coughing and panting, damp with slime. Maasha Kaatra stood over her, intent, feeling her arms and legs for broken bones. Tanalabrinu was pressed against the rock, eyes wide with evident terror.

Catherine clambered up, bruised but unharmed, and looked down the hill after the salamander. The lights were getting away, apparently unable to float high enough to be completely out of reach, but able to move slightly faster than the salamander could run, at least on this uneven terrain.

Then the ground rumbled again, and a shower of dirt and rock exploded ahead of the lights. A hole opened in the earth, and a second salamander wriggled out of it. The lights tried to veer, but it snatched a huge mouthful of them. The rest whirled left to evade it, but a third salamander burst out of the ground, and then a fourth.

Catherine started running down the hill, heedless of Maasha Kaatra's cries. "Quick!" she said. "Or they'll all be dead."

The salamanders were effective predators. They knew how to corral their prey, creating an ever tighter clump of lights that allowed them to fill their jaws with each lunging mouthful. Catherine threw rocks at them as she ran, but if any of them struck home, the salamanders were not diverted.

Even with quintessence, her options were limited. She could

produce light, bright enough to start a fire that could burn just about any substance. It was a powerful weapon, but not a very focused one, and it might hurt the spirits more than the salamanders. Besides that, she could make her body light, jump high in the air, move incredibly fast, and walk through solid objects—all useful skills, but not very helpful for driving off massive predators.

If she did nothing, however, all the spirits would be dead. She reached inside for the quintessence power and blazed out with it, just as she had done a year ago to drive the manticores away from the settlement. The salamanders stopped immediately, sliding to a halt with their legs splayed. Then all four salamanders turned toward her, eyes intent and huge mouths dripping.

Dirt sprayed from their hind legs as they charged at her, churning up the ground. In panic, she increased the intensity of the light, and nearby trees burst into white flame. The fire gave off no heat, but it devoured the wood quickly, shooting up the trunk and into the leaves.

The salamanders didn't pause. When they came into range, they ignited, but they kept coming. Catherine scrambled backward and tripped on a root. The lead salamander lunged at her, but then Maasha Kaatra was there, scooping her up in his huge arms and dragging her away.

"Turn it off!" he shouted at her. "It just attracts them!"

She obeyed, quenching the light. As soon as she did so, the salamanders stopped chasing her as if she had disappeared or ceased to exist. Instead, they leapt on each other, all of them still on fire, licking and gnawing at each other's skin, crushing bushes and felling small trees as they rolled and wrestled. The fire didn't consume them like it did the trees. In fact, it seemed to make them larger.

By this time, a crowd of manticores had gathered, watching the spectacle. Tanalabrinu stood next to Catherine. "The deeps are rising," he said. "The tribes are choosing sides for war, and the earth snakes are walking beneath the sky. It is the *chithra*. The end of the world."

Catherine turned to him. "I will help you," she said. "But first, take me to Matthew and my parents. They need to hear what's happening, and they need to know I'm alive."

"I have already told your father I have found you safe."

"Please, just take me to them."

TORRES hated these manticores already, and he suspected the feeling was mutual. Rinchirith wanted only one thing from the Spanish: as many matchlock rifles as could be provided. He insisted that Torres's men train the manticores on proper loading and firing techniques. Given the number of creatures that Rinchirith commanded, it was hard to strike a fair bargain, but Torres had resisted actually handing over any quantity of weapons. He had also concealed from the creature the superior wheellock rifles he had onboard. Before he gave Rinchirith anything of real value, the manticore would have to fulfill his side of the bargain.

When it came down to it, the manticores could probably massacre them all and take the weapons, permission or no. Torres knew the trick of covering the bullets with wax; that information had been passed along through Juan Barrosa, from the last group of Spaniards who had come to this island, before they died. Even so, they would only be able to kill a fraction of the manticore force before they were overwhelmed. But Torres wasn't willing to simply give Rinchirith everything he wanted. He hadn't become Capitán-General without the ability to bluff. He had a mission to fulfill, and superior force or no, the manticores were just a tool for that purpose.

Torres needed to mine this island's riches, and to do that, he first needed to find the English colonists. Most of them could be killed outright. They were apostate, so that didn't bother Torres's conscience. But he would need to capture enough of them alive to learn everything he needed to know about the island's magic. Then, once he understood what was important to bring back with him, they would die, as he had been ordered.

The manticores were a means to an end. He didn't care if they lived or died, or whether Rinchirith was the king of the island or some other beast. Eventually, the Spanish would send enough power to enslave or kill them all. He just had to keep them happy in the meantime.

"We need more guns to train," Rinchirith said, having come up on the deck of *La Magdalena* yet again to complain. He was flanked, as usual, by two smaller manticores, one white and one a dirty yellow, neither of whom ever spoke. For that matter, he could be accompanied by dozens more, invisibly swarming the deck, and Torres would have no way to know.

Torres glared at him and tried to seem implacable, not that this creature could probably pick up on his facial expressions. "Not a single one more. In fact, your people won't fire a single shot more until you fulfill your end of the bargain. I want those colonists."

"They may have help from other manticores. Unless my brothers are armed and trained, we cannot be certain of victory."

"You said they were on the run. Fleeing, living in caves. If we wait, they may gather allies, become more entrenched. I say the time to fight is now."

Rinchirith snapped his pincers together with a sharp clap, and Torres had to steel himself not to jump. "If you insist."

"Good," Torres said. "Now, what can these colonists do, and what can the manticores do who might be defending them? I don't want to charge into battle without a good idea of the enemy's power."

Rinchirith arranged his tails in an expression that meant nothing to Torres, but from the tone of his voice Torres imagined a self-satisfied smile. "They can do many things, but they will die quickly."

Rinchirith opened a pouch made of some kind of plant material. Inside were a dozen balls made of what looked like a dark wood. Torres plucked one out and turned it in his fingers. It was very hard, but definitely not made of metal. It appeared to have been made of two halves glued together with an adhesive, making him wonder if there was something hidden inside.

"What is this?" Torres said.

Rinchirith made the same twining movement with his tails, and Torres was pretty certain this time that it was the equivalent of a smile. "Victory," Rinchirith said.

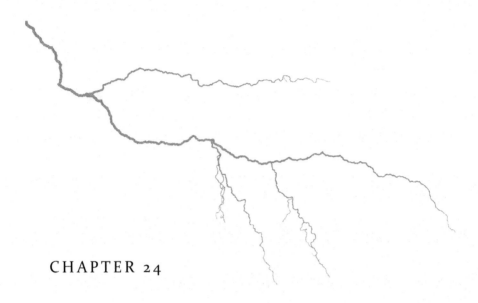

CHAPTER 24

MATTHEW was ready to strangle someone. Elizabeth's council, as she called it, was a disaster. Everyone had different priorities, different grievances, and each saw this change of leadership as a chance to get their way. There was no reasoned debate, with argument matched with rebuttal. Instead, each new speaker changed the subject to bring the conversation around to his own pet complaint.

It disgusted him. This was Princess Elizabeth, the rightful queen of England. They should be asking her for advice, not squabbling for attention. It wasn't that Matthew was so impressed by royalty. But here was a clear chain of command, someone who could command with authority and make irrelevant any arguments about who should be governor. So why were they still bickering and getting nowhere?

Ramos sidled over to stand next to Matthew. It was disconcerting to have a member of the Tavera family here, despite his apparent good will. Only a year ago, Ramos's brother had tortured Matthew for the secrets he knew, and had shot Catherine in the head. Ramos had a different build than his brother, but the resemblance was still there.

"Don't worry about all this," Ramos said, indicating the noisy and increasingly belligerent council. "I've seen monarchs do it before."

"What are you talking about?"

"This isn't really a decision-making discussion. She called it a council, but she has no intention of taking any of this advice."

"So why is she doing it?" Matthew said.

Ramos watched her while he answered. "She's taking everyone's measure. She doesn't know these people. This way, she learns their names, learns their dispositions, discovers who is wise or foolish, rude or gracious, devious or forthright. I've been serving kings and queens for most of my adult life. Trust me, she knows what she's doing."

Matthew shook his head. "It drives me crazy."

Elizabeth looked up sharply. She raised a hand, and the room fell silent. Matthew followed her gaze to see Stephen Parris, on his feet, his face ashen.

"What is it?" Elizabeth said.

"Catherine is alive." Parris's eyes didn't focus properly, as if he were in some other place, watching a different scene unfold. "She is safe, and . . . Maasha Kaatra . . ."

Matthew stared at him in consternation. He knew Parris was bonded to Tanalabrinu, that what the manticore saw and heard, Parris could too. The claim that Catherine was alive made Matthew's heart pound, but Maasha Kaatra? He'd been dead for more than a year. Was this a true vision, or some kind of reverie?

Parris's eyes snapped back to the present. "Rinchirith is coming. The Spanish conquistadors, hundreds strong, and thousands of manticores, are on their way here, right now, with plans to kill us all."

The room erupted into noise. Ferguson jumped to his feet. "We'll fight them," he said. "Fear not, your Grace. We will defy them to the last man." Others jumped up as well, shouting once more.

"Silence," Elizabeth said. Her voice cut like clear crystal over the din. "They are too many. We must flee." She tilted back her chin and caught Matthew's eyes over the crowd. "Matthew Marcheford, where are we to go?"

Matthew gaped. She was asking him? Of course, Elizabeth had no knowledge of the geography of this place, so she would have to ask someone. Ramos shot him a subtle, told-you-so smile, while everyone waited for him to speak.

"North, into the mountains," he said. "As far from the bay as possible. We should find higher ground, with a defensible position."

"North it is," Elizabeth said. Her tone was imperious, and although she had walked out of the forest with no explanation, they all moved to obey her, gathering their supplies for another exodus. Matthew marveled at her poise and strength of authority. She had been here an hour at most, and already she commanded more complete obedience than any governor had ever managed.

TORRES'S men were well-disciplined and marched in a formation designed for forest terrain. Torres himself rode at the front with the cavalry, following the manticores. The creatures, however, did not travel in straight lines. They seemed to roam randomly, following some pattern of the terrain that Torres couldn't see, sometimes on the ground and sometimes through the trees. If they were following a path, it was not one suitable for humans. The manticores led them down into ravines and back up again, through thick brambles, into marshy areas that squelched underfoot. Occasionally, they had to leave their guides and strike out on their own to take some easier path, trusting that the manticores would find them again and lead them on.

It occurred to Torres that this could be intentional on the part of the manticores, and that they were laughing at the humans from up in the trees. If so, there wasn't much he could do about it. As long as they eventually led him to what remained of the colonists, he could handle a little delay.

The real problem was that he wasn't commanding any respect from these savages, nor had he managed to intimidate them with his technology. This was not a good start in a relationship where he had intended to dominate and exploit them. The only leverage he had over them was his guns. He had given them a few dozen as a gesture of good faith, but he would have to start trading them for more concrete goods.

First things first. He had to find the original colonists, force them to tell everything they knew, and then kill them. That done, he would have a better idea of what he needed. Shekinah flatworms, to be sure, and quintessence pearls, probably some living animals and plants. More of those eels Barrosa had showed him that could turn things into gold. That alone would make his trip a great success. He didn't have to worry about subjugating the natives, not on this trip anyway. Eventually, they would need a proper colony here, with a fort and a regular garrison guarding the bay. There would be plenty of time to teach the manticores proper respect, and to set them to some useful task.

They reached the foothills of the mountains, and the march grew more difficult, though somewhat straighter. The slope was steep, and the ground was made of loose, rocky soil with treacherous footing. Finally, they crested a rise and found a clearing. The mountain rose up again on the other side of the clearing, but there were fissures in the rock face that looked like they might be the openings to deep caves. In the clearing itself was evidence of construction: wooden beams and stone blocks partially assembled or stacked in piles. They checked the caves, and found the remains of cookfires, but no people.

"Where are they?" Torres demanded.

"They were warned of our coming." Rinchirith said.

"Who warned them? Did one of yours betray us?"

Rinchirith ignored the question. "They have no stealth, no skill. They leave a trail as bright and stinking as a—" He made a clicking, coughing noise that was no language Torres had ever heard, and gestured with two of its tails.

"What does that mean?" Torres said.

"It means we can track them."

WHEN Matthew and the others had migrated to these caves in

the first place, their line had been scatted, stretched thin as those who couldn't travel as fast trailed behind.   This time, Elizabeth insisted on a formation, keeping everyone close, with ranging scouts both ahead and behind.   Elizabeth herself had difficulty with the pace; she was new to the strength and agility quintessence gave her body, and so was unused to using it.   Ramos adjusted more readily, and he carried his daughter Antonia along as easily as if she were made of straw.   Before they left, he had circulated among the colonists, distributing the supply of salt he had brought with him from England.   Combined with what they had been able to scrape hastily from the deposits in the cave, they were all well-supplied.

They climbed steeply uphill through forest, and the speed at which they traveled made it imperative to watch for roots and branches underfoot. Matthew remembered the vulnerable, straggling line from their first migration, and felt foolish.   It hadn't even occurred to him to keep everyone together as a group for safety. Though, why should it have? He was young, not even married, not a leader. He wasn't responsible for their protection. In fact, he was such a terrible leader he had destroyed their entire settlement. So why did people always look to him when there were decisions to be made?

A sharp whistle came from behind them, and one of the scouts ran up past him and addressed Elizabeth. "Conquistadors on our trail," he reported. "They left the caves and are marching this way, though their speed is much slower than ours."

"How did they know which way to go?" Matthew's father asked.

The scout shook his head. "We must have left signs. Footprints, maybe."

It seemed unlikely to Matthew—the ground near the caves was rocky and packed hard—but perhaps the Spanish were better trackers than he expected. "Where are the manticores that were supposed to be with them?"

"Could be a hundred, and I wouldn't know it," the scout said. "No skink tears."

"We press on," Elizabeth said.   "If you see any sign of the manticore force, report immediately."

The scout nodded and bowed, but it was the last thing he did. A crack sounded from somewhere to their left, and when the scout straightened, a bright red stain bloomed on his chest. His eyes wide and glassy, he coughed once, spraying blood onto Elizabeth, and collapsed to the ground.

AS CATHERINE and Maasha Kaatra traveled with Tanalabrinu, more and more manticores joined them. First it was just a dozen, serving as a kind of honor guard, but they kept appearing out of nowhere, and every time Catherine turned around, there was a larger group. She gradually became aware that there must be a vast company of manticores moving through the trees behind and around them. An army.

"Why are so many coming with us?" she said.

"They would follow the star-bird," Tanalabrinu said.

"What are you not telling me?"

At first, Tanalabrinu did not answer, and Catherine wondered if he would refuse. Then he said, "Rinchirith's army has already reached your human colonists. They are surrounded and overwhelmed. I fear we may be too late to make any difference."

A knot of dread fell into Catherine's stomach. "How far away are they?"

As if in answer, they came to a rocky outcropping devoid of trees, allowing them a view of the ground below. The view was tremendous, vast stretches of forests and plains carpeting the landscape. They were much closer to the sea than Catherine had realized, close to the eastern cliffs where the water pounded against the rocks, impassable for any ship. On a slope far below them, she could see a horde of manticores pouring into a stretch of forest while even more held back, keeping their quarry surrounded. It was a hundred times as many manticores as there were humans on the island. She couldn't see them well enough to pick out any individuals, but the roar of their attack filtered up to her ears faintly on the wind.

"We have to save them!" Catherine said.

"The path goes to the right," Tanalabrinu said. "It follows the curve of the mountain and comes out at the base of those trees, there."

"Too slow. Look at them all! My family and friends will be massacred."

"It's the only way. My warriors are swift. We will soon engage the enemy."

Catherine looked down at the manticore army far below. The drop was not sheer, exactly, but it was very steep and strewn with loose boulders. "Not swift enough. You go that way if you want."

"What do you intend?"

"To rescue them."

With a shout to give herself courage, Catherine ran forward and careened over the edge. She flew faster than she ever had before, half running and half falling, trying to avoid scree that could trip her up. One mistake and she might simply fall the rest of the way and crack her head open on a rock.

A ululating war cry behind her told her that Tanalabrinu, at least, had followed her over the edge, and soon a roar like an avalanche came from behind her. She dared not look back, needing to keep her eyes on her footing. Either it *was* an avalanche, disturbed by her feet and rushing down to crush her, or else Tanalabrinu's army was plunging down the slope after her. Either way, she had no choice but to keep running and keep her feet.

Finally, the slope smoothed out toward the horizontal, and she found herself careening straight into the rearguard of Rinchirith's manticore army. She kept running, turning her skin to iron and blazing out with quintessence fire. They fell back as she and the hundreds of manticores behind her smashed deeply into their midst.

The two manticore armies collided with a noise like the ocean thundering over the edge of the world. They fought in two planes, able to pass through solid objects, but still able to strike each other in that insubstantial second world. The battle was only partly about the humans now. It was a battle for dominance over Horizon.

THE WHINE of bullets filled the air. Matthew whirled, trying to see where their attackers were. The forest seemed to be full of invisible enemies. Colonists threw themselves on the ground or took cover behind trees, though it was hard to tell which direction the shots were coming from. For all they knew, they were surrounded. With skink tears, they would have at least been able to see them, but their stores of the blue liquid had all been lost when the settlement burned.

Something was very wrong. The dead scout now bleeding out onto the ground had quintessence in his veins, just like the rest of them. Matthew had seen men heal from bullet wounds, from burns, even from accidental amputation. But this man *hadn't healed.*

Blanca screamed and went down with a bullet in her shoulder. Matthew knelt and pressed his hand against the wound. It kept bleeding, showing no sign of the miraculous quintessence healing they were all so used to expecting. The bullet had punched a hole right through her shoulder and out the other side, and Matthew saw what looked like a tiny half-circle of wood on the ground behind her. He picked it up. The wood was cracked. On the inside, there was a reservoir with a small amount of metallic liquid that Matthew recognized immediately. Mercury.

The manticores were firing mercury bullets. Mercury counteracted the effects of quintessence, dousing its power just as salt inflamed it. With mercury in the wound, the quintessence couldn't heal it as it usually would.

Blanca clutched his arm and gritted her teeth against the pain. "I'm okay," she said. "You should fight!"

By this time, the colonists were rallying. Even without skink tears, even surrounded and caught by surprise, they were far from helpless, thanks to Ramos's salt. Skin transformed into iron, and bullets ricocheted harmlessly away. The colonists formed a rough circle around the wounded. As quintessence light blazed from their skin, trees caught fire, and some of the attacking manticores became visible as their fur ignited.

Somebody pressed something into Matthew's hand. It was Stephen Parris. Matthew looked down to see a small glass vial with a tiny amount of blue liquid in the bottom. Skink tears.

"It's all I have," Parris said. "You'd better take a look."

Matthew poured out the last dribble from the vial and spread it into his eyes. He shut his eyes firmly through the brief moment of burning pain, and when he opened them again, he could see.

Thousands of manticores. They were everywhere, all around them, as far as he could see, both on the ground and in the trees. Dozens of manticores were dead or on fire, but there were always more to take their place. A burning manticore made it through the fire and threw itself onto a colonist, driving a pincer edge through his unprotected eye. The man dropped, and more manticores ran for the gap.

Matthew looked back down at Blanca, frozen with indecision.

"I'll take care of her," Parris shouted. "Go!"

Matthew hastily took the fallen man's place and closed the gap before the manticores could break through the circle.

Elizabeth touched his shoulder, standing behind him and using his iron body as a shield. "What do you see?"

Matthew told her, shouting over his shoulder.

"Should we surrender? Will they take us alive?"

Parris, doing his best to clean the mercury out of Blanca's wound, was close enough to hear. "They are here to slaughter us, your Grace. They will leave no one alive, white flag or no."

"I'm sorry you came here," Matthew said. "We meant to save your life, not take it."

"My life is in God's hands, not yours," Elizabeth said. "We will surrender, and pray that you are wrong."

"Help is coming," Parris said. "Only a little longer, your Grace."

"What help?" Matthew said.

"Tanalabrinu, of course. And Catherine."

The sounds of the battle changed, and Matthew scanned the forest, trying to see what was happening. For a while, it was all confusion, the smoke from the guns and the quintessence fires obscuring his vision. Then he saw them, manticores fighting other manticores, the newcomers dancing and weaving through the trees to avoid the deadly guns.

Matthew kept blazing out from the circle, using what quintessence power he had left to drive manticores back from their position. He had no other weapon, and he would be no match for a manticore fighting hand-to-hand. The only defense the colonists had was this quintessence fire.

It was difficult to tell which manticores were on their side. Only a small number of the attacking group had matchlocks; the rest fought with claws and pincers, leaping on their enemies and stabbing them through. But something was wrong. As far as Matthew could tell, more of Tanalabrinu's manticores were dying than Rinchirith's. In fact, many of Tanalabrinu's seemed to be falling over for no apparent reason. It took Matthew a few minutes to figure out what was happening.

It was the mercury-filled bullets. Depending on how close the bullet came to striking the quintessence pearl at the base of a manticore's skull, it damaged not just the manticore it hit, but all those bonded to it. Just as whole schools of ironfish could be killed by dropping a pearl from a single fish into a vial of mercury, so whole memory families of manticores were being killed with a single shot.

Matthew spotted Parris, now holding a position on the other side of the circle. He was still standing, for now. But Parris was bonded with Tanalabrinu. If the manticore was shot and killed with a mercury bullet, Parris would die along with him.

FROM Catherine's perspective, it looked like a star blazing out from between the trees. It was only when she drew closer that she could make out the circle of colonists, barely keeping the manticores at bay. Unlike a year ago, when she had driven back the grays from their attack on the colony, the manticores knew what the humans were doing. They knew it wasn't supernatural, and worse, they knew the humans couldn't keep it up forever. Hundreds of manticores might burn, but at the end of it, the humans would all be dead.

Though, not if she could help it. Catherine glanced back over her shoulder at the other army of manticores that had followed her here, united by the symbol of her rise from the depths. There had been manticore battles of this magnitude before, passed down in the memories of their families, but not within the lifetimes of any now living. A decisive victory would mean great power for the side that won. The enemy survivors would be forcibly incorporated into memory families, their tribes erased. More likely, though, at least if history was any judge, there would be huge casualties and no clear victor, meaning a great amount of blood would be spilled for no clear purpose.

Catherine couldn't worry about that. She didn't want manticores to die, but when it came down to it, she was loyal to her own family and her own species.

Despite her skills with quintessence, Catherine was no warrior, any more than the rest of the colonists were. The best she could do was blaze out with a light of her own. The circle of fire kept the manticores back more than it made any significant impact on the battle. But Catherine's goal wasn't to kill. She just wanted to reach her family.

When she finally made it inside the human circle, her breath was knocked away by the simultaneous embraces of Matthew and both her parents. They hugged her and touched her face and Matthew kissed her full on the lips, an act that back in England would have meant scandal, engagement or no. At the moment, though, not even Mother seemed to mind. Matthew didn't say anything. He just looked at her, eyes shining.

She kissed him again, remembering that afternoon on the sand by the bay, when they had played with the principle of substitution and watched the tortoises. Happier times.

Then she saw Blanca, lying on the ground, her shoulder torn and bloody, and dropped immediately to her side. "What happened?"

"Shot," Blanca said weakly.

"They're using mercury bullets," her father said. "The wounds don't heal. I've got this one nearly cleaned out, and it is healing, though slowly. She'll live. If any of us do."

Blanca looked past her, just for a moment, at Matthew, and Catherine saw an expression of loss register briefly on her face. It was gone in a moment, making Catherine wonder if she had imagined it.

"We could use some help!" bellowed another colonist, and Catherine saw that the circle was failing, the power of its light dimming. The human dead were everywhere. There was a time to greet friends and family, but this was not it.

She rejoined the circle with Matthew and her parents, adding their quintessence light to its strength. It was a losing battle, though, Catherine could see at once. Rinchirith's manticores were fully engaged in fighting Tanalabrinu's at the moment, but even so, their light would only last so long, as would the iron skin that kept the mercury bullets from killing them.

"We have to make a barrier!" Catherine said.

Matthew knew what she meant at once. Just as the settlement had been protected from manticore incursion by an invisible barrier, they needed protection now. This was a beetlewood forest. A rough wall could be made by snapping green branches off of the trees, drawing out the quintessence threads, and wrapping them around neighboring trees, thus creating a weave of living quintessence threads. But all of the trees in their vicinity were on fire, caught in the destructive blaze that was keeping the manticore assault at bay. There was no way to climb them or pull off the branches, if the trees were even still alive.

They had no way to douse the fire, either. It would burn until it had nothing left to burn.

"How?" Matthew said.

In answer, Catherine leaped as high as her quintessence-fueled legs could carry her, aiming at a branch that seemed relatively unaffected by the fire. She caught hold and made her body heavy again, dragging it down. The branch broke, but didn't entirely detach from the trunk, swinging her down toward the deadly fire. She released her grip just in time and fell heavily to the ground.

"That's not going to work," Matthew said. "Even a little of that white fire on your skin . . ."

She knew he was right. There was no stopping that fire from

burning once it touched something. But if they did nothing, they
were all going to die anyway. Already, Tanalabrinu's manticores were
falling back from Rinchirith's, some of them turning to run back the
way they had come. Many of Rinchirith's manticores were howling
and racing off in pursuit, but others were turning back toward the
small knot of humans.

Catherine leaped again and yanked at the branch. This time, it
peeled away, and she fell back down with it in her hands.

It was all she needed. She ran around the next tree, stretching the
quintessence thread and wrapping it around, then heading to a third.
She snapped it and threw one half to Matthew, who did the same
thing, in and out, weaving the threads together to make a barrier.
The quintessence firelight reflected off the strand, making it visible to
Catherine, even without skink tears.

But it was taking too long. They would need thousands of passes
to make it thick enough to serve. By then their salt would be
exhausted, and the manticores would be upon them.

"We can help," said a voice in her ear.

It was Antonia, bobbing gently near her head. Catherine looked
up and saw thousands of the spirit lights flitting through the air.
How had they followed her? The spirits couldn't see normal matter;
they hadn't even realized they were in the natural world. Perhaps
they could see her spirit in some different way than normal sight?

"Can you interact with matter?" Catherine said.

"I don't think so, but I'm not sure I need to." Antonia's light flew
to one of the threads and spun, seeming to wrap herself in it. When
she came away, the thread stretched behind her. She flew around a
tree branch, dragging a taut thread behind her in the air.

"Perfect!" Catherine said.

The lights all joined in. Catherine could hear their tiny voices
speaking to each other in a dozen languages, translating instructions,
and soon dozens of spirits were weaving their way in and out of the
trees surrounding the surviving colonists, dragging bright strands
behind them. They zigzagged in and out, tangling the strands around
the trees like a giant spiderweb. Eventually they were surrounded by
a shining wall, thicker and more intertwined than the settlement wall

had ever been. They couldn't see the fighting anymore, and even the crack of gunfire and the battle screams of the manticores grew muted. They were wrapped in a glowing cocoon of protection while the war raged on.

Many of the colonists collapsed to the ground, out of salt and out of strength. Catherine's father circulated among the injured, wrapping wounds, examining the damage. In some cases, he tried to cut out the mercury from their flesh. When he succeeded, the quintessence in their bodies took over, healing the wounds rapidly until there was no sign they had been any injury at all. For some, however, it was already too late.

"What's happening out there?" Matthew said. "We can't stay behind this barrier forever."

"It all depends on who wins, and we can't do anything about that," Catherine said.

"We should be able to." Matthew cracked a fist into his palm. "I hate feeling so helpless."

A imperious looking young woman with almost no hair and exhausted-looking eyes was deep in intense conversation with Matthew's father.

"Who's that?" Catherine said. It was odd to see a stranger. They had been isolated on this island for over a year; new people didn't just stop by.

"You won't believe it," Matthew said.

"Try me."

"It's the Princess Elizabeth. She was very nearly executed in England, but she escaped with the help of a few loyal friends, including one who had been studying the quintessence brought back by the Spanish ship."

"That ship made it back home? How do you know?"

Matthew ran his fingers through his hair. "A lot has happened since you left. There's a lot to explain. Yes, the ship made it back, with a few pearls and a shekinah, and this man Ramos de Tavera was studying it."

Catherine felt a chill. "Tavera?"

"I know, I know." Matthew waved it away. "One thing at a time.

Blanca figured out that we could send *objects* across a quintessence thread, not just information. When Elizabeth escaped, she and Ramos and his daughter made it through. They traveled along a thread from England to here, in moments. And one other man, though he died."

It was too much to take in. Catherine had so many questions she didn't know which to ask first.

"Let me introduce you," Matthew said. He beckoned, and a dark-haired Spaniard walked toward them, drawing a teenage girl by the hand. "Catherine Parris, this is Ramos de Tavera."

"Pleased to meet you," he said. The resemblance to the Tavera who had tyrannized and tortured them was disconcerting. Ramos smiled reassuringly. "And this is my daughter, Antonia. She won't acknowledge you; she can't really speak, or at least she can't hear you."

Catherine studied the girl's face, thinking of the spirit that had been here only a moment ago. "Her name is Antonia? Antonia de Tavera?"

Ramos opened his mouth to answer, but he was interrupted by a tree, one of those that supported the barrier, suddenly toppling and falling away from them onto the ground with a crash. The barrier unraveled, suddenly revealing a battlefield strewn with manticore dead. And a legion of armed Spanish conquistadors, surrounding them.

A tall man with the insignia and cap of a captain spoke rapidly in Spanish. An officer translated. "My name is Alvaro de Torres. In the name of His Majesty, King Philip, surrender immediately, or we will kill you all."

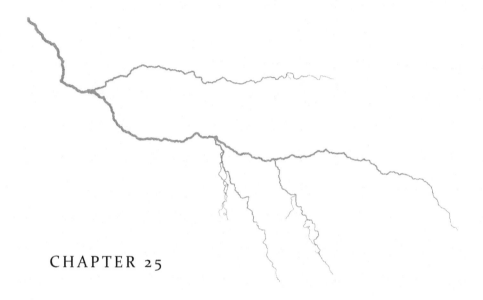

CHAPTER 25

RAMOS had to act fast. The colonists, exhausted and surrounded, didn't have much energy left to fight. They were out of salt and out of strength. They knew the presence of the Spanish meant that their manticore allies had either been killed or had fled. They had no will left to resist.

Ramos knew what the captain's orders were. He would kill them all eventually, even if they did surrender. He would torture them to be sure they told him everything, and then he would kill them.

"Capitán-General de Torres," he called out, speaking in Spanish. "I come from His Majesty, King Philip."

Torres looked startled. He raised a hand and looked for the source of the voice.

Ramos stepped forward, trying to appear confident despite his torn and filthy attire. "I am Father Ramos de Tavera, Jesuit and chief astronomer to His Majesty and advisor on Horizon and quintessence. I have replaced Juan Barrosa as your liaison."

Torres's eyebrows furrowed, trying to make sense of it. "What is this?" he said. "Witchcraft, like all the rest?"

"On the contrary. You have received no word from the king or Barrosa through the bell-box lately, have you?" Ramos knew he had not, because until recently, the box had been in his possession.

"What has happened to Barrosa?"

"Alas, my lord. He is dead."

"How could you learn such a thing, or know the king's wishes, since you are here, and they are not?"

Ramos gave him a haughty look. "Do you think that box is the only magic the king controls? This morning I stood in London; today I am here."

"If the king had such a magic, why did he send us to voyage for months on treacherous seas?"

"The passage I traveled was dangerous as well, and only one man may pass it at a time. To benefit from this island, we must have a shipping trade, controlled by the strength of Spanish might. Your task is a vital one, and the king will reward you well for success."

Torres was still suspicious. "How do I know you aren't reading my mind?"

Ramos stepped even closer and looked into his face. "Come, man. You've seen me at court before. You know my face. I am brother to Diego de Tavera, who negotiated the king's marriage contract."

He saw a glimmer of recognition, and hoped it would be enough. He clapped Torres on the back. "Good man. The king wishes these colonists returned to England along with the goods, so their knowledge of quintessence and this island can be fully extracted. They are not to be touched in the meantime; he wants them unbroken."

Ramos held his breath, not sure that Torres was going to buy it. If he had thought ahead and anticipated this meeting, he might have stolen the king's seal, or prepared a letter of some kind, to strengthen the deception, but he was making this up as he went along.

Torres nodded slowly. "Secure the prisoners," he said.

Ramos let his breath out. It was going to work.

The soldiers circulated among the colonists, confiscating what few weapons they found and tying the colonists' hands. "Walk with me,"

Torres said.

They walked away through the woods, stepping over manticore corpses and around pools of blood. Torres grilled Ramos, asking question after pointed question about Spain and England and the king. Ramos had no trouble answering any of them. After all, he really had been in London that morning, and he really had been working with Barrosa in King Philip's service. He spun a creative tale about the technology used to send him here, how it was a one way trip, but had been imprecise in place and time. It had dumped him far from the bay, he said, and he had only just caught up with Torres and his men.

They walked a long way, with two conquistadors flanking them like an honor guard, until the circle of colonists were out of sight. "What happened to all the manticores?" Ramos asked.

"The renegade manticores fled," Torres said. "Those loyal to the crown pursued them into the mountains."

Ramos didn't quibble with his terms. He was pretty sure he had Torres convinced, and he didn't want to ruin it. "So may it be with all the king's enemies," he said. "When I was in England, Philip was anxious to send armies into the field. He will be eager to see what power you can bring home to him."

Torres raised a pistol and pointed it at his head. "And when you were in England," he said, "was the Protestant princess there as well?"

Ramos swallowed. He was caught. Torres had recognized Elizabeth, and knew she must have come with him. He wasn't convinced at all. He had just been toying with him all this time, trying to find out who he really was and what he knew.

"She was there," Ramos managed to say.

"Then how is it that she was also here, fighting against my men with the Protestants?"

"Oh, that girl," Ramos said. "I saw her, too. She does look rather like the princess, in the right light."

The finger on the trigger twitched. Ramos reacted. He wasn't terribly good at using the quintessence power in his body, but he made his body as heavy as possible. He was hoping this would work like the trick that the others did, making their skin into a protective armor that could deflect bullets, but all it did was drag him to the ground, suddenly too heavy to lift himself or even move. Torres's bullet whined over his head, just missing him. Ramos struggled for breath, unable to lift his crushingly-heavy chest. If he wasn't careful, he was going to kill himself before Torres had a chance. He reversed the effect, making his body lighter, and ran.

Unless he had another pistol, Torres would have to reload before he could shoot again, but that wasn't true of the two conquistadors. "Shoot him!" Torres shouted.

A gunshot cracked behind him, followed closely by a second. Ramos cringed, expecting to be hit in the back, but the shots whistled by him. He weaved as he ran, trying to create a more difficult target and putting trees between him and his attackers. Soon he heard running feet behind him. He tried to use quintessence to make his body light and increase his speed, but he didn't have the knack for it. The ground was uneven and treacherous, and he couldn't control it. He twisted an ankle painfully, and crashed into the ground.

He was up again in a moment, afraid he had injured his ankle, but quintessence had already healed it. He ran on, risking a look back, and saw that the conquistadors had almost reached him, their bayonets held out in front of them. They were strong, young, and athletic, and he was none of those things. He darted away again, breathing in short gasps.

Ramos had intended to run back to the circle of colonists. He had no plan, in particular, except the vague thought that he might distract the soldiers long enough for the others to do something. Soon, however, it became clear that he had no idea which direction the colonists were. He was lost.

The conquistadors raced behind him, cursing at him in Spanish. The trees became smaller and closer together, making them harder to avoid, and the undergrowth grew thicker. He crashed through bushes, losing speed. There was a gap in the treeline ahead, a place where the sun shone through. Perhaps it was an open area, a field where he could use try quintessence again to run faster and leave his pursuers behind.

He broke out into the clearing, and suddenly there was nowhere else to go. It wasn't a field. He was at the top of a rocky cliff a hundred feet high, and beyond it, the endless ocean, as far as he could see. At the cliff bottom, enormous waves crashed against the rocks, driving up spray. His back to the cliff, he turned to face his attackers.

They came at him together, bayonets cutting the air. The twelve inch blades glittered in the light, and Ramos knew the quintessence wouldn't help him if they drove those blades up into his heart. Their faces were grim, purposeful. One of them thrust at his midsection, and he sidestepped, narrowly avoiding it, but in the process, he stepped back to the very edge of the cliff.

"Nowhere to go," the other one said. "Time to say your prayers."

Ramos thought of Antonia, still a prisoner with the colonists, and his conscience pricked him. He had left her, helpless, in the control of killers. Elizabeth, too, he had rescued from execution only to abandon her to Spanish soldiers. It wasn't fair, and he knew it—he had done the best he could to try and save them all—but it didn't stop him from feeling like a coward.

The conquistador stabbed, and this time Ramos couldn't get away. The point of the bayonet cut deep into his belly. He cried out and stepped backwards involuntarily, his foot finding nothing but air. The soldier pulled the blade back out, and Ramos fell backwards into space. The cliff was not completely vertical. He dropped, flailing with arms and legs, then struck against a steep slope, caroming away and falling again. He struck a second time and tumbled headlong, half falling, half sliding on loose gravel, battering himself on rocks on the way down. Another free fall, and he struck with jarring force against a rock ledge, biting his tongue and lancing pain through his skull, but stopping his fall. He tried to get up, but his head was ringing with the impact, and his vision narrowed and went black.

MATTHEW sat in the dirt with the rest of the colonists, hands tied. He felt helpless and stupid and afraid. Catherine was alive, but in a few minutes, she might wish she had died at the bottom of the manticores' cave shaft. It was clear that Torres was planning to find out what they knew, and Matthew knew from painful experience what a Spanish interrogation could be like.

The barrier was gone. Torres had destroyed it through the simple expedient of chopping down all the trees that supported it. Those trees he had further chopped into firewood, which several soldiers were now stacking into a tall pyramid. Matthew knew what that was. It was a pyre.

Horizon had taken its toll. There were now fewer than fifty colonists left alive, of the hundreds who had traveled with them from England. Some had died on the journey, some from predatory animals or poisonous plants, some by the hand of Diego de Tavera, still more in the first battle with the manticores over the settlement. Today's battle had claimed still more, though looking out across the field, the English dead was nothing compared to the enormous number of manticores killed.

Ramos had told Torres that the colonists were not to be touched; presumably that was because Torres's actual orders were to kill them. They had no energy or salt left to resist. It would be Diego de Tavera all over again: torture, or the threat of harm or death to others, in order to extract information. Matthew knew there was no resisting it. The year before, he had endured punishing pain to his own body, only to crumble when Tavera started killing random people to force him to talk. He had ultimately told them everything he knew, which was why the Spanish had been able to get a ship back to England with any treasures at all. He had no illusions about his chance of survival, either. Once Torres had what he wanted, he would kill them. The only hope they had was rescue, and who could rescue them now?

Torres had Elizabeth off to herself, where he was questioning her. She maintained her regal pose, even when he slapped her, and Matthew suspected she was making no secret of her true identity. Torres had obviously recognized her anyway.

The conquistadors stood over them, preventing conversation. Matthew was nearest to his father, with Parris and Ferguson not far away. Catherine was on the other side of the group, too far away even to try any surreptitious conversation. Matthew felt a stab of dread in his chest at the thought that, after she had so recently been restored to him, she might die before he could even speak with her again. She was tied next to Ramos's strange daughter, Antonia, who didn't even seem to know where she was. Matthew had heard from Ramos how so many in Europe had fallen under this same madness, though none had on Horizon. It was as if some central part of herself had gone absent, leaving her alive, but no longer present.

It reminded Matthew of when Catherine had bonded to Chichirico on the ship, before any of them had any experience doing so or knowledge of what was happening. Her consciousness had been entirely immersed in the manticore's, such that she could hardly differentiate herself from him. That had been different in many ways; Catherine had been unconscious, not able to be led around like Antonia was, but there was that same sense of someone missing an essential part of herself.

Matthew caught a brief glimpse of something bright glowing in Antonia's thick black hair. He peered, trying to make it out. Most of the time he couldn't see it, but—there—a flash of light. In fact, he realized that Catherine was whispering, not to Antonia, but to the glow in her hair. It was one of those spirit lights. Matthew glanced at their Spanish captors, to see if they'd noticed, but they gave no sign that they'd seen it.

By now, the sun was descending toward the horizon, red and gigantic, as close to the Earth as it ever came. Despite the cover of the trees, the air was hot, and Matthew felt a droplet of sweat slide down his back. It was not the first evening the conquistadors had spent in this place, but the huge sun clearly unnerved them.

They erected three pyres in all, each with a post in the center driven into the ground. Torres grabbed a handful of Elizabeth's dress and yanked her to her feet. The once-white gown was dirty and torn. He pushed her up against one of the posts, and his men tied her wrists tightly to a notch high on the post, forcing her to lean against it with her hands high in the air, her feet only barely touching the ground.

"Two more," Torres said. He pointed to Catherine and Antonia. "These two will do."

Blanca screamed and tried to shield them, but the conquistadores knocked her roughly to the ground. They pulled Catherine and Antonia to their feet. Catherine twisted and fought, but they overpowered her and led her toward one of the posts.

They stretched Catherine's arms high and hooked her tied wrists over the notch in the post, just like they had with Elizabeth. Antonia went willingly, making no complaint, and was similarly tied to the third post.

Matthew couldn't tear his eyes away from Catherine. Her eyes were locked to his, wide with panic. After all this time, fearing her lost, not knowing whether or how to grieve, was he really going to lose her like this? It seemed impossible that he could do nothing. A month ago, he had so much power. Power to heal, power to fight, a settlement like a fortress and what seemed like infinite stores of salt. Now he had nothing. He was just a mortal man, helpless, able to do nothing as his love was tortured and killed. He couldn't bear to watch, but it seemed like a betrayal to look away. If he couldn't hold her hand, at least he could hold her gaze.

His father poked him in the back, hard. "Do something," he whispered.

"What can I possibly do?"

His voice was like a hiss, spoken out of the side of his mouth. "I've seen you do the impossible more than once. Don't tell me you're just going to stand there and let this happen."

Matthew wanted to punch him. The situation was bad enough without his father blaming him for it. "Why are you asking me?" he said bitterly. "Why don't you just pray?"

"I *am* praying. I'm praying for you to rescue them."

"I can't."

"Stop it. Stop feeling sorry for yourself and do what needs to be done."

Matthew gritted his teeth. How could his father think so much of him and so little of him at the same time? His hands were tied behind his back, he had no salt, and they were surrounded by armed soldiers. What did he expect Matthew to do?

And then Matthew knew. It popped into his head as obvious as his own name.

He waited for just the right moment, when Torres was reaching for a torch, and moved as quickly as he could. He jumped up, off-balance, and ran to Catherine's pyre. Before anyone could stop him, he kissed her passionately, knowing he had mere seconds. As he expected, the conquistadors tore him away from her and shoved him roughly to the ground.

"How touching," Torres said, chuckling. "The lover steals a final kiss before the end." He lit his torch and held it above Catherine's pyre. "I was going to burn the princess first, but this is more tragic, don't you think? Young love, cut short." All he had to do was drop the torch. There was no oil, nothing to make the wood burn quickly. Worst of all, the quintessence water still in Catherine's veins would continue to heal her as she burned. It would be a slow and horrible death.

"Stop!" Matthew said. "You don't have to do this. We'll tell you whatever you want to know."

"I'm certain you will," Torres said. "I find that tongues are loose once their owners witness the horrors their heresy has earned them. I will burn your love, and then you will have a chance to speak. If I am not satisfied, I will burn the next in line."

"I can teach you how to use quintessence," Matthew said. "I can show you where to find shekinah flatworms, how to preserve them for the trip back to England. I'll show you how to make your body fast and strong, like ours, and how to create the quintessence fire."

"You will lie to me," Torres said. "And then I will burn your friends, and only then will you tell the truth. I wish to skip the lies. I take no joy from it, but it was you who chose to set your faces against the Lord. As it says in Holy Scripture, 'He shall crush you with a scepter of iron; he shall break you in pieces like a potter's vessel.' God laughs at your pitiful rebellion. When you see your princess burn, you will know there is no hope in defying Almighty God."

It was a twisting of Psalm 2, and a horrible one. Matthew struggled to stand, but a soldier kicked him and he fell back to the ground. Ferguson looked dazed, staring in shock and denial. Parris had his eyes closed in apparent calm, and his lips were moving. Was he talking to Tanalabrinu across their bond? Or praying for divine rescue?

"We will never tell you anything," Catherine said from her pyre. "Your cruelty will buy you nothing but God's judgment."

"Such brave words," Torres said. "But we will see how fast your defiance turns to begging for mercy." He turned back to look at Matthew. "Any last words for your young love?"

Matthew glared at him from the ground. "You're a monster. Is this what serving Christ looks like? The torture of young women?" He had no doubt that Torres had picked out Catherine and Antonia simply because they were young and beautiful, and thus their gruesome deaths would be that much more shocking. His goal was to crush any hope of resistance or rescue, in order to be sure the information he extracted from the rest was true and complete.

Torres shook his head in apparent regret. "This is the price of heresy," he said. He tossed the torch into the wood at Catherine's feet.

CHAPTER 26

RAMOS woke with a throbbing headache. He was on a narrow ledge, maybe thirty feet above the crashing waves. He looked back up the way he had fallen. There was no way he could climb it. He was alone in this vast and strange world with no resources, no plan, nowhere to go. Antonia and Elizabeth and the others were doomed. As soon as Torres extracted the information he needed from them, he would kill them. Burn them for heresy, probably. Ramos knew how it worked. He would burn some so that the others would talk, and then burn the others anyway.

He had to do something, had to save them. But what could he possibly do? He was just one man, an astronomer, not even a warrior. He had no weapons, no quintessence tricks. He was stuck on a ledge with no way off. Everything he ever knew had been taken away from him. His church. His country. Now even his niece.

And what if he could find a way off this slope? What then? He could make a hero's suicide charge and rush into the circle shouting for Antonia. But for what purpose? So she could see him cut down with gunfire just before she burned?   He could turn himself in peacefully, but again, why? So he could watch her die in agony?

Ramos staggered to the edge and looked down at the ocean. It was, possibly, the most beautiful sight he had ever seen. The sea was turquoise and stretched out sparkling to the edge of vision. Great waves dashed themselves against the cliffs, throwing spray high in the air. A flock of birds with long, dagger-like beaks plummeted into the water from hundreds of feet up and emerged, dripping, with wriggling eels impaled on their beaks. The successful ones gathered on an outcropping to tear their prey to pieces, while those still hunting wheeled high overhead. Clouds turned fiery with reflected sunlight streaked the sky.

He found that he was crying.   What was happening to him? Where had he gone wrong? He had turned from the Church, yes, but only to avoid torturing a youth, giving up his daughter to be burned, or condemning a young princess to her death. Was God punishing him for those things?   For rejecting his Church and his divinely ordained king? Perhaps he was reaping what he had sown. Or more precisely, Antonia was reaping it. Perhaps he should have obeyed in silence, content to follow the pope and the king without question.

On the other hand, why should he think that this situation was brought about by God? His discoveries had taught him that the world was a machine, gears and cogs meshing together, everything from rocks to human beings made up of random, mindless atoms. In such a universe, why should he expect good deeds to be rewarded? Perhaps the atheists were right. Perhaps there was no such thing as God after all.

A noise from above caught his attention. The birds with the dagger beaks were squawking, taking awkward flight and abandoning their half-eaten eels on their rock. Something was scaring them away.

Their outcropping was unreachable from where Ramos stood, separated by one of many cracks jutting into the cliff face. He could see clearly, however, when a huge creature emerged where the birds had stood a moment before. It was a salamander, grossly bloated, its translucent skin gorged and dragging on the ground. A faint glow emanated from inside its flesh, as if it had been feasting on fireflies. It bellowed, a guttural sound like a retching cow. Then, incredibly, it ran off the edge of the cliff.

It fell gracelessly, end over end, and collided with the water with an audible slap. Ramos thought it must surely be dead, but he could see it shake itself off and swim out to sea, its splayed legs frantically churning the water. He was too busy watching it to notice the second salamander until it, too, had pitched itself into the ocean.

Ramos looked back up at the cliff to see a third and fourth salamander, each as bloated and fat as the first, launch themselves in ungainly leaps into space, only to fall like a stone. They were followed by two more, and then a multitude, like a river of salamanders cascading into the sea. Ramos watched them, transfixed.

Not all of them survived the fall. Some slapped against the water and then floated motionless, while others survived the splash but were crushed by the weight of the next creature landing on top of them. What were they doing? His consternation only increased when he saw the first group of salamanders, those who had made it farther out into the water, disappearing under the waves. An enormous back crested nearby, revealing the existence of some truly gigantic predator.

One of the salamanders had drifted off course and was paddling away, but the sea creature erupted from beneath it, its enormous mouth swallowing the salamander whole and throwing tremendous waves of water into the air. The breach revealed the monster's shape: an enormous fish with a head like a stone tower, black crested, with a mouth full of gleaming rows of teeth. Ramos had never sailed in these waters, but he had heard of such giants. One had nearly destroyed the ship that brought the original colonists to Horizon. They had called it leviathan.

Ramos knew enough about animals to know that they valued their own lives. What possible survival instinct would drive this group of salamanders to hurl themselves into the sea to die? He had no idea, but the scene seemed particularly poignant, given his own circumstances. Whatever drove them, these creatures must have felt that they had no choices left. The other options open to them must have seemed worse than this insane act of self-destruction.

Ramos stepped right to the very edge of his own precipice, his toes over open space, looking straight down at the rocks and the spraying mist from the crashing waves. There was no smell of salt; this was Horizon, after all. He swayed slightly, his sense of balance compromised. It would be so easy. So simple, just to fall forward. Hardly a decision at all. A brief and terrifying fall, and then it would be all over. What was his life, after all? He had failed Antonia. He had failed Elizabeth. He could do nothing for them. Better to die here, alone, than to give his enemies a chance to use his death to coerce others.

And yet, he couldn't do it. It was more than just the fear of committing a mortal sin; he was well beyond that. It was just that, even now, he thought of life as precious. Antonia's life was precious. He couldn't let her die. Helpless rage surged through him. If what he was doing was right, why was it all turning out so wrong? Was God truly just an architect who had started the machine of the world and then let it go? Didn't he care about the evils being committed in the world right now?

If God truly cared about the events of this world, then wasn't this a time to intervene? Ramos's faith was slipping away like salt through his fingers. He didn't know what to think anymore. He had the Scriptures, yes, but what did that mean for him, now? Gideon had asked for a sign in a fleece, and God had given it to him. That's what Ramos needed. Some hint, some sign, that God cared about the good and evil deeds men did, and that all that was happening was part of his great design.

A giant wave crashed against the cliff face below him, sending another crest of spray into the air. But this time, it was no natural wave. It was the leviathan, leaping out of the sea directly below Ramos, just like it had done to swallow the wayward salamander. Its massive bulk cleared the water entirely, a fish leaping to catch an insect, only the fish was as big as a building, and the insect was Ramos. Before he could move, the leviathan's huge jaws had enveloped him. Its enormous body smashed into the earth, its teeth tearing through rock, rending away a piece of the cliff with a sound like an avalanche, swallowing Ramos whole.

ANTONIA knew her body was close. Catherine had told her so, although she couldn't see it herself. The world around her was a mystery; she couldn't see it like the people did, not through physical eyes. She could sense the people around her, track their movements, but her own body was as invisible to her as the air. With Catherine's guidance, she flitted around it, even passed through it, but she couldn't enter it, couldn't marry her spirit to her body. She couldn't become herself again. It was maddening.

And there was fire. She couldn't see it or smell it or feel its heat, but she could tell it was there. Just a smolder at first, dry wood slowly heating and catching the flame of the torch. It spread from branch to branch, licking upward, smoking, gathering around Catherine.

Antonia screamed in frustration. These men were burning Catherine, and she could do nothing about it. They would probably burn her own body as well, before she had a chance to get back into it. She didn't even know if she ever would, but she certainly couldn't if it was burned away. She was so helpless, unable to rescue Catherine or douse the fire or even call for help.

Help. Maybe she could get help. It wasn't just those people close to her whom she could sense. Maasha Kaatra was far away, still with Tanalabrinu's manticores, but she could see his spirit. If she could reach him, if he and the others could come before it was too late, then maybe there was hope.

She flew toward him. She moved at a frustratingly slow pace, but at least it was in a straight line. Tanalabrinu's manticores had retreated to high ground, where they had reached a kind of stalemate. The mercury bullets had long since run out, but Rinchirith's manticores had them surrounded and pinned. Fierce fighting continued, but Maasha Kaatra sat far from the front line, on the edge of the Gorge, his legs hanging over the side.

Antonia rushed to tell him what was happening.

"What can I do?" he said. "Death is the fate of all men."

The roars and cries of battle seemed strangely faint here. The land around was quiet and still.

"You can fight!" she said. "You can stand against oppression and rescue the innocent."

Maasha Kaatra turned his head slowly, wearily, to face her. "Ten years ago, I watched as my girls were murdered by Portuguese sailors. I was ready to take my own life then, but Christopher Sinclair convinced me there was another way. He told me stories of an island with magical powers, where the dead could come to life. I knew these stories already. I had read them in the books of Jabir ibn Hayyan. A recipe for the creation of life. So I knew they were true.

"I traveled here with Sinclair, and I watched him make those stories live. He healed the dying, and brought the dead back to life. But I learned something. Death does not belong with life. Death cannot be reclaimed, except at a cost greater than one is willing to pay. So I sought, instead, to die.

"All I want is to be with my girls again. It's all I've ever wanted. Yet, I entered the void to find them, and they were not there. What if I cross the river into death and do not find them there either?"

Antonia huffed in frustration. If they stood here talking much longer, it would be too late. "Catherine is dying as we speak. She's being murdered, just like your daughters were. If you must die, do it for a reason. Your girls are dead, but she's not, at least not yet, and neither am I. Would they want you to sit by and do nothing? Stop trying to die for them, and *live* for them instead!"

Maasha Kaatra's body straightened, and his eyes focused. An intensity started to burn there, a sense of purpose. He stood up. "You are wise, little one."

He drew his curved sword out of the scabbard at his belt. He hefted it, raising it high above his head and back down again.

"Go!" Antonia said. "Or there won't be anything left to save."

He ran toward the battle, bellowing his daughters' names. Antonia rose higher. She could see him charge into the fray, whirling and spinning with his great sword. He was just one man against a multitude, but the manticores had seen him emerge from the deep.

He represented the power and strength of the earth snakes. Tanalabrinu's manticores surged down around him, fighting with renewed fervor.

The Gorge under Antonia suddenly glowed red, and a salamander crawled out. Antonia flew as high as she could, hoping it wouldn't sense her. Then another came out, and another. They loped down the hill toward the fighting, lunging and snapping. All through the battlefield, more salamanders erupted out of the ground.

Rinchirith's troops, convinced it was Maasha Kaatra calling them forth to fight, fled in panic, while Tanalabrinu's troops pursued them, now gaining the upper hand. The salamanders seemed willing to attack either side, but they, too, were running down the mountainside, giving the impression that they were chasing Rinchirith's fleeing manticores.

Antonia didn't know if Maasha Kaatra could get there in time to stop the burning, but she had done all she could. She was just thinking this as a salamander leaped high and snapped its jaws around her, plunging her into darkness.

RAMOS was the leviathan. His body was gone, crushed and digested within seconds, but he still remained. And he was not the only one. He knew now that the salamanders throwing themselves over the cliff were sated with the spirits they had devoured, all of which now vied inside the leviathan's mind. Ramos fought, hardly knowing how, his spirit battling instinctively for dominance.

Most of the spirits were passive, resigned to their fate, but one was strong and wild, the spirit of the leviathan itself. It was not an intelligent creature, not aware of itself as an individual, but it was young and fierce and full of life. Ramos fought to keep his sense of self, waging a war with no weapons, no strength of arms, just the power of his spirit struggling to survive.

He was himself, and he was the leviathan. He saw what the leviathan saw, felt what it felt, swam where it swam. But he could not overcome its instincts. It was a fish, not a man, an animal driven by the need to eat and reproduce and survive. These needs drove its actions, and so Ramos—the leviathan— continued his feast, feeding on the bodies of salamanders living and dead. With each bite came a rush of fresh spirits, and yet Ramos maintained control.

It was the quintessence, not the spirits themselves, that this creature craved. And yet, there was more to it. Just as the manticores' minds could connect through a quintessence bond, so this great beast was connected to every salamander it had ever devoured, and through it, to every shekinah flatworm those salamanders had devoured in their turn.

In fact, this act of grasping and chewing and swallowing and digesting was not really feeding at all. It was a stage in the life of this extraordinary creature, as it developed from a host of shekinah flatworms to a handful of salamanders into a single leviathan. Through its mind, however simple, Ramos could see the whole picture.

It began as a shekinah, just one of many, born of starlight in the trunks of the beetlewood trees. Its light shone out, generating a quintessence field that affected many other plants and animals. Over time, however, as its starlight poured out, a residue of salt built up in its body, and its light waned. Finally, it migrated to the mountain caves, leaving trails of salt behind it on the ground.

Deep within those caves, its overheated body cooled by the rock, it excreted salt and starved for lack of starlight. Finally, unable to live without the light, it devoured its neighbor. Eating the neighbor did not mean the neighbor's death, however. The two merged flesh and mind. Combined, it grew in strength, but also in need, and soon ate a third, and a fourth, vying with other devourers and eating them in turn.

Thus it entered its second stage of life, that of the salamander, eating shekinahs for the little light that remained in them, and excreting the extra salt that had built up in their bodies. This is the salt that made its way through streams and rivers into the earth, where plants drew from it, and were in turn eaten by the animals who needed the salt as well.

The salamanders were more mobile and could roam the caves,

seeking quintessence that had become trapped in rocks or pools. But soon they began to devour one another, merging yet again. As one gained ascendency, the other salamanders submitted to being eaten, eager to join their minds and strength into the greater whole. Fully developed, now, with fins and a tail, the leviathan would splash down into the deep mountain streams that emptied, at long last, into the sea.

The part of Ramos that was not the leviathan struggled to make sense of this. Why would such a complex multi-stage being exist? Why the move from the land to the sea? What benefit did it gain?

Then this, too, became clear to him through the leviathan's memories. The ocean abounded in quintessence. All the quintessence that flowed into the world from the stars and filtered, unused, through land and water, eventually found its way here, to the edge of the world, where it collected and reacted with the salt, making the water fresh and giving it its power to heal. Here the leviathan could glut itself on the quintessence it could find by sifting the water through its jaws, or by eating sea creatures smaller than itself.

And this was the truly remarkable discovery for an astronomer: quintessence was not infinite. The stars did not generate an unending supply. Quintessence had to be *returned* to the sky as part of an ancient cycle, one that combined the actions of sun and stars and land and animals.

The leviathan surfaced. Its deep bellow echoed against the cliffs. Then it began to glow.

It was nothing like the simple glow of a shekinah. This was a spotlight aimed at the stars. Quintessence flowed thick and heavy, like liquid gold, pouring out of the leviathan and into the sky. The spirits, except for Ramos and the leviathan itself, flowed up with it. They were returning to their constellation, perhaps even following the quintessence threads right back to their own bodies in England and Spain and Africa and Cathay.

And Ramos knew, too, why the island had been covered by storms that blocked the stars, why the salt deposits in the ground were running out, and why a miasma had been seeping up into the lowest spaces where quintessence no longer reached. Maasha Kaatra had interrupted the cycle. He had usurped the place of the leviathans and torn quintessence down from the sky. He had broken the connection between the human spirits and the stars under which they had been born.

The leviathan knew nothing of the great cycle. It felt no need to replenish the heavens with quintessence. It was just a beast, following its own instinctual behavior. As his beam of golden light illuminated the sky, Ramos could see other beams, farther away, blazing up out of the sea.

Driven by instinct, Ramos swam towards these with great strokes of his tail. The lights converged, hundreds of them, and soon the water seethed with leviathans. They swam over and under each other, each demonstrating the strength and color of its quintessence light, trying to attract a mate. Before long, Ramos's leviathan had paired with another, and the mating began.

Ramos began to drift. He was not a leviathan, and had no wish to live like one. Perhaps now he would die. Perhaps he would rise and become part of the heavens. He didn't know. Part of him noticed that now, as the leviathans mated, the rays of light were speckled with thousands of tiny specks, drifting up into the sky. Ramos had no doubt that, in some fashion, these specks would find their way back down to Earth in beams of starlight striking the beetlewood trees, from which tiny shekinah worms would begin to grow.

Relinquishing his hold on the leviathan, Ramos floated up with them, born aloft with the force of the golden river. He could see the whole island and, beyond it, the sharp curve of the edge of the world and the desperate empty blackness of the void beyond. Then he ascended past the clouds and into the dark sky.

And now he knew what quintessence was. It was spirit-stuff, the material of souls, of life itself. He could see the threads passing through the stars and back, around the world, toward the people who lived in Europe and Africa and Asia. The quintessence that returned to the sky here, near Horizon, spread out over the whole world. It fell to Earth as starlight and fueled all living things. He saw the glowing spirit lights flit down those threads, flying fast toward home. But

Ramos had no home, no body to return to. His physical body lay crushed and digesting in the leviathan's stomach.

He flew higher still, above the stars. He saw the intricate way they turned and spun, exactly as Copernicus had predicted, driven by the quintessence that flowed into them. It was a revelation greater even than those he had seen so far: the stars, the very heavens, operated by the same natural rules as things on the Earth. The world was, after all, a machine. Even the stars were part of the same mechanism that made water freeze or boil, dropped objects fall to the ground, wood burn and wax melt, rocks hard and flesh soft, and blind seeds break to send shoots springing out into the light.

He had always been taught that the stars, closer to heaven, were heavenly in nature: unblemished, flawless, traveling in perfect circles. But here he was in the heavens, and he couldn't see God. All he saw was a self-winding watch, a system that ran itself. Quintessence—life itself—was a natural cycle, self-perpetuating. The stars were ultimately no different than rocks or centipedes.

He flew even higher. The great machine of the world dwindled to a single point of meaning, surrounded by looming, infinite void. It was transient, a device that would exist as long as its gears kept turning and then submit to the darkness. But no. Ramos refused to accept that there was no more purpose to his life than as a tiny cog in the churning of a great machine. He wasn't ready to die, nor was he willing to let Antonia and Elizabeth go helplessly to their deaths. Their persecution wasn't just the meaningless shifting of a gear; it was evil. There was right, and there was wrong, regardless of how the machine ran.

And suddenly, he could see something new. There was a fabric, light and strong, twined through everything. The world was made of the fabric. The rocks, the water, the air, the humans and manticores, the animals and plants, the stars, even quintessence, was simply painted dye, and the fabric, the fabric was everything, so finely woven as to be nearly invisible. Even the *void* itself, the very darkness, was woven from it.

Ramos touched it. It thrummed and sang. He ran fingers through its strings, and knew that every one of them, a thousand thousand

thousand, had a name. The choices of kings, the rise and fall of nations, even the throw of a pair of dice, was in the strings. The fabric held the machine together. The sun rose and set, animals were born and lived and died, because of the shape and weave of the fabric.

If the fabric shifted, would the machine change? Would the natural laws of the universe reverse themselves and take new shapes?

Ramos had asked for a sign, and here it was. He couldn't see God, but he could see what God saw. He could see that the machine was not a machine in truth, but merely an expression of the shape of the fabric. And what could the fabric itself be but an expression of the will and character of God? Here, at the end of everything, Ramos found his faltering faith gaining strength again.

He had been so concerned about the machine, but underneath it, all the time, was a deeper layer. He might study the clouds and the sun and the wind, and understand why the rain fell on a particular day, but underneath that was another reason, governed by the shape of the fabric. And who was to say that under the fabric was not a deeper layer still, and underneath that, still more?

And now, he had a choice. Above him, in the distance, he could see a light. The light called to him, promising beauty and goodness and rest. He could drift away, continuing this journey to where it ended, and perhaps see God in truth, in all of his glory. Perhaps, there, he would see all the layers, and understand them all.

On the other hand, he could take hold of the strings. He touched them, feeling them vibrate, and knew that, for this moment at least, he had power to command, more power than any human before had ever held, save one. All of the quintessence in the world was nothing compared to the power of these strings.

He looked up again, and the light flooded his eyes, so beautiful it made his heart ache, so right and whole that he nearly let go. But it wasn't time yet. He had work to do.

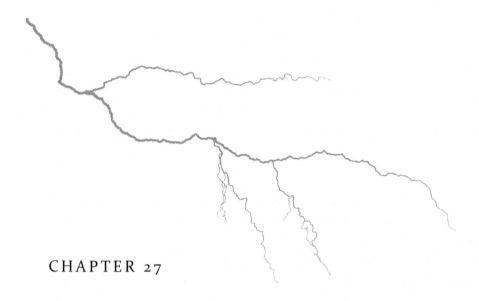

CHAPTER 27

THE FIRE under Catherine was slow to spread. Her father fought to reach her, to stamp out the flames, for all the good it would have done. Torres would simply have lit it again. But the soldiers held him back, laughing, and the flames steadily grew.

She felt the heat of the fire, but no pain, not yet. She wondered how long it would take for her to die. Hours? *Could* she even die from fire, or would her body burn and burn and then heal itself only to burn some more? She was trying to be brave, but she didn't feel brave, not facing this.

Matthew was holding her gaze, and it felt like a lifeline. He wasn't leaving her alone, though there was nothing he could do to save her. Her concerns about marrying him seemed baseless now; she knew he would listen to her and respect her. It was who he was. It was why she loved him. Though now she would never get the chance to find that out.

His mouth moved in the shape of a word. What was he saying? I love you? No, it hadn't looked like that. The crackling of the fire under her was making it hard to think. He tried again, and this time she understood the word: *substitution*. She knew what it meant, of course. It was the basis of the heat exchanger, and a memory of that day on the bay, when they had kissed and traded the sensations of their bodies.

Then it hit her. The kiss. It hadn't been a tragic, last symbol of love. He had pushed his tongue into her mouth, taking enough of her saliva to make a connection. He was taking her pain on himself.

She had only just comprehended his meaning when he clenched his teeth and turned away from her. She knew it had worked. The fire was higher now, but she felt nothing. Matthew was feeling the agony that ought to be hers, the flames that even now were licking at her feet.

She spoke, making her voice calm and confident, loud enough that everyone could hear. "Are you done with this charade yet, Captain Torres?"

Torres smiled at her, but there was uncertainty in his eyes. "Very bravely spoken. Perhaps the devil gives you strength. But even the devil cannot stand against hell."

"You are mistaken," Catherine said. "We are God's elect. Have you not heard of the three friends of Daniel, who walked in the furnace and were not burned?"

"True. But God does not rescue heretics. And the devil is not above twisting the words of holy Scripture."

The fire was rising fast. Matthew must be suffering terribly, but he lay unmoving on the ground, not betraying his anguish. Catherine hated to do it, but she knew she must. It was what Matthew wanted. She lifted her foot and thrust it into the heart of the flames. She saw Matthew's foot jerk, but he didn't cry out.

She turned away from him and faced the Spanish. "You cannot hurt me. We will tell you nothing. Repent of your violence and greed and release us, and perhaps God will forgive you. Perhaps he will allow you to return to your own country in peace."

It was the best she could do. It couldn't possibly fool them for long. They would just hurt someone else, or they would wait long enough that Matthew would cry out, or the substitution would wear off, and she would burn. Torres's eyes were wide. If he were a monster like Tavera, this wouldn't work. He would keep pressing until someone suffered. If he were devout, though, doing this out of a twisted sense of godliness, then, just maybe, it would have some effect.

Torres pulled a long branch out of the fire, its other end hot embers. He reached over the fire with the stick and pressed the embers into her cheek. It sizzled, and she smelled her own flesh burning, but she felt nothing. She forced herself not to look at Matthew. Instead, she smiled. "Stop this masquerade. Would you fight against God?"

The conquistadors were backing away, crossing themselves, clearly terrified. Torres dropped the stick. "Stand your ground!" he shouted at them. "This is not God's work, but the work of the devil. They are witches and demon worshippers. Do not listen to them."

Catherine could have cried. She looked at Matthew now, still curled on the ground, trying not attract attention. It was intense bravery, and she loved him for it. Loved him for taking her agony, if only for a time, and for being willing to give his life in an attempt to save hers. Even if it hadn't worked.

It was too late now, anyway. The fire was burning too hot and too high, and there was no water; the Spanish couldn't put it out now even if they wanted to. The smoke was thick, making it hard to breathe, and she coughed violently. It occurred to her that even if the flames never harmed her, she could die from breathing the smoke. If the flames spread high enough that they burned the ropes around her wrists, she could walk out unharmed. But her wrists were tied above her head. By the time the fire reached them, Matthew would be dead, and the effect of the substitution would end. They would die together.

She wished that, before they died, she could at least see his face one last time. Then, as if hearing her wish, Matthew stirred and raised his head, astonishment written on his face.

THE PAIN was worse than Matthew had imagined. He moaned through gritted teeth, trying to keep silent. His legs were in searing, blistering agony. He refused to writhe, refused to scream, giving Catherine a chance to make this desperate attempt work. When she held her foot in the fire, he opened his mouth to scream, only to feel the strong, knotted hand of his father clamp firmly over his mouth.

His father's voice whispered urgently in his ear. "Don't give up now. You can do this."

Matthew clenched his teeth again, focusing on the pain, trying to disassociate what he was feeling from the reactions of his body. The fire consumed him. It became hard to remember who he was or what had been so important to him a moment ago; the world contained nothing but pain. It was colored lights flashing behind his eyes, a buzzing in his ears, a suffocating stench. There was rhythm to the pain, a throbbing, pulsing beat that threatened to split him open.

Then, suddenly, it stopped.

One moment, excruciating pain; the next, nothing, as if it had never been. Afraid for Catherine, Matthew snapped open his eyes and lifted his head to look at her. If the pain had left him, it would be back to her.

But no. She was looking at him, still unaffected. Yet he felt nothing. What was happening?

The fire rose quickly now, crackling loudly, filling the air with smoke. Catherine coughed violently, but she still seemed unaffected by the heat of the fire.

"Look, in the flames!" Ferguson shouted. He pointed, and Matthew looked. There, standing in the fire with Catherine, was a man. Torres saw it, too. He fell to his knees, unable to tear his eyes away. "What have I done? Get water, quickly! Douse the fire!"

The man in the fire raised his arms, and a giant salamander leaped out of the flames. It was twice as big as a man, and its flesh was ablaze. It fell on a conquistador, its gleaming mouth agape. The others scrambled back, but they weren't quick enough. More salamanders leaped from the fire, burning like torches but unaffected by the flames. They chased down the soldiers, fast and relentless, and where they touched skin and cloth the men were engulfed in fire.

Only Torres escaped, running past his screaming men and into the forest beyond.

The ropes holding Catherine's wrists broke, and she stumbled out, coughing and gasping for air, but otherwise unharmed. The man whom they had seen in the fire was gone.

MAASHA KAATRA fought like one possessed. He had always been fast and strong, but today he felt invincible, his sword slicing cleanly through flesh, the manticores' pincers and tails unable to touch him. Even so, it was the salamanders, not him, who turned the tide. Rinchirith's manticores thought he had called them out to war against them, and many of Tanalabrinu's seemed to think he had as well. The enemy panicked, and once they were on the run, their advantage was lost.

Tanalabrinu's army pursued them down the slopes, but they scattered, retreating in every direction. Maasha Kaatra didn't veer to help track them down. Antonia had sent him on a mission, and he would not be diverted. He could see the smoke pouring into the sky above the trees, and he headed that way. He was sure he would be too late. With that much smoke, the fire must be large, but he wouldn't give up now. He kept running.

As he drew close, he heard screams and the grunting sounds he now associated with the salamanders. Had they reached the spot before him? If so, who were they attacking?

His answer came quickly, as a conquistador with a captain's insignia on his helmet came running toward him through the trees, hardly looking where he was going. Maasha Kaatra didn't stop. He swung his curved sword in a familiar arc and took the man's head off his shoulders.

When he reached the clearing and the fire, he saw that there was nothing left for him to do. The battle was over.

The fire still burned, not a cool, white quintessence flame, but a roaring furnace of heat that made the air shimmer. The salamanders were everywhere, leaping and devouring, but Maasha Kaatra wasn't afraid of them.   He couldn't tear his eyes away from the fire.   It beckoned to him.   He looked into its depths, mesmerized.

The power that was in him, keeping him alive, that he had drawn from the stars, wanted to be in that fire.   It was as if he was a key and the fire was a lock.   He knew he would fit perfectly into it, would click and turn and spring open.   Instinct took hold, the instincts of the two leviathans he had entered and overtaken.   He thought he had conquered them, but that wasn't entirely true.   They had entered him as well.   He had overcome them for a time, but he couldn't hold back their fate forever.

He needed that fire, and it needed him.   He stepped toward it, unafraid.   He heard someone calling his name, but he didn't stop.   He walked into the fire.

There was no pain.   He felt, distantly, that his skin was burning. He licked his lips, but his tongue was dry.   Light was leeching out of his pores.   There were beams of light, far away, shining up to the sky from the ocean, and he joined them, a golden river of light springing up out of the fire, with him borne aloft on it, leaving his body behind to burn.

He left the island behind in a moment, and then the Earth itself grew distant as he was lifted into the realm of the stars.   A great flash of light seemed to incinerate everything he could see, and then it was dark. Utterly dark. The void.

Was this it, then? Was this where it ended? A pinprick of light broke the darkness.   Maasha Kaatra shielded his eyes with his hand, and was surprised to discover that he had eyes, and a hand.   There was motion in the light.   He walked toward it.

In the distance, he saw two figures, young, female.   The light streaming behind them made it hard to make out their features. "Girls?" he said.   He whispered their names through dry lips, but they heard him anyway.   He could see it in their postures, in the way they turned their heads, and then they ran to him.

"Papa!"

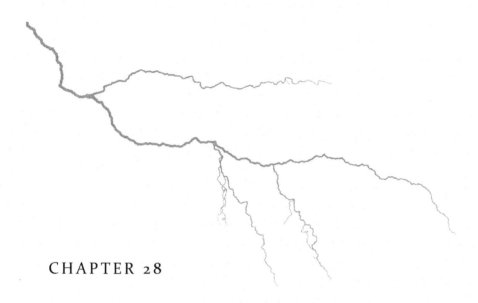

CHAPTER 28

MATTHEW threw his arms around Catherine. They both watched in horror and amazement as the burning salamanders attacked their enemies but left the colonists unharmed. The man who had walked in the fire with Catherine was gone.

"Maasha Kaatra!" Catherine screamed. Matthew followed her gaze and saw the big man walking toward the fire, heedless of the fighting around him.

"What's he doing?"

"I don't know," Catherine said. She shouted his name again, but he didn't pause. Without changing expression or stride, he walked directly into the flames. His clothes and hair caught instantly, but the intent expression on his face didn't change. Sweat poured from his body, and then, incredibly, light. The light shone out blindingly in every direction, and then became a column pointed at the sky. Maasha Kaatra's legs gave way, and he collapsed into the embers. The light blazed upwards, apparently from his body, which burned away rapidly. Finally, when there seemed to be nothing left, the light faded and disappeared.

The salamanders, however, were burning hotter than ever. The conquistadors dead, they stood still, feet planted, flames roaring high from their skin. It didn't seem to harm them, or to burn any part of them, until Matthew noticed that the closest one seemed lighter, more insubstantial, as if . . .

"It's burning them from the inside out," he breathed.

The salamander nearest to them exploded in a blast of ash that floated on the wind. It was swiftly followed by each of the others, until a cloud of ash filled the clearing like snow. It swirled around, as if driven by the wind, but its eddies grew tighter, the ashes spinning closer together until they formed a shape that gradually took the appearance of a man. Then the ashes coalesced, and left in their place a real man of flesh and blood.

The man from the fire. He was youthful, strong, his face smooth and unlined. His skin was impossibly clean, shining like a newly-forged sword. He was smiling broadly, and despite his strange appearance, Matthew recognized him.

"Ramos?" he said. "Ramos de Tavera?"

Ramos laughed. "Yes, it's me, my friend."

A realization struck Matthew. "It was you in the fire!"

Ramos shrugged and nodded.

"And those salamanders were your doing?"

"In a manner of speaking."

Matthew grasped Ramos's arm—as real and solid as his own—and introduced Catherine. "This is my fiancée," he said. "We owe you our lives."

Ramos shook his head. "It was your substitution that made it possible. I simply transferred the link."

"I don't understand."

"You and Catherine were linked by a quintessence thread, just like the one I passed through from London to Horizon. The threads are more like tunnels that reach into the space beyond; they can transfer just about anything. I simply took that thread and reconnected it to a group of salamanders that hadn't yet found their way to the sea."

"But . . ." Matthew gaped at him. "How could you possibly do such a thing?"

Ramos smiled, and there was a gleam in his eye of some deep understanding. He was a man at peace with himself and with the world. "Honestly?" he said. "I have no idea."

Matthew wanted to press him on it, to hear his story, but by then the other colonists had crowded around, shaking Ramos's hand and clapping him on the back.

Catherine drew Matthew away. "Plenty of time to get your questions in later," she said. She pulled him toward her. This time, they made the kiss last. Matthew never wanted to pull away, but eventually she pushed him back. "I have to breathe, you know," she said, laughing.

Matthew saw a young girl pushing her way into the crowd. "Look," he said.

Catherine saw her. "Make way!" she called. "Everybody stand back!"

The crowd parted, and Ramos saw her, too. "Antonia?" he said.

A smile split her face, now filled with intelligence and awareness of her surroundings. "Tío Ramos!" she said.

They ran into an embrace.

Matthew buried his face in Catherine's hair, breathing in the scent of her, smoke and all. "It's over," he said.

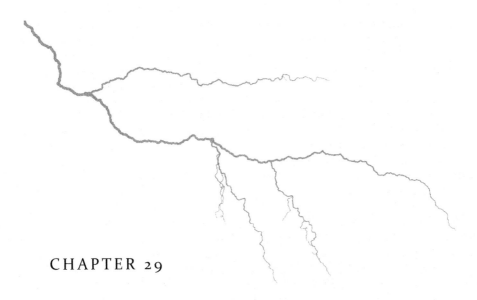

CHAPTER 29

CATHERINE'S wedding dress wasn't white. They had no white cloth to use, and no way to whiten it, even with quintessence. It was one of a long list of details that was causing her mother heartache.

Catherine hoped she was happy, despite all the complaints. Before coming to Horizon, her mother would have expected her to marry a nobleman in a cathedral, exquisite in the best dress money could buy. She had, in fact, pushed hard to find such a match back in England, thinking that the way to ensure Catherine's future happiness and security—not to mention the happiness of her grandchildren— was to land her with a reliable and lavish income. This, like so many other things, hadn't turned out as Catherine's mother had planned.

"And the flowers are all wrong!" her mother said. "A wedding is supposed to have rosemary and roses; it's how it's always done."

"But roses don't grow on Horizon," Catherine said. "Nor does rosemary. We do have some lovely red blooms, though."

"It's not the same. And look at your dress!"

It was probably the tenth time she had exclaimed about it. The dress was a dark gray, stitched by Joan herself from a silk tablecloth found in Captain Torres's cabin aboard *La Magdalena*. It had a square-cut neckline, flowing sleeves with lace snipped from another of the Spanish captain's amenities, a tightly-fitted waist, and a skirt over layers of petticoats that poured out like a waterfall in every direction. Catherine thought it was beautiful.

"It's perfect, Mother. You did a wonderful job."

"But there's no church! How can you get married without a church?"

"True," Catherine said. "But how many girls get to have a Princess of England as a bridesmaid?"

Her mother beamed despite herself. Catherine knew that she was fiercely proud of this fact, even though there was no pecking system here and none of the aristocratic ladies with whom her mother used to interact were here to be impressed. Back home, it would have been the highlight of her mother's year to be *spoken* to by the princess; for Elizabeth to actually be in her daughter's wedding made up for any number of other deficiencies.

Catherine's father strode into the room. He was getting better at managing his bond with Tanalabrinu; he didn't seem so distracted all the time. "Did you tell her, my dear?"

Joan's smile vanished. "I couldn't do it," she said.

"Tell me what?"

Her father sighed. "We won't be coming with you after the wedding."

"What do you mean? We're all going back to England, just like we agreed. It was your idea."

Her father met her eyes. "Most are going. But not your mother and I."

"I don't understand. There's nothing left here. We talked about this. We decided!"

After bringing so much disaster, they had come to the hard conclusion that there was no place for human colonists on Horizon. It was inhabited already. Their presence had disrupted manticore politics and nearly destroyed the whole island itself, more than once. A small colony was only the start; with the generations, it would grow, and their children and grandchildren would be always be at war with the manticores, until one side or the other was completely destroyed.

It had been Catherine's father who had helped them all see that, bonded as he was to Tanalabrinu. There was no happy ending where manticores and humans could mix and live in peace. One of them would have to win the island entirely, and the manticores were here already.

"That was the plan," her mother said, rolling her eyes. "But your father had other ideas."

Catherine's father took her hands in his. "Tanalabrinu asked us to stay. Just because we leave doesn't mean no humans will come to Horizon. There will be more ships, and more colonists, and more soldiers. Once the power of this place becomes known, every country on Earth will send troops to take a piece for themselves. Tanalabrinu wants to be ready. He wants me to help him make Horizon into a nation, one other countries will recognize and respect, even if they don't like it. He wants to be strong enough to fight off aggressors, but diplomatic enough not to have to, at least not always. To do that, he needs ambassadors. People who understand how to communicate effectively between manticore and human."

"And that's you." Catherine couldn't keep the sob out of her voice. This meant she wouldn't see her parents for years. She might never see them again in her whole life.

"Your mother and I, and Matthew's father as well. We're going to stay, and live among the manticores, and treat with the humans when they come."

"Does Matthew know?"

"I don't think so. We only decided for certain this morning."

Catherine wiped her eyes. "I want to stay, too."

Her father squeezed her hands and gently shook his head. "You and Matthew have chosen well. Elizabeth needs supporters she can trust. Most of all, she needs people who understand quintessence and how to use it. If she's going to win back her throne, she'll need the two of you. This power is going to change the shape of the world, and you and Matthew are going to be at the forefront." He kissed her.

"But I will miss you terribly."

Joan started to cry in earnest, and then Catherine couldn't hold back the tears. They clutched each other, and Catherine stroked her mother's hair.

"A fine wedding celebration this is shaping up to be," Catherine said.

"Nonsense." Her mother pulled back and looked her in the eye. "This is your day. Forget about what comes after. And forget about the roses and the dress. We're going to make it a day you'll remember—with joy—for the rest of your life. Understand?"

Catherine nodded her assent, and a smile escaped through her tears. "Yes, mother."

MATTHEW was packing a small satchel with supplies for a short journey when Blanca found him. He hadn't spoken to her since Catherine had returned. To tell the truth, he'd been avoiding her.

"Please let me talk to you," she said.

"Of course. I'm sorry," he said.

"I really am glad Catherine is back. You know that, don't you?"

He set the satchel down. "Yes, of course I do. She's your closest friend."

"And I'm happy for you both. You're so in love. I'm glad she's found someone. She's had a lot of hard things in her life, and . . ." She trailed off.

She was truly beautiful, soft and uncertain, her eyes expressive in that exquisitely carved face. But despite her beauty and kindness and gentle grace, he could say without hesitation that she was not for him. Catherine fit him perfectly. She could be brash and impatient, but it was just what he needed sometimes, when he tended toward self-pity. And her strength and intensity reminded him of what was true and right and mattered in the world. He loved Catherine.

But Blanca was hurting. He had to respond. If their situations had been reversed, Blanca would have had the perfect encouragement, known just the right thing to say.

"There is someone for you," he said. She started to object but he held up his hand. "Somewhere there's a man who is fervent and wild and passionate and needs your gentle strength to ground him. Someone bright and good who fits you like Catherine fits me. Believe it. You're not limited to this island anymore. You'll have all of England and France and Spain and beyond to choose from."

She gave a wavering smile. "I'm fine on my own. I don't need a man."

"But somewhere there's a man who needs you."

She squeezed his hand. "You're a good friend," she said.

Matthew tied his satchel shut and went in search of Ramos. They had a job to do, and not much time in which to do it. In fact, he probably shouldn't be doing it at all this close to his wedding; Ramos could handle it on his own. But Catherine knew how much he wanted to, and didn't object.

Ramos was down by the water, on a stretch of sand. The Spanish ships still floated at anchor in the bay. He had the stick that was connected, by quintessence thread, to a chicken bone in London. Parris was there, too, with a small vial of vitriol.

Ramos placed the stick on the sand. "Ready?" he said.

Matthew nodded. The stick was such an ordinary piece of wood, by appearance, but it was their only link back to Europe, the only means by which they could make this work. Parris poured a drop of vitriol, and the void sprang into being.

Now that he was standing here, watching it grow, Matthew realized how incredibly brave Elizabeth had been to leap into it for the first time, especially knowing as little about it as she did. Even Matthew, knowing it had been done successfully before, had a hard time looking into that black hole and deciding to jump into it. Parris split another stick in half and threw half of it into the void. He would stay here, with the ability to come after them if something went wrong, and they didn't return.

Ramos went first, and once he had gone, Matthew could hardly fail to follow. He took a deep breath and plunged into the darkness.

He fell out of the void onto a stretch of country road under a blue sky. Ramos had just stepped out of the way, avoiding a collision. The destroyed carriage had been dragged off the road, where it lay rusting and forgotten, but apparently the chicken bone Ramos had used to anchor to the thread had fallen out here. Ramos kicked around in the dirt and found it. He bent and picked it up, then put it in his pocket.

It felt strange to be in England again. Everything looked both familiar and foreign. The sun seemed remote and cool, the air dry, the trees exotic with their broad green leaves. It was everything Matthew had grown up with, but after more than a year living on Horizon, it was surprising how different it all looked.

There was no one in sight. Their task was simple: to make sure the connection was still working, and to find a safe place to put the bone so that when the larger group came through with Elizabeth in a few days, they could be reasonably certain they would arrive safe and unnoticed. There was no guarantee, of course, but Matthew and Ramos wanted to minimize the chance of surprises.

They turned east, away from London, and began walking down the road. They hoped to find a village of some kind, perhaps an inn with a room they could rent for several days. Matthew darted glances at Ramos while they walked. He had hardly known the man before the battle, but it was disconcerting to see his flawless skin and newly-youthful face. Ramos had explained what had happened from his perspective, but Matthew barely understood it. He got the impression that Ramos barely understood it himself.

They each had several shekinahs with them, keeping them alive, as well as giving them all the quintessence abilities they had enjoyed back on the island. They broke into a run, easily covering as much ground as a horse might, and without feeling tired. They passed small farm after small farm, each scratching out a subsistence in the muddy earth. In the distance, Matthew saw a stone barn with weathered edges and a half-collapsed roof.

"How about that?"

Ramos skidded to a stop, kicking up a cloud of road dust. "The barn?"

"It's large enough for a group, and it looks abandoned."

They jogged across the field and examined the building more closely. The door hung askew on broken hinges. Inside, moldy straw and spider webs were all that was left of what must have once held a large number of animals. Matthew suspected a large number of rats now lived there, but that no humans had been here in some time.

"It will suffice," Ramos said. "It's large, and remote enough to cause little comment. We can clean it out, and with your building methods, it should be a simple matter to repair the roof. For a few days, at least, while Elizabeth contacts her supporters, we should be safe enough."

"Why did you convert?" Matthew said.

Ramos frowned. "I beg your pardon?"

"You're Spanish, but you support Elizabeth. I never asked you, and I wondered what made you convert to Protestantism."

"I'm no Protestant," Ramos said. He spoke sternly, but he didn't seem to mind the question. "Any problems the Church has—and she does have them, I admit freely—should be resolved inside the Church. It does no good to splinter the Holy Faith into a thousand pieces, each of them free to pursue their own heresies."

Matthew was taken aback. "But . . ."

"But why do I support the Protestant princess?" Ramos shrugged. "She convinced me."

He dropped the chicken bone on the floor and kicked some straw over it. It seemed strange to leave something so precious lying around on the floor of a barn, but then, it had most recently been lying in the middle of the road. It was the sort of the thing that was safer if no attention was drawn to it.

A drop of vitriol opened up a void. It had taken all of Matthew's courage to step into it the first time, having seen and experimented with its destructive power, even though he knew that Ramos and Elizabeth had successfully made the trip before. This time he hesitated less, but it still made him nervous. He closed his eyes, took a breath, and stepped through. He fell and fell, no less terrifying for having done it before, but after what seemed like only moments, he crashed hard onto the stone floor of the caves. He was back on Horizon.

Strong hands pulled him to his feet. Parris brushed the dirt off of Matthew's front. "I thought you were only going to be gone a moment," he said. "Are you trying to miss your own wedding?"

THEY were married at the edge of the world. Bishop Marcheford stood with his back to the precipice, while the guests—both human and manticore—gathered closer to the tree line. Catherine didn't care about the color of her dress or the kind of flowers in her bouquet. Standing here, the sky almost close enough to touch and the breeze caressing her face and hair, she felt beautiful. Matthew clearly thought so, too, the way he couldn't tear his eyes away from her. His hair was askew, testament to his hasty preparations, but she didn't mind. He was back safely, and all was well for their return.

Blanca stood next to Catherine, and Elizabeth beyond her. On Matthew's side were her father and Tanalabrinu. The manticore looked awkward; the rite of marriage was completely alien to him, and Catherine couldn't guess what he felt about it. He had agreed to participate, however, and accepted it as the honor it was meant to be.

"Dearly beloved friends . . ." Bishop Marcheford began.

The sky was clear and blue for the first time in what seemed like months. Now that the quintessence cycle was restored, the novas had faded from the sky. The violent storms that had wracked the island were gone, and the soil, though not yet returned to its former levels, was increasing in salt content. Even the miasma was gone, the blighted hollows in the ground restored to quintessence life.

Catherine knew that all this had been Maasha Kaatra's doing. It had been he who had caused the novas in the first place, but by walking into that fire, he had set it right again. He had concluded the cycle that should have been completed by the leviathans whose power he had usurped. She hoped he hadn't suffered.

". . . and forsaking all others keep thee only to her, so long as you both shall live?" Marcheford said.

Matthew gazed at her face, his eyes alight. "I will," he said.

Catherine responded in kind, flashing him a quick grin. Matthew struggled to keep his expression solemn, as fitted such a holy occasion. She winked at him on the western side, where no one could see it but him, making him bite his lip to keep from smiling. They were giddy with excitement and love.

"I, Matthew, take thee, Catherine, to my wedded wife," he said seriously, glaring playfully at her, "to have and to hold from this day forward, for better, for worse, for richer, for poorer, in sickness, and in health, to love and to cherish, till death us do part, according to God's holy ordinance, and thereto I plight thee my troth."

The wedding vows were the new ones, taken from a copy of The Book of Common Prayer that Bishop Marcheford had smuggled out of England. They had been written by Thomas Cranmer less than ten years earlier, back when Edward VI was still alive and it was still safe to be a Protestant in England. Catherine repeated the words, hastily memorized and unfamiliar on her tongue. ". . . and thereto I plight thee my troth."

There was a lot more for Bishop Marcheford to read from the book, prayers and blessings and psalms. She and Matthew knelt and recited the Lord's Prayer, and there were more prayers and liturgical readings, which seemed to include a great deal about a wife submitting to and reverencing her husband, obeying him and calling him lord, and being mild and quiet in the home. Catherine wanted to pinch Matthew to make sure he wasn't taking it all too seriously, but she restrained herself. Enough time for that later.

The wedding concluded with the signing of the marriage contract between Catherine's father and Matthew's father. Matthew had objected to that bit of tradition, arguing that it was not their fathers who were getting married, but it was such an established part of custom and legal practice that he hadn't been able to make the objection stick. Their fathers both signed with a flourish, and the deed was done. They were married. Catherine put the wedding garland on her head, whooped, and threw her arms around her new husband.

The celebration afterwards was raucous and merry. In England, they would have had sweetmeats, baked peacock, and large quantities of wine, but none of those things were available here. They had sand pastries sweetened with honey instead, and roast diki, and some strong ale that one of the colonists brewed in the salvaged remains of

Sinclair's alchemy laboratory. There was singing and dancing, both in the English style and in the manticore style, which none of the humans could come close to imitating.

It was the first day of pure joy there had been in months. The time since the battle had been a time of grief, burying the dead, becoming reconciled to the destruction of their home, and trying to make plans for the future. The dead were not forgotten, but for this brief moment, they were able to set their sadness aside and enjoy this new beginning. It wasn't just Catherine who felt that way; she looked around at the survivors and saw real smiles on their faces. She was glad her wedding could provide such a badly needed respite from sorrow and regret.

Matthew left her side only for one brief moment, when he approached his father, tentatively at first, then with determination, and wrapped him in an awkward hug. They didn't say much, but Bishop Marcheford's hands were strong against his son's back. Tomorrow, Matthew would be leaving for England, and his father would be staying here. The two of them might never agree, but she was glad to see this reconciliation before they parted.

Matthew came back to her, and she took his hands. She gestured with her eyes, and they slipped away, not even saying goodbye to their guests. No one tried to stop them. After all, they only had this one night together before they returned to England. She longed for a month or a year with him, living peacefully in some secluded spot, getting to know each other as man and wife. But it was not to be. Tomorrow was a new day, and a new life.

THE NEXT day, before they left, another ceremony was held, just as well attended if more solemn. Catherine's father and Tanalabrinu had together drafted a letter declaring Horizon to be an independent nation. They had outlined a rough policy allowing limited human immigration, but not colonization, and a desire to build alliances and open trade. All the tribes were at least loosely unified now, under Tanalabrinu as a kind of king, and all the chiefs had agreed to the main points of the letter.

The ceremony was for Elizabeth, having declared herself the rightful queen of England, to sign and ratify the letter, the first European monarch to officially recognize Horizon's status as a nation and Tanalabrinu's title as king. Catherine smiled and clapped as Elizabeth signed. It was a bit of a sham, perhaps, since Elizabeth was not really a queen, and had no real authority to recognize anyone. But it was an important moment nonetheless, as it represented her promise to honor the alliance if she did manage to take the throne.

After signing, Elizabeth stood with Tanalabrinu on the raised dais built for the occasion and looked out over those who had come to witness it. There was clapping from the human contingent and that eerie rhythmic clacking from the much larger crowd of manticores.

The applause was loud, but Catherine was close enough to hear Elizabeth say to Tanalabrinu, "You really should execute him, you know."

Catherine knew she was referring to Rinchirith, who had sworn allegiance to Tanalabrinu and had been given no punishment that Catherine could see. In fact, he still seemed to be chief of the gray tribe.

"He is part of my memory family now," Tanalabrinu said, as if that explained everything.

"Aren't you afraid he'll rebel? That others will follow him again?" Elizabeth said.

Tanalabrinu's gesture was obscure. "He tried only to unify the tribes, as I have done. I fear him, certainly. But I will not kill him."

Elizabeth shrugged. "Your blood be on your own head. For my part, though, I hope you succeed."

"And you as well," Tanalabrinu replied.

The signing was the last event planned before the return to England. Crates had been packed with shekinah flatworms and other useful Horizon materials, animals, and plants of every kind. A few of the remaining colonists were planning to stay, but most of the survivors, about forty of them, would be returning to England with Elizabeth. The plan was to split up once they arrived, dividing the quintessence materials and traveling around England, raising support for Elizabeth's claim to the throne and training an army in the use of the quintessence power.

It was thrilling to be part of such a plan, though Catherine knew it would be dangerous. She believed in the cause, believed that Mary's religion and union with King Philip were destroying England, and that she needed to be stopped. Matthew was just as motivated, though Catherine knew his reasons were different. He didn't care about the religion. He wasn't convinced that Protestantism was necessarily any better than Catholicism for England. But he trusted Elizabeth, and knew she cared about truth more than tradition. That was enough for him.

Catherine looked around at the gathered colonists. Each of them probably had their own reasons for following Elizabeth. Nearly all were Protestants, so of course they supported the Protestant princess, but they had different goals, different visions for what England should be. Some probably just wanted to get home to their families and be able to live in their own country without fear of persecution.

Matthew opened up the void and let it grow large to accommodate so many people. Even though she knew Matthew had gone through it and come back only yesterday, it was frightening to look into that black nothingness and consider leaping into it. There was no indication that it would lead to England or anywhere else. What if the link on the other side had been destroyed? Would they fall through the void forever?

Suddenly, it was time to go. Catherine wasn't ready for it. She clutched her parents, crying. Matthew came and wrapped his arms around all three of them.

Finally, they released each other, and Catherine's father shook Matthew's hand. "When you get there, you must destroy the link. Cut the thread or burn the bone, whatever you need to do to make sure no one can come through it again."

"No!" Catherine said. "If we do that, we can never come back. I'll never see you again."

Her father put a hand on her arm. "It has to be this way. The link is a secret now, but it won't stay that way. Someone will be captured, someone will talk. If it falls into the wrong hands, we'll have armies coming through here. The only way to protect the island is to cut the link entirely."

Catherine felt fresh tears coming, but she held them back. Her father was right, and she knew it. She couldn't risk the lives of countless manticores for her own personal wishes. She had done that often enough already. If Horizon was really going to be a manticore nation, then they had to be in control of who came and went. Even if it meant keeping her from her own parents.

She hugged her father again, and then her mother. "Thank you," she said. "I'll think of you every day."

"It's time," her mother said. "Now go."

Most of the colonists and all of the baggage was already through. Catherine took Matthew's hand, and together they stepped into the void.

Also available from David Walton

TERMINAL MIND

winner of the Philip K. Dick Award for best paperback science
fiction novel of the year

CHAPTER 1

*Daddy sent me a message. He gave me a job to do but he said don't
do it yet. He said just wake up and be ready. I'm awake but there's
nothing to do. He left me in the dark. He said he'd come but that was
seconds and seconds ago. I can do it Daddy I really can. Let me try.
Where are you Daddy?*

MARK McGovern would have traded his inheritance to escape this
party. Any political event meant flashy mods and petty gossip, but
this one seemed worse than most. Out here on the balcony, he found
some momentary relief; the night air cooled his face, and the sliding
glass door muted the sounds of the party inside. Below him, the
Philadelphia Crater sparkled like a bowl of diamonds. Mark switched
his eyes to a higher magnification and watched headlights chase each
other up and down Broad Street.

The door slid open.

"Tenny, there you are," said his father.

Mark grimaced. Tennessee—his real name—sounded pretentious,
but "Tenny", his family nickname, was even worse.

"Tenny," said his father, "there's someone I'd like you to meet."

"Yes, come here, dear," said Diane, his father's latest, a woman
with no more right to call him "dear" than his landlord. Mark
followed them inside.

Bejeweled and betuxed ladies and gentlemen stuffed the room,
sintered into a living mosaic of high-class biological modifications.

He squeezed past a woman with earlobes molded into ringlets that draped over her shoulders, past a man with violet skin, past a woman who'd traded hair for a moist moss wreathed with tiny white flowers. They all held wine glasses with wrists at the same angle. They all looked at him.

Mark flashed the requisite smile. He hated this song and dance, the perpetual games of ambition and insincerity. None of these people had any interest in him beyond the attention they could bring to themselves. He spotted his great-grandfather at the bar, his arm snaked around a woman swathed in what looked like designer plastic wrap. Great-granddad was well over a hundred now, but with regular mod treatments, he seemed to age in reverse. His choices in women had grown younger, too, though for all Mark knew, that shrink-wrapped floozy might be sixty.

Jack McGovern, Mark's father, dominated the room, a wide-shouldered giant with a ferocious smile. He was the reason Mark was here. The press expected it, his father had said. The heir-apparent to the McGovern fortune must make appearances.

Mark's father crushed him in a one-armed hug and waggled fingers at those closest. "Tenny, you know Councilman Marsh and his wife Georgette, and this is Vivian DuChamp from *Panache*, but this— I don't believe you've met our newest artist, Dr. Alastair Tremayne. The man's a genius. With mods obviously, but he's made a few heads turn with some of his inventions as well. Patented a process to give net mods to a fetus, if you can believe that. Teach your unborn baby to read, show him pictures of his family, monitor his health, that sort of thing. Quite a hit with the maternal crowd. But I'm sorry—Dr. Tremayne, this is my son, Tennessee."

Over two meters tall, with silver hair shimmering like Christmas tinsel, Tremayne seemed hyper; he kept bouncing on the balls of his feet. Mark wasn't impressed. Tremayne would be like all his father's new discoveries: a fad for a time, then forgotten. He noticed his younger sister, Carolina, eyeing Tremayne like a hooked fish. Another fad for her then, too.

Mark worried about Carolina. At eighteen, she had a perfect figure, clear skin, golden smart-hair that arranged itself becomingly in any weather, and the very latest in eyes. Her eyes glistened, as if constantly wet with emotion, and their color—gold—shone with a deep luster like polished wood. But mods like that attracted men who were only interested in her appearance. Or her money.

Who was this Dr. Alastair Tremayne? It was impossible to tell his age. He looked twenty-five, but he could be as much as seventy if he was good at his craft.

"Councilman McGovern!" Three men crowded Mark aside and surrounded his father. A cloud of drones hovered over each shoulder, identifying them as reporters. "Mr. McGovern, we hear you're sitting on a new revelation, some synthesis of mod and fabrique technology."

Mark's father beamed. "You won't wring any secrets from me. Come to Friday's demonstration at the South Hills construction site."

Mark caught Carolina's eye, smiled, and flicked his eyes at Tremayne. She shrugged.

Isn't he cute? she sent. The words passed from her implanted Visor to his, allowing him to hear the words in his mind.

How old is he? Mark sent back.

What does that matter?

I don't want to see my sister mistreated. There are things more important than cute.

Carolina's lips puckered into a pout. *You're no fun. Stop playing the big brother.*

Mark blew her a kiss, pretending it was all just banter, but he made a mental note to find out something about this Dr. Tremayne. He loved Carolina, but that didn't mean he trusted her judgment.

". . . a stunning fractal filigree," Mark's father was saying, "Insouciant, yet unfeigned. Don't you think so, Tennessee?"

Mark snapped around, trying to figure out what he was supposed to be agreeing with. Everyone was staring at Diane, so he did, too. That's when he noticed her skin. It seemed to be alive. Looking closer, he saw the pigment of her skin was changing, subtly, in shifting spiral patterns. He'd never seen anything like it. How was it done? A bacterium? He couldn't look at her too long; the patterns made his eyes swim.

"Very nice," he managed.

"Very nice? It's an unrivaled tour-de-force of neoplasticism!"

Mark thought his father had probably practiced those words ahead of time for the benefit of the writer from *Panache*. He needed to get away from this circus.

"Come now, Tenny. You can do better than 'very nice.'" His father's goatée had turned black. Mark watched it kaleidoscope through brown and gray, then back to blond. His father's mood changed accordingly, and he laughed for the crowd. "Well, well, we can't all have taste."

"That's quite a mod you have yourself," Mark ventured, nodding at the goatée, which rippled into blue.

"That's Tremayne's work. Took two liters of celgel—it probably has more smarts than I do." Appreciative laughter. He turned to Mark. "What do you think of that?"

Mark glanced at the gaggle of cognoscenti and their sycophants, then back at his father, and decided: why not? He was twenty-four years old; he could say what he pleased.

"I think the Metropolitan Hospital ER could have made better use of it," he said.

The goatée blackened. For the first time in Mark's memory, his father opened his mouth, but nothing came out.

Dr. Tremayne spoke instead. "Idealism is so charming in the young."

Carolina said, "Daddy, leave him be. You know he has that Comber friend."

She caught Mark's eye. *That's your cue*, she sent.

Mark frowned, then understood. "Oh yes, Darin Kinsley," he said loudly. "I spend lots of time with him, down in the Combs."

His father's goatée turned a surprising shade of pink. "Wonderful, Mark, very nice. Now perhaps you could . . . ah . . . retire for the evening? Yes?"

Mark sighed in relief and nodded his thanks to Carolina.

You owe me one, she sent.

Out the door, he broke into a run. At the back of the house, where the arches and terraces faded into shadow, he lifted his jetvac off a hook and unfolded it into aluminum seat, handles, footrests. The vacuum motor whispered to life, lifting him off the ground. He squeezed the throttle, and the jetvac shot forward, skimming up the slope behind the house.

Finally free. Darin would have been waiting for half an hour now, and he wasn't likely to find Mark's Rimmer party a good excuse. Darin railed against Rimmers almost as often as he breathed—how they prettified themselves with technology better used to cure disease, how they controlled ninety-five percent of the resources while doing five percent of the work. Yet he refused to accept anything Mark tried to give him—even a ticket for the mag. Darin despised charity, thought it weakened those who accepted it. Once, he'd even stopped Mark from giving money to a beggar in the Combs. "Leave him some dignity," he'd said. When Mark asked if the man was expected to eat his dignity, Darin had responded, "Better to starve than to cower." It made Mark ashamed of his wealth, but what could he do?

Mark's night-vision kicked in, illuminating the top of the hill: he saw Darin first, lounging back against the hillside. Another figure hunched over Darin's telescope, and Mark recognized Praveen Kumar. He had known Praveen since they were boys; their families traveled in the same circles of society, but whereas Mark had always chafed against his family privilege, Praveen was a model son: hard-working, obedient, polite. So what was he doing here joining in a cracker's prank?

Mark touched down, refolded his jetvac, and slung it over his shoulder. Darin, spotting him, jumped up with arms spread wide.

"Prince Mark," he said. "You honor us with your presence."

Mark ignored the jibe. "What's he doing here?"

"I invited him."

"You didn't ask me," said Mark. "What if he tells someone?"

"Stop worrying," said Darin. "He'll be fine."

"This isn't exactly legal," said Mark.

"But what fun would it be if we didn't show it to anyone?"

Mark sighed. He'd long since given up on winning an argument with Darin.

"Praveen knows more astronomy than either of us," Darin continued, "and he can video the fireworks while we make them happen. Of course, I still didn't tell Praveen *what*'s going to happen."

Mark allowed a smile. He wanted to ask what Darin *had* told Praveen, but by that time Praveen joined them.

In recent years, Praveen had darkened his skin and hair to accentuate his Indian heritage. A double row of lithium niobate crystals studded his brow: a state-of-the-art Visor that rivaled Mark's own.

"And here's the genius in person," said Darin. "Can you actually be seen with us, Praveen, or will your agent bill us for the time?"

"You flatter me," Praveen said in a musical Indian accent he never had when they were young.

"Nonsense. Apparently you wrote quite a paper. You deserve the praise."

Praveen waved aside the compliments, but he was obviously pleased. His physicist grandfather, Dhaval Kumar, had established some of the theoretical principles behind non-attenuating laser light, the applications of which made Visor technology and the world-wide optical network possible. Praveen, who idolized his granddad, had recently been published himself in a prominent physics journal—one of the youngest ever to do so. Most of his peers didn't recognize what a triumph it was for him.

"You brought your camera?" Mark asked him.

"Yes, of course. But for what? Darin did not tell me."

Darin crouched in the grass, ignoring the question.

He unzipped a pouch at his waist and began laying out his netmask and its sensory apparatus—a cumbersome bio-electronic interface that connected eyes, ears, and mouth to a net interface. Mark had offered, more than once, to pay for a Visor, but of course Darin wouldn't hear of it.

Mark busied himself with the telescopes. The zoom mods in his eyes were no more adequate to view an astronomical event than one of those tiny camera drones was to holograph it. He snapped a memory crystal into the back and worked to calibrate the lenses. On the far side of the crater, he could see the hydroelectric dam that provided most of the city's power shining white in the darkness. Above it, a few stars twinkled faintly.

"Had a little trouble getting here," said Darin. Something in his voice caused Mark to turn around.

"Why?"

"Merc at the corner of 28th and Hill," said Darin. "Almost wouldn't let me pass."

"Were you polite?"

"As a politician. I guess he didn't like the look of my telescope."

"He's just there to keep the peace."

"He wouldn't have stopped you," said Darin. "He only stopped me because I'm a Comber, not because I was doing anything wrong. Rimmers are too attached to their comfortable lifestyle—you hire mercs to protect it, and call it 'keeping the peace'."

"They're preventing violence, not causing it. That's peace-keeping in anyone's book."

"Who causes violence,citizens who stand up for their rights, or those who take them away?"

Mark let it drop. Lately, Darin argued social philosophy at any provocation. They'd been school friends long before they understood the class differences, Mark's father having chosen public school over private tutors for political reasons. Even now, Mark agreed with Darin's perspectives more than his Rimmer peers', so it frustrated him when Darin's accusative pronouns shifted from 'they' to 'you'.

"Please," said Praveen, "I must know what am I photographing. I can not set my light levels unless I can estimate intensity and contrast."

Mark glanced at Darin, who was busy louvering a sticky lens into one eye. The back of the lens bristled with tiny fibers that Darin labored to keep free of tangles., "Tell him," he said.

"It's a flare," said Mark. "A NAIL flare."

He watched, amused, as Praveen's face went through a series of confused expressions. Praveen certainly knew more than they did about the various NAIL constellations of satellites. NAIL stood for Non-Attenuating Infrared Laser, and accounted for almost all of the optical net traffic in the country. The satellites were renowned for their half-mile-wide main antennas, umbrella-like dishes coated with a reflective material. When the angles between sun, satellite, and observer were just right, a burst of sunlight was reflected: a flare, lasting up to ten seconds and reaching magnitudes between minus ten and minus twelve—much brighter than anything else in the night sky. Amateur astronomers scrambled around the world to the sites the flares were predicted to appear.

Praveen rolled his eyes. "Just because it flies over does not mean you will see a flare. I cannot believe you dragged me out here. The next good flare is not for months, and I think it is only visible from Greenland."

"Don't put that camera away," said Mark. "Darin and me, we don't like to wait for months. And Greenland's too cold."

"Ready," said Darin.

Praveen's face changed again. "You're hackers? I don't believe this."

"We're nothing of the sort," said Mark. "Hackers are criminals. Hackers break into nodes to steal or destroy. Crackers, on the other hand, are in it for fun, for the thrill of the race, for the intellectual challenge. And this," he smiled, "is a crackerjack."

"A fine distinction."

"No time to argue," said Mark. "Just man that camera."

Darin sat up, a grotesquerie of celgel-smeared fibers protruding from eyes, ears, and throat. Mark simply relaxed against the hillside and unfocused his eyes. Billions of information-laden photons, careening invisibly around him, were manipulated into coherence by the holographic crystals in his Visor. The feed from the crystals spliced directly into his optic nerve, overlaying his normal vision with the familiar icons of his net interface.

Using slight movements of his eyes, he navigated deeper into the system, found a procedure called "Connect NAIL Public Portal", and executed it. At its request for a pass-image, Mark envisioned a regular icosahedron, faces shaded blue, and it granted him access. Most people chose familiar faces for their pass-images, but Mark preferred geometric shapes. They required a good spacial mind to envision properly, reducing the chance that someone else could hack into his system.

Mark checked the satellite he was connected through, verifying it was not the one they were targeting. Wouldn't do to lose a connection before they were able to clean up. A few more queries told him the NAIL satellite now entering the eastern sky was a dedicated one for federal military use. So much the better. He opened the account directory and chose an entry. It didn't matter which, since he didn't intend to complete the call. At random, he selected a recipient at the Navy base in Norfolk, Virginia.

You there, Darin? he sent.

Right in here with you.

Mark paused. Despite his bravado out on the hill, this would be the most ambitious jack they'd ever attempted. If they crashed it, the security agents would snag their IDs, and well, the federal government didn't have much clout anymore, but it could still lock them away for a long time. But hey, where was the rush without the risk? He took a deep breath, and placed the call.

No turning back now. In order to call, the software had to access the encryption algorithm, which meant opening a socket—a data hole—into the command level. The hole would be open for less than a microsecond, but a hole was a hole.

Mark watched the process logs: account lookup . . . server handshake . . . message collation . . . Sensing the open socket at the precise moment, his software reacted, opening a chute to prevent it from closing normally.

Chute is holding, Darin reported, and then, *Dropping caterpillar.* Another cracker, one of Darin's, copied itself through the chute into the system beyond.

Mark hoped the caterpillar would be quick. Written to resemble a worm, which the security software agents fought on a daily basis, the caterpillar was bait. Thinking it was just a worm, the software agents would kill it, and the caterpillar, just before dying, would fire back crucial information about the agents to Mark and Darin.

At least, that was the plan. Mark always feared the worst: that a top-flight software agent would sniff the jack and follow the trail right back through the chute. A caterpillar had to be quick, or the risks outweighed the gain.

Anything yet? he sent.

I knew you'd snap.

Have not. I'm just falling asleep waiting for your junkware.

The caterpillar spouted a stream of data. Mark studied it to see what they would be up against. Looked like a few sentries, a strongman, and . . . *Scan it!*

What?

A nazi. They've got a nazi. That's it, I'm collapsing the . . .

Keep your panties on. We've got a few seconds—drop your kevorkian.

But—

Drop it!

Cringing, Mark obeyed.

Nazis were the most feared of security agents, but common lore said their weakness was in their strength. They were so powerful that they were equipped with fail-safes, mechanisms to put them to sleep if they started attacking friendly system code. A kevorkian played off this concept, faking data to convince the nazi it was doing serious damage. The nazi then killed itself, and would remain dead—they hoped—until a sysadmin could take a look.

Mark had written this kevorkian himself, and was proud of it, but it had never been tested against a genuine nazi. He cringed, expecting at any moment to see a surge of data that would mean disaster.

You got him, said Darin.

What?

You got him.

Mark swallowed the acid that had been rising in his throat. *Of course I did. Now jump in there and get this bird turning.*

MARIE Coleson knew enough about slicers to be careful. Despite practically living here at the Norfolk anti-viral lab for the last two years, she'd never handled software so volatile. The slicer reacted unpredictably to every test, and never the same way twice.

Because it was human. Not a person—Marie refused to believe that it could genuinely think or feel emotion. But generated from a human mind, and just as complex and flexible and,well, intelligentas the original. Marie's job was to break it down, understand its inner workings, and write tools to defeat it. Fortunately, she'd caught it just as it went active on one of the city's rental memory blocks. If it had distributed copies of itself on the open net, it would have been much harder to contain.

She stood, stretched, and walked to the coffee machine. It was past nine, but that was hardly unusual. Since she'd walked into a Navy recruitment center last April, she'd spent most of her time in this tiny room, with its faded paint and ten-year-old promotional posters. In the six decades since the Conflict, the federal Navy's volunteer list had declined as rapidly as the federal government's power, so she figured they were desperate for anyone. Uncle Sam would have grown her a soldier's armored body, but by the time her turn came up, she'd proved so useful in the lab that she was assigned electronic security detail instead.

It didn't matter to Marie. Not much mattered to her anymore. Not since a flier accident two days before Christmas had killed her husband and son. Two years ago now. She mourned Keith, but didn't miss him; the marriage had been falling apart anyway. That last year, he'd rarely been home, and when he was, they'd done nothing but fight. But Samuel, little Sammy, her angel, her peanut: what could be worth doing now that he was gone?

Sometimes, late in the evening, alone in the lab like she was tonight, Marie fantasized about becoming a mother again. It wasn't impossible.The fertility treatments that had produced Sammy had left an embryo unused. It was still there at the clinic, kept in frozen possibility. But she was forty-two years old, for heavens sake. Too old to consider starting such a life.

This was her life now, this lab—fighting viruses, worms, phages, krakens. Investigating, classifying, designing anti-viruses, sometimes for twenty hours a day. Any time not required for other military duties, she spent here. It kept her mind busy, and that she desperately needed.

She sipped her coffee, staring through the faded walls into her memories of the past. She was still standing there when Pamela Rider peeked through the door. Pam worked for Navy administration in the next building over, but she stopped by whenever she could.

"Don't you ever go home?" Pam said.

"Hi, Pam."

"Or out?" Pam sat the wrong way around in a swivel chair, the backrest between her legs and her arms crossed on top. Her tan was smooth and permanent, and her elegant legs had been lengthened and tapered by regular mod treatments. In a cotton flower-print dress, she cut a striking image, making Marie feel frumpy in her plasticwear overall.

"When was the last time you saw a guy?" asked Pam.

"You know I'm not interested."

" It's been two years, Marie. Two years! It's not healthy. Leave Keith already."

"No, that's not—"

"Listen, if the guy were still alive, you'd have dropped him ages ago. Relationships don't last that long. If you ask me, three months is ideal—any less, and you've hardly gotten to the good parts, but any more, and he starts to feel like he owns you."

"Pam—"

"Come on, I remember Keith. He wasn't worth that kind of loyalty even when he was alive."

"Seriously, it's not Keith. I just don't want to go looking for another guy now."

"It's the kid, isn't it."

"The kid," Marie echoed. Yes, it was the kid. Sammy had been born three weeks early and had never looked back. He was quick to walk, quick to talk, quick to form complete sentences. He'd loved construction vehicles and chocolate candy.

"Come out with me tonight," said Pam.

"I can't."

"Come on. This is a Navy base. They line up for miles to talk to a pretty woman, which you are. A hundred tasty slabs of manflesh, just dying to be eaten up. You'll be mobbed before you take a step."

"Are you looking at the same woman I see in the mirror?"

Pam cocked her head. "You could use some sprucing up, I won't deny it. But nothing I can't manage."

"I don't know, Pam. I'll probably work late tonight. I flagged a data spike on one of the city's rental memory blocks. Turns out it's a slicer."

"Yeah? What's a slicer?"

"It's a person. Was a person. They slice down into someone's brain, copying it neuron by neuron into a digital simulation. The original brain doesn't survive."

"Get out of town. People do that?"

"It started as an immortality technology—you know, flash your mind into crystal and live forever. But it doesn't work. The trauma's too much for the mind; it goes insane."

Such a grisly practice appalled Marie, but also fascinated her. What could ever drive a person to make a slicer? She assumed a group, one member of whom sacrificed his life for the endeavor, must create them. Terrorists, maybe, or cultists of some sort? Marie knew what it was like to wish she were dead, but she couldn't relate to that kind of commitment to a cause.

"Somehow, the people who create it can control it," she said. "I'm trying to figure out how."

"Well, finish up, and then come out with me tonight."

Marie laughed. "We're talking about a slicer, here, not some teenager's porn virus."

"Like that means anything to me."

"Tell you what. Give me an hour to run some tests and send it off to a colleague, and I'll come join you."

"One hour. Promise?"

"Promise."

"Don't stand me up, now. I'll hold you to it."

Half an hour later, Marie thought she had the answer, though it made her a little sick. The slicer seemed to be controlled through pleasure and pain. A little module ran separately from the main simulator, a master process that could send signals to the pleasure or pain centers of the mind. Since the slicer wasn't limited by a physical body, those sensations could be as extreme as the mind could register. It was a revolting concept, like torturing someone who was mentally handicapped.

She didn't understand the whole process, though. She needed another opinion. She decided to send the slicer out to Tommy Dungan, a fellow researcher at the army base at Fort Bragg. Transporting malicious code could be dangerous, but their dedicated NAIL satellite used isolated channels, and she trusted Dungan to keep the slicer secure once it reached his end.

Just as she logged into the NAIL system, she saw an incoming call on the lab's private channel. She answered it, but the sender had already disconnected. Wrong number, probably. Marie sent the slicer to Dungan, logged off for the day, and went out to meet Pam.

MARK fiddled with the settings on his chute analyzer, watching for any sudden change in data rate—the online equivalent of pacing the room. His kevorkian ought to have knocked down that nazi for good, but what if a sysadmin happened to spot it and cycled it back up? If the data rate across that chute so much as *hiccupped* . . .

He looked back at the analyzer just in time. An enormous surge of data was pouring back across the chute toward him.

Abort, abort! He couldn't collapse the chute until Darin pulled out, or he would hang Darin's session inside, leaving a wealth of information for sysadmins to find and track at their leisure.

Abort! Get out of there!

Done. I'm out.

Mark opened his eyes, breathing hard. Darin tore off his netmask.

"A close one," said Darin.

"We should have been caught. That nazi had plenty of time to ID us. Plenty of time."

"Cheer up. We made it." Darin pointed to the eastern sky. "Let's enjoy the show."

While Praveen made final adjustments to the camera, Mark overlaid a corner of his vision with a digital countdown.

"Five," he said. "Four. Three. Two. One."

Several seconds passed.

"Zero," Mark said, belatedly.

The eastern sky remained dark. Darin grunted.

"What happened?" said Mark.

"Don't ask me. You did the calculations."

"The calculations were correct. We did three simulations; you know they were."

"But the bird turned! I saw the telemetry before I jumped out; it was all correct."

"I don't get it," said Mark."You mean you got it wrong?" said Praveen. "I knew I should not have come. I could have been working this evening instead of hauling all this gear up to the rim for nothing. Next time, don't . . ."

A brilliant flash of light leapt at them from the east. Mark opened his mouth to cheer, then shut it again. There was no way that light was from the satellite. It was too far north, and besides, it was too red.

Mark could only say, "Looks like an ex—" before he was cut off by a deafening boom that echoed off the hillside. The base of the eastern mountain seemed to be on fire.

He dialed up his vision to maximum and saw fire and smoke, and behind it, a torrent of rushing water.

"It's the dam," said Mark, disbelieving. "Someone blew up the dam."

CPSIA information can be obtained at www.ICGtesting.com
Printed in the USA
BVOW08s1148140615

404553BV00007B/67/P

9 781492 938477